THE LOYAL TRAVELER

WE ARE WATCHING
NOTHING IS SAFE

THE LOYAL TRAVELER

BRIAN SCHAN

UPDYN BOOKS

ATLANTA

Published 2008 by UpDyn Books.

Visit our website at *www.theloyaltraveler.com*

Library of Congress Cataloging-in-Publication Data

Schan, Brian.

The Loyal Traveler / by Brian Schan

P. CM.

ISBN: 0-9822588-0-1

ISBN 13: 978-0-9822588-0-4

For my parents...
my heroes and inspiration

CHAPTER ONE

"Good morning, sir. Welcome to Ravens Valley Country Club. Golf clubs in the trunk?" asked the valet.

I replied in the affirmative.

"Are you Ethan Kravis? Seven-thirty tee time with Judge Lawrence?"

"I am indeed."

"I was told to tell you that you have a message waiting for you at the pro shop. If you follow the slate path, you'll eventually run right into it."

The valet looked at me and for an infinitely small second, I thought I picked up on a tiny smirk. That smirk told me all I needed to know. Judge Lawrence wasn't coming. Why then was the valet taking my clubs out of the car? Trying not to ponder the fact that I had gotten up at the crack of dawn on only a few hours of sleep to get out here in time, I made my way to the pro shop.

Although most people wouldn't notice, I was acutely aware of the tight surveillance I was under from the moment I pulled into the long willow-lined driveway. Every square inch of the place was covered by closed circuit TVs watching my every movement. Given the extremely high profile of the club, the system it had in place was light-years ahead of the ever-present CCTV system installed in major cities like London.

I entered the pro shop and was greeted by a tall, well-tanned gentleman. Without my saying a word, he walked over to me, extended his hand, and said, "Hi, Mr. Kravis, I'm Henry, the club pro."

I shook his hand and could feel the power in his grip, which was most likely the result of many years of gripping the club.

"I'm sorry to have to tell you this, but the judge was unexpectedly called into an important meeting this morning. He apologizes and would like very much if you would consider playing a round without him. Typically it would never be allowed, but the judge and his family is some of our oldest and most respected members, so the golf committee has made this one exception. I've been here twenty-five years, and I can't remember it ever being allowed."

I wasn't sure if Henry threw that last part in to make me feel special or to ensure he had it on record to cover himself in the event there was an uprising in the club elite. I replied, "How would it work? Would I play as a single?"

"Actually, we had an unexpected out-of-town member come in this morning. In my twenty-five years of running the golf shop here, I've never met Mr. Michaels. Apparently he was going to join you and Judge Lawrence. I'm surprised that the judge didn't mention it to you."

I got a feeling I had not had since my army days, the feeling that something outside my purview was unfolding, but to which I was not aware. Most people call it a gut feeling, but when you have seen what I have seen and been through the types of situations I have been through, it was more than a gut feeling. I looked at Henry to see if I could pick up on any subtle expressions that he knew anything further about the situation. My read was that he didn't. My instincts said to ask some probing questions. The situation seemed very odd to me that not only was I invited there, but that the invitee was not showing up. Equally odd was that a rule in the place that had never been broken before was about to be broken. To top it all off, a person who has never shown up was there. The whole episode contained too many inconsistencies. I couldn't fathom why I felt it, but it was there. Danger.

"I think I'm going to pass. I wanted to discuss some items with the judge, and since he's not here, I think we'll just cancel for today."

The door to the pro shop opened. In walked a short, older man. He looked to be in his late sixties, maybe early seventies. He obviously noticed Henry and me, smiled politely and started to approach. He was wearing a Hawaiian print shirt and khaki shorts. His attire must have been on the fringe of acceptable for a club like Ravens Valley. Seeming to sense my thoughts, he said, "If the old farts at this place can't appreciate style, then screw 'em."

Henry winced as if he had bitten a bone in his fish. Clearly he hoped that no one had heard the offensive comment.

The old man continued. "Are you Ethan Kravis?"

"How could you tell?"

"Well, the judge told me to look for a six-foot-four guy in his mid-thirties with short brown hair and who has the build of a beach volleyball player. Since the average age of the people I have seen since I arrived here is around a hundred and thirty-seven, I took a wild guess."

Oh boy. Whoever this guy was, I could tell immediately that he was the type of person the old geezers at the club didn't invite to bridge night. I smiled and said, "Your powers of deduction are unrivaled. I am indeed Ethan Kravis."

I glanced over at Henry. He clearly looked nervous when addressing the human tornado who just entered his pro shop. "Mr. Kravis was just expressing to me that he doesn't feel like an exception to the club rules should be made for him, and that this morning's round should be called off."

It was a good attempt to stave off a potential career-threatening problem for Henry, nicely worded so that he wouldn't have to break the rules while also allowing me to leave.

"Hogwash. If anyone gives you any problems what-so-ever, you come to me, and I'll deal with it."

Henry seemed to be relieved by the public statement, but I could still sense a bit of hesitation.

"Ethan Kravis, I'm Garrett Michaels. I'm an old friend of the judge's. Just like him that he would invite us both here and not show up. Let's say we make the most of the situation, shall we?"

I wasn't sure if it was his boisterous southern drawl or his unimposing stature, but for some reason Garrett Michaels' rebellious attitude had a way of putting me at ease with the situation. My earlier thoughts that something was wrong could have been a false positive. I decided to continue as planned, without the judge.

"Hi Garrett, I think it would be great get out there on this beautiful course and enjoy some fresh air. Are you sure you don't mind? I feel as if I'm imposing."

Garrett regarded my statement for a moment and slightly shook his head, almost as if he knew that I sensed something was off about the situation.

"Imposing? Not in the least. I've traveled pretty far to meet up with the judge and play some golf. I know I won't get to see my old friend the judge, but it would be a real shame if I couldn't even get out there and stretch my legs. So wha'd ya say, you in?"

I gave a forceful nod and a smile.

"Great. Meet you out front in five minutes."

Henry said, "You can change your shoes in the men's locker room there." He pointed to a staircase.

I quickly changed my shoes and headed toward the rear of the pro shop building, the first chance I had to look at the magnificently manicured course. The pro shop was elevated above the eighteenth putting green. From that vantage point I could see the signature eighteenth hole. The 590 yard par five named "Lynny" was daunting for players who didn't have length to their shots. The massive golf hole was an especially cruel way to end a round.

In a trancelike state looking over the amazing course, I snapped back to consciousness when I heard the words, "All set?" behind me. Garrett was in a golf cart with a single bag of clubs attached to the back.

"I'm all set, but would you happen to know where my clubs are?"

Seeming to have anticipated the question, Garrett said, "Here at Ravens Valley, you have to take a caddy, as long as you are able to walk and don't have medical issues. I'm an old man, so I have an exemption to this rule. I know it might be a little awkward; do you mind?"

Not having a choice in the matter, I replied, "No problem here."

Garrett smiled and registered a look of relief. Perhaps his age was the reason why Garrett never came to the club. Maybe the old-timers didn't want to play with Garrett because they would lose the opportunity to walk and talk while they played. Not knowing Garrett at all, it didn't matter to me.

"Great. Then we're off. This way," Garrett said.

Garrett drove off and I walked behind him. We made our way to the first tee. Waiting there was a man who appeared to be in his mid-thirties.

"Ethan, this is Jonah. Jonah will be your caddy today. Jonah, this is Mr. Kravis."

I nodded to Jonah. I observed that he was not dressed with the same blue caddy shirt the rest of the caddies wore.

Garrett said, "I brought Jonah with me this morning. He's a

trained paramedic, among other things. He'll double as your caddy."

I looked over to Garrett and contemplated what health issues he had that necessitated such precautions. Surely the club had medical facilities and enough member doctors to cure the ills of several small countries. Equally as curious to me was Garrett's use of the phrase "other things" when describing Jonah's duties. I wasn't sure how to take it, but we continued on.

CHAPTER TWO

Garrett and I arrived at the sixth hole. Up to that point, my golf game was less than impressive. I typically play to a nine handicap, but that day I was a bogey golfer. A variety of factors may have contributed. Although I was in good shape, perhaps it was the walking instead of riding in a cart that may be the cause. Perhaps it was Garrett's slow play or the anxious feeling of the morning's events that I couldn't shake. Whatever it was, I decided to press on and enjoy the weather and the course.

Garrett had taken the liberty of driving his cart slowly so that I could walk by his side and engage in conversation. I glanced over to him and asked, "So how long have you known the judge?"

"Let me see. I guess it has been about forty-five years. We were in the same class at Yale together."

"Wow. You kept in touch all these years? That's pretty impressive."

"After we graduated, we lost touch for a while. The judge went to law school and I moved back to Atlanta to run my family's business."

"How did you reconnect with him?"

"Actually, I read the story of how your S.T.A.R.E. system saved his life. I called to make sure he was all right. The judge couldn't stop praising you and your security system."

At the tee box of the sixth hole, Garrett gingerly got out of his cart. He looked at the fifth hole and then glanced around probably to see if anyone was in the vicinity. We were reasonably alone, and he approached me.

"So, I really don't know the first thing about computers, but how exactly did your system identify that the man was going to try to kill the judge?"

Was this it? Was this the reason why the judge had paired Garrett and me together? Maybe Garrett wants to buy the company? Or perhaps he wants to install my system somewhere? Without trying to sound too salesman-like, I replied. "The system didn't actually know the suspect was trying to kill. It took several factors into account and determined that there was a perceived threat. It took in the data that it could collect through its multitude of sensors and used its logic to act."

"What an amazing world we live in. When I was in school, the calculator was a brand-new invention. It was the size of a laptop computer and did simple arithmetic. Now you tell me you developed a system that gives a building a mind. Fascinating."

I never thought of putting it that way, but I would have to make a mental note and use it in my next sales pitch.

Garrett continued, "I have someone you really must meet. He is very smart at this computer stuff. Perhaps he could use a unique talent such as you."

There it was. This is how people like the judge pay back a good deed. Did the judge set this all up so that Garrett could plug me into the crowd that inhabited clubs like Ravens Valley?

I said in an excited voice, "I'd love to meet your friend. Do you know what technology field he's in?"

Garrett looked at me. He could probably see that he had my full attention. He smiled at me before he replied. "Like I said, I'm not too familiar with computer speak, but I think you'll be impressed with this particular friend."

It wasn't what he said, but how he said it that made the hairs on back of the back of my neck stand at attention.

Garrett continued, "As a matter of fact, I spoke to my friend, and he's very interested to meet you as soon as possible. It's not very often he would extend this type of interest in someone. You should feel good about that."

"Is that so? Well, if he is a friend of yours and the judge's, he must be a good guy."

"So?" Garrett asked.

"So what?" I said.

"So would you like to meet with him?"

"Sure I would. We can set some time up for whenever–I'm sorry, what did you say your friend's name was?"

Garrett's eyes widened and a broad smile crossed his face. "I didn't say his name. I'll let him introduce himself. Would you be OK if we saw him today?"

"When? After golf?"

"I was thinking a little sooner than that," Garrett said.

"Now? We are on the hole farthest away from the clubhouse. Is he out here on the course?" I looked around and didn't see a soul on the course. Something was eerily strange about Garrett's questions.

"He's close by. I thought we could take the cart and drive to meet him. Would that be all right with you? I think the trip may be worth your time. I have no doubt you would enjoy yourself. What do you say? It'll be only a couple of hours out of your life. You'll be back before we would've finished our round. I have the feeling you like adventures."

Something in me felt compelled to trust the old man. I don't know why, but I did. My entire career was built on computers and logic. The whole episode this morning defied logic, yet I was compelled to go with it. I said to Garrett with a half-hearted smile, "Against my better judgment, I'm in."

"Wonderful," said Garrett. He looked over to Jonah and nodded.

Jonah put down my golf bag, raised his hand to his mouth, and began talking to his wrist. Jonah must have had a micro transmitter in his cuff like those secret service agents use in the movies. I overheard what Jonah was saying.

"Package is wrapped. Request satellite sweep, one-thousand-foot radius. Regular observation is a check. How about thermal? Check. Clear to proceed? Check. Send the trailer cart."

Jonah looked over at Garrett, gave a nod, and said, "We are clear, sir."

Confused at what was going on, I turned to Garrett and said, "What the heck was that?"

"Jonah was just checking to see if there was anyone in the area who might be a threat."

"Threat? What do you mean, threat?"

"Ethan, please try to relax. You must trust that you will be fine. Are you ready?"

Ready for what, I thought. Jonah walked over to the golf cart. It was very strange, but when getting into the golf cart, Jonah ducked much lower then he needed to get in and then he raised his legs up high as he got into the cart. Weird dude I thought.

"Ethan, please get into the passenger's side of the cart," said Garrett.

I walked over to the cart. Before I got in, Garrett said, "Jonah, make sure Mr. Kravis gets into the cart safely please."

Jonah said, "Mr. Kravis, please watch your head."

This was very strange. I've gotten into and out of golf carts for twenty years. Were these guys crazy? Just as I thought that, I smacked my head on something hard. It felt like I hit my head on the roof of the cart, but surely I had ducked low enough.

"Careful," both Jonah and Garrett said in unison with an "Oh, that had to hurt" expression on their faces.

Jonah reached out and put his hand on the top of my head as I was getting in. He applied downward pressure to ensure my head was low enough.

"Now lift your legs up higher then you normally would," said Jonah.

Remembering how Jonah had gotten in before, I tried to replicate his actions. I lifted my legs as if I were stepping over an invisible tripwire. I was finally in. I yelled out to Garrett, "Where are you going to sit?"

Jonah looked at me and said, "This has room for only two people. Garrett is going to go and have lunch at the clubhouse."

I looked back and saw that Garrett was getting into a cart with a man who had driven up. Is that what Jonah had meant by "send the trailer cart"? Garrett waved and smiled at me.

I looked back at Jonah and asked him, "What the hell is going on?"

Jonah faced me and said, "Just relax. You remember the first time you had sex? Well, this is going to be like that multiplied by a thousand."

I wasn't sure what Jonah meant, but he started talking. "Comm check."

A voice came from a speaker I couldn't see. It was like surround sound in a movie theater. "Roger. Comm is go."

"Comm, this is the package. Preliminary sweep is complete. Request secondary sweep."

"Roger. Commencing secondary sweep. LM Sat five hundred is a check. LM Sat one thousand is a check. LM Sat two thousand is a check. You are a go to move dark."

Jonah looked at me and said, "Pucker up your asshole and hold on, 'cause we're about to go bye-bye."

Jonah reached in front of him and flipped the forward/reverse switch of the golf cart. I suddenly felt a strap tighten across my chest, like an amusement park ride. Next an instrumentation panel materialized out of thin air. I blurted, "What the fuck?"

Jonah put his hand on my arm and said, "Calm yourself. Everything will be fine. The cart has electro-chromatic skin. For lack of a better explanation, it's like a chameleon. It can blend into the environment around it. The outside will be invisible. Inside here, the true vehicle will become visible again."

I saw two doors come down from the top of the roof like a gull-wing car door closing. I heard two latches lock on the doors. A slight hiss came from the sides of the golf cart.

"We have to pressurize the cabin prior to taking off," said Jonah.

"Taking off? What do you mean take off? This thing flies?"

With a smile, Jonah said, "Sort of."

An electronic voice announced, "Fully pressurized. You are a go for takeoff."

Jonah said, "This is where it's going to get interesting for you. I'll take it slow because it's your first time."

He slowly pushed forward the joystick that was between his legs. I was in absolute and utter shock. We gently floated off the ground. There was no sound. No shrill of an engine. The only audible thing I could hear was a very low, barely noticeable humming that came from below my feet. I was speechless. I could only stammer out one ridiculous question. "Is this–like a hot air balloon?"

Jonah seemed to consider the question a moment, and then

turned to me and said, “Do you think a hot air balloon can do this?”

He pushed the joystick forward quickly about four inches, and we accelerated at an unbelievable speed. I saw the altimeter on the dash. It was rising at a dizzying rate. I looked out the window, and I saw the ground getting very small. I saw the New Jersey shore, and then I saw the entire state. I got a queasy feeling in the pit of my stomach. I looked over at the altimeter again. It read 198,000 feet. I did the simple math. If an airplane flew at 38,000 feet, we were more than five times higher and still climbing. All I could get out of my mouth was, “How high?”

Jonah said, “We are going to start orbit when we reach nine hundred and ninety-four miles. We should be there in about fourteen minutes. Total flight time will be roughly thirty-two minutes. How are you feeling?”

Barely able to comprehend the question, my only reply was “Peachy.”

Jonah snickered, faced me, and said, “Take off your golf visor.”

I raised my hand to my visor and slid it off my head.

“Let it go.”

I let the visor go, and it stayed there, floating, weightless.

CHAPTER THREE

A black Maybach sedan pulled up to a small office building in the Earls Court section of London. It was minutes prior to the agreed upon meeting time. Not since the formation of the group thirty-two years before was there an unscheduled meeting of the council outside of the annual summit. This was a cause of great concern to Member Number Seven. He knew that the reason for this impromptu meeting must have been tremendously important. Coordinating an unscheduled meeting of the seven-member council was not an easy task. Controlling ninety percent of the world's oil was more than a fulltime job.

These seven men are the puppet masters. They had both direct and indirect influence on the extraction and production of almost all of the world's most valuable natural resource. They knew their secret, which had been meticulously constructed over decades, was one of the biggest covert actions ever in the history of man. Their singular goal when they formed the council in the late 1970s was simple. They would set out a series of world events to corner the oil market. To achieve such an enormous goal, they had to work in the background. They needed to exert nearly invisible influences on the market to manipulate situations to their desired outcome. Over the past thirty years they had mastered the craft. None of the men on the seven-member council existed in the eyes of the world. The extraordinary wealth the men had accumulated had allowed them to cover their tracks completely. No hint of their existence was ever made public. Their God-given lives had vanished on that cold autumn day thirty-two years before. They assumed new lives outside the convention of normal society. They were the unexplained forces that moved the world's financial markets.

Number Seven grinned as he thought of this notion. It was unfathomable how, after all these years, the council had been able to operate undiscovered. Through carefully crafted and elaborate misdirection, the council had successfully changed the perception of the entire world. The ruse it had meticulously constructed was that the royal families in the Middle East controlled the majority of the world's oil. Number Seven knew it to be an absolute lie. The illusion was an elaborate front that the council had put in place years earlier. Number Seven was about to meet with the only people on the planet that knew the true organizational structure of the oil industry.

The Maybach pulled into a small garage two blocks south of the Earls Court tube station. Parked in the middle of the garage were six other cars, arranged in a circle with the headlights facing each other, like spokes on a wheel. Number Seven told his driver to pull up and park in the missing spoke. The driver eased the car into the empty space between the silver Rolls and the stretch Mercedes limo. Number Seven rolled his eyes and thought that this ritual was a little strange, but who was he to change the way it had been done since the beginning?

With the circle of cars complete, the driver's door of each car opened simultaneously. Each of the drivers walked back and opened the passenger left-side door. The council members emerged from their vehicles at the same time and walked to the middle of the circle while the drivers took their position in front of the cars.

The men were all impeccably dressed in hand-tailored suits. Although it had been only eight months since last they met, Number Seven noticed that all of the men, who were approaching their seventies, had aged well. The wonderful advances in science and the means to employ them had allowed the men to maintain above-average health.

The nationalities of the group spanned the globe. Each member was from a different continent. The members would handle the business that came out of their regions. Any business that crossed over between regions would be handed off through a specific process that ensured absolute secrecy.

Each man had a number assigned according to when he was invited to join the council. No true names would ever be spoken or documented in council communications. The numerical system was one of the many precautions the group had adopted to maintain the anonymity of the council. These and many other rules and processes had to be followed to the letter, or the consequences would be immediate termination, without discussion or vote. These steps had allowed the council to survive undiscovered. At first, the multitude of rules frustrated the members of the council. After a while, the rules became second nature. Once the men all arrived in the center of the circle, Number One began to speak.

"Thank you all for coming on such short notice. Everyone knows the process. Please remove any electronic equipment and place it in the tray. All armed escorts are to remain in their respective cars for the duration of this meeting."

None of the men moved. Knowing the standard operating procedures, they had anticipated this step in the process and left cell phones and other electrical devices in their cars. After a minute or so passed without movement, Number One spoke again. "We will now perform an electronic sweep."

Number One raised his hand to signal his driver to commence the sweep.

After about thirty seconds, the car door of Number One's Rolls Royce opened. "We are all clear, sir," said Number One's driver.

Number Seven was relieved that the council no longer had to change clothes prior to the start of a meeting, the process used in the early days of the council. With the advent of electronic detection devices, this precaution was no longer needed.

"Gentlemen, if you will follow me, please," said Number One.

The men walked over to an elevator at the rear of the garage. One by one they leaned forward to a panel next to the elevator. First each positioned his eye in front of a retinal scanner, and then pressed his thumb on the thumbprint reader. Next was the facial recognition scan. Once all passed the biometric tests, a green LED above the elevator began to blink. The elevator door opened.

Number Seven knew the multitude of biometric tests were unnecessary. The security forces in place would have never allowed anyone not on the council to approach within one thousand feet of the garage. Each car emitted a scrambled signal that ensured the correct cargo was in tow. If any car without the correct signal approached the garage, it would have met with quick and decisive demise.

From outward appearances, the elevator looked old and worn. Once the doors opened, it revealed a wood-paneled elevator with plush carpeting that one might find in a high-end office building. The men got on the elevator and the door closed. The elevator moved slowly at first, and then dropped faster. Number Seven knew of this meeting place. It was 1,100 feet below street level. The council had purchased the garage many years before and slowly constructed an advanced meeting facility far below the city of London. The council used one of the many shell companies under its control to carry out the construction of the underground fortress. Although the first time it used this specific location, the council had similar meeting places in many cities around the world. All the structures were impervious to electronic signals, both inward and outward. They had no Internet connections or phone lines. Once the council members locked themselves in the belly of these elaborate sanctuaries, they could be assured of absolute privacy. The cost to construct and maintain these facilities were astronomical, but well worth it for the extreme privacy they provided.

The elevator slowed slightly, signaling its approach to the underground bunker. The door opened, and the council members entered into a large marble-floored foyer. Deep-grained wood paneling covered the walls. Expensive paintings hung on the wood paneling. The bunker décor rivaled that of a five-star hotel. Number Seven thought it to be excessive, but given the limitless wealth that the group had amassed, it spared no expense on any of the comforts the world had to offer. The group of men walked confidently down a long hallway and into an executive conference room. At the center was a round table made of the finest Brazilian rosewood money could buy. Each of the members took his assigned seat. The plush black leather of the high-back chairs swallowed their bodies in a gentle caress. Once each of the men was settled, Number One spoke.

“Again I want to thank you all for agreeing to meet on short notice. Because of our communication protocols, I know the subject of this meeting is unknown to you at this time. I assure you all that only the gravest of concerns could break protocol and necessitate a meeting outside our norm.”

Number One paused for effect while he looked at each of the council member's faces. Number Seven noted a growing look of concern on each of the men. Number One continued.

"Approximately five years ago one of my advanced research companies detected a slight geomagnetic anomaly in the Mid-Atlantic region of the United States. For those of you who do not know, geomagnetics is the study of the earth's magnetic field, which is responsible for a great many things. The field has small influences, such as making a compass work, to very large influences, such as deflecting solar winds from the sun. The detected disturbance was very small, barely detectable by the research company's high earth-orbit satellites. At first the researchers passed over the anomaly in the data. An incident report was created, and they all but forgot about it. An internal audit of the company's projects was done for budgetary purposes about a year later, which is when the report resurfaced and came to my attention. The wording of the report was curious to me. I decided to establish a project to study the disturbance and classified its status as 'Above Top Secret.' The charter for this project was to work independently from the research company and get me some answers."

Number Three cleared his throat. "Pardon my interruption, Number One, but was your involvement with this project direct?"

Number One looked put off by the question and annoyed at the interruption. He gathered himself and said coolly, "All interaction was indirect and transacted through an intermediary."

This response seemed to please Number Three and the rest of the council. The group's survival depended upon one item above all else. Discretion was to be used in all facets of business, and absolutely no direct ties to the shell companies could be made back to the council.

Number One continued. "Throughout the next three years, the project team discovered a way to detect these anomalies after they happened, but could not predict when and where they would occur. Unfortunately even after three years and seventy-two million dollars, they were no closer to understanding why the disturbances were happening. Just as I was about to cancel the project, a young, new researcher named Dr. Gene Resman joined the research team and made very interesting progress. Because of the unique signature the anomaly produced, he inferred that the anomaly did not occur naturally. This means that a man-made process or device was causing the interruptions in the earth's magnetic field. After many months of determining possible uses for such a device, Dr. Resman concluded that there was only one practical reason that this type of technology would be created."

The council members were deadly silent. Number One continued. "Somehow, in some way, someone has developed a way to repel the earth's magnetic field away from an object. Although this technology was thought to be theoretically possible, there is no evidence that any known scientist is even close to discovering how to achieve this outcome."

Number One paused for a moment while the council members caught up to what he had just said. The silence was broken by a question from Number Four. "Number One, I think I can speak for several of us at this table when I say that I'm not sure I understand what this all means. Are you saying that there is a threat to the earth's magnetic field? Did our group in some way cause this threat?"

Number One explained, "Think of the earth as one giant magnet. If you have a magnet that is positively charged and you hold a negatively charged magnet near it, the two magnets are drawn to each other, right?"

The council members nodded.

"Have you ever seen two magnets that move away from each other as they got closer?"

The men nodded again.

"That happens when you have two positively or two negatively charged magnets. Well, someone has figured out a way to use the earth and a device as two magnets that have the same type of charge."

The members stayed silent, so Number One continued. "Someone has developed an anti gravity machine."

The council members looked at each other in disbelief. The men started talking loudly amongst themselves. Number Seven overheard Number Six and Number Four talking.

"An anti gravity machine that doesn't use a gas engine? If that is the case, the demand for oil is going to drop like a rock if this ever becomes public," said Number Six in a frantic, elevated voice.

Number Four quickly responded, "We need to do something about this now. We need to nip this in the bud. This type of invention could put us out of business."

The conversations were growing more heated. Number One yelled, "Order gentlemen, order! I'm sure by now you understand the threat this type of discovery has on our business interests. The good news is that we have uncovered this development before it becomes public. I move for a vote to evoke Plan Alpha."

The room went so silent that the only sound was the air moving through the vent on the wall. Plan Alpha was a big step to take for an unsubstantiated finding. The plan was constructed around one under lying principle; Use all the considerable resources the group had at its disposal and eradicate the problem by any and all means necessary.

Without hesitation or pause, Number Six said, "I second the motion on the floor."

The vote passed unanimously. The council had released the dogs of war.

CHAPTER FOUR

The flight was the most majestic sight I had ever seen. When I watched the Discovery Channel I hadn't even gotten a glimpse of what I experienced during space flight. The first thing that moved me to awe was the intense brilliance of what seemed like billions of stars. The most remote areas of the world that I had ever been could not prepare me for how radiant the stars could be without the interference of the earth's atmosphere. I glanced in the opposite direction, back down to the earth. White swirls blanketed the deep blue oceans that covered much of the planet. The picture from a satellite would not come close to conveying how vivid the stark contrast of the white clouds meshing with the green and blue backdrop could be.

A shiver shot down my spine when I saw what happened next. Just beyond the curvature of the earth I saw a white cap peeking over the horizon. I must have been in shock, not registering what it was at first. As it slowly climbed over the dazzling blue ocean, I realized what it was. At that moment I felt very small. I knew that I was witnessing something that only a handful of very fortunate people had ever seen from this vantage point. The moon was rising over the earth. It was such a beautiful sight I felt my eyes start to moisten. Before the tears began to fall, I was jolted back to reality by Jonah.

"Surreal, isn't it?" he asked.

My body had not caught up with my mind yet. All I could get out of my mouth was a stuttering, "How?"

Jonah regarded the question for a moment. I could almost hear a tinge of jealousy when he spoke. "I remember my first flight. I wish that feeling I got could be replicated every time. Although I don't get that feeling anymore, I know enough to give you a couple of minutes to enjoy it before we talk."

I barely heard what Jonah had said. I was in a trance-like state. Not even the most powerful drugs created by man could come close to the euphoria that I was feeling. I worked hard to imprint as many details of this experience my mind could handle. I never wanted the feeling to end. I knew it would eventually. I just prayed that I could somehow later recall the inexplicable feeling I had.

Because I was completely submerged in my thoughts, I lost all perception of time. Jonah began to speak after what seemed to be a couple of hours, but in reality was probably only a couple of minutes.

"I can't really explain how."

Not remembering what I had asked a couple of minutes prior, I responded, "What?"

Jonah continued, "You asked the question, 'How'?"

"I did?"

Jonah smiled and said, "You asked me how. I assume you meant 'how did we achieve orbit nine hundred and ninety-two miles off the earth's surface?'"

This question snapped me back to full awareness. I needed to know the answer. Fully in charge of all my faculties once again, I responded. "That's not nearly the only question I have." Processing the day's events, I continued.

"In addition to how we somehow traveled in near silence nine hundred and ninety-two miles off the earth's surface in an invisible spacecraft, I'd like to know a couple of other things. First, who's Garrett and how is he involved? Second, who the hell are you, Jonah? Lastly, what the hell is this all about, and why have I been chosen?"

Jonah calmly replied, "I know you have many questions. The fact is that you have many more questions than I have answers. The man we are going to see is the best person to answer all of your questions."

Seeing that Jonah was just the help hired to carry out the task of transporting me to a meeting, I decided to lighten up on the questioning. A moment passed, which allowed some of the tension in the spacecraft to settle a bit. When I felt the rush of confusion and anger had passed, I calmed myself and asked in a levelheaded tone, "Can you at least tell me who we are going to meet?"

This was one question Jonah seemed prepared, or even authorized, to answer. "I can't really tell you who he is. To be completely honest, I don't know. No one knows who he truly is. What I can tell you is that he is unlike anyone you will ever meet in your life."

In a normal situation, a response like that one would be greeted with skepticism or even disdain; however, given where we were and what had transpired until now, I decided to trust what Jonah was saying.

Jonah continued, "He's felt by many and known by none. He's an intensely private man. That's the reason we are traveling such a great distance to meet him. The only thing I can tell you with absolute certainty is that he is exponentially smarter than anyone you have ever met. When you do meet with him, you should keep that thought in the back of your mind, because he'll know instantly if you are not truthful with him."

His statement struck a nerve. It sounded like a cheesy line from a movie I had seen weeks before. The conviction with which it was said made it sound legitimate. Jonah laughed and let out an exacerbated grunt like he himself was in disbelief about what he had said.

I thought the guy was crazy or knew something that genuinely shocked even him. I decided to probe his curious reaction. "What?" I asked.

Jonah had given me more information than he was authorized to give by his inadvertent display of emotion. He immediately tried to backpedal.

"Nothing," he said.

"That wasn't nothing. What do you know that you are not telling me?" I almost wined like a kid whose parents not allow him to go to the video arcade.

I continued, "C'mon, Jonah. You have to realize that every single thing that has happened today is completely confusing to me. I really need any information you can provide. Please tell me anything you know."

I think that Jonah was resigned to the fact that I had picked up on his outburst. He answered. "Well, you could fill the Library of Congress with what I know."

His cocky response was not at all unexpected. It did show a side of Jonah that had not been revealed on the golf course. I knew that there was a lot I didn't know about Jonah, so I let him continue without interruption.

"I was just thinking that to my knowledge, the man we're going to meet has never directly requested that a specific individual be brought to him. As a security measure, he's never let an outsider into his world. You must be something very special for him to have broken his cardinal rule."

I decided not to respond. My hope was that by my silence, Jonah would continue.

"The only reason I can think of for him to break his rule is that you have something he wants. After all, you have the same background as he does."

"What do you mean, the same background?"

Without pause, Jonah turned his head to me and looked dead in my eyes. With an eerily ominous smile, he said, "You are both experts in the field of science and technology."

A voice came from the speakers from within the vehicle. "Package, this is Comm. Thirty seconds to reentry. Stir the tanks for retro-rocket burn on my mark. Three-two-one, mark."

Jonah leaned forward and depressed a switch located in the middle of the instrumentation panel. A stirring noise came from above our heads that sounded like a kitchen appliance mixing dough. The noise continued for about five seconds and then stopped.

"Comm, this is package. Tanks are stirred. On standby for retro-rocket burn on your mark," Jonah said in a calm and practiced voice.

"Roger, wait thirty."

Jonah turned to me and said, "I hope you haven't eaten much today, because this is where it tends to get a little messy."

I suddenly felt like we were rising up the slow incline of an amusement park ride, the feeling that comes from knowing that the first drop on the ride was nearing. My muscles tensed. My mouth went dry, and my heartbeat quickened.

The voice from the speaker said, "Arm retro-rockets."

Jonah replied, "Retro-rockets armed."

"Plug in geomagnetic coordinates at one-niner-niner feet."

Jonah leaned forward and typed in 199,000 into the keypad on the center instrumentation panel. He turned to me. "We need the help of the rockets to break through the atmosphere. Once we reach one hundred and ninety-nine thousand feet, the unique propulsion system that got us into orbit will take over and slow our descent."

My eyes darted around and Jonah must have seen that I was nervous. He said, "At first it will be a very strange sensation. You just have to go with it. Don't fight it. Just relax as best you can. The minute you start fighting it, you will become sick and could blackout."

I had some appreciation for Jonah waiting to tell me this information until the very last possible moment, like ripping off a Band-aid. Instead of ripping it off slowly and telling me what to expect early in the fight, he decided to let me enjoy the wonders of space travel and save the impending bad part of the flight to himself.

The speaker came back alive. "Burn retro-rockets in five-four-three-two-one. Go for burn."

Jonah flipped another switch on the center dash. At first, all I heard was a slight hissing. The vehicle inched its way closer to earth. I thought, "If this is all that happens, then it should be no problem at all." As the earth grew increasingly bigger in the window, I decided to take one more look at the stars. When I looked out into the infinite heavens, I started to feel as if my body were trying to float out of the seat. I turned back to the earth and saw it getting bigger and bigger. My front-row seat to the beautiful big earth was then distorted and replaced with an orange and blue glow. We were plummeting to the earth like a fireball moving twenty times the speed of sound. The cabin shook. The warmth of the orange glow came through the window. After what seemed like an eternity, I felt the familiar slow hum from beneath my feet. The orange and blue glow faded and the cabin stopped vibrating. The feeling of being lifted off my seat was replaced with a slight tug from beneath my butt, as if the seat were pulling on the lower half of my body. The vehicle finally slowed. My stomach felt like it wanted to continue the supersonic descent back to earth. Remembering Jonah's words, I decided not to fight the feeling. I took several deep breaths, so deep that I felt as though I might start hyperventilating. Conscious of this fact, I tried to gain control by taking in a breath and counting to three to exhale.

Once a couple of minutes had passed, a feeling of serenity washed over me. The vehicle seemed to float back down to earth like a leaf in the wind. I had to infer that the worst of the ordeal was over. A couple of deep breaths allowed me to regain my senses and bring my heart rate down to one level below the "exploding in my chest" level.

I had the audacity to look back out the window for the first time since plummeting back to the earth encased in a fiery ball. I saw only the deep blue ocean. There was no cloud cover in this area. I could see thousands of miles in each direction. Off in the distance I could make out some landmasses. They looked too far away for them to be our final destination. I couldn't believe that we would travel so far only to land smack dab in the middle of an ocean.

Just as the thought crossed my mind, a barely discernable pinprick of green started to emerge from the vast ocean. It appeared to be a tiny island. There was no indication of any landmasses even remotely close to the island. A secondary glance at the surrounding area confirmed my thought. This must be where we were going to land. Jonah startled me when he began to speak.

"I have to say that I'm very impressed. Although not too many people have done what you just did, I'd estimate that ninety-five percent of the time there would be chunks of vomit on the dash when a rookie is involved. Thank you for sparing me that."

The voice from the speaker shot through the cabin. "Package, this is Comm. You have been reacquired. Continue on present course at your current rate of descent. Touchdown has you at five minutes, fifteen seconds. Copy that?"

"Roger Comm. Maintaining current rate of descent. Touchdown

in five minutes and counting. We are five-by-five for approach."

"I want to know what this is all about right now!" I said in an angry tone.

Jonah let out an exaggerated exhale and said, "Today has been an emotional roller coaster. I understand that. But you've come too far to freak out now. Just a couple more minutes to go, and you'll get all the answers you need. Please relax, and we'll be on the ground in a couple of minutes."

"Relax? Relax? How can I possibly relax after plummeting through the atmosphere at fifteen thousand miles an hour?"

I knew it was no use going into a prolonged rant. Jonah was a cool customer. No sense in making the rest of the short ride miserable for him. I decided to be quiet the rest of the ride.

Just as we were about to touch down, Jonah broke the silence.

"Remember what I said. This man is infinitely smarter than anyone you have ever encountered. Just be truthful and everything will be fine."

Given Jonah's unique skill set of space flight and God knows what else, I decided to take his statement as a serious warning. What had I gotten myself into?

CHAPTER FIVE

"Can I get you a drink, Mr. Bouchard?" Albert entered the main cabin conference room. Albert was the personal aide to the man referred to by the council members as Member Number Seven. Member Number Seven's name was Dean Bouchard. He had come from a very long line of Bouchards. The Bouchard line was one of the oldest bloodlines known to man. Descended from European royalty, the family would make a fateful decision to break off its ties with the Monarch and start a life in the newfound land named America back in the 1700s. Just like investors who get in on the ground floor of a company that has a meteoric rise to greatness, the Bouchards got in on the find of all time. America, with its great vastness, promised to be a land that had an overabundance of everything. The lands were supple for farming. Each passing year new natural resources lay almost in plain sight, waiting for someone to plunder its riches. The Bouchards took full advantage of the opportunity and quickly became one of the richest families in the world. Generation after generation, the strong male patriarchs of the family steadily built on this growing wealth and power. The family's tentacles reached far and wide over the entire country. Over the years, it had cultivated many business interests in its burgeoning empire. In addition to a multitude of businesses, the family was deeply intertwined in government. This relationship was only natural, as no great business grew to the size of the Bouchard's without the strong backing of the United States Government.

Dean's family background was the reason why the council had approached him. His family's influence and wealth became so extensive that it provided a perfect cover to conduct council business unhindered. Although the Bouchard family had all the money it could ever need in a lifetime and thousands of generations to come, it was engrained in Dean's DNA to want more. The lust for money and power was an inherited trait. The undeniable desire was an involuntary response that was programmed into him ever since he could remember. It was this need for supreme power that drove him to accept the council's invitation. With that acceptance came trillions of dollars. His fortunes grew to such a staggering amount that the paltry sixty billion or so that *Forbes* magazine had claimed the world's richest man had was interest Dean collected in a year. If this were ever to become public, most people would ask why someone needed that amount of money. Dean knew the answer. For him, it wasn't about the money. It was about the game. It was him and six other individuals against the world. To date, they were decimating the opponents.

Dean looked up at his personal aide and replied, "Some Pelligrino, if you would, Albert."

"One cube with a slice of lemon. Yes, sir," said Albert.

Dean smiled at this reply by his faithful aide. Albert had been with Dean Bouchard for almost thirty-five years. He was the only one in the world Dean could trust completely and without a second thought. Thirty-five years prior, Dean had met Albert at an orphanage where he was about to make a sizable contribution. As Dean strolled around the home taking in the misfortunes of the children who inhabited the place, he came upon a boy playing by himself far away from the commotion of Dean's visit. Dean knelt down next to nine-year-old the boy who was sitting in his bunk bed. Dean introduced himself and asked the boy his name. The boy replied, "My name is Albert. I know who you are, Mr. Bouchard."

Struck by the boy's bluntness, Dean continued, "Do you know why I'm here at the orphanage?"

"You have lots of money and we have none. You are here to give us life."

Dean was dumfounded at what the quiet, nine-year-old boy said. Dean had negotiated with heads of state and Fortune one hundred CEOs on a regular basis. This simple expression out of a nine-year-old orphan floored him and left him speechless. After talking with Albert for another thirty minutes, Dean reached a simple conclusion. Dean would donate the money needed by the orphanage if the orphanage would allow him to adopt Albert. The director of the orphanage jumped at the opportunity not only to get the much-needed funding, but also move the headcount down by one.

Dean took Albert under his wing. He cared for him as a father cared for his child. Albert was spared nothing. He was entitled to very best of everything. Dean was proud of what Albert had accomplished with his life. Although Dean had wanted Albert to use his first-rate education to follow his own interests, Albert persuaded Dean to allow him to become his personal aide. At first, Dean was adamantly opposed to the idea. He didn't want Albert corrupted by the often immoral and illegal activities necessary when one rose to the level of power at which he had attained.

Over time, Dean warmed to the idea of Albert joining him on council matters. The council had all but forced Dean to withdraw from public life, which required that Dean become invisible to the media. He wrapped himself in an insulating cocoon of protection so that what he and the council were doing remained unknown to the outside world. That type of isolation was very difficult for Dean, who yearned for a friend he could confide in. The double life was taking its toll on his emotions. Against his better judgment, he requested and received the council's permission to bring Albert into certain aspects of the council's business. There was a stern warning given at the time by the council. Dean's failure to adhere to the council's warning meant certain death for both him and Albert. Although Dean knew he could never fully divulge all the inner workings of the council, he also knew that the council would eventually grow old and need to hand the reigns to a new generation of members. Albert was Dean's heir-apparent. One day, all that Dean had accomplished would be handed over to him.

Although Dean had three sons from which to choose, all of them for one reason or another would not have the internal fortitude required to take his seat on the council. Growing up with enormous wealth had spoiled his sons. They did not possess the discipline it would take to fill a role on the council. Dean knew it early on. Albert was Dean's last chance to raise a child and mold him into a man who could take his spot when the time was right.

Albert sat down across from Dean. The conference room in which they sat was located at the heart of the converted Boeing 747. The plane was the flagship of Dean's private fleet of airplanes. It was the plane he most often used. When the runway at the destination was too small to accommodate the large jetliner, Dean used a smaller jet in his personal fleet to fill his need. This plane, however, was outfitted with all the luxuries of home. Bedrooms, workout facilities, a conference room, a dining room, and a fully stocked galley made sure of a comfortable journey. The jumbo jet was also outfitted with a communications system that rivaled that of Air Force One. Dean could feel safe and secure about conducting any type of business from this mobile fortress.

"Today's messages, sir." Albert handed Dean some pink slips of paper.

In the beginning, when Albert first started working for Dean, Dean had insisted that he be addressed by his first name. Albert refused such informality while under Dean's employ. From then on Albert always addressed Dean as sir or Mr. Bouchard. Given how close they had become over the years, Dean found it a little awkward. After several years, Dean had become accustomed to Albert's formality. Dean took the messages and flipped through them slowly. Albert did a terrific job at filtering unimportant items, so Dean knew that any messages Albert provided would require his attention.

As Dean reviewed the messages, Albert inquired, "How did the meeting go, sir?"

Dean knew this question would be coming. Albert was the one who had driven Dean to the meeting. He knew that it was a council meeting and that it was not planned. Although Albert didn't know exactly what the council did at these meetings, he knew from past experience that they were held once a year. Because the last meeting was held eight months before in Germany, Albert knew that something important had arisen.

Without looking up, Dean replied to the question. "I'm afraid a storm is brewing on the horizon, Albert."

Albert didn't rush the conversation or press for more details. It was ingrained in his training that when extracting information from an unwilling party, you allow him or her to guide the conversation.

Dean smiled to himself. His protégé had learned well. He knew that the absence of an immediate response was a tactic that he had taught Albert. He decided to play along. "It appears as if the egg of our golden goose has been found."

Albert's patience had been rewarded. That response told him all he needed to know. Not needing to extract any further information, he was free to engage in dialogue. If the dialogue produced any additional details, it was considered a bonus. If not, he had enough information to make a next step in this cat-and-mouse game. Albert shook his head at the comment. He replied, "How much do they know?"

Dean was concerned that Albert knew too much about the situation. If the council had ever found out how much Albert really knew, heir-apparent or not, Albert would be killed. This was a risk both Dean and Albert were willing to take.

Dean replied, "They are further along than I would have thought. They know it exists and they have a way of knowing after it has been used. I would doubt very seriously if Number One divulged all he knew to the council. Like any good businessman, he let the council hear exactly what he wanted the members to hear. I'm sure he has other plans that he didn't share with the council."

"What do you think he will do?" asked Albert.

Dean looked at Albert. The way Albert handled himself reminded Dean of himself when he was Albert's age. Although physically they did not look alike, the mannerisms Albert displayed and the way at which he approached and manipulated a conversation was very familiar to Dean. Dean showed no outward emotion at this realization. Instead, he decided to test his young protégé.

"What do you think he will do, Albert?"

Albert considered this reversal. He identified the meaning of the question immediately. It was a mental joust. A challenge laid down by his teacher. This was a test to see how he would react to an unknown situation. With the experience of an expert poker player, he was sure not to provide any tells to his teacher that he was onto his game. He simply replied, "Misdirection."

Dean liked the response. Short and open for interpretation. Give a little, take a lot. At that moment he was very proud and impressed with Albert. He had spotted the challenge and acted appropriately. He took the tiny pieces of information Dean had given him, processed them, and came up with the same conclusion Dean had reached while leaving the council meeting hours earlier. Dean nodded and said, "I think so as well. Number One has upped the ante. The council initiated Plan Alpha. The directive was clear. Hunt down and destroy the threat. I'm afraid our plan now needs to be expedited."

Albert showed a crack in his façade. Plan Alpha was a major reaction. It was like putting out a match with a fire hose. Days earlier, Albert had been confident that the work that he and Dean had been doing over the previous five years was undetectable by the council. However, with a full blitz from the council, anything was possible. If the council had found out about what they had been doing, they would be terminated without a second thought.

Although Dean could not see Albert's concern, after so many years with Albert he could feel it. As any good father would do in this situation, he decided to comfort his son. "God will see us through this, Albert. God will see us through this and the world will never be the same again. This will be my lasting contribution to humanity, and you will be there to ensure it stays the course."

CHAPTER SIX

I was extremely relieved to have both of my feet firmly planted on solid ground again. Jonah and I exited the vehicle that had just provided me the ride of a lifetime. I walked a couple of feet away and looked back. The vehicle that I had mistaken for a golf cart now showed its true form. It was roughly the size of a golf cart but was altogether different. Upon a cursory glance, one might mistake the vehicle for one of those tiny two-person Smart Cars you see in Europe. On closer inspection, I saw several differences. The most noticeable difference was that at the base of the vehicle there was a metallic oval bumper that encircled the entire car. This metallic disk appeared to cover the whole under carriage of the vehicle. I crouched down close to the ground and saw four small wheels that were barely discernable.

"This way, Ethan." Jonah walked along a lit path away from the landing pad.

Deciding to ignore Jonah, I continued to explore this tiny machine that had given me an incomprehensible journey. I circled the vehicle as a lion would stalk his prey. My technical background opened a floodgate of thoughts about how this machine might have worked. I casually walked to the back of the vehicle. I looked at the roof and saw two nozzles. The cup-shaped nozzles must have been the retro-rockets that gently nudged us out of orbit. I continued my way around to the driver's side and saw a slight color change on the skin of the car. This skin appeared to cover every inch of surface. The skin must have some type of pixilation like that of a TV. It was able to change colors in very fine detail to disguise its true form. Jonah had used the term "electrochromatic" to describe it. I'd heard of various uses for such technology. I'd actually seen this type of technology in use by a prospective client. The windows that surrounded the executive boardroom in this client's headquarters building made use of it. At the flip of a switch the clear glass walls of the conference room became frosted. The client made it a point to show how technically advanced the walls were. Blinds would have done equally as well and cost less than one percent of the fancy glass. If those corporate lackeys could have only seen what I was looking at right now, they wouldn't be nearly as smug as they were during that meeting.

I could have spent the next several hours studying this technological marvel. It was so far beyond anything that I had ever seen that it ate away at the curious side of my brain. The sun was setting, and the lack of light on the landing pad was making it more difficult to make my observations. Then it struck me. The sun was setting. It was about nine in the morning when Jonah and I started this journey. Jonah said that the flight time was thirty-two minutes. Where the hell are we that the sun was setting? This thought snapped me back to full alertness. This was the first time I had taken my eyes off the vehicle that had gotten us here.

I looked around at the surrounding area. It was hard to judge the size of the island during our descent. I looked around the periphery of the landing pad. All I could see was miles and miles of ocean. The sun setting caused tiny reflections on the vast ocean. It looked like millions of orange fireflies dancing on the water. It was a natural wonder nearly as impressive as the image of the moonrise that had been seared into my mind twenty minutes prior. This image put me in a relaxed hypnotic state. I felt as though I was the last person on earth. This is probably the reason why I was startled when I felt a hand on my shoulder.

"Beautiful, isn't it?" Jonah stood next to me and took in the magnificent sunset for a moment. He then continued. "We really must get going. We don't want to keep the old man waiting."

I was torn between wanting to stay to watch the Monet-like sunset and my desire for some answers. My logical side won out. I followed Jonah down a well-groomed slate path. It was the first time I noticed a series of interconnected dwellings on the interior of the island. From high above, the island had looked like an uninhabited forest. At eye-level, it was altogether different. The dwellings appeared to be dug into the jagged rock faces of the island, which provided near invisibility from above. Whoever designed these structures clearly wanted to provide the appearance that this island was uninhabited.

Jonah and I continued our journey down the path. Eventually we approached the grand entryway to what appeared to be the main dwelling. As we got closer to the dimly lit entryway, I noticed two massive wooden doors. If I had to guess, the doors were four times my height. At first glance they appeared to be normal, solid-wood doors. As we drew closer, I noticed that the entire height of the door was adorned with intricate carvings of figurines. For some reason my mind flashed to the famous sculpture named "The Gates of Hell" by the French artist Rodin. I stopped and took a closer look at the doors. Rodin had tried to depict what the gates of hell would look like. He carved faces of demons, goblins, and lost souls trying to escape from the doors. The scene on the doors in front of us painted an altogether different picture. It was a series of men, women, and children working in unison to build a great city. The figurines looked happy in their roles within the society. The craftsmanship was breathtaking. Thousands of figurines covered the doors. It seemed like an exact opposite to the "Gates of Hell." If I had created such an amazing work of art, I would have named it, "Gates of Utopia."

Just as I was about to reach out to feel one of the figurines, a screeching sound came from behind the doors. Slowly, each of the massive thirty-foot doors opened.

On the other side of the doors stood a slender man dressed in a hand-tailored three-piece suit. Jonah glanced at him and said, "Hello, David, are we ready?"

Before answering, David looked at Jonah briefly then gave me a once over. For some unexplained reason, I didn't think that David was the man I had come here to meet. It may have been Jonah's lack of formality or David's demeanor that gave me this impression.

David responded as if I were not standing in front of him. "Dinner will be served in ten minutes. Please escort Mr. Kravis to the master guest room. He can freshen up and change into something more suitable if he likes. There is a wide selection of evening attire in the armoire."

David used his eyes to scan me from head to toe. I thought I saw a hint of a smirk on his face. The way he had said it and the look he gave made it clear that he thought I was underdressed for the occasion. I wondered if David was privy to my kidnapping from a golf course earlier that day. Trying not to let it get under my skin, I nodded, smiled, and said thank you.

David did an immediate about face, and with his chin held high in the air, he walked away. Jonah motioned me to follow him and said, "David comes off as a massive snob at first, but he really is an all right guy once you get to know him. He has been with the old man for a long time."

I pondered what Jonah had just said and decided to ask, "Do you think I will be around here long enough to get to know the real David?"

Jonah looked back at me and raised his shoulders in an "I have no idea" type expression. As we walked down the long corridor, I was taken aback by the finishings of the building. It had all the elegance and beauty of a royal European castle. The thirty-foot high cathedral ceilings featured wood beams and, the floors had intricate patterns of custom-laid marble. It was amazing to me that an edifice of this detail and eloquence could have been constructed in the middle of the ocean. It must have taken more wealth then I'd ever seen to pull something like this off. After taking a ride in an invisible spaceship halfway around the world, I had a feeling that the meeting would be icing on the cake.

Jonah and I reached what I could only surmise was the master guest room. Jonah opened the door and swung his arm through the threshold, as if to signal that I should enter. Jonah spoke. "You are right in here, Ethan. We have about ten minutes. Not much time to relax. Throw some water on your face, and I'll be back to escort you to the dining room."

I decided upon landing that I would reserve my numerous questions. Although I had many questions, I knew that Jonah would not be the one to answer them. Without a word, I stepped past Jonah into the guest room.

Master guest room was right. I was staring into a room that was easily as big as my apartment in Olde City Philadelphia. It was furnished with what appeared to be English and French antiques. The furniture was intricately carved mahogany polished to a mirror shine. There was a flat screen TV mounted above a grand wood-burning fireplace. A Queen Anne-style writing desk with a brown leather high-back chair placed on one side of the room. The room was the type of room you might see roped off in a museum. I was hesitant to touch anything, sensing its high dollar value.

Given that I had only a couple of minutes before Jonah was going to come by and pick me up, I decided to make the most of the time. I walked over to what I thought may be the door to the bathroom. I opened it to discover a secondary room with a sauna in it. Realizing the mistake, I looked toward the opposite end of the football-field-sized room. I located the French doors that led to the bathroom, walked across the room, and entered. The outer chamber of the bathroom was about four hundred square feet. Along the back wall was a double vanity. I walked over to the vanity and turned the knob. Instead of a normal faucet, the sinks had a curved metal bar where the facet typically was located. The water ran evenly over the curved bar and created a waterfall effect. "Cool," I said out loud.

I spent the next couple of minutes cleaning up. I splashed water on my face and dried off. I relieved myself of some excess fluid. I had thought about what snobby David had said about evening attire and decided to see if any of the clothes in the armoire struck my fancy. Before I could make my way to the armoire, I heard a knock on the door.

Jonah peeked in and said, "You ready to get some answers, Ethan?"

Deciding that it would serve as a nice poke in the eye to David, I skipped the change of clothes. I walked over to the door and said to Jonah, "Apsa-freakin-lootly!"

Jonah led the way through the maze of corridors. The complex was much more extensive than one could observe from the outside. It took us a good ten minutes, but we finally reached the entrance to the dining room. I could feel my anticipation rising. Whoever had set this meeting up went to tremendous lengths to do so. I didn't know what to expect.

Jonah opened the door and ushered me inside. I looked around and saw that there was no one in the massive dining room. The room itself was rectangular. Two doors on opposite ends provided the only entryways. The walls of the room were wood paneled. Huge portraits of men hung around all available wall space. I felt their cold stares penetrating my body. In the center of the room was a French-style dining table made from dark wood. Its scalloped edges and bowed legs gave me the impression that it was centuries old. The table could comfortably seat twenty people with the capacity for more. I heard "good luck," as Jonah slowly exited the dining room closing the door behind him.

As I was taking in the beauty of yet another breathtakingly furnished room, the door at the opposite end of the room began to open. There was a strong contrast between the dimly lit dining room and room that lay on the opposite side of the door. The difference barely allowed me to make out a silhouette of the man entering. As he drew closer, more and more facial details emerged. When he was fully in focus standing ten feet in front of me, a sudden surge of adrenaline shot through my body. I recognized the old, fragile man standing before me. All I could say was "You?"

The man smiled and was visibly happy that I had remembered him.

"I know you." I said in complete astonishment.

"Our meeting was very brief and many years ago, Ethan. I'm glad I made such an impression," the old man responded.

Getting used to the feeling, I was more in control than I had been in the other speechless situations that day. I continued, "Who are you, and what is this place?"

The old man's eyes widened, and with a broad smile replied, "Let me show you."

CHAPTER SEVEN

Dean Bouchard disembarked his plane and walked across the tarmac of the private airfield toward the sleek black Maybach that awaited him. The Maybach was a specially designed mobile fortress that had been withdrawn from the belly of the converted 747 moments earlier. Albert stood by the passenger door and opened it as Dean drew closer. Dean entered the vehicle, and the door was closed behind him. Albert walked to the opposite side of the car and got in the passenger-side door.

Although Jason Owens had been Dean's trusted driver for many years, Dean raised the partition between the front seat and the passenger compartment, the final step needed to completely secure the passenger compartment from prying ears.

Comfortable that he could speak freely, Dean said, "Brief me on this." Dean held up one of the messages that Albert had given him during the five-hour flight back from London. The message simply said, "Contact – 6:43 A.M. EST."

"Our Spectra-star fifteen satellite picked up on the signature earlier this morning. We were able to get a strong fix on the location. The signal emanated from a golf course located thirty minutes north of here in Bryn Mawr, Pennsylvania," said Albert quickly and concisely.

Dean replied, "Were the teams dispatched to the location?"

"Teams are on standby, but there is a wrinkle, sir. The golf course is located at Ravens Valley Country Club," said Albert in a hesitant tone.

Dean knew Albert's hesitation was well warranted. If Albert were to have given the go-ahead to the special operations team to raid the area, it would have sent shockwaves through the socially elite who inhabited the prestigious club and shown up as a big blip on the council's radar. Many of the club patrons traveled in the same circles as council members. It would not have been long before one of the council members somehow discovered the stories of the commando-style raid. What Dean could not understand was why Albert had waited so long to brief him on the event.

Albert preemptively addressed this concern. "I put the team in a holding pattern until we made contact with a friendly inside the club. Just as we were disembarking the plane, we heard back from our source. Our source told us that a twosome starting playing golf at 7:30 A.M. Eastern Standard Time. Typically this would not have been out of the norm, but the makeup of the twosome aroused some suspicion. One of the men in the twosome was not a member of the club. A member invited him as a guest. The member's name was Owen Lawrence. A quick background check revealed that Owen H. Lawrence is a federal Supreme Court judge for the Commonwealth of Pennsylvania. As far as we can tell, he is clean as a whistle. Apparently the judge did not show up to meet his guest."

Dean knew better than to interrupt and let Albert continue his winded explanation.

"The judge invited Ethan W. Kravis. Kravis owns a small security company and operates out of Center City, Philadelphia. Although his resume is quite impressive, from all outward appearances he's an average Joe. As far as our analysts can tell, he has no ties to anyone of importance. The judge and Kravis were not what interested our source. His suspicion grew when a second member he had never seen before showed up in the judge's place. The second member's name was Garrett Michaels. Quick background check on Michaels turned up nothing. No financials. No affiliations with covert government agencies. No history whatsoever."

Dean started to understand where Albert was taking him. It was nearly impossible these days not to leave a digital footprint. Through Dean's vast enterprise, he was plugged into the most extensive sources of data on the planet. If his analysts could not pull background on someone, it was an automatic red flag. Dean pondered this discovery and become obsessively curious about who this Michaels character was.

This discovery was intriguing to Dean, but it still didn't ensure that there was a connection between the sighting of the signature and this unknown quantity that goes by the name Garrett Michaels. Dean needed more data on the situation to make an informed decision. He couldn't approve a special operations raid based on what Albert had just told him. Dean interrupted Albert's briefing and said, "Although this information is curious, it doesn't provide enough information to take action. These anomalies can be explained by any number of factors."

Albert smiled and continued his briefing. "I agree with your assessment. This is why I took no action until now; however, I just received some new information that sheds additional light on the situation."

Albert was clearly excited when he began to speak. "A secondary signature was captured forty-seven minutes ago. The signal was triangulated to the sixth hole of the Ravens Valley Golf Course. Shortly after the signal was detected, Garrett Michaels returned to the clubhouse in a different golf cart and without Ethan Kravis. If you allow for an average of fifteen minutes per hole, that puts Kravis and Michaels at the sixth hole forty-seven minutes ago."

Dean felt something he had not felt in a long time. He felt a rush of excitement. He used to get this feeling when he closed a deal that would add billions to his coffers. That type of action no longer gave him a jolt of adrenaline. He cherished the feeling for a moment and said, "Very interesting indeed, Albert."

"What are your orders, sir?"

Dean contemplated this question for a moment. He knew the time for caution was coming to an end. He had to seize this golden opportunity.

"This is the best lead we have had over the last five years. We need to act decisively. With the initiation of Plan Alpha, we may not get another opportunity like this again. Contact the special operations team and have them devise three covert extraction plans. Give them the details of the terrain. The mission objective is to capture and extract Garrett Michaels. Stress to the team lead that this extraction is to be done without anyone at that club finding out. I want these three plans in my hands in less than fifteen minutes. Indicate that mission silence is the highest priority of the team. I don't want any ripples in the pond. I'm authorizing a twenty-million-dollar bonus for the team lead and a five-million-dollar bonus for each team member, if the mission is a success. No one at that club is to be collateral damage. If the mission goes sideways, they are to abort and hightail it out of there ASAP. Get to it."

Having received his instruction, Albert immediately picked up the SAMSAC satellite phone from the armrest. He spoke with a sense of urgency into the phone. "Go secure. Scrambled loop for black op team one."

Albert paused as the satellite phone opened an impervious connection with the black operations team leader. He heard the familiar high-pitched squeal of the signal scrambler. A moment later, a voice answered.

"Go for team lead," said the special operations team leader.

Albert spent the next couple of minutes relaying Dean's instructions to the team lead. Confident that the team lead understood the delicate nature of the pending operation, Albert gave Dean a reassuring nod. Albert ended the conversation with the team lead by saying, "When you have developed the three extraction plan alternatives, pick up the SAMSAC and relay the following code to the operator: Echo-Lima-Niner-Niner-Alpha-Echo. The operator will patch you back directly to me. Upon review of the plans, I will provide further instruction. Get it done!"

Albert hung up the SAMSAC phone and said, "The ball has been set in motion."

Dean knew he was in a race against time. He had to act swiftly before the council's minions destroyed his simple plan. The timing was curious to Dean. What were the odds of receiving the best lead he had ever received on the same day that the council had been made aware such a technology existed? Dean would have to explore this thought in more depth at a later time. For now, he had to focus on the task at hand. He had to be successful in carrying out the plan that he and Albert had devised five years before when they first discovered the geomagnetic disturbances. He had to capture this technology for himself before the council could erase any sign that it had ever existed.

The plan was simple. If he could capture this technology and own it; he alone could own the world. He would be the last man standing on the council. With his abundantly deep pockets, he could fund the rapid expansion and development of replacing every engine on earth with his technology. Who knew what other areas of technology this invention would impact? He had the means to maintain control over this invention. It would work its way into every crevice of human existence. He would grow to be a god among men. People would speak his name for all time. This lasting legacy is the prize he so desperately sought. Nothing would stand in his way of achieving this goal. He would need to focus and execute his plan with extreme precision if he wanted to pull this nearly impossible task off. All these thoughts gave Dean an untapped inner strength. Extremely confident that he had mentally prepared himself for the battle that was looming on the horizon, he said to Albert, "We'll use the house as the command post."

Albert nodded and spoke into the car's internal intercom. "To the estate".

The driver's voice came through the small speaker mounted above the partition and said, "Right away, sir."

CHAPTER EIGHT

My mind was in danger of overheating. I was trying desperately to figure out who this man really was. I'd met him only once seven years before when my company was just starting out. At that time, biometric devices were bulky, expensive, and had extremely limited functionality. My company was created to expand the scope of how these devices could be applied to real-life situations. This type of work didn't come cheap. Within a year, the company had burned through what little capital investment we had. I'd used the insignificant money we had left to secure a demonstration booth at the Comdex technology convention in Las Vegas. Las Vegas was defiantly the appropriate place to hold the conference. My company was on the verge of bankruptcy, and this would have been my last opportunity to roll the dice and get some much-needed cash to stay afloat.

The entire first day of the conference yielded zero prospects. Only a couple of stragglers passed by the booth. After suffering such a failure the first day of the conference, I gave serious consideration to not even showing up for the second day. I had everything riding on that convention. If I left the state of Nevada without securing some funding, the doors to my office would not open the following Monday.

The second day of the convention was much like the first. Almost the entire day passed without a single person stopping by the booth. It wasn't until about an hour prior to the convention closing down that my booth received its first visitor. The frail-looking man wandered over in a nonchalant manner. He stopped directly in front, giving me the impression he wanted to talk. Excited to get even a single person to stop and actually talk, I gave the visitor my full attention. It was odd at first, because he didn't follow the normal introduction process that emanated from the surrounding booths. Instead he simply said something that stuck with me to this very day.

"You should focus less on the device and more on the logic behind it. The device itself is nothing without someone thinking for it. You should create a logic hub that polices multiple devices like a person using his five senses".

Without my being able to say a word, this strange little man strolled off. I don't know why, but I took what this odd man said to heart. It made sense to me. Not thirty minutes after the strange encounter did my Hail Mary pass finally pay off. The convention was nearly closing, and a second visitor came by the booth. His name was Frank Watkins, and he was an angel investor. Frank invested in tiny companies like mine before the venture capitalists came in. We talked briefly, and within twenty minutes, my company had secured enough funding to keep us afloat for an additional three years.

It wasn't until I saw this odd little man again did I realize why Frank Watkins had stopped by and been our saving angel. It made perfect sense to me now.

The old man spoke. "I see that you put the money that Frank gave you to good use. I have been following your progress with great interest over the years."

All I could say was, "Who are you?"

"I'm sure you have many more questions than that," replied the man in a comforting voice. "If it's all right with you, we'll skip dinner. I'd like to spend some time with you to answer your questions and tell you why I have brought you here to my island. In order to do so, we must start right away. It's important that we get you back to the golf course before your absence arouses suspicion. Would it be acceptable if we retire to a more intimate setting? This dining room table is only good for when you don't want to talk to your guests."

I noticed that the old man had found some humor in his last statement and let out a small chuckle. "We can talk in the next room. This way, please."

He led me through the door he had come through moments before. We exited the dining room and entered a small study. In the center of the study were two leather recliners and a small couch. He motioned for me to take a seat in one of the recliners. I sat down and he sat across from me in the adjacent recliner.

He began to speak. "I know you have a great many questions. Please allow me a couple of minutes to speak. If what I say doesn't answer your most pressing questions, you will then have the opportunity to ask me some questions. If I'm able to provide answers, then you will receive them. Is that understood?"

I noticed something strangely familiar with the way this man had spoken. His words were direct and to the point. They followed a very logical thought process. His use of the terms "if" and "then" in his sentences reminded me of the millions of lines of computer code I had written. This man was either a robot or he had spent extensive amounts of time writing computer code. As I pondered this instinctive thought, he continued.

"Let me first say that I'm glad to see that you accepted Garrett's invitation. I doubt very highly that you would have accepted the invitation had you known what was involved in getting here. I'm glad you arrived unscathed. I'm also confident that the ride was something you will never forget. I'm delighted to finally have you here. As I am sure you have deduced by now, I have had my eye on you for some time.

Born Ethan William Kravis June 7, 1975, you were raised by your parents Lynn and Lawrence in suburban Philadelphia. You showed advanced propensity for science and mathematics at an early age, so your parents enrolled you in Grame Academy for gifted students. Graduating top of your class, you were awarded the Truman scholarship and given a full ride at the Massachusetts Institute of Technology. At MIT you developed groundbreaking logic protocols still in use by semiconductor companies to this day. After graduating from MIT with honors, you attended Harvard, where you received both an MBA and a juris doctorate simultaneously. Against your parents' wishes, you were offered and accepted a job with Upward Dynamics. This was an advanced think tank funded by the United States Army. Much of the work done by Upward Dynamics was classified above top secret. There you perfected the art of psychological warfare with the advent of the PsyPass system. The system was so effective during the first Gulf War that funding for the think tank was scaled back in the mid 1990s. It was then that you decided to start your company. The work being done by your own company was so advanced that many investors did not see its potential. Funding issues arose, and that's when I decided to get involved."

I sat absolutely still. Although most of the information this man had just spoken was matter of public record, PsyPass was known to very few. Only the highest levels of the US Army and government were privy to the details of this project. Whoever this man was, he had access to the US government's deepest and darkest secrets. Equally impressive was the fact that he had committed all of this information to memory. He did not need the aid of a file in front of him as he spoke.

I decided to heed the old man's words and let him continue uninterrupted.

"It looks as though my trivial amount of funding paid off," he continued.

A flat panel TV screen rose from what appeared to be a chest in the corner of the room. What was displayed on the screen was unmistakable. It was what I had spent the last five years of my life on. I looked at it in astonishment. It was the source code to the S.T.A.R.E security system. I was speechless to see it sitting there in its naked form. I went to extraordinary lengths to ensure that the source code never got out into the open. It was the only competitive advantage my company had, and I would protect it in every way I knew how.

All changes to the program were done offline. Not being connected to the Internet while making changes was just the first step in a long list of steps taken to protect my system. Specially built copper plating in the walls around the lab killed any signals both in and out of the lab. Required body scans were routine for the staff both entering and exiting the office. When the system was about to be installed, a triple obfuscation of the code was done before it was loaded onto the servers. Typically a single obfuscation of the code scrambled it so completely that there was no chance for a hacker to see the true code. Scrambling the code a further two times made it flat out impossible to revert it to its naked form.

Too many things I had seen and heard today just didn't make any sense to me. I had always had the unique ability to solve the unsolvable. The toughest puzzles my teachers and colleagues had posed to me could often be answered with relative ease. The series of inexplicable questions I had asked myself that day had taken their toll on my psyche. The flaunting of the source code I had so desperately tried to protect had broken me.

I started to feel dizzy and nauseated. My loss of situational awareness had thrown me completely off balance. I could feel my cheeks flush and perspiration form on my forehead. I hadn't even realized it, but the old man had stopped talking, gone over to the wet bar, and gotten a glass of ice water. He extended the glass to me and said, "Please drink this and do try to calm yourself. Everything is going to be just fine once you have some answers."

I grasped the glass and took a big swig of the ice-cold water. It was the best-tasting water I had ever had. I imagined that if I was stranded in the desert for three days without water, this is what it would taste like when I finally found some. The coldness of the water helped me regain some composure. The hot flash on my cheeks subsided. Feeling better, I took the opportunity the pause had created to ask my first question. "How did you get my source code?"

Probably seeing that I was one step away from going completely crazy, he answered. "I do have to give you credit. You took every precaution you could have to protect your code. What if I told you that I have invented a way to pass in and out of any computer system without ever being detected, regardless of whether or not it was networked?"

Looking at the old man like he was a suspect in a liquor store robbery, I replied, "I would say that you are full of shit."

The old man smiled at this blunt and unadulterated response. I noticed then that the flat panel TV that had displayed my source code had nothing but a big black zero displayed. I guessed someone was listening to our conversation, because the old man did nothing to change what was displayed on the screen. He went on to say, "I have taken a look at yours; now I would like to show you some code of my own."

He directed my attention to the monitor. A freakin' zero in the middle of a screen? This was his code? This guy must be one beer short of a six-pack.

He began to speak. "Very few people in the world know what you are about to hear. In fact, you are the third person who will know. All computer software is built on one underlying architecture, as you know. It is built upon binary code. It is built on ones and zeros. In computer speak, these ones and zeros are referred to as bits, of course. They are the smallest units of information on a computer. What if I told you that I have developed a way to take a single bit and store an infinite amount of data within it?"

This certainly caught my full attention.

The old man continued. "Here on the screen we have a single bit of information represented as a zero. Embedded in the zero are three hundred and eighty-six separate and distinct data cubes."

The zero shattered into hundreds of little cubes. One cube was isolated on the screen, while the others moved off to the side. The cube rotated ninety degrees and was cut in half. A cross section of the cube was displayed. There in the cross section of the cube was an unmistakable sight, several pages of my source code.

"Within each of the three hundred and eighty-six cubes are pages of raw data. Embedded in each of those pages of data are thousands of additional bits. Each of those bits can be split into three hundred and eighty-six additional cubes of data. And so on and so forth. Within this single bit of data, we can compress an infinite amount of information. This is the cornerstone of all the technology I have developed. This includes the technology for Alexander One, the spacecraft that brought you here. I call this technology Packet Assimilation Synthesis System, or P.A.S.S technology for short. It gives us a free P.A.S.S to walk into and out of any network on the planet."

The beauty was in the simplicity of it. It was astonishing to me. For what seemed like the millionth time that day, I was speechless with what had been explained to me. All of the data in the world contained in a single bit of information. It was a hard concept to wrap my head around. This opened up an entirely new line of questions. I sensed somehow that if I were to be trapped with this man in this room for ten years still wouldn't allow me enough time to have all my questions answered. I was so overwhelmed that I felt my brain starting to shut down.

"I'm sure by now you have many questions for me."

With an open mouth, I nodded my head with the obvious statement.

The old man continued. "Unfortunately we are rapidly running out of time. Perhaps we can spend what little time we have left explaining why I brought you here."

Not bothering to wait for a response, he continued. "I'd like to give you a very special gift. Your background puts you in a unique position to accept this gift. I would like to give you the rights and knowledge for you to bring a scaled-down version of the Alexander One to market. You and you alone will be responsible for introducing the world to the first geomagnetic vehicle. You will take the credit for having created the most important invention in the history of man. Think of the impact it will have. You will be responsible for saving the planet.

Mankind has accelerated its consumption of natural resources at an unsustainable rate. Mankind is bleeding this planet dry much faster than you are led to believe by the governments and media. In the past one hundred years, the world population has ballooned from one billion to seven billion. Think about that for a moment. In one hundred years humans have grown seven times in size than the previous twenty thousand years. Instead of measuring our annual consumption of oil in the tens of thousands of barrels, we measure it in the billions of barrels. In less than ten years, this keg we call Earth will be sucked bone dry, if something drastic isn't done about it.

The current solutions to the problem are just as dangerous as doing nothing. If corn crops are used to produce ethanol, it will eventually lead the world into famine. If hydrogen fuel cells are used, it will quickly lead to the depletion of yet another natural resource. If electricity is used, the demand for it will skyrocket. This will necessitate more coal and oil be used to produce the electricity. The Alexander One is the only sustainable solution. Without getting bogged down in the details, I can tell you that the Alexander One will not deplete the earth of her natural resources the way the other current solutions would."

The old man paused for a moment. He then continued. "I'm growing old, and I fear that I will not be around much longer to see that this is taken care of properly. That coupled with your background made you the perfect candidate for a task such as this. While I have no doubt you will grow to have more money than you would ever need, I think that you will do this for all the right reasons. This is why you are here. I need someone who is brilliant, caring, and most of all, uncorrupted. Will you take this very special gift that I'm prepared to give you?"

Save the planet and get incredibly wealthy at the same time? It sounded way too good to be true. I wasn't sure how to respond. If someone were to invite me into his office and described this scenario to me, I would have laughed all the way back home. But I had seen and felt the Alexander One in action. This was not a theoretical conversation. It was fact. If I hadn't witnessed all of these inexplicable events with my own eyes, I would have declined the old man's "gift." If he had let me into his secretive world and shown me all that he had already, why would it be hard to believe that what he was saying was true?

Perhaps seeing the angels and demons battling it out on my shoulders, the old man started speaking again before I had a chance to respond.

"Before you answer, I must paint the other half of the picture for you. It wouldn't be fair to you if I didn't."

The demon on my shoulder laughed. He knew the "but" was about to be coming.

The old man said in a serious tone. "Please don't think that I'm doing you any favors by giving you this opportunity. Make no mistake about it. There are ruthless men in this world who will stop at nothing to ensure that the flow of oil remains unhindered. Wars have been started over the black gold from the earth. If these men feel threatened, they'll kill anything or anyone in their way. The risk in accepting this opportunity is finite. It may cost you your life. The reward, however, is limitless to mankind. If it helps with your decision-making process, I will lend every resource available to me to aid in your protection. As you may have been able to tell, I have quite a bit of resources. I can't say with absolute certainty that even my vast resources will be able to protect you fully."

There it was. The rub. I have known this crackpot for less than an hour and he wants me to risk my life for him? It seemed like a near impossible sell. I needed to stall for a little bit more time to process all of this information.

"Is now a good time to ask some of those questions we talked about earlier?"

The old man replied, "We have about fifteen minutes before I need an answer. Ask away."

There were so many questions to choose from, I didn't know where to start. I started with the thing that amazed me most about today. "How does the Alexander One work?"

I'm sure he could spend years explaining the answer to this open-ended question. I hoped he could contain his answer so that I would have the opportunity to ask more questions.

He responded. "There are many ways I can answer that question. For the sake of time, I'll choose the short version. It works on a fundamental concept that every fifth grader has heard many times. Opposites attract and likes repel. Sir Isaac Newton gave us this simple blueprint when he defined the laws of action and reaction. This is the concept that the Alexander One was built upon.

The earth is one big magnet. It has a magnetic North and South Pole. All I did was create a super magnet to repel the polarity of the earth. As I am sure you know, passing an electrical current through metal creates a magnet. At the core of the Alexander One is nuclear-fission-powered engine. The engine puts out a tremendous amount of power and converts it to electricity. The electricity is then channeled to a series of specially designed wires that surround a high-density liquid metal. The electrical charge is regulated, allowing the driver to control the repelling power of the craft. This fluctuation of power causes the Alexander One to move up and down off the earth."

"Holy shit," I said to myself. There is no way the world will allow mini nuclear bombs to drive around the planet. I immediately interrupted. "Nuclear? Did you say nuclear?"

"That's the power plant for the craft you rode in today. The model you would be presenting to the world is drastically scaled down. Our goal is to replace wheeled vehicles at first. For this, you need only a limited amount of electricity to get the vehicle off the ground. We have designed a self-replenishing power source for the vehicle you would introduce to the world. It would never need refueling and would not be nuclear. It will be completely safe," reassured the old man.

"Why do you need me? Why don't you just introduce the Alexander One to the world yourself?"

"The world needs someone it knows to present this discovery. There is plenty of public information on you and your achievements. People would have no problem believing that you had invented the Alexander One. My background, on the other hand, is a little less clear. There would be too many unanswerable questions if I stepped out into the public eye."

This last answer sounded a little ominous. I decided that this question was defiantly worth exploring. I pressed on. "Ah, yes. There's the real question. One that I have been asking myself all day. Who are you? Don't hand be that crap Jonah tried to pawn off on me, either. 'Felt by many and known by few.' You have to tell him not to say that garbage again. He can't pull it off."

The old man let out a roaring laugh that made me flinch. He then continued. "Yes, Jonah has a flare for the dramatic. The simple truth is that I'm no one. I don't have citizenship in a specific country. The name my parents gave me vanished long ago. My identity vanished so long ago that no one knows that I still exist. I have dedicated my entire life to humanity. I don't consider myself to be good or evil. I only try with all my might to bring lopsided situations back into balance. I do this for all humanity. I do it so that the world can grow beyond its adolescence before it annihilates itself."

Geez, I thought. That sounded a lot like how my Sunday school teacher defined God. If I weren't so impressed with everything I had seen that day, I would have said that this guy was delusional. But his accomplishments were so groundbreaking that I figured he must truly believe what he just said. I could feel myself starting to buy into his mission. The truth was that he was absolutely correct in his assessment of the pending natural disaster. I wasn't sure if what he said about running out of oil in ten years was accurate, but I knew that when we did, the world economy would collapse.

Just as I was about to ask another question, the old man said, "Look, Ethan. I know that fifteen minutes is not a lot of time to consider a life-shattering choice; however, our fifteen minutes is almost up. Whatever you choose is fine with me. No harm will come to you if you choose not to take this opportunity. I sincerely hope that what I've shown you so far ensures that what I'm offering is very real. You're my number-one choice to carry out my legacy. Although you have only known me for an hour, I've been following you for quite some time. I'm certain you are the right person for what I've asked. Is this gift something that you would accept knowing full well the potential risks and rewards?"

I knew the answer before he laid on the thick sell. I answered, "I'd be happy to take the journey with you wherever it may lead, only if you answer one more question. What's your name?"

With a beaming expression on his face he replied, "You can call me Loyal, and I'm very pleased you've decided to come along for the ride."

CHAPTER NINE

It had taken the black Maybach nearly twenty-five minutes to reach the Bouchard estate. The drive from the airport had provided ample time for Dean and Albert to receive and study the three alternative plans provided by the special operations team lead. The plans had been sent to them through secure Email using the SAMSAC satellite terminal.

They approached the towering cast-iron gates of the estate. The gates started to open automatically when the car came within one hundred feet. Dean's private security forces kept a twenty-four-hour satellite fix on him. The highly paid security force knew his global position at all times. In addition to personal security that was more advanced than that of the president of the United States, it afforded Dean small luxuries, like never having to stop and wait for the gates of his sprawling estate to open. The car didn't slow its brisk pace as it turned into the mile-long driveway.

Dean's extensive estate had been in his family since the late 1700s. After his great-great-great grandfather had made millions in the coal and cotton businesses, he purchased one thousand acres of pristine land in the area of Pennsylvania currently known as Haverford. Taking almost five years and thousands of laborers to complete, the main house was a true architectural marvel.

Measuring more than two hundred thousand square feet, it was still among the largest private dwellings on the planet. With sixty-seven bedrooms and ninety-eight bathrooms, there were many areas of the house that had not been traveled by its inhabitants in years. A full-time staff of fifty-two included maids, butlers, landscapers, and handymen who kept the massive house in pristine working order. A secondary house was built for the onsite staff in the mid 1800s a half mile south of the main house. Moving the staff to the secondary house had meant that the Bouchard family would live alone in the house that could comfortably sleep a small army of people. This was one of many excesses that the Bouchards came to expect over the years.

The car reached the two-story external rotunda that acted as the main entrance to the estate. Sensing that they had arrived at their destination, both Albert and Dean knew that any conversation they were engaged in would have to stop until they were in the Lockbox. The Lockbox was a specially designed, secure room that was constructed out of an old bomb shelter deep in the bowels of the estate. The bomb shelter had been constructed as an add-on to the house during the Civil War. Two hundred fifty feet below the lowest level of the house, it was the perfect setting in which to conduct highly confidential business.

Dean had contracted a specialized firm to retrofit the facility with ultra modern equipment. At a cost of nearly ninety million dollars, it was a bargain for the privacy it guaranteed. Unlike the bunkers constructed by the council that prevented any data signals in or out of the facility, the Lockbox was Dean's nerve center. It had the most advanced communications systems money could buy and ensured unhindered secure contact with anyone in the world.

Dean and Albert exited the car. They bounded up the marble

steps that led to the front door. Waiting there to greet them was Dean's primary butler, Andrew. Andrew greeted Dean with his customary, "Good to have you back, Mr. Bouchard."

Seemingly ignoring Andrew, Dean whisked past Andrew and said in a firm tone, "We are not to be disturbed."

With Albert directly behind him, Dean took long strides across the tremendous foyer and down the main hallway. After expertly negotiating a maze of hallways and staircases, Dean and Albert had reached the exterior entrance of the Lockbox. Waiting outside the door to the Lockbox was Dean's chief of security. Albert had phoned ahead and commanded that Brad Resniki be waiting for him and Dean at the entrance of the Lockbox.

Brad was retired Delta force. He was a master of covert military action. His resume was long and impressive. It spanned more than twenty-five years and he had planned and executed thousands of special operation missions. This reason alone wasn't why Dean had hired him for such an important job. What had cemented Brad's position within Dean's empire was his track record. Brad had never failed to meet an objective. Thousands of missions, and he had never encountered a situation that prevented him from succeeding. Brad was a winner, and Dean felt lucky to have such a talented asset.

"Sir," said Brad as he stood at attention awaiting Dean's arrival.

Without a word, Dean walked over to the door of the Lockbox. He went through the numerous steps required to open the door. After the battery of biometric challenges had successfully been completed, the foot-thick steel-reinforced door let out a crashing thud and slowly began to open. Moments later, Dean, Albert, and Brad were safely inside. Dean slapped a big red button on the interior wall directly next to the bank-vault-style steel door. As the door slid closed, a bone-crunching crash was followed by the short pinging sound as each of the six-inch reinforcement bars encased within the steel door locked into place. A green light on top of the door flashed and indicated that the three men were locked in. Not even a direct hit from a nuclear-tipped ICBM would harm the inhabitants of the Lockbox. If the two hundred fifty feet of soil didn't stop the bomb blast, then the three-foot-thick steel box that surrounded them would.

Given the green light to proceed, Dean got right down to business. "Brad, I know that Albert could not fill you in on the details for this particular operation. We took the first step and contacted the special operations team to get the ball rolling."

Brad clinched his teeth. The vein in his neck protruded as he gave a begrudging look to Dean. "Sir, we have discussed this many times. I'm your chief of security for a reason. I thought we agreed that you would handle the politics and I would be fully in charge of the operational aspects of all military-type missions."

Dean ignored the complaint and continued. "The operation is an extraction. The target is one individual. The dilemma is that he is located in a very sensitive area. The parameters of this extraction are to accomplish the mission undetected by anyone in the target area."

Albert opened his briefcase. He withdrew the three alternative plans that the team had Emailed to him in the car. He placed the plans on the long conference table in front of the three men and spread them out.

Dean continued. "We need to determine which of the plans will give us the greatest chance of success."

Brad scanned through the documents with blurring speed and efficiency. After spending two minutes reviewing the plans, he said confidently, "Plan Beta. It's the plan that is the most direct with the least amount of moving parts. Fewer moving parts means less of a chance of the situation breaking down. As with all missions, the timing of the intel will be the key. Based on the two technology-driven factors in obtaining this real-time intelligence, I can say with certainty that we have the technical capability to accomplish the plan."

The plan was fairly simple. The most challenging part was obtaining eyes on the situation in real time. To get this much-needed situational awareness, the team would have to tap into the closed-circuit security TV system that blanketed the club. Additionally, it would have to monitor the point-of-sale system in the dining room. The biggest obstacle that the team faced was that it didn't know what Garrett Michaels looked liked. There was no public record of the man, which meant no photo.

The plan called for three two-man teams. Team One would sit outside the club and be responsible for tapping into the hard-line of the closed-circuit TV system. Once completed, it would maintain surveillance on the main entrance of the club. Team Two would perform the actual extraction. Team three, perhaps the most important team, would be responsible for eyes and ears on the situation. It would also be the team that had operational command in the field.

Team two would infiltrate the club posing as garbage men. Garbage was collected once a day from the dumpster in the rear of the main clubhouse thirty-two feet away from the rear door of the main kitchen at the bottom of a service ramp. The garbage truck would have to reverse down the ramp and back up to the dumpster. A staircase next to the dumpster provided an easy way to get to the long slate path that stretched from the front of the main entrance to the golf pro shop. It was on this path that Team Two would intercept and capture Garrett Michaels. Speed and timing were the keys. If the operation went off without a hitch, the whole thing would take less than ten minutes to complete.

Confident that they had arrived at the right choice, Dean gave the final order. "Brad, please take overall operational command and execute Plan Beta."

Without a word, Brad walked to the operations room. Dean and Albert followed.

The room looked like the command center of the Kennedy Space Center in Houston. Three ten-foot by twenty-foot movie-theater-size screens formed a "V" high on the wall in front of them. Brad sat down at the main console facing the large displays. Dean and Albert sat ten feet behind the console on an elevated grandstand. They would have front-row seats to the operation as it unfolded. Brad flipped a switch causing various displays on the console to come to life. Once the instrumentation panels of the console fully booted, he typed a pass code into the main terminal. As soon as he pressed the Enter key, the display on the main screen turned on. An electronic voice then narrated what was being displayed on the screen.

"Locating–locating–locating."

A map of the world came into focus. With each passing "locating" the electronic voice said, the display zoomed closer to a point on the map. It first zoomed down to the East Coast of the United States. Then farther down to the state of Pennsylvania. Then down to the Philadelphia metro area. The final image was coming into focus. The picture was crystal clear. It was a real-time image of the Ravens Valley Country Club. On the northernmost tip of the picture, a van was parked just outside the country club gate. Directly behind the van was a garbage truck.

The electronic voice continued. "Target acquired. Opening secure data tunnel. Tunnel established. Commencing encryption algorithm. Secure tunnel opened at one thousand, seventy-four-bit encryption."

The voice stopped. Less than ten seconds after Brad typed the code into the SAMSAC terminal, the stationary high-earth orbit satellite had located and opened a secure line of communication with the special operations team. "We have come so far," Dean thought.

Once connected, Brad began to speak. "This is the Lockbox. Go for team lead."

The immediate response could be heard through the speakers with startling clarity. "This is team lead."

"Team lead, you are a go for Plan Beta. Please confirm."

"Roger that. We are a go for Plan Beta. Good to have you on this one, Skip."

Dean smiled at this last comment. He knew that it was a slight dig aimed at him. He knew what it must have been like to take military orders from someone like him instead of Brad. Brad had handpicked his special operations team. He had extensive experience with each and every man on the team. Having been through many difficult situations with the men on the team, it was fiercely loyal and gave Brad enormous respect for his past accomplishments. Dean knew that no matter how much he paid these men, they would never work directly for him without someone like Brad. Respect was something that was earned in blood with these types of people.

Brad didn't acknowledge the team leaders quip. He replied, "Roger that team lead. Give me a status."

"All teams are ready to go. We have requisitioned a garbage truck and the proper uniforms. Commencing with Plan Beta."

Operational control was now in the hands of the team lead. Dean, Albert, and Brad were spectators. Although no further commands would be given from the Lockbox unless something went wrong, they were fully plugged into all aspects of the operation. The team leader then started giving orders.

"Team One. Get me some eyes."

The satellite display in the Lockbox showed the passenger side door of the van opening. A man quickly made his way to the exterior stonewall that bordered the golf course. He scaled the wall and located a camera that was facing the golf course. He clamped a device to the wire that extended out of the rear of the camera.

A voice passed over the airwaves. "This is Team One. Sniffer secured."

"Roger that, One. Eyes coming online now. Wait, One," said the team lead.

The large displays in the Lockbox danced with many camera images. The sniffer that was attached to the back of the camera diverted the electrical current that carried the cameras images to the security monitors within the club. The intercepted electrical signals were sent wirelessly to a receiver within the van. Because the system was closed circuit, once someone had access to one camera, he had access to all cameras. It was a major design flaw that many believed was done on purpose by the security firm that installed the devices.

"Affirmative. Nice picture, Team One. Return to the van."

The man who had planted the sniffer device casually walked back to the van and got in the passenger-side door.

The team lead continued. "Last known intel puts the target in the dining room. Scanning for dining room cameras."

Various camera perspectives scrolled through the display. The screen eventually stopped at a picture of the dining room. The dining room had roughly twenty-five guests. This number could be drastically reduced, given what information the team had received from its source within the club. The team knew that Garrett Michaels was an older gentleman and that he was dining alone. There were three diners that fit that description. Now it was up to the team to determine which one he was.

The team lead spoke again. "We have eyes on the dining room.

Team One, you are a go for point of sale intrusion."

"Roger, team lead. Opening connection now. Locating point of sale server on the network. Server found. Looking for vulnerable ports. UDP Port identified. Attempting first intrusion. First time is a charm; we are in."

Because the system that recorded food orders in the dining was not high up on the security totem pole, Dean knew that breaking into the system would be relatively easy. He was just relieved that it could be done on the first attempt. Time was the most important factor in a special operation. He was proud to have a man on his team that could effortlessly hack into any system so quickly. It took Team One only an additional thirty seconds to find what it was looking for.

Team One reported its findings back to the team lead. "The targets sales chit has been located. The target is at table number nineteen."

There was a pause in the line. Dean knew the problem immediately after Team One had made his report. It had identified the table at which Garrett Michaels was sitting, but had no way to determine where table nineteen was on the seating chart. This was the type of situation Brad had become famous for negotiating. He had run into many problems during the multitude of operations over the years. His biggest asset was his ability to adapt and overcome. Dean sat back as Brad took control of the situation.

"Lockbox for team lead," said Brad.

"Go for team lead."

"Team lead, if a seating chart is not obtainable, proceed with the next step in the plan."

Brad let out a big exhale. The next step would make or break the mission.

"Roger that, Lockbox" said the team lead in a downtrodden voice.

The team lead then continued, "Team One, plant the seed."

"Roger that team lead. Planting the seed."

A dial tone then crept through the speakers within the command center. A number was dialed and the line rang twice before the call was answered.

"Good morning. Ravens Valley Country Club. How may I direct your call?" said the perky voice of the receptionist.

The familiar voice of the man on Team One spoke in a nearly perfect fake British accent.

"Yes, good morning. Could you connect me with the dining room, please?"

"One moment please," said the polite receptionist.

"Good morning. This is the dining room. How may I help you?"

The man from Team One continued, "Yes, good morning. I would like for you to relay a message to a guest in your dining room, if you would. I was wondering if you could tell Mr. Michaels that Mr. Kravis has arrived early and was wondering if Mr. Michaels could meet him at the golf pro shop."

The man that had answered the phone in the dining room responded, "Yes. I see Mr. Michaels. I will give him the message right away"

"Thank you so much. Ta!"

The phone line went dead. All eyes were on the surveillance camera. If Michaels did not take the bait, the mission would be over before it started. This "seed" as the team lead had called it was a big gamble. If Michaels knew that Ethan Kravis was not going to return to the club, then the message would alert him that something was wrong. It was a risk the team had to take.

From the right side of the surveillance picture, an oversized man walked across the dining room floor. He stopped at a table where one man sat. He briefly spoke to the man, turned around, and left. Dean watched the monitor with growing anticipation. The man at the table signaled a waitress. The waitress produced a slip of paper from her apron and placed it on the table. The man signed the paper, took one last drink of his iced tea, and stood.

An excited voice came from the speakers in the Lockbox.

"We have a fix on the target. He's on the move. Team Two, you are a go," said the team lead.

"Roger that. We're rolling."

The sidewall display in the command center still had the real-time satellite imagery on it. The garbage truck from behind the van pulled out onto the street. It turned into the main entrance of the club and headed toward the clubhouse. It pulled around to the back of the clubhouse and reversed down the ramp toward the dumpster.

One of the men from Team Two spoke. "Team Two in position."

"Roger that, Team Two. Target is moving to rear exit. Contact with extraction point has an ETA of one minute. Exit vehicle and wait at the base of the stairwell. Go for extraction on my command."

Dean's stomach was in knots. He was so nervous he couldn't move. He sat with his eyesight transfixed on the overhead screens.

"Wait one. Friendly is on course to intercept."

Dean's eyes darted around the screen. He knew that if anyone else at the club were in a position to see the extraction happen, then the mission would have to be aborted. At the corner of the screen, he saw an old woman come into the view of the surveillance camera directly over the extraction zone. At that instant, as if by some act of God, the old woman did an about face and headed back toward the pro shop.

The team lead spoke. "Friendly is moving out of range. Team Two, get ready for extraction."

The rear exit to the clubhouse opened. The man identified as

Garrett Michaels exited. He slowly started walking down the slate path.

"This is team lead. Target is forty feet from extraction point. Team Two, go wrap the package. Eyes are going blind. Radio silence until mission is in the clear."

Dean almost fell out of his chair when the surveillance video screen went blank. He asked in an excited tone, "What just happened?"

Brad turned around and shot an annoyed look at Dean. As he started adjusting some of the buttons on the center console, he calmly said, "You don't want any evidence that we carried out this mission, do you? We had to bring down the cameras so that we weren't recorded."

As Dean sat back and composed himself, he saw the middle overhead display change from a blacked out picture to the satellite imagery. The satellite zoomed in with dazzling clarity until it was approximately twenty feet over the head of the man known as Garrett Michaels. One man of Team Two approached Garrett Michaels from the south. When the man from Team Two was about fifteen feet away, he paused. Garrett Michaels looked like he was fainting. The man from Team Two ran over to the falling body of Garrett Michaels and caught him before he hit the ground. The operative from Team Two heaved the old man over his shoulder and quickly headed for the stairwell.

"We got him," Dean thought. He watched the scene unfold in real time. Sensing that he shouldn't get overly excited until the teams were safely away, he calmed himself.

The man carrying Garrett Michaels glided down the steps. At the bottom of the stairwell, the second man from Team Two met him. They quickly wrapped their precious cargo in what appeared to be a body bag and gently placed him in the rear of the garbage truck. Within seconds the two men were in the truck and driving up the ramp.

Dean watched as the seemingly harmless garbage truck exited the main entrance. The satellite image zoomed out to its original size. A man hopped out of the van, scaled the same wall he had before, and removed the sniffer device. The images of the closed-circuit TV system sprang back to life. The man dropped off the wall and got back into the van. The garbage truck stopped for a split second next to the van. Two men got out of the garbage truck and transferred the filled body bag into the van. The men got back into the garbage truck, and both vehicles drove off in opposite directions.

Ten seconds later, the familiar voice of the team lead came over the speakers. "Lockbox, this is team lead. Target has been extracted. Mission was a success. Target is en route to final destination."

Brad yelled, "Roger that team lead. A big whowa to you and the boys. First beer is on me tonight."

Brad turned to Dean and gave a thumbs up. Dean clapped at the performance. The fifty-five million dollars in bonuses was the best money he had spent in a while. He couldn't wait to unwrap his present and talk to the mysterious man known as Garrett Michaels.

CHAPTER TEN

Loyal? I knew that this was a popular name at the turn of the twentieth century, but I didn't know too many people with that name these days. A unique name for a unique man I suppose.

Loyal and I exited the small study, and he led me back to the main foyer. The walk gave me another chance to take in the magnificent home. Waiting for us in the foyer was David, the head butler, and Jonah.

Without a word, Jonah walked over to Loyal. "Sir, you have a message."

Jonah handed Loyal a slip of paper. Loyal read the contents of the piece of paper and nodded as if he were agreeing with the message's contents.

Loyal then spoke. "I think you've had enough space travel for today, Ethan. Maybe it would be best if you spent the night here and return to Philadelphia in the morning. I'm assigning Jonah to you full time. He'll act as your guardian and ensure your safety. Perhaps you could spend some time with him tonight while he briefs you on some of the safety precautions we would like to take."

I looked around at the faces of the three gentlemen. A little confused at the change in plans, I asked, "I thought I needed to get back to the golf course before my round of golf was supposed to be over. Won't it make people curious if I disappear?"

I sensed that Loyal had a look of satisfaction on his face. Maybe he was happy at how quickly I had adapted my thought pattern to someone with self-preservation on the brain.

"I'll send word to Garrett. He'll make something up if anyone should ask. He can say that you had an urgent call and had to leave early. I doubt very highly that anyone at the club will care."

Considering all that my mind and body had been through, I figured that if Loyal was all right with not going back right away, then I should be too. I responded, "That sounds good with me. It is only about ten in the morning where I'm from, so I won't be tired for some time."

Glad to see that I was amenable to the change in plans, Loyal said, "Great. I will leave you in the hands of Jonah and David. I have to take care of some business before I turn in for the night."

Before Loyal could turn and walk away, I asked him, "Since I'm no longer bound by the constraints of time, could we talk a bit further? I still have many questions I'd like to ask you, Loyal."

I glanced over at Jonah and David. For the briefest of moments, I thought I saw a wince of pain on their faces when I spoke Loyal's name.

Loyal responded, "I understand that you still have questions. I'm afraid that a pressing matter has come up, and it will require my full attention tonight. You and Jonah will most likely be gone by the time I wake up tomorrow. Given our conversation tonight, I'm confident that you and I will have many conversations in the coming years. You'll see that throughout time, all of your questions will be answered. I promise that all will be revealed in due time."

Not wanting to press my luck, I decided to back off. I merely nodded and said, "OK."

"Great, then. Once again, I'm extremely pleased that you have decided to join us."

He turned to Jonah and said, "Jonah, make sure you look after Mr. Kravis. He is now one of most cherished assets."

Loyal turned back to me. "Have a very pleasant evening. Do try to get some rest, and we'll talk again very soon."

Loyal turned around and walked away. David did not say a word to me or even glance in my direction. He simply followed Loyal down the long hallway.

I glanced back at Jonah and raised my eyebrows. Jonah chuckled and said, "Are you tired?"

I shook my head and said, "Not in the least. A warm shower might do me some good though."

Jonah said, "I was thinking the same thing myself."

I couldn't tell if Jonah was trying to tell me that I smelled or that he too wanted to shower. Before I had the opportunity to ask, he said, "Let's grab a quick shower and meet in an hour or so. Sound good to you?"

I nodded. Jonah escorted me back to the master guest bedroom. Before he closed the door, he said, "I'll be back in an hour. You should have everything you need. There is a change of clothes in the armoire, if you want."

I thought back to what David had said when I first arrived and Jonah's comment made me smile. I knew Jonah was being sincere when he said it, but it made me smile just the same. I gave Jonah thumbs up, and he closed the door.

I took half of the hour I was allotted and stood in a scalding hot shower. The entire roof of the shower was like one giant faucet. Thousands of tiny holes on the ceiling of the shower gently rained down water on me. It was so relaxing I didn't want to leave. Not wanting to expend too much of the precious water supply on the tiny island, I decided that it was time to end the shower.

As I dried myself off, I wandered toward the armoire. I took a peek inside and saw a wide selection of clothes to choose from. I was amazed to see that all the clothes were my size. I picked out a sweat suit and threw it on the bed. I figured comfort was better than fashion. I slipped on the sweat suit and laid down on the bed. It was the first time that I had a chance to reflect on what had happened.

I replayed the series of events in my head. There were still too many unanswered questions about today. I was the type of person that could easily go insane when I couldn't solve a problem. Now I had so many things that I couldn't solve, it cause a tremendous inner-conflict.

I spent the next thirty minutes thinking. Deep in my thoughts, I barely heard the knock on the door. Jonah entered and said, "All set?"

Hoping that Jonah's briefing could help further my understanding of the situation, I replied, "Let's get to it."

Jonah motioned me to follow him. I got off the bed and quickly caught up to him as he walked down the hallway. He led me to a conference room. "Take a seat."

I took a seat and noticed that a large plastic case sat at the end of the table.

Jonah walked over to the case and slid it in my direction. He sat down next to me. He opened the case and began to speak. "I'm sure your conversation with the old man was enlightening. I was glad to hear that you accepted his proposition."

That last statement by Jonah made me question how much of the details he already knew.

Jonah continued. "As I'm sure he explained to you, the nature of your mission may put you in harm's way. That's where I come in. I have some items here that will help me to protect you."

Jonah pulled some of the items out of the case and gently placed them on the conference table. The first thing he showed me was a Rolex watch.

"Nice", I thought.

"Here is a Rolex Submariner watch. Embedded in the watch face is a micro-burst GPS transmitter. It will allow us to locate your position at all times. If you turn the dial to nine o'clock and press the winding mechanism, it will broadcast a distress signal. My team and I will respond within thirty seconds."

I interrupted and said in my best Sean Connery expression, "How very James Bond of you, Moneypenny."

Jonah looked back at me with a blank expression. He had probably heard that comment, or something like it, a million times. He continued with a demonstration of how the distress signal could be triggered. Five seconds after he had demonstrated how the watch worked, two large men barreled through the door. Jonah raised his hand and yelled, "Demonstration, fellas."

The two men rolled their eyes and quietly left the room. Jonah shot me a funny expression and said, "Works pretty well, doesn't it?"

I had no doubt that this was all staged for my benefit. I decided to play along with Jonah's attempt at humor. He went on to say, "The watch may be James Bond, but this little baby is definitely Star Wars." Jonah took out a small metal case that appeared to be a contact lens holder. He placed the case on the table in front of me. I made a motion to pick it up, but Jonah reached out and put his hand on my arm. He said, "This device is going to blow your mind. It'll take you some time to master its functionality. Until you get the hang of how to use it, it will defiantly cause some irritation."

I looked at Jonah and became a little nervous. Not sure what to do,

I just sat there.

A moment passed and Jonah began to speak again. "Are you up for this?"

I was a little confused and replied, "I haven't the foggiest on what 'this' is yet. Let's drop the cloak-and-dagger stuff and just get on with it, shall we?"

Jonah raised his shoulders in an "OK, I tried to warn you" fashion. He reached forward and opened the case. Sitting in a clear liquid was what appeared to be a contact lens. For some reason I thought that this was no ordinary contact lens.

Jonah began to explain. "This is something the old man cooked up. I think he developed it so that one day he could replace cell phones. The old man refers to it as the EyeWonder. I'm not really sure how to explain it. I think you are just going to have to see for yourself. Carefully place it in your right eye as you would a contact lens."

I leaned forward and extended my pointer finger. I felt the thin lens stick to my finger using the capillary reaction that the solution had on my fingertip. I never had the need for glasses, so I had a lot of trouble trying to get the thing in my eye. With every failed attempt, I could sense Jonah wince. After the third failed attempt to get it on my eye, Jonah barked out, "Stop! Stop. Just stop right there. Put it back into the solution."

Doing as Jonah had said, I placed the small clear disk back in the solution. In a frustrated tone, Jonah went on to say, "For a genius, you sure aren't very smart. Let me do it."

Jonah rubbed the disk in the solution to ensure that all the debris from my finger was washed away. He raised the disk on the tip of his finger so that it was next to my head. He tilted my head back and used two fingers from his other hand to pry my eyelid open. He gently placed the disk on my eyeball. He moved back. "Give it a second to power up."

A moment passed, and nothing happened, and then something totally unexpected happened. It was such a foreign feeling to me that my whole body stiffened, and I put my palms on the table in front of me to brace myself.

I saw a tiny computer screen. The screen was very opaque and did not really distort my view. I had tried out a PC monocle once; however, it was a bulky eyepiece that blocked my entire field of vision. It was connected to a dorky headband, which in turn was connected to a battery pack the size of a DVD player. This EyeWonder device was hundreds of generations ahead of the relatively new technology that I had played with.

The tiny screen displayed what appeared to be my vital signs. The display was dazzling, but I had the feeling it did more. I decided to ask Jonah. "Very cool, but what does it do?"

Jonah replied, "Think of a question, and don't say it out loud. Just think it."

Not sure what Jonah was saying, I did as he instructed. I asked myself the question, "Where are we?" As soon as I thought the question, the tiny screen displayed, "Question not understood." Not seeming to comprehend the fact that this little clear disk had just read my thoughts, I said to Jonah, "It says that the question was not understood."

"What was your question?"

"I asked 'where are we?'"

"Right. You need to ask questions in terms a computer would be able to understand. I think the term "we" might have thrown it off. Try asking something like, 'What is my current position?'"

As soon as I thought the question, the computer screen came to life. It displayed a map of the world and had latitude and longitude coordinates in the upper right had corner. In the middle of the Pacific

Ocean, there was a blinking red dot. I couldn't believe what I was seeing. I wondered how in the world this thing could have read my mind. All of a sudden, the map disappeared, and the tiny screen displayed, "Question not understood." I let out an explosive laugh and said, "No freakin' way!"

I don't know if I was in shock or what, but I just continued to let out a giddy little laugh. I guess it was contagious, because Jonah started to laugh as well. Could this be real? "Question not understood" displayed once again on the tiny screen. Wow!

Jonah interrupted my girlish little laugh and said, "To turn it on and off, all you have to do is think 'EyeWonder on' or 'EyeWonder off'."

I thought "EyeWonder off." The tiny little screen in my eye turned off.

Shaking my head in disbelief, I asked Jonah, "Do you know how it works?"

Jonah replied, "I'm sure the EyeWonder could explain it a lot better than I can. I can provide some basic background for you, though. First off, it is completely safe. It will not harm your eye or any other part of your body, for that matter. It's powered by drawing a slight electrical current from your body. After extended use, you may start to feel a little tired, but like I said, it will not be harmful in any way.

The device works much like a WI-FI-connected laptop. Instead of connecting to an Internet service provider, it connects by satellite to the servers at this facility. Suffice it to say that the servers here are unlike anything you have ever seen. You'll have to trust me on that. The thing that makes it so powerful is the vast amount of information it can process. I think the old man showed you how a limitless amount of data can be compressed in a single bit of information, didn't he?"

I nodded.

Jonah continued. "Well, the EyeWonder takes full advantage of the P.A.S.S. technology. That's all I really know. Don't ask me how the thing reads your mind, because I have no idea."

"Craziness," I thought. All I wanted to do at that point was go back to the master guest suite and ask the EyeWonder every possible question I could think of.

Seeming to have read my mind, Jonah said, "Well, I'm getting a little tired. We have a long day ahead of us tomorrow. If it's all right with you, I'm going to hit the sack. You should really try to get some rest yourself."

Jonah gave me a smirk. He probably knew exactly what I'd be doing all night. He got up and walked me back to my room.

"Have a good night, and I'll see you in the morning," Jonah said as he let out a large yawn.

I quickly shut the door and jumped into the bed. There was only one thing I could think of.

I thought to myself, "EyeWonder On!"

CHAPTER ELEVEN

Still groggy and unsure at what had just happened to him, Garrett Michaels didn't recognize the huge room in which he was sitting. Although his vision was slightly blurred, he noticed that the display of his EyeWonder would no longer respond to his commands, which caused him great concern. He had grown accustomed to using the ingenious device, especially in times of danger. He reached for his wristwatch. His wrist was bare. A sinking feeling settled into his stomach.

"Looking for these?" said a voice from directly behind Garrett.

Garrett attempted to turn around to see who else was in the room. He noticed that when he tried to turn his head, his neck was very sore. Garrett winced in pain and massaged the back of his neck with his hand. The sudden movement had caused his head to throb uncontrollably. Deciding not exacerbate his growing headache, he sat as still as possible as he continued to message his neck.

Dean Bouchard walked around the couch where Garrett was sitting. Dean was carrying a clear plexiglass case. In the case was all of the personal property Garrett had on him at the golf course. The man, whom Garrett did not recognize, began to speak as he sat down in a floral-patterned chair across from him.

Dean placed the items on the coffee table between the two men and said, "When we brought you here, we couldn't take any chances that you were bugged. I had you stripped of all your personal property. The GPS transponder in your watch was easy enough to identify. It wasn't until we did a full body scan that we realized your contact lens was emitting a very low frequency signal. This clear box will prevent any signal from escaping."

The man gestured to the box on the coffee table. In the box, Garrett saw his watch, wallet, some golf tees, a ball marker, a divot tool, and the EyeWonder. Garrett's heart fluttered when he saw the EyeWonder. He knew that without it, he was powerless. His only comfort was in the fact that this man would have no idea of its capability. Each EyeWonder was custom made for each individual. The device wouldn't turn on if someone other than the intended owner tried to use it. Garrett also knew that the device would destroy itself if anyone tried to reverse engineer it. Although Garrett was happy that the device was built with such security precautions, he hoped that he would never have to be in a situation requiring that they be tested.

At that point, Garrett felt defeated. His one saving grace was the fact that he was still alive. Not sure how much longer that would continue, he grew nervous. He sat very still and waited for the man to continue.

"My name is Dean Bouchard, Mr. Michaels."

Garrett thought the name sounded familiar, but couldn't place it.

Dean continued to speak. "I do apologize for the way in which you had to be brought here. The effects from the tranquilizer should continue to dissipate. In a normal situation, I'm confident that two civilized men such as us could have found a gentlemanly way to meet. Given certain factors, I decided to expedite the meeting using a rather distasteful method."

Garrett observed a reverence to the way that Dean had spoken. He dismissed the idea that Dean was a common thug out to steal his wallet. He glanced around the room for the first time. He was sitting in a room that he could describe only as a great room. It was roughly the size of a football field. The room was adorned with old, yet exquisite furnishings. He immediately judged that Dean Bouchard was a man of extraordinary wealth. Garrett's nervousness had subsided a bit and his curiosity grew. He knew exactly what Dean wanted, but was curious about who he was and where he fit into the situation. Garrett was fully alert now. He listened intently at what Dean was saying.

"Mr. Michaels, I'm afraid that your life is in grave danger. I'm just happy that I was able to save you before any harm should have befallen you. I'm your friend in the strange situation we find ourselves in at this moment. There are some dangerous men after you, Mr. Kravis, and anyone else who has come in contact with the special vehicle you saw at the golf course today."

There it was. Garrett had expected as much. Somehow the man knew about the Alexander One. It didn't take Garrett long to realize that Dean Bouchard was a man who could not be messed with. He had the resources not only to know of the Alexander One's existence, but also had the means to act very quickly when it was identified earlier today. That, coupled with the fact that he could kidnap someone from a highly secure facility, gave Garrett all the reason he needed to take the man very seriously.

"Please help me help you. I want to ensure that you make it through this situation unharmed. The only way I can protect you is for you to give me information. I need to know what this vehicle does and how it works."

Garrett knew that this wasn't a scene from the movies. He would not be the character to give his life for the secrets that he had in his possession. The simple fact was that he was caught. Unless some of his protectors broke down the doors within the next thirty seconds, he had to play ball. The truth was that he knew very little about the mysterious communications he had received over the past several years. He didn't know who they came from. He didn't know all of the cryptic series of events that occurred when he received the messages. The messages merely contained confusing instructions. Garrett carried out the confusing instruction, and in return, he received generous amounts of money.

The only thing that Garrett knew was that he was now caught up in a festering mess. He would take what little information he did have and barter for his life. He decided to use the one thing he did know to test the waters.

"The Alexander One," Garrett said in a glum voice as he made eye contact with Dean for the first time.

Dean displayed a look of confusion. He asked, "Excuse me?"

Garrett went on to explain, "The vehicle. The name it has been given is the Alexander One."

"What is it?" asked Dean.

Garrett thought about answering the question. He knew that he had piqued Dean's interest. He took a moment to construct his reply. When he was comfortable with the words that he had chosen, he said, "I need some proof that I will not be harmed if I provide you the answers to your questions."

Dean replied, "Mr. Michaels, if you can prove to me that you have valuable information on the subject, then I will have no choice but to keep you alive. I'm confident that if you have this type of information, the people you work for would prefer that I kill you as soon as possible. Even if I were to release you this very instant, your life would still be in extreme danger. If your employers don't kill you, I know some men who would do anything to see that any information that you had never became public. I'm your new best friend. I can protect you from these evils."

Garrett Michaels knew he had to talk or he was dead. If he didn't talk, he would be thrown to the wolves and most certainly not be treated as kindly as Dean was treating him. Garrett considered all that Dean had said. He knew he only had one option. Before he provided everything he knew to Dean, he would try one last time to negotiate for his safety.

"I fully understand what you have explained. But what is to stop you from killing me as soon and I tell you what you want to hear?"

Dean replied to Garrett's offer. "I'm a man of extraordinary wealth. When you strip away all the material possessions I've accumulated in this lifetime, all I have left is my word. My word is my bond. I give you my word that if you provide me with all you know, I will guarantee that you not only live through this ordeal, but you also prosper because of it. As a show of good faith on my behalf, I will wire two hundred and fifty million dollars to a numbered account of your choosing. Half will be transferred immediately and the remainder will be transferred upon the capture of the vehicle–ah, Alexander One as you have called it."

Two hundred and fifty million dollars, Garrett thought to himself. This was more money that he could ever hope to accumulate doing random tasks assigned to him by whoever was sending him cryptic instructions. He cherished the thought of living the rest of his life in extreme wealth. Garrett's family always had money. He had lived a comfortable life. This was his opportunity to live like a king without ever having to worry about money again.

The only question that he could not answer was that of trust. Could he trust this mysterious man whom he had just met to keep his word? At the very least this man stood to lose one hundred and twenty-five million dollars once the first wire transfer took place. The money would be irretrievable once it reached the Swiss bank account Garrett had at his disposal. Deciding that this was indeed an acceptable show of good faith, Garrett responded to the generous offer. "Transfer the first one hundred and twenty-five million dollars, and then we'll talk."

Dean motioned for Albert to come over. Albert was standing in the corner of the room and had gone unnoticed by Garrett. Garrett was startled when Albert approached him from around the couch.

Without saying a word, Albert placed a laptop on the coffee table and sat down in a chair. Dean then asked, "Do you have an account number that you would like the money to be transferred to, Mr. Michaels?"

Garrett provided the necessary account details. Albert worked furiously on the laptop. Thirty seconds went by. Albert looked up at Dean and gave him a nod. Dean then spoke, "The first one hundred and twenty-five million dollars has been transferred. Please use this phone to call your bank and confirm."

Dean handed Garrett a cell phone. Garrett dialed the number to the bank. After several challenging security questions, Garrett got through to a bank operator. Within minutes he received the confirmation on his balance. The money was in his account. Garrett let out a big exhale and smiled.

Dean took this as a positive sign. "I take it you're satisfied with our arrangement. You have confirmed that I have lived up to my part of the deal; now it's your turn. What is the Alexander One and how does it work?"

"I have only seen it a half dozen times or so. If you are asking how it works, prepare to be disappointed. I have no idea how it works. What I can tell you is that it's unlike anything you have ever seen."

Dean sat motionless, hanging on every word.

Garrett continued with his briefing. "The Alexander One is a nearly silent aircraft. It has the ability to turn invisible and disappear from the area at great speeds. I have to assume that it travels at a very high altitude. The only reason that I suspect this is because when it takes off, all you can hear is a rush of wind and a very faint humming sound. The rush of wind is not like the wind produced by an airplane engine. It's more like the sound you may hear from a baseball rushing past your head. The baseball has no moving parts, but you hear the rush of air as it moves past you. It's hard to explain the sensation you get when it takes off. I hope that baseball analogy makes sense."

Dean asked, "When you say it turns invisible, what do you mean?"

"Exactly what it sounds like. The skin of the Alexander One has some way to blend in with the background of the surrounding area. It does this prior to taking off. It's really an impressive sight."

Dean continued to question Garrett for the next two hours. Dean would ask the same questions over and over again to see if there were any variations in the answers. Garrett had been mostly truthful until that point. He knew that was about to change when he heard Dean's next question.

"Who created the Alexander One?"

Garrett knew the question coming. He had prepared his answer over the last two hours. He had hoped that the last two hours had built some trust between himself and Dean. He knew the answer he was about to give was a lie, but he had no other choice. Garrett answered, "I don't know who he is, but I know how to contact him."

CHAPTER TWELVE

It had been eight hours since Jonah had escorted me back to the master guest room. I was still lying in bed and had not even moved to get up to go to the bathroom. I was up the entire night asking every question I could think of, using the EyeWonder device.

Although I was unsuccessful in phrasing the questions in the correct syntax at first, after a couple of hours, I got the hang of it. The information the EyeWonder provided was astounding. It answered many questions that had been generated based on the previous day's events. I did notice, however, that even though some of the questions I had asked were in the proper phrasing, the response from the EyeWonder came back as "Access Restricted."

The types of questions that had restricted access primarily had to do with personal data. I wasn't able to receive any personal background on Jonah, Loyal, or Garrett Michaels. I tried every permutation and combination of question I could think of in hopes at arriving at some answers. Nothing had worked. However, I was able to get some very interesting details on both the Alexander One and the EyeWonder.

The details of the Alexander One were not very different than what Jonah and Loyal had explained. The basic concept behind how the Alexander One worked was simple enough to understand. It was exactly what Loyal had described as "one giant magnet." However, being the scientist that I am, I was fascinated in the details of the science behind the spacecraft.

The first thing that truly impressed me was the way in which the Alexander One determined the repelling power needed to achieve certain heights off the earth's surface. It used an ingenious equation that I had never seen before. It took hundreds of factors into consideration. Wind speed, the force of gravity, total weight, current altitude, electrical flow, relative position on the earth, proximity to the magnetic North and South Pole, phase in the moon cycle, humidity of the outside air–the list of factors was endless. It took all of this raw data and processed it faster than any computer that I had ever seen. Eventually, it would boil all of these factors down to a number that regulated how much electricity was passed through the wires surrounding the liquid iron ferrite composite metal that resided at the base of the craft. It processed hundreds of these factors millions of times a second to achieve flight. Simply incredible.

The second most amazing function of the Alexander One was its electro-chromatic skin. The skin itself was made up of billions of advanced photocells that acted much like a video camera. It would take a snapshot of the surrounding area on one side of the Alexander One and simultaneously display the picture on the corresponding photocell on the opposite side of the craft. Each of the microscopic photocells acted as both the camera and the display. The clearest picture on an average high definition television runs at one thousand eighty lines of resolution. If one were to try to equate that to the skin of the Alexander One, the skin would have more than one billion lines of resolution. The resolution it produced was so fine that even when I was right next to it, I didn't have an inkling that my eyes were deceiving me.

The design of the Alexander One was mind-blowing indeed. It wasn't until I started asking questions about the EyeWonder that I realized how insignificant any of the groundbreaking work that I had participated in really was. The EyeWonder literally and figuratively opened my eyes to new concepts and sciences that had never been documented. Einstein, Newton, Pasteur, Faraday, and all the other great scientists who had worked so brilliantly to create the laws of science would be shocked to find out that many of their discoveries were thrown out the window when creating the EyeWonder.

In its creation, brand-new branches of science were born. I couldn't even follow a fraction of the science behind the tiny device. The only parts that I could glean were that the device operated off a form of molecular computing. Billions of tiny computers the size of molecules worked in perfect harmony to allow the EyeWonder to function. Each of these billions of microscopic robots had the processing power of the most advanced computers I had ever worked with. Each molecule had a specific purpose. I knew that I had barely touched on the device's full potential over the last eight hours. The only thing I knew with absolute certainty was that Loyal had a mind like no one else on the planet. His work was so far beyond anything the world had seen that it guaranteed it would take the world decades to catch up.

Jonah had been right last night when he warned me that prolonged use of the EyeWonder would make me tired. After eight continuous hours of use, I was exhausted. I had to push myself to the very limits to continue to use the EyeWonder. I just couldn't stop. I fought off the exhaustion because the device was so phenomenal. Using the EyeWonder was like taking an addictive drug. I just couldn't stop. Information was my heroin. My only fear was that I would soon overdose if I abused the EyeWonder too much. Having made the decision to stop, I thought to myself, "EyeWonder off." The tiny computer screen turned off, and I chuckled to myself, still not believing the amazing device really existed. I tried to close my eyes in hopes of getting some much-needed sleep. As soon as I closed my eyes, I heard the knock at the door. I laid still hoping that the person who had knocked would go away. No such luck. Jonah peeked in and said, "Time to get going."

"Great," I thought to myself. "How much time do we have?" I asked Jonah in a tired voice.

"What's the matter? Didn't sleep well?" Jonah said in a clearly sarcastic tone.

"Not a wink."

"I figured as much. I can give you a half hour to get ready. Once we get back to Philadelphia, you can sleep until Tuesday. Your journey doesn't begin until then."

"What am I doing on Tuesday?"

"I'll brief you later. Don't worry. It isn't anything too crazy like the last twenty-four hours have been."

"What was so crazy about the last twenty-four hours?" I said in a joking voice.

Jonah smiled and said, "I'll be back in thirty minutes." He closed the door.

It had taken me a while to get motivated and peel myself off the bed. I decided that a quick, cold shower might wake me up a bit. After the shower, I put on fresh clothes and lay back down on the bed. While waiting for Jonah, I realized that the EyeWonder was still in my eye. I made a mental note to ask Jonah how often I needed to take it out and wash it. I doubted very highly that Visine was the cleanser of choice.

Jonah arrived at my door exactly when he said he would. He asked, "Set?"

I sprung off the bed and walked through the door. As we walked toward the main entrance, I asked, "Any chance of seeing Loyal this morning?"

"I don't think so. He sleeps pretty late."

It dawned on me that I didn't even know what time it was. I looked down at my new Rolex watch, and it appeared to be set for Philadelphia time. I realized that the answer to my question was staring me right in my eye. I turned on the EyeWonder, got the local time, and turned it off. Given our location in the South Pacific, the local time was 5:34 A.M. Literally half a world away, that meant that it was now 5:34 P.M. on the East Coast of the United States. However, it was still Saturday there, not Sunday like here. Jonah and I had traveled halfway around the world in thirty-two minutes.

Jonah headed out the front door and down the slate path in the direction of the landing pad. As we walked, I looked around. The raw beauty of the island had escaped my attention the night before. Not much of the lush vegetation and coconut trees were visible in the fading sun. Now that the sun had risen, I could truly appreciate what a fantastical place this was. At that moment, I had hoped that I could live out the rest of my days in a place like this island.

Lost in that pleasant thought, I hadn't realized that Jonah and I had reached the landing pad. There she was. The Alexander One stood there in all her splendor. Before we entered the Alexander One, Jonah turned to me and said, "Are you ready for this again?"

"What choice do I have? I would miss out on whatever is planned for Tuesday if I had to swim back to Philadelphia."

Jonah smirked at the wisecrack. He produced a syringe from his pocket so quickly I didn't have time to react. He jabbed the needle into my neck and pressed down on the plunger. Once the contents of the syringe were emptied into my neck, he removed the needle. Before I had a chance to protest, I felt a warm sensation spreading from my neck to the rest of my body. My hand immediately covered the spot where he had jabbed me. Doubling over in pain, I started to stumble backwards. Jonah yelled out, "It will pass in a second or two."

I felt some of the warmth that had coursed through my veins subside. I yelled out, "What the hell was that?"

"Sorry I sneaked that one on you. I thought it best that we get that out of the way as quickly as possible."

I was no longer in any pain. The warm feeling that I had experienced moments earlier was replaced by a slight tingling sensation that ran all over my body, like a mild case of pins and needles.

Jonah continued his explanation. "We didn't get to that last night. After I saw how excited you were to start using the EyeWonder, I cut our session short. We didn't have a chance to cover this last security measure."

"What was in that syringe?" I yelled at Jonah.

"Well, I'm sure you researched what the EyeWonder was all about last night, right?"

I nodded.

"Then you know that the EyeWonder was built on a molecular computing platform."

Jonah had said this as a statement rather than a question, but I decided to answer anyway. "Yes."

"Well, the contents of the syringe are what the old man calls Nanobiotics. It's like an antibiotic, but based on the platform of the EyeWonder."

"You mean I have microscopic computers running through my veins?"

Jonah nodded his head and said, "Exactly."

"Why didn't you just tell me you were going to give me the shot?"

Jonah's face stiffened. He was dead serious. "Forget about why I did it the way I did it. Listen to me very carefully. While the Nanobiotics can repair small issues within the body, they cannot help you if there is a catastrophic event. For example, the Nanobiotics can kill viruses, pathogens, harmful bacteria, and even cancers. However, if you suffer a catastrophic event like a gunshot wound, the Nanobiotics will not be able to repair the damage in time to save you. Do you understand?"

Seeming to grasp what was just said, I replied, "So I'll never get cancer?"

Jonah said simply, "Ask your EyeWonder. Come on, let's go."

Jonah turned and started walking toward the Alexander One. Still in shock at what had just transpired, I didn't follow right away. Was it really possible that I could live a sickness-free life? I immediately turned on the EyeWonder to try to answer that very question.

"Come on. Let's go!" Jonah yelled from the driver's seat of the Alexander One.

I quickly got into the passenger side. Jonah then turned to me and asked, "Ready to go home?"

"Not really. I would have liked to explore the island a little more."

Jonah ignored me and flipped the start button on the main console. Within seconds, we were airborne, on our way back to Philadelphia.

CHAPTER THIRTEEN

There was no choice in the matter. Garrett was backed up in a corner and had to lie to Dean. Garrett's only hope was that the person responsible for today's elaborate meeting had now realized that Garrett had disappeared. It was now way past the time that Garrett was supposed to meet Ethan back at the golf course. Garrett was counting on this fact, and he knew his life depended on it. Garrett reasoned that if the mysterious sender of the instructions knew that he was not there to greet Ethan Kravis when he was due to return to the golf course, something was wrong. Perhaps his anonymous employer knew much earlier, based on a report from the security detail that was assigned to Garrett to prevent an occurrence such as kidnapping.

This last thought struck Garrett. It wasn't until many hours after the fact that Garrett thought about his single man security detail assigned by his unknown employer. The security had picked up Garrett in a secondary golf cart after Jonah and Ethan had taken off. He dropped Garrett off at the clubhouse dining room and was supposed to keep an eye out for danger. Why hadn't he been there when Garrett was abducted? Security details had been assigned to Garrett before. He had seen their capability and knew them to be extremely reliable. Why had there been a breakdown in security? Perhaps the detail became lax because there was already such tight security at the club.

Garrett started thinking a little deeper about this particular assignment. It was very different from most of his previous tasks. For one thing, it was much more elaborate than any of the previous assignments. It had many more moving parts. Garrett's previous dealings with his unknown employer had always called for doing something, then quickly leaving the scene of the task. Today's assignment was the first time that Garrett had been instructed to stay at the scene after the main objective had been completed. The main objective was for Jonah to take Ethan Kravis to the meeting.

At the time of committing the instructions to memory, Garrett thought it completely natural to stay at the scene and wait for Ethan to return. This step was needed so that no suspicion was aroused at the club. Reflecting on this thought, Garrett wasn't sure if the seemingly omniscient planner of these tasks hadn't made a serious error in judgment by allowing Garrett to stay after Jonah and Ethan had taken off. Garrett dismissed this thought. He was sure that the planner had thought what Garrett had fully believed. He was confident that the Alexander One's use was untraceable to the world at large.

Trying not to cause a brain aneurysm, Garrett decided not to beleaguer these inconsequential facts. The fact was that none of it mattered any longer. What was done was done. Garrett's only thought now was self-preservation and the $250,000,000 prize waiting for him at the end of the tunnel.

As all of these thoughts crossed Garrett's mind, he turned to Dean and said, "I can contact the person responsible for the Alexander One through a mutual acquaintance."

"Who is the mutual acquaintance?" Dean asked.

"The judge that Ethan Kravis was supposed to meet at the golf course."

Dean shook his head and responded, "No. I had my team of analysts do a deep background check on Judge Lawrence. There was nothing to suggest that he is involved in this situation."

Garrett was impressed. Dean was very thorough and must have access to tremendous amounts of information to dismiss the judge's complicity in this situation. It was part of Garrett's instruction to contact the judge and convince him to invite Ethan Kravis to the golf club. Although Garrett had told Ethan that he was a longtime friend and classmate of the Judge, the truth was that it was all part of the cover story. Contained in the instructions were some details of an extramarital affair that the judge had participated in. If this information had become public, it would be very embarrassing and damaging to the federal judge. It was all that was needed to persuade the judge to follow Garrett's request.

Garrett responded to Dean's insightful statement. "You're absolutely correct. The judge has no knowledge of anything that has gone on today; however, if I know anything about the man who set this all up, it is that he is extremely thorough. Once he realizes that I'm not where I'm supposed to be, he will cast a very wide net to find out where I've gone. I'm extremely confident that he'll be monitoring calls received by the Judge. I can call the judge and relay any message you want to the man who will be listening."

Dean asked, "What's to stop me from making that call myself? Why do I need you to make the call?"

Garrett was prepared for this question. He calmly replied, "My voice. My voice will flag the wiretap computers. I have no doubt that they will be able to determine that my speech pattern is authentic. Once they realize that it's actually me on the other end of the phone, they'll listen intently to anything that I say. If you were to make the call, I doubt that the computers would flag your voice."

Garrett hoped that this was enough to convince Dean. If it wasn't, Garrett knew what could happen. He sat quietly to see if Dean bit on the idea.

Dean responded. "OK. We'll try this course of action." Dean turned his attention on Albert. "Albert. Work up a script for Mr. Michaels to follow when he makes the call. Within the script, provide a subtle way for our mystery man to contact us. The method of contact that you choose needs to be untraceable. Also, set up a way for Mr. Michaels to make the call to the judge using a line that cannot be traced back to us. I don't want to give any unneeded information to our mystery guest. Brief Brad on the operation. I'd like his feedback on the plan. Let's be prepared to make the call tomorrow morning. No sense in disturbing the judge's Saturday night. Also, have Brad create an operation to track down Ethan Kravis. If Ethan Kravis pops up on our radar again, I want Brad and his team ready to scoop him up quickly and quietly."

Albert stood up and exited the room. Dean turned back to Garrett and said, "I hope for your sake that this little plan of yours works."

Garrett prayed to himself that Dean was right.

CHAPTER FOURTEEN

The second flight on the Alexander One had been equally as impressive as the first had been. I didn't feel nearly as faint or queasy when reentering the atmosphere. Perhaps my body had known what to expect. I dismissed this thought. All the preparation in the world could not condition your body for something like that. Plummeting to the earth at that rate of speed was an overwhelming assault on your senses. The only other explanation I could think of was Nanobiotics.

Somehow the Nanobiotics did something to my body to quell the sickening feeling of the rapid descent. Although I thought to use the EyeWonder to answer some questions about the Nanobiotics during the flight back, once we took off I shrugged off the urge so that I could once again give my full attention to the wonders of space flight. It wasn't until our final approach that the questions about Nanobiotics again swarmed in my brain.

As I was about to turn on the EyeWonder, Jonah began to speak. "We have about six minutes until touchdown. As another security measure, we cannot allow you to go back to your apartment. Arrangements have been made for you to live in a new location. I know that this is an inconvenience, but I'm sure you will be comfortable in your new home."

Given all that I had seen at the island, I had no doubt that Jonah had spoken the truth. The place that they had set up for me was probably several notches above my current home.

I had grown accustomed to my small home in the newly rehabilitated section of Philadelphia known as Olde City. The small three-bedroom two-bath brownstone was in terrible shape when I decided to purchase it back in late 1990s. The section of Philadelphia in which it was located was pretty run down at the time. Once a vibrant part of Philadelphia that accommodated many of city's warehouses, it had turned into a ghost town when the factories moved farther outside the city. The reason I had chosen to buy a home there came down to simple economics. Without much demand for homes in that area, it was one of the only places I could afford to live. I had decided to lease some cheap office space a couple of blocks from the brownstone. Not wanting to have to make the grueling commute into the city daily, I decided to purchase the fixer upper on Third Street.

Over the next several years I was happy to see an influx of young professionals in the area. Almost overnight, many of the old warehouses in the area had been purchased and converted into artsy loft-style apartments. It was very fashionable for young professionals in Philadelphia to live in big open spaces with unfinished brick walls and exposed HVAC ductwork. Within five years, Olde City Philadelphia had transformed from a rundown industrial part of town to a hip and desirable place to live. My timing for buying the little brownstone could not have been better. I paid next to nothing for it. I recently had it appraised and was astounded to find out that I could get at least twenty times what I had paid for it just ten years prior. The real estate agent who had done the appraisal even commented on the foresight I must have had when making the investment. I told her that I wished I could've been so lucky with all my investments.

Jonah interrupted my daydream. "I know that you must like your home and that this will be tough for you."

It dawned on me then that I must really have a bad poker face. It was the third or fourth time that Jonah had seemingly read my thoughts. His comments always seem to be right on point. He had found similar reassuring words when we were in orbit the day before. He had cut our meeting short the night before when he sensed that I wanted to start exploring the EyeWonder. Now he was sympathizing with the fact that I would not be able to return to my home. I guess it didn't take a rocket scientist to figure all this out, given the specific situations. He always seemed to react just when I was thinking it. If my mannerisms did indicate what I was thinking, then Jonah was a master at picking up on the subtle tells. Jonah could no doubt take this perfectly honed skill and make a killing in Las Vegas.

"Any idea when I might be able to move back into my house?" I asked Jonah.

"It's hard to say. I guess when we know the situation is safe. After you see the new place, you may not want to go back to your old life."

Eager to see what Jonah had meant, I was slowly building high expectations for the new living location.

"We're about to touch down. Are you ready to see your new house?"

I looked out the window and saw that we were roughly thirty feet above a rooftop. I looked around at the neighboring streets. I had a sense of where we were. Just above the tops of the surrounding buildings, I could make out the spire on top of Independence Hall. We were descending on an area of Philadelphia known as Society Hill.

Society Hill was not too far away from my brownstone on Third Street. It was a small neighborhood only about a twenty-minute walk from Olde City. In the twenty minutes that it would take to walk there, the area drastically changed from a nice up-and-coming neighborhood to one of the oldest and most prestigious areas in the country. The row homes located in Society Hill were known the world over. Almost all the homes in this area of Philadelphia had historical significance. Little plaques were affixed to each house indicating that someone famous had once lived in the modest row home. Although the homes did not appear to be much from the outside, the insides were often a very different story.

I had toured a couple of these magnificent structures over the years. The homes that I had seen were perfectly maintained and had retained the beautiful craftsmanship that came out of the late 1700s. Meticulous handcrafted woodworking and the very best materials were used during the construction of these homes. As you walked through them, you could not help but to sense that these wonderful homes once belonged to many of the men who gave independence to America. This pedigree didn't come cheaply. For those who wanted to own a piece of American heritage, the price tag usually started in the tens of millions. It was not very often that one of the homes went up for sale, but the couple of homes that I had heard were for sale started a bidding war. If I remembered correctly, one of the homes sold for close to forty million dollars. My heart skipped a beat at the thought. I got excited. I asked Jonah. "Society Hill?"

Jonah turned to me and smiled. He didn't bother to respond. He turned his attention back to the task at hand. Like an egg falling on a stack of pillows, the Alexander One gently touched down on the rooftop.

As soon as we landed, an awning extended over our heads. Before Jonah spoke I knew the purpose of the awning. It provided cover for the Alexander One, and also would allow us to enter and exit the craft unseen by prying eyes who might be watching from other rooftop decks.

Jonah confirmed my suspicion. "The awning is to keep nosy neighbors at bay."

Jonah powered down the Alexander One. The gull-wing doors opened and we exited the craft. Approximately fifteen feet away was a door. Jonah headed toward the door and I followed. I heard the popping sound of a dead bolt unlocking. Jonah reached out his hand to open the door. "The door has a proximity sensor. When you are within three feet of it, it will unlock automatically. After you enter and are out of range, it will rearm."

We entered the door, and a steep staircase greeted us. Jonah and I walked down the steps and I heard the dead bolt of the door slam shut behind us. Because I was in the biometrics security business, I figured that the door had some type of facial scanning device mounted somewhere on the rooftop.

As we walked down the stairs I started to see the first glimpse that the house was indeed one of the upper-class town homes in Society Hill. Inset in the wall next to the staircase was a stone statue of a little boy holding an American flag. The statue itself was not so impressive. My thoughts were more of the details surrounding the reason for placing the statue in such an odd place. This statue could have served as a centerpiece in an average person's home. In this house, it was displayed in a place that was probably rarely traveled. I couldn't wait to see the rest of the house.

At the bottom of the stairwell, we entered a door that put us out on a mezzanine level of the home. Immediately, I fell in love with what I saw. The home appeared to have three levels. We were standing on the third level. I glanced around and saw a U-shaped mezzanine that surrounded an open atrium that extended down to the first level. Overhead was a stained glass skylight that covered almost all of the open space on top of the three-story atrium. The light shining through the stained glass projected a broad spectrum of colors on the surfaces below and caused a slight kaleidoscope effect on the deep-grained hardwoods that made up the mezzanine floor. Intricate carvings in the wooden banister caressed the open void created by the mezzanine. I let out an involuntary whistle and said, "Ah, yeah. This will do nicely."

"Follow me. There are some things we need to discuss before you tour your new home."

Jonah walked down the open hallway of the mezzanine and turned at the corner. I had the sense that he was familiar with the layout of the house, because he hadn't stopped to look around. We arrived at a fifteen-foot-wide staircase that led to the second level of the home. In keeping with what I had seen so far, even the staircase exuded a sense of wealth. This extra-wide staircase was made from dark wood. Each step was dressed with a paisley rug that extended down the length of the staircase. A gold bar held the rug firmly in place on each step. The intricately carved banister that surrounded the mezzanine extended uninterrupted down the sides of the staircase. This gave the appearance that one long piece of banister snaked throughout the entire house. It was a stunning display of craftsmanship that must have taken years to create.

Jonah and I descended down the staircase. When we reached the second-floor mezzanine, Jonah crossed over the landing area and continued down to the first floor. It was then that I fully appreciated the architecture of the magnificent home. I had never seen anything like it before. The staircase was basically one long staircase that extended the entire height of the house. For some reason, the staircase had made me think of the side of a pyramid.

We reached the first floor. The staircase deposited us into a huge open foyer toward the back of the home. I looked up and saw the stained glass skylight three stories above. I turned my attention to the foyer. Instead of the hardwood floors that blanketed the rest of the house, the foyer had pink marble floors. The foyer was approximately sixty by sixty feet. The open space above gave the foyer the appearance of being much larger than that.

Jonah negotiated the round table in the middle of the foyer and walked towards an open door off to the side. We entered a den. In the center of the wood-paneled room was a seating area. Jonah motioned me to take a seat. A large manila envelope lay on the coffee table in front of me.

Once Jonah and I were sitting, he began to speak. "I'm sure that you are eager to explore your new home and relax a bit. You'll have the next couple of days to do so at your leisure. I wanted to brief you on a couple of things before I leave you."

Jonah picked up the manila envelope and dumped its contents on the coffee table.

"The old man thought it best that you have a second identity. If people were to somehow know of your involvement, this cover identity should help provide some protection. Your temporary new name is Steve Hamilton. You recently sold your investment firm and are actively looking for new business opportunities."

Jonah handed me some items from the envelope. "Here are a couple of forms of identifications and some credit cards. If by some chance your new identity is run through the system, it'll all check out."

Jonah then reached below the coffee table and produced a small cardboard box. "In addition, here's twenty thousand dollars in various denominations. Don't be afraid of running out, because there's more if you should need it."

Jonah handed me the box. I had a flashback to a movie I had recently seen. It was one of the many spy movies where the lead character leads a double life. I almost laughed at the fact that I was now in this same situation. What the heck did I know about being a spy? I'm a scientist, for gosh sakes!

"Don't worry. We are not expecting you to go into East Germany and flip assets for us. This is strictly a security measure. The truth is that you probably won't have much need for your new identity. We just felt better giving you this option in the event you find yourself in a position to have to use it."

Again, Jonah had seemed to sense the very thought I just had about the spy movie and addressed the concern. Jonah continued. "All right. Any questions?"

"Once we are done here, where will you go? Are you staying here with me? I'm sure I could find some space for you."

Jonah chuckled at my little joke. "I will not be staying here, but I'll be close by. I want to give you some space. My job is to look after you and make sure you don't get into any trouble. I can do this from a safe distance. You just go about your business and pretend that I'm not there. This probably won't be too difficult to do, because you probably won't see me. When I need to, I'll make contact with you. If you need me, use this."

Jonah handed me a key chain with a couple of keys on it. "These are the keys to your new home. You can call me by pressing the button on the key chain. The watch is your panic button if you are in danger. Activating the key chain device just means that you want to talk. Got it?"

I nodded at the description. "What are we doing Tuesday?"

Jonah paused for a moment. "I think you could use some rest. Let's hold off on that for now. Let's meet back here Monday night at six o'clock. We can have some dinner and then I can brief you about Tuesday. Sound like a plan?"

"Yeah, that sounds good."

"Good. Before I leave you, I cannot stress enough how important it is not to draw attention to yourself if you should happen to leave here. Try to avoid anyone you might know on the street. If you happen to run into someone you know, say that you are late for something and leave as quickly as possible. Try to stay in this neighborhood, and don't venture too close to Olde City. We probably should have put you up in a house in a different city, but we thought it would be best if you were familiar with the area. The kitchen is fully stocked. There are new clothes for you in the closet of the master bedroom. In reality, there should be no reason for you to have to leave the house; however, you may want some fresh air, so feel free to take a walk around the neighborhood. If for some reason you need the use of a car, let me know, and I can arrange it. Any more questions?"

"What about my business? People will be worried if I don't show up on Monday."

"Don't worry about that. We have taken care of that for you. You are taking some time off to attend to personal matters. You left Bret in charge until you get back."

Jonah had thought of everything. How did he even know who Bret was? Who was I kidding? This guy knows everything.

The comfortable leather couch that I was now sitting on accelerated the tiredness I now felt. I let out a yawn when I spoke. "You guys think of everything."

Jonah rose to his feet. "I can see that you are tired. I'm going to leave you now. Get some rest, and we'll meet up again on Monday night. I'll let myself out."

Before I could respond, Jonah had left the room. I could feel my eyelids get increasingly heavy. It didn't take me long to reach that barely conscious state just before being fully asleep. As I felt myself falling deeper and deeper into sleep, I thought to myself, "Tomorrow I start the first day of my new life."

CHAPTER FIFTEEN

Dean spent the majority of the morning in his home office. Because of the council meeting and yesterday's other events, he now needed to spend some time to ensure that his empire was still sailing in the right direction. Even though it was Sunday morning, he had no problems calling several of his key lieutenants who handled the day-to-day operations of his oil enterprise. Confident that his interests had stayed the course during his brief absence yesterday, he realized that it was almost time for Garrett to make his call.

Before Dean got up from his French-made antique desk, he decided to check to see if there had been any additional communications from the council that came out of yesterday's impromptu meeting. Dean located the fingerprint scanner installed on the underside of his desk. He placed his index finger on the device for three seconds. The device then triggered two events. First, the door to his home office was double locked ensuring that no one accidentally entered. Second, Dean heard the unmistakable popping sound that came from the middle drawer of his desk as it disengaged its internal lock. He opened the drawer to his desk and took out a small black laptop. He placed the computer down on the calfskin blotter that protected the desk from pen etchings. He flipped up the screen on the small laptop. The familiar slight whining sound of the internal hard drive spinning was heard. A red laser began to emanate from the top of the device. The laser passed up and down Dean's face. Once Dean had passed the facial recognition test that the device had just preformed, the computer challenged him with a question. "Please state your name"

"Dean Edward Bouchard," said Dean as he leaned toward the device. The electronic voice continued. "Please speak your pass code."

"Number Seven. Echo-Charlie-Foxtrot-Four-Two-Seven-Alpha."

Within a second, the laptop processed the voiceprint analysis and authenticated Dean's responses. The laptop then opened the inbox of the specially designed Email program the council had developed to transmit its highly private communications.

Dean looked at the screen with growing anticipation. Moments later, he was disappointed that no new messages had been broadcast by the council. This was either a good thing or bad. He needed to be kept abreast of any actions that emanated from the initiation of Plan Alpha. The lack of communication either meant that no new details had emerged or that Number One knew something, but just didn't share this with the group.

Dean decided not to send a message to inquire if any action had been taken. Dean knew that the first details of any action should come from Number One. If Dean were to send a communication prematurely, it might arouse some suspicion. Deciding to lie low for a while, Dean shut down the laptop. He placed the device back into the secure middle drawer and used the fingerprint scanner to lock the laptop back up.

Dean reassured himself that he was much closer to solving the unexplained events that surrounded the use of the Alexander One than the council was currently. Dean smiled and said, "The council doesn't even know that what it's looking for is called the Alexander One." He was sure that he had more actionable intelligence about the situation than the council did at this moment. "Let's go solve another piece of the puzzle."

Dean got up from behind his desk, exited the door to his office, and headed to the great room. When he arrived at the great room, he noticed that Albert and Brad were facing Garrett as he read from a piece of paper. Dean determined that Garrett was practicing the script that Albert had prepared for the call. Dean interrupted Garrett's recitation. "Are we ready to make the call?" Dean said in a booming voice as he entered the room.

The three men flinched. Albert looked up and said, "We are ready, sir."

"Good." Dean turned his attention to his chief of security and asked the trillion-dollar question. "Brad. What steps have been taken to ensure that the call cannot be traced?"

"We are using the SAMSAC terminal to connect to a remote server that is not affiliated with us in any way. The server will then route the call through several more remote servers and will eventually place the call. Any trace preformed should stop at the server that physically makes the call to the judge."

Dean pounded his fist on the coffee table and yelled. "Should? Should? I don't pay for should. I pay for will. Can you tell me that trace will stop at the first server?"

Dean looked at Brad with fire in his eyes. The explosive reaction to what Brad said was unlike Dean. He had always tried to remain calm, even during the direst of situations. The situation was becoming critical and Dean knew better then to take his frustrations out on Brad. Not only was Brad a trusted employee, but he was a man of action. Dean, on several occasions, had seen Brad get upset. It wasn't a pretty sight. If Dean treated Brad with this type of disrespect often, it wouldn't be long before Brad jumped over the couch and snapped Dean's neck. Brad was a trained killer. He solved his problems through the use of force. With this in mind, Dean listened to Brad's response.

"This is the most technically advanced option we have. No known tracing techniques will allow the call to be tracked. Unless there is a technique that the NSA has not discovered, we will be secure."

This response seemed to calm Dean down. He knew that he should not have publicly berated his trusted security chief. He could feel the gravity of the situation and the importance it had on the desired outcome. He decided that when the call was over, he would take Brad aside and apologize, but first it was time to address the matter at hand. In a placid voice, Dean said, "Make the call."

Brad nodded his head and began to work on the laptop in front of him. The phone signal was bouncing through the external servers chosen for the task, so he said to Garrett, "Pick up the handset. The call will be placed in ten seconds."

Garrett did as instructed.

Albert then spoke quickly. "Remember not to deviate from the script. If the conversation goes awry, just hang up."

Everyone in the room went deadly silent. Garrett placed the handset to his ear. The familiar ringing of a call being placed could be heard through the speakers of the Lockbox. After the second ring, a woman with a thick Spanish accent answered the call. "Jello. Lawrence residence. Can I jelp you?"

Garrett began to recite the script that had been prepared for him. "Good morning. Could I speak with Judge Lawrence please?"

"May I tell jim who is calling?"

"Please tell him that it's his friend from the golf course yesterday."

There was a brief pause in the line and Dean's heart fluttered.

Within a couple of seconds, a man came on the line and said in a low whisper, "I thought we had agreed that you would never contact me again. I did what you asked. If you think you can continue to blackmail me–."

Garrett cut the judge off in mid-sentence and began to recite the script. "Judge Lawrence, this is Alexander One. If Mr. Kravis would like to speak with me, I can be reached through an alternate number. Tell him that he can use–ah."

Garrett stumbled a bit in his reading in the script. He quickly composed himself and continued. "Tell him that he can use encrypted channel 154.121.103.742 on high band fourteen."

"What the hell are you talking–?"

Before the judge could continue his protest, Garrett hung up the phone.

"Killing the connection," said Brad as he punched keys on the laptop.

The four men sat silent for a moment before Dean started to speak. "Are we secure?"

Brad said, "There was evidence of an immediate back trace when the line was established. Someone was definitely listening. They didn't get very far with the trace. They were able to penetrate only the first of fourteen servers. We're in the clear."

Brad stressed the last sentence. Dean knew that Brad did so in response to the public scolding from earlier. Dean said, "Good job all."

Dean then looked at Garrett. He appeared to be visibly relieved when the call had gone well. Dean was sure that Garrett had no idea what the message meant, but he was glad that Garrett's simple task was over.

Brad had indicated that someone had tried to tap the line. Dean just hoped that it was the person the cryptic message was intended for.

Hearing the message and acting on it were two different stories. Dean prayed that the person listening on the other end would understand the instructions embedded in the message. The Internet protocol address encoded in the message was a secure gateway to establish communication with the unknown listener. If the IP address were used, it would be flagged and answered by the SAMSAC terminal. The terminal would prevent the caller from getting a trace on the person who answered the call. Additionally, Dean would be able to use the open line to have the Lockbox computer locate the caller's origin. All Dean could do now was wait and pray that he received the call from his mystery guest.

"Brad. A word if you please."

Dean motioned for Brad to follow him. He led Brad out of the great room and back to his office. Once the two men were comfortably sitting, Dean began to speak.

"You must know by now that I consider you to be a highly trusted and valued asset in my organization. You know I would never want to publicly embarrass you like I did back there. This situation has me on edge. There is a lot riding on its outcome. I never meant to fly off the handle like that. I hope you can accept my apology."

Dean delivered the apology with conviction. He always considered apologies a form of weakness. In this case, Dean felt it was necessary. The last thing he needed was for Brad to fail him because of personal differences.

Brad said, "I appreciate that this is a difficult situation for you, sir. Although it is completely unnecessary, thank you for the apology."

Dean was pleased that his trusted employee was not overly offended by his public berating. He smiled and started to rise when he thought the conversation had been concluded.

Brad began to speak again. "I was waiting to tell you this until after we had made the call."

Dean sat back down in his chair.

Brad continued. "At roughly eight o'clock this morning I received some new intel pertinent to this situation. Our computers didn't pick up on it right away. Our techs said that the delay was caused because of the urban topography. Apparently, the computers identified another signature produced by the Alexander One."

Dean's eyebrows arched as if to signal a response. Dean felt the anger building inside him. He worked hard to suppress the outburst he knew was coming. On the inside, Dean was fuming. Dean's exterior did not betray his emotion as he just sat there and listened intently.

Brad continued. "Apparently the signature was well disguised by the urban clutter of the high-rise buildings. It took several hours for the computers to recognize the broken signal."

Dean then asked, "Were the computers able to get a fix on the location of the signature?"

"The clutter made it impossible to get an exact fix. They were able to get an approximate location. The signature was detected in and around the city of Philadelphia. It looks like Kravis might have been brought home."

Dean could hardly contain the excitement at this latest discovery. A million thoughts raced through his head. His first excited response was, "Send a team to extract Kravis."

"The team was dispatched at 8:02 this morning. They have already raided Ethan Kravis's home and found nothing to suggest that he has been there since yesterday."

Dean was a little deflated by this last comment. He knew that he wasn't going to be that lucky. While he pondered what his next action should be, Brad interrupted and provided the answer.

"We will maintain surveillance on the house. I have also instructed the team lead to send out reconnaissance teams to hunt for any sign of Kravis. They'll use a circular sweep pattern emanating from Kravis's home. This technique is extremely effective in locating a subject."

Dean considered this plan of action. He thought of one additional step that could be taken in the team's effort to track down Ethan Kravis. He said, "Tap into any known surveillance cameras in the area. If Ethan Kravis walks by, I want one of our analysts to identify him."

"Already done, sir."

Dean nodded his head in approval. He knew one thing for sure. If he were able to capture Ethan Kravis, he would have something that he desperately needed in this situation. He would have leverage.

CHAPTER SIXTEEN

I had woken up from the deep, coma-like sleep in a place that I didn't immediately recognize. Still blurry-eyed, I rubbed my hand over my face and looked around. What I thought had been a dream, turned out to be reality. The prior night's sleep had been so intense, it took me a couple of minutes to adjust to my new surroundings. Everything came back to me like a boomerang once I saw the wood paneling of the den.

I was still fully clothed and lying on a tan leather couch. I had slept on many couches in my lifetime; however, none had been as comfortable as this one had been. I couldn't tell if it had been the comfortable couch or the past day's events that had knocked me out so completely. I rose off the couch, stretched, and let out a loud yawn. Not knowing what time it was, I stumbled out of the den to look around. I entered the large pink marble foyer. I looked up at the three-story atrium and saw the stained glass skylight.

"I guess it wasn't a dream." I headed toward what I thought to be the way to the kitchen. After a couple minutes of aimlessly wandering around, I arrived at the kitchen. I opened the door to the refrigerator. The refrigerator was brimming with food. It dawned on me that I hadn't eaten since golf the day before. I didn't feel overly hungry. I knew it would be in my best interest to eat something and quickly identified a bowl of fresh-cut fruit and some raspberry yogurt in the refrigerator. I placed the items on the kitchen table and turned on the flat-panel TV mounted on the wall. As had been my morning ritual for many years, I turned the TV channel to a twenty-four-hour news network. I inhaled the fresh fruit and yogurt and listened to the sexy newscaster I had a crush on for many years.

"In today's other top headlines, yet another oil production facility has been attacked in Nigeria. For further details, we turn to our reporter in the field, Lindsay Freemont. Lindsey, what can you tell us about the latest attack?"

"Good morning Erin. It has been yet another day of unrest here in the African nation of Nigeria. Early this morning there was an explosion at the Hanati oil production facility in the port city of Calabar. At 3:15 A.M. local time a huge fireball erupted from the facility. Many of the local residents heard the explosion and caused a near riot reaction. The facility is owned by the oil giant Petro United. It was severely damaged by the explosion. It took firefighters here over six hours to get the flames under control. This is the third attack in as many weeks on Petro United facilities around the world. The people responsible for the attacks are still unidentified. We contacted the company for a statement about the attacks, but were unable to reach anyone who would comment.

The shutdown of the facility caused panic in the world oil market this morning. News of the explosion caused a significant jump in the price of oil. Last we checked, the price of oil was up almost ten dollars a barrel. Now trading at close to one hundred and fifty dollars a barrel, it is unlikely to go down anytime soon. The Hanati oil facility produces one hundred twenty thousand barrels of oil per day, ten percent of Nigeria's total oil output. The latest attack makes it even more difficult to keep pace with the growing demand for oil around the world. Reporting live from Calabar, Nigeria, this is Lindsay Freemont."

"Thank you, Lindsay. Indeed the oil markets have taken another blow with this attack. Turning our attention to a more positive story, a baby seal was rescued in the oddest of places. Stay tuned to find out where."

I had heard enough depressing news for one day. I turned off the TV and finished the rest of my breakfast in peace and quiet. I continued to shovel the delicious morsels of fruit into my mouth. I thought about what Loyal had said about the Alexander One. Although I was aware of the growing cost of oil, I hadn't really paid attention to the reasons why. I only noticed that the price for a gallon of gasoline had gone up roughly thirty percent in the last twelve months. "The world has started wars over this black gold from the earth," I thought to myself. Loyal sure did have a way with words.

Deciding that I had eaten enough, I slipped the cover back on the fruit and placed it back in the refrigerator. "Now what?" I asked myself as I stood in the silent kitchen. I looked up at the large wall clock just beyond the kitchen table. I was stunned to see that it was already ten o'clock in the morning. I typically slept only seven hours a night at most. I must have been tired to sleep nonstop on a couch for thirteen hours. Feeling a bit lazy because of this, I decided to take a shower and go out for a walk around my new neighborhood although Jonah had advised against it.

I left the kitchen and bound up the massive rear staircase at the back of the house. I headed for the third floor in search of the master bedroom. After making almost an entire loop around the mezzanine, I finally arrived at my destination. I walked through the double French doors and was surprised at what I saw. The master bedroom was nearly identical to the master guest room back on the island. This sight threw me off balance. It was like déjà vu. I guess the old man liked the setup enough to have it recreated here.

I took a long hot shower and changed into some fresh clothes. I was pleasantly surprised that the clothes fit perfectly. I put on a white T-shirt and a pair of blue jeans. A new pair of running sneakers completed the outfit. I grabbed a sweater but doubted very much that I would need it at this time of the year.

I went back down to the den and grabbed a little cash out of the cardboard box. I slipped the cash in my pocket along with my new credit cards, my new identification, and the new keys to my house. Steve? Do I really look like a Steve? Not being able to answer the question, I headed toward the front door.

I stepped out the front door and took in a deep breath. The fresh air filled my lungs. The temperature outside was perfect. Not too hot and not too cool. A perfectly sunny day to take a nice walk.

I'm the type of person who needs to have a plan before I act. Knowing that I couldn't just walk around aimlessly and enjoy the day, I decided the purpose for this walk would be to get a copy of the Sunday paper. I glanced in both directions to get my bearing. Turning right would send me north towards Olde City. Heeding Jonah's warning, I turned in the opposite direction and started walking. The night's rest had done me good. I felt fully rested. In fact, I felt better than I had in years. I wondered if the Nanobiotics had anything to do with the way I felt. Realizing that my EyeWonder was still attached to my eye, I decided to be productive with the time. I went to work to learn more about the tiny robots that now flowed through my veins.

I walked a couple of blocks and turned left on Walnut Street. I knew the area well. There was a convenience store across the street from Washington Square Park. I walked the couple of blocks while reading up on the Nanobiotics. Similar to the EyeWonder, I really didn't understand most of the science behind the Nanobiotics. From what I did understand, the Nanobiotics basically hunted down and killed things that shouldn't be in the body. It was amazing to me that something so small could not only identify a threat, but also had the logic to take it out. Knowing that I would probably give myself a headache if I tried to delve too deeply into the technology behind the Nanobiotics, I determined that I knew all that I needed to know on the subject. It was a good thing to have these little robots in my body protecting me.

I reached the entrance of the small convenience store and went in. The newspapers were stacked in a bin next to the front door. I bent down to pick up a paper. Once the paper was in hand, I turned to the cashier counter to pay. When I looked over at the counter, I almost dropped all several hundred pages of newspaper on the floor.

Her beauty hit me like a shockwave from a bomb. It was the first time in a long time that I was instantly attracted to someone. She was standing in front of the cashier engaged in a small argument with the man behind the counter. I decided not to get in line, but rather observe the disagreement from a distance. I moved to my left next to the cases of soda that were piled up from the floor to eye height. This wall made of soda allowed me to take in her captivating features without fear of being spotted.

Staring at her was like staring at the sun. It was nearly impossible for me to look away. She was shorter than me by at about twelve inches. Her curly hazelnut hair bounced as she spoke to the man behind the counter. She was wearing a floral patterned sundress that hugged her ample breasts tightly. Her arms and legs exposed a deep tan that accentuated her firm body. She wore dark rimmed glasses that made her look like one of those sexy librarians every heterosexual male has fantasized about at one time or another. I glanced down to the left hand as had been my standard response when I saw a good-looking woman. No rings! Could it be that this remarkably striking woman was not married? Not possible.

I needed to get a better look at her face before I fell completely in love with this perfect stranger. I inched my way over a couple of feet so that I was positioned at a forty-five degree angle from her. When I looked up, it confirmed what I had already suspected. She was as breathtaking as the moonrise I had seen the day earlier. The dark rimmed-glasses covered her pale blue eyes. As she spoke, I noticed her glistening white teeth that were protected nicely by her full pink lips. My gaze traveled down her body. A small gold chain caressed her ankle. She was wearing open-toed sandals that exposed her painted red toenails.

I made the decision right then and there that I had to find out more about her. I had never been one of those guys who could waltz up to a girl and strike up a conversation. Although many of my past girlfriends told me that I had above-average looks, I always lacked the courage to initiate a relationship. This time would be no different. The knockout was about to pay for her items. I decided to see how effective the EyeWonder could be in a real life situation.

As soon as the man behind the counter swiped her credit card, I commanded the EyeWonder to pull a list of credit card transactions for the store. The tiny monitor in my eye came alive with pages and pages of data. There! I had identified the last transaction. From the last transaction, I was able to obtain a name. The name of the cardholder was Risa Castleberry. Risa, I thought to myself. What a beautiful name to go with a beautiful woman. I challenged the EyeWonder further. I asked for a background report on Risa Castleberry. The EyeWonder ripped through the data with incredible speed.

A very detailed background report on this mystery woman was displayed on the screen. I felt a little bad for using the EyeWonder for such a ridiculous purpose. If anyone were to ask about it, I would say that I was just practicing using the device.

I scanned the summarized background report. Risa Castleberry was thirty-two years old. She did not have any arrests on her record. She was current on her taxes and had minimal credit card debts. Her occupation was a school teacher. She taught third grade at a public school not too far away from here. She lived in the Riverside apartment complex on Front Street. There was no record of her ever being married. I scanned the rest of the report and came to an interesting section of the report titled, Other Facts. Under this section, it said that the origin of her name was Spanish. When translated, it meant "laughter." This was a little odd to me. She did not appear to be Hispanic. Her last name did not sound Hispanic. "Laughter," I said out loud.

"Excuse me?" I heard as I read over the report again.

Being so focused on the report, I hadn't realized that I was blocking the exit to the store. She was standing right in front of me. Her beauty paralyzed me. Barely able to speak or move, I somehow managed to get out a barely audible, "Oh, sorry," as I moved to the side.

But Risa just stood there looking at me. She said, "Did you just say 'laughter?'"

Realizing now that I had said it out loud just as she was exiting the store, I didn't know how to respond to the seemingly easy question. I lied and acted dumb. I said, "I'm sorry, what?"

Risa responded, "I could've sworn that you just said the word 'laughter.' That's so funny, because that's what my name means in Spanish."

Was it even a remote possibility that this woman who was causing my heart to literally skip a beat was flirting with me? The mere fact that she had even stopped to say anything was a good sign. Our eyes locked, and she held my stare. We both stood there looking into each other's eyes. Not a word was spoken for what seemed like an eternity.

She finally spoke. "Risa," she said as she continued to look in my eyes.

I was sure she felt something, as I had. Something inside me broke. I had an animalistic urge to pounce on her right then and there. As this feeling nearly buckled my knees, she spoke again.

"That's my name. Risa." She spoke in a wispy, almost distant voice. It was like she was in a trace while staring into my eyes.

All I could say was, "Beautiful."

Then I heard the most unexpected three words I had heard in my life. She simply said, "Yes, you are." She displayed an unmistakable smile.

What was the probability of this, I wondered. In twenty-four hours I had flown in outer space, learned of new technologies that I never thought could exist, made a life-changing decision to lead the introduction of an new technology that may well save the planet, moved into a house that in my wildest dreams I could never hope to afford and, now this chance meeting with someone I could conceivably spend the rest of my life with. It was hard to fathom, but it had all happened. I caught myself just as I was about to slip and say that my name was Ethan.

"Steve. I'm so glad I finally found you."

Before I realized what I had just said, I immediately wished I could have taken it back. I didn't want Risa to think that I was psychotic freak. But it was the truth. I knew as soon as I saw her that she was the one I had been looking for all these years. If someone asked me how I knew this, I wouldn't have the faintest idea how to answer him or her. I just knew. I knew the way a newborn horse knew to stand. I knew the same way the sun knew to rise in the morning. I knew that this was going to be the start of something very special. As with most things in life, timing was everything.

I cursed myself that I had finally met someone I was so sure was the right person. My newfound purpose in life was going to make it difficult to start seeing Risa. Even worse, I might put her in harm's way. I didn't know what to do in that moment. I sensed that moment was one of those critical moments in life. It was like a valve in a pipe that could send you in two completely different directions based on which way it was turned. I couldn't run the risk of not having the opportunity to find out if Risa was the one. I had to see where this might lead. I was relieved that my last comment hadn't sent her screaming out the door. She just continued to stand there in front of me, making love to me with those big blue eyes.

She finally responded. "What do we do now?"

"I really don't know."

It was if the words we spoke meant nothing. I felt like we were floating around the store engaged in a waltz.

"I was about to head over to Washington Square Park. Would you like to come?"

I placed the Sunday paper down on the stack of soda cases and said, "Absolutely."

We held each other's stare for one more fleeting moment. Never wanting it to end, I finally turned to the door and started to walk through the exit. Risa followed right behind me as we left.

We reached the sidewalk and I turned to face her. We again looked in each other's eyes. I decided to be absurdly blunt with her and said, "This is the start of something special, isn't it?"

Before she responded, I felt a walloping sting on my right shoulder, like a big wasp jabbed its stinger in me as deep as it could go. I raised my left hand to my shoulder. When my hand arrived at the area of the stinging sensation, I felt a dart sticking out of my shoulder. I grabbed the tiny dart and yanked it out of my body. My shoulder started getting warm. The next series of events happened so quickly that I couldn't process what was happening right away.

I looked at the dart in my hand. Out of the corner of my eye, I saw a man who was standing next to the convenience store fall to the ground. A split second after the man fell to the ground, I heard something that sounded like a gunshot ring out. Risa was falling to the ground. I reached out for her and caught her before she hit the pavement. A car sped towards us and slammed on its brakes. A large man jumped out of the passenger's seat and wrapped his huge mitts around both Risa and me. With crushing force, he flung us into the back seat of the car. The car sped off, and I heard a familiar voice yelling. "Are you hurt? Are you hurt?"

Jonah was in the driver's seat. He repeated his question. "Ethan, are you hurt?"

"No. I don't think so. I was shot in the shoulder with this."

I held up the dart for Jonah to see.

He barely looked at it and said, "Tranquiller dart. Do you feel a warm sensation where it struck you?"

"Yes."

"Good. That means the Nanobiotics are working."

I looked over at Risa. She was unconscious. A quick search of her body, and I found it. A dart had struck her just below her neckline. I pulled it out and threw it on the floor.

Jonah took the corner at a very high speed. He reached down to the radio and turned it on. Within seconds, we were airborne, floating high above the City of Philadelphia.

I looked over at Risa. She looked so peaceful sitting there. A sudden wave of guilt hit me. What had I gotten her into?

CHAPTER SEVENTEEN

Dean slammed the big red button to lock the door of the Lockbox. He walked into the command center where Brad and Albert were sitting.

"What'd we got?" asked Dean as he entered the grandstand seating behind the console.

Brad and Albert looked at each other. This pause told Dean all he needed to know. It was clear that the news was bad. The slight look Brad and Albert gave to each other indicated that neither of them wanted to present the update to Dean. He was growing impatient with the unresponsiveness. Dean took a deep breath and said, "I don't care which one of you tells me. Just get on with it. Brad, what is going on?"

Brad reluctantly responded. "Sir. We made contact with Ethan Kravis a couple of minutes ago."

Dean's face lit up and asked, "Did we get him?"

Brad paused. Dean cursed himself for getting so upset before. His team was now hesitating when providing much needed information. He gave assurances to Brad. "Forget about what happened before. I won't get mad, I promise. However, I'll get mad if you don't tell me what has happened, so get on with it. Did we capture Kravis?"

"No, sir. He got away with the help of a team of men who were watching over him. We lost an agent in the process."

Dean couldn't control himself. His assurances went right out the window and he said, "Brad! What the hell do you mean he got away? What the hell happened?"

Brad took a deep breath and provided some of the emerging details about the situation. "Information is still coming in, but it appears that our agents located the subject at a convenience store near Washington Park. They sent a man to the side of the store to tranquilize and extract the target. The team lead thought it best to do this out in the open once the target left the store. This is what I would've ordered as well. Waiting until the target left the store would allow the team to capture the subject within seconds. If they were to have attempted to tranquilize the subject in the store, there would've been many witnesses. There would've been people on the street that would've seen the agent walk out of the store with a man over his shoulder. By performing the extraction on the street, the whole operation would've been done by the time anyone had noticed."

Dean ignored all of the small details Brad had just provided. Dean's business interests have grown to be so vast, that he didn't have time for trivialities. He almost cut off Brad's explanation when he spoke. "Were you able to follow where he went after your team failed to capture him?"

Dean saw Brad cringe at the word "failed." He had never used the word before when discussing a mission under Brad's command. This episode was the first blemish on Brad's spotless record since he came to work for Dean. The mistake couldn't have come at a worse time.

"No, sir. We lost contact with the car that picked up the target when it rounded the corner of Spruce Street."

"What do you mean lost contact?" Dean said in an indignant tone.

"They entered a blind spot in between two public cameras. The camera they were heading toward never spotted them coming down the street."

Dean shook his head in disbelief. Deciding that he had jumped too far ahead too quickly he said, "Wait. Let's back up a second. Take me through the whole series of events. Show me what you do have."

Brad turned to the console within the command center. He pressed several buttons on the console, and video footage was put up on the main screen overhead. He then started his briefing.

"We're still receiving the footage from all available cameras in the area. Here's what we have been able to piece together so far. At 11:07 A.M. one of our remote surveillance experts located the target entering the Quik-E Mart on the corner of Walnut and Sixth Street in Philadelphia."

Dean saw video of a man walking into the convenience store.

Brad continued. "A two-man team was immediately dispatched to the location. The team was on the scene within four minutes. The driver parked his car on the street and the man responsible for intercepting the target took up a position along the south face of the store."

Dean watched the video footage and saw a man walk to the side of the convenience store.

"At 11:12 A.M., the target left the store with a woman. Facial scan revealed the woman to be Risa Castleberry, a local schoolteacher with no discernable ties to the target. As they exited the store, our agent shot them both with a tranquilizer dart. Within a second of shooting the tranquilizer darts, our agent went down to the ground from what appeared to be a gunshot wound from a high-caliber bullet. Before our man on the street had time to react, both the target and the woman were placed in this BMW 750I, and it sped away."

Dean watched the video of the fast moving event. He saw a black BMW speed up to Ethan Kravis and the woman. A large man jumped out of the passenger's seat, grabbed both Kravis and the woman, threw them in the back seat, and the car sped away. The whole event took less than three seconds. He then noticed something in the video. "Brad. Can you rewind the video to the point at which the agent shot the target with the tranquilizer dart?"

Brad expertly navigated the console and rewound the video.

Dean continued. "Good. Now, can you slow the playback down right at the point the darts would have made contact with the target?"

Brad did as he was asked.

"There!" Dean yelled and jumped out of his seat.

"Rewind it and go extra slow. There! Did you see that?" Dean pointed up to the large screen.

Both Brad and Albert squinted while looking at the screen. Dean saw that they didn't see what he was seeing. Dean clarified, "They were both stuck by a dart. First Kravis was struck then the woman. Kravis pulls the dart out of his shoulder, there!"

Brad shrugged his shoulders. Dean took this as a sign that Brad still didn't understand what he was pointing out. He paused for a moment to allow Brad to comment. Brad just sat there staring at the screen without saying a word. Dean looked over at Albert. He too was looking at the screen and didn't appear as if he was going to comment.

Dean continued, "Ethan Kravis was struck with the dart but doesn't go down. A split second later, the woman takes a dart to her neck and starts to fall. Kravis than catches her, and the man in the BMW grabs them both and throws them into the car."

The three men in the Lockbox reflect on this thought for a moment.

Dean continued his thought pattern. "Ethan Kravis is wearing a T-shirt. The dart would have easily passed through to his skin. Why didn't the tranquilizer knock him out?"

All three men pondered this mystery. A moment had passed before Brad offered his opinion. "Perhaps the dart was a dud?"

Dean shot Brad a look for wasting his breath to expel such a stupid comment. Dean continued to concentrate on the question. He said, "Run the video back one more time."

Dean watched the events unfold again in super slow motion. He didn't know how to explain the occurrence, but he knew that it was important.

Albert spoke his first words since Dean entered the room. "The dart clearly pierces his skin, because he winces as he pulls it out. Somehow he was immune to the dart's effects."

Dean knew that Albert was onto something, but he couldn't figure out what. He was hoping that Albert had more to offer, so he asked, "How do you think he could be immune to a neuro-inhibitor?"

Dean desperately hoped his protégé would impress him with an insightful comment. He looked over at Albert in anticipation. He watched as Albert struggled to find the appropriate words. All eyes were on Albert when he said, "Well, what do we know about neuro-inhibiters? We know that as soon as they are introduced to the bloodstream, they basically cause a short in the electrical impulses in the nervous system. Somehow, something in Ethan Kravis's body stopped the short circuit from happening."

Dean considered the vague explanation. He made up his mind that there was something very different about Ethan Kravis. "I get the feeling that the Alexander One is not the only secret Ethan Kravis is carrying."

He smiled at his protégé, and then turned his attention to Brad. "I don't care what it costs. Scour the earth for this man. If he is hiding in a single-man bunker in a small village in Iraq, I want us to be there to grab him!"

"Yes, sir!" Brad said forcefully.

Dean sat back down and asked, "Is there any additional footage of the event?"

"We have two more pieces of footage, sir. One is from within the store and one is from the last camera to have picked up the car as it sped away. Which one would you like to review first?"

"In the store," Dean said without hesitation.

Dean watched as Brad pulled up the footage and let it run. Brad let the video run without commenting. Dean saw the woman known to be Risa Castleberry at the cashiers counter paying for her items. Off to the side, he could barely make out the top of a man's head from behind a stack of soda cases. The woman paid for her items and signed the sales receipt. She started to exit the store. She disappeared behind the stacks of soda and stopped for a couple of minutes as she talked to a man. The clock at the bottom of the video screen showed that they talked for two minutes and fifteen seconds before they both left the store. Dean then realized that the man behind the cases of soda was Ethan Kravis. The video didn't appear to provide a lot of details.

Once the video was over, Dean began to speak. "Run it back again."

Brad rewound the video and played it again.

Dean immediately interrupted. "Pause it."

Brad paused the video.

"Did you see that?" said Dean in a quizzical voice. "Play it in slow motion."

Brad did as he was ordered. Dean then exclaimed, "What is he doing with his right eye?"

There was a small twitching in the barley visible right eye of Ethan Kravis. Dean surprised himself when he picked up on the subtle detail. The motion of Kravis' eye was so slight, that he doubted Brad or Albert even noticed. Dean was unsure if this movement was significant. He continued to watch the video in silence until Brad responded. "Maybe he has a nervous tick."

Dean became annoyed at Brad's comment. So far, Brad fumbled the capture of King and was now compounding his failure with ridiculous comments. Dean tried not to overreact. Dean simply dismissed the comment by saying, "Nothing in his medical file indicates that he has a facial tick. Did the techs ever find out anything further about the contact lens we pulled out of Garrett Michaels's right eye?"

Albert responded to the question. "They determined that it was just a contact lens. They couldn't explain why Michaels was wearing only one or why we detected a signal emitting from it."

Dean shifted around in has chair so that he was mimicking the direction of the man on the video screen. He held up his right arm and said, "That's his right eye that he's twitching, correct?"

"Yes, sir." Albert shot back.

"The contact lens was pulled from the right eye of Michaels, correct?"

"Correct. Do you think the two things are related? I know that you have an attention for detail, but Michaels's contact lens and Kravis's eye twitch is a big leap. Do you think you could be over analyzing this occurrence, sir?"

Dean went further to ask, "And the techs said that it was just a contact lens?"

"Correct, sir."

Perhaps Dean was over-analyzing the situation. He was grasping at straws. He decided to move on but keep this observation in the back of his mind. He turned back towards the screen and said, "All right. Maybe it is nothing. Continue to roll the video."

Brad pressed play.

Once again, Dean interrupted. "Pause it."

Brad paused the video at the time when both individuals were behind the cases of soda for two minutes and fifteen seconds.

Dean asked, "Are there any other camera angles from within the store?"

"No, sir," said Brad.

Dean knew that with no other angles, there was no way to determine what was being said behind the wall of soda. He remembered Brad saying that there were no known ties between Kravis and Castleberry, so what were they talking about? Why had they left the store together? He didn't have a clue, so he decided to ask the men in the room.

"You said that there was nothing to suggest that Kravis and Castleberry knew each other. Why then did they stop and talk?"

"Look at her."

Dean looked at the woman and said, "All right. So I'm looking at her. So what?"

Brad continued. "She is a hottie. I think our Mr. Kravis was trying to scoop a little ass."

Dean was repulsed by this vulgar comment. As tasteless as the comment was, there was some truth to it. The young woman was exceedingly attractive. Could it have been as simple as that? Could Ethan Kravis have been wooing the young woman in hopes of kindling a romantic relationship?

Brad pressed on. "Sure. Look at it. Ethan Kravis is a young, attractive guy. He notices a hot little number up at the counter. He hides behind the soda and does a little peeping-Tom routine. He can't take his eyes off her. He has some wild thoughts about this woman and gets so excited his eye starts twitching. It's happened to me many times."

Dean didn't dismiss Brad's comment right away. He let the idea swirl around in his head for a while. Even though Brad's comment was not all together idiotic, Dean didn't want to give Brad the satisfaction of a letting him know that fact. He decided that instead of hearing anymore jock-like comments, he would shift focus to the last remaining tape.

"OK. There's nothing much on this video. Bring up the last video."

Brad was clearly disappointed that Dean hadn't acknowledged his take on the situation. Dean would reserve such praise for when Brad's men captured Kravis. Dean watched as Brad turned to the console and played the last video of the event.

The video was only two seconds long. It showed the back of the BMW as it sped off. Brad replayed the video a couple of times and then paused it.

"There is nothing there." Dean said in a disappointed voice. He then started to ask some questions to which he already knew the answers. "So the car sped off and was never picked up by any other cameras in the area?"

"Correct, sir. We lost them as soon as they turned the corner."

"Was there any signature picked up in that area around the time of the disappearance?"

"It's the same as before. The computers think they identified a signature, but the urban clutter camouflaged it."

"Garrett Michaels said that the Alexander One was the size of a golf cart, not a BMW," Dean said in a rhetorical fashion. No one in the room responded. He went on to deduce the obvious. "They have several of these vehicles in various sizes."

The men sat quietly for a moment. After a couple of seconds, Dean was the first to speak. "This event shows that there is a lot more we don't know about this situation. Kravis is under close protection, yet he returned to an area where his protectors knew we would be looking. Why?"

Dean paused as if trying to figure out the answer to his question. He continued his thought pattern. "What did the protectors hope to gain by allowing us to almost catch Ethan Kravis? It doesn't make sense. The people who are smart enough to create such an advanced technology should be smart enough to know we would try to capture Ethan Kravis, just as we captured Garrett Michaels. Why would they put his life in danger by letting him stroll around the city of Philadelphia? Why?" Dean's voice trailed off.

Just as Dean arrived at an answer, Brad interrupted. "It was a test."

Dean knew Brad was right. He pointed to Brad and said, "Exactly!"

Dean knew it was a tactic. He had seen it many times in the boardroom. It was a way to obtain intelligence on a situation. Just like in chess, each action had a purpose. Dean's opponent had advanced one of his pieces to see how Dean would react. His opponent had obtained a tremendous amount of information from the move. He learned about how the team operated and type of training it must have received. He would be able to see the team's movements during the situation. Most importantly, the opponent would be able to gauge the response. The opponent now knew that Dean had no interest in surveying the situation. If a piece on the board were carelessly moved out into a vulnerable position, Dean would pounce on the opportunity to capture it.

This said a lot about both sides of the playing board. He was dealing with a very cunning and formidable advisory. It was then that Dean realized that he would have to adapt his tactics in order to beat his opponent. He reveled in the heated match he now found himself in. He ordered his next move in this fast-moving match of strategy and action. "Extend the search to include Risa Castleberry. Find the girl, and we find Ethan Kravis."

CHAPTER EIGHTEEN

I sat in a chair next to the bed in which Risa was now lying. She looked incredibly gorgeous and peaceful while she slept in her drug-induced unconsciousness. I don't know what was so compelling about this woman that I had met for only the briefest of moments, but something inside of me made it impossible to leave her side. I was an unmovable sentry that would keep a watchful eye over her.

Jonah had made the decision that the situation was too dangerous for us to remain in Philadelphia. He took us to the one place he knew would provide refuge from the dangers that lurked in the world. It took us less than forty-five minutes to reach the safe haven of the island. There was very little said during the short flight. My full attention was on Risa. I nearly broke down in tears as she lay on the bed of the master guest room. I was conflicted about what had happened. The selfish side of me was happy that I had met her. I was glad that she was with me and safe. The other side of me was guilt ridden. I had exposed her to a situation that would make it impossible for her to return to her normal life. I couldn't forgive myself.

The only thing Jonah had said during our flight back to the island was that the effects of the tranquilizer should wear off within a couple of hours. It had been about an hour since she had been dosed, so it could be another hour or two of waiting by her side before she awoke. As I sat there and watched over Risa, I heard a knock at the door.

Jonah entered the room. "She will be fine. Don't worry."

"That isn't what I'm worried about."

I could sense that Jonah knew what I had meant. He then asked, "Why didn't you follow my instructions? I told you that if you ran into someone you knew, to make up an excuse and leave as quickly as possible."

I understood the full meaning of what Jonah had asked. I felt so bad about what I had done to Risa, I responded to the question in a way I knew I shouldn't have. "I didn't know her."

"What?"

"I didn't know her. You said that if I were to run into someone I knew, that I should make up an excuse and leave as quickly as possible. I had never met Risa before in my life."

Jonah didn't find my response amusing. "If you never met her before, how did you know her name was Risa?"

I looked up at Jonah the first time. He had caught me with an obvious question. I remembered back to the explanation I worked out in the store. "I was testing the capability of the EyeWonder. I'm telling the truth when I say that I've never met her before. I used the EyeWonder to pull a background report. She happened to be the subject of the test."

I knew the excuse was lame, but it was mostly true.

Jonah went on to ask, "Why did you choose her to be your test subject?"

I would have thought the answer was obvious to Jonah. One look at her and I was sure that he could've put two and two together. I continued to stay with the story I was feeding him.

"She was the first person I came in contact with when I went for a walk."

I could see from Jonah's expression that he wasn't buying the story. "Yeah right, whatever you say, Ethan. I have to say that I'm very disappointed. The old man is confident that you're the right person for this assignment. Based on today's events, I'm not one hundred percent sure of that anymore. You must learn to follow my instructions. They only exist for your protection. Now you see what happens if you stray off course. You get someone else involved who shouldn't be. Because of your lack of control, you must now suffer the consequences of your careless actions."

I would've been really pissed at that moment, but what Jonah was saying was absolutely true. I couldn't be angry at anyone but myself for what had happened. I became choked up and almost started to cry when I asked, "What should I do now?"

Jonah could see that I was on the verge of tears. He spoke with a calm and reassuring voice. "I can see that you care for this woman that you just met."

I nodded my head.

"Well, if you don't want to see her get hurt, there's no other option than to keep her here on the island. I fear that if we bring her back to Philadelphia, she will be in danger from the same men who tried to kidnap you today. By now I'm sure that they have reviewed the situation and know of Risa."

I should have been more concerned about why and who had tried to kidnap me, but my only thoughts were of Risa. This stranger that I'd met for only a microsecond in a chance encounter now ruled my thoughts.

"I'm going to leave it up to you to explain the situation to her. You can provide her as many or as few details as you see fit. There will be times that you'll need to leave the island and she'll have to stay. Please prepare her for that. Who knows? Maybe her reaction won't be as drastic as you might think. After all, being trapped on a tropical island with someone catering to your every desire isn't so bad. Wouldn't you agree?"

Jonah had done a great deal to lift my spirits given the situation. Again, he seemed to know just what to say at the right time. I looked at him for a moment. It was at that moment that I regarded Jonah less as my protector and more as a friend. I smiled at Jonah and I could see he was relieved that I was starting to cheer up.

"Good. That is what I like to see. This is all going to work out for you, I promise. Even if the budding romance between you two doesn't work out, you will both get through this in one piece."

This last comment threw me off balance. Jonah was much more observant then I gave him credit for. Perhaps he too at one time had felt the incredible feeling of love at first sight, or maybe he used those innate powers of perception and could see that I'd already fallen in love with the girl. In any event, the method wasn't important. He signaled to me that he understood the situation.

"I'll leave you now. Good luck. I hope that you can smooth this situation out with Risa. If you need anything, pick up the phone, and someone from the wait staff will respond promptly. When your guest wakes up, feel free to walk around the island with her while you explain what is going on. It may also help to relieve the tension if you weren't here when she wakes up. It would be more than a little unsettling to see a man she just met staring at her after she wakes up from being drugged.

"Oh boy" I hadn't really thought of it before, but it would be very awkward. No more awkward than finding out that she is halfway around the world. I nodded to Jonah and said in a sarcastic tone, "Thanks for the advice."

Jonah turned around and left the room.

***

Jonah exited the master guest room. He walked toward the back of the main dwelling. He approached a seemingly random door. When he was three feet away, the door automatically disengaged the lock. He opened the door and started to walk down the long concrete hallway. The hallway was a passageway to a secondary dwelling that branched off from the main house. As he reached the end of the hallway, the door on the other end unlocked. He walked through the threshold, and the door slammed shut behind him. He was now standing in a massive open room. He had been in the room many times before.

Loyal was sitting behind the main console of the massive command center. "Did you smooth things over with Ethan?" asked Loyal.

"He seems to be holding up pretty well."

Loyal looked concerned for a moment.

Jonah raised his hand and said, "Everything went according to plan. Ethan fell for Risa very hard. The Nanobiotics made sure Ethan would fall head over heels for her. Did you have any problem keeping her at the store until Ethan arrived?"

Loyal responded, "I declined her credit card four times as she was trying to pay for her items. It looked as though she might have walked out if her credit card was rejected again. We got lucky."

Jonah responded, "I hope we did the right thing getting the girl involved with this project. She's just an innocent schoolteacher."

"Her psychological profile matches up perfectly with Ethan. There's no doubt that she fell in love with him the moment she saw him. When she wakes up, it'll be unsettling for her. It will take some time for her to see past the fact she was drugged and abducted. But biology is biology. Her chemical composition guarantees that she falls in love with Ethan unconditionally. I'm confident that we made the right choice. Her profile suggests that she has a strong enough will to survive this ordeal," said Loyal in a confident tone.

Jonah looked at Loyal. He knew that choosing someone that they had never met before was a risk. Loyal's profile of Risa's personality was a perfect match for Ethan. Still, love was something that science couldn't quantify. Jonah showed hesitation regarding the decision. He needed to reassure himself that the right choice was made. "Are you sure about this?"

Loyal said, "We have been over this several times before, Jonah. The match had to perfect and unhindered. Ethan must fall in love with the girl. If the girl knew it was her role in the project, there's a greater risk of the relationship failing."

Jonah's demons were getting the best of him. He replied, "We could have used someone we knew for the assignment. We don't know this girl at all. Are you willing to risk the entire project on her emotions?"

"We have no other options at the moment. I fear that if we take Risa away now, it may distract Ethan from the task at hand."

Jonah agreed with Loyal's assessment. Without belaboring the subject, he said, "Are you ready to make the call to the person who is holding Garrett captive?"

Loyal inhaled deeply and replied, "Ready as I'll ever be."

Loyal began to work the controls of the console. He typed in the IP address that had been provided in Garrett Michaels's call to Judge Lawrence. After he opened the secure gateway, the line began to ring. The call was answered by the mysterious man who had captured Garrett Michaels and who was most likely the person behind the attempted capture of Ethan Kravis.

Loyal nodded to Jonah. Loyal sat in silence as the man on the other end of the phone began to speak.

"I'm so happy you decided to call. To whom am I speaking, please?" said Dean Bouchard.

CHAPTER NINETEEN

Dean was nearly in shock when he received the call. He was lucky that he happened to still be in the Lockbox when Brad gave him the unexpected news.

"Sir, remember to keep the caller on the line for as long as possible so that we can complete the trace."

Dean waved his hand as if to indicate for Brad to be quiet. He walked over to the SAMSAC terminal and answered the phone.

"I'm so happy you decided to call. To whom am I speaking, please?"

There was an uncomfortable silence the other end of the phone. Dean became nervous. This call was his best opportunity to try and strike a deal with his unknown opponent. Dean was growing tired of the cat-and-mouse game. Above all else, he was a businessman. His hopes were that he could negotiate some type of mutually beneficial arrangement. He knew that he would never live up to any agreement that was made. Dean knew that the tactic would be used to only draw his opponent out into the open. Dean was relieved to hear a response.

"You may call me Loyal. To whom am I speaking?"

"It's good to finally talk to you, Loyal. For our conversation today, you may address me as Mr. B."

"All right then, Mr. B. Perhaps you can explain to me what you want."

Dean appreciated the fact that this man didn't want to engage in small talk. He also wanted to get right down to brass tacks. Dean continued. "I think you are smart enough to know what I want. I believe you call it the Alexander One."

"What is the Alexander One?"

Dean knew Loyal was fishing for information. He decided to divulge some of the information he had obtained through Garrett Michaels. Dean hoped that by giving a little, so would Loyal. "I suspect you know perfectly well what the Alexander One is Loyal. After all, you are probably the one who built the magnificent aircraft."

"How do you know about the Alexander One?"

If it had been any other situation, Dean would have hung up the phone for wasting his time. He knew that he might never get an opportunity like this again. He decided to lay it all out for Loyal. "If it will help expedite our conversation, I'll tell you all I know about the aircraft. In return, I hope that you will listen to the generous proposition I'm prepared to offer you. Is that acceptable to you, Loyal?"

Dean prayed that he had not been too direct. After all, he knew nothing about Loyal. He doubted very highly that Loyal was actually the man's real name.

"Very well, Mr. B. Please tell me all you know, and you have my word I'll listen to your proposal."

Dean didn't fully trust this man he only just met. On the other hand, what harm could it cause? After all, he was convinced that everything he was about to say, Loyal already knew. He was hoping for an easy solution to this issue. If the outcome weren't to Dean's liking, he would use the line trace to hunt down his opponent and destroy him.

Dean continued. "I know that the Alexander One is a geomagnetic vehicle that uses the earth's magnetic polarity to fly. I know that it has been in active use for at least the last five years. I know that it has a skin that allows it to become invisible. I know that it could revolutionize the transportation business. Lastly, and most importantly, I know some people who will stop at nothing to see that its existence never becomes public." Dean paused to allow his last statement to have a greater impact.

"It seems you know quite a bit, Mr. B."

"Indeed I do, Loyal."

"And how did you come by this wealth of information?"

Dean thought briefly before he spoke. "Well, Loyal. As you probably could tell from the past twenty-four hours, I'm a man with exceptional means. I have invested a lot of money to uncover the breadcrumbs that you have been leaving. I must say that I'm very impressed with not only the Alexander One, but also your ability to keep it a secret for so long. You and I could combine forces to make a wonderful partnership."

"Do the exceptional means you speak of include the kidnapping and attempted kidnapping of two of my dearest friends?" responded Loyal.

Dean needed to extinguish the flame before it grew into a raging fire. "Loyal, I can assure you that no harm has befallen your friend. I merely wanted to talk to him so that I could better understand the situation. If there were an easier way to have made contact with you, I would have much rather taken that route. Unfortunately, you are a very difficult man to get in touch with. You have my word that Garrett Michaels will not be harmed in any way."

"And Ethan Kravis? What about his health?"

"I can guarantee that if we could somehow come to an arrangement, absolutely nothing will happen to Ethan Kravis."

Dean quickly regretted making this statement. The wording of the statement may have been construed as a veiled threat. Dean thought about clarifying what he said, but it was too late.

"Does this mean that if we are not able to come to an arrangement, Ethan Kravis's life would still be in danger?"

Dean cursed himself. He knew he had to backpedal fast. "Not at all, Loyal. You have my word that nothing bad will happen to Ethan Kravis. I merely meant that I would like very much to explore a partnership with you. I understand the impact that your creation will have on this earth, and I would like to see you succeed. That's all I was saying."

Dean sensed that the conversation was drawing to a close. He was starting to mentally prepare himself for the sales pitch of a lifetime.

"All right, Mr. B. You have explained to me what you know about my invention. As a man of my word, I will now listen to your proposition."

Dean took a deep breath before he leaned into his sales pitch. If he could end this intense game that he now found himself in, he would seize the opportunity. "First, let me say that I'm relieved that you have decided to keep your word. Over the years I have created a vast business enterprise. As a result, I have developed a sort of sixth sense about people. I can tell from our brief conversation that you are a man of principles. You gave me your word on something and you kept good on your promise. I'm always on the lookout for honest people such as you. I would be delighted if you and I could form a business relationship. My only fear is that you may be in some danger. I assure you that I'm not the cause of this danger. As I said earlier, my business interests have grown to be very large over the years. When a business grows to be as large as mine, you indubitably meet some unsavory people. I have it on good authority that I'm not the only one who has discovered your invention. I have specifically spoken to some of these dangerous men about the subject. I didn't initiate these conversations; I only listened. I'm afraid that your invention directly conflicts with these men's interests. They expressed to me that they would stop at nothing to destroy both you and the Alexander One. These men want to destroy, while all I want to do is help create. I would like to extend my hand of friendship to you so that I can help navigate you through this difficult situation. I would like to help introduce the Alexander One to the world. Would you be open to the possibility of forming a partnership?"

Dean thought that he had done a good job at providing a summarization of the situation. He hoped that Loyal would take his warning seriously. He waited eagerly for a response.

"Well, Mr. B, I do appreciate your candidness. I also thank you for warning me of the dangers that exist in the world. You made some excellent points, and I understand that we may very well have the same goals in mind. I'll need some time to digest all that you have said. I'm not denying your proposal outright. I'm simply asking that you provide me a couple of days to think it through. If after those couple of days I see that you are a man who can be trusted, then I will contact you with an answer. Would that be an acceptable course of action, Mr B.?"

Dean knew that he couldn't forge a concrete deal based on one conversation. It was completely fair to allow Loyal to take a couple of days to think it through. After all, what choice did Dean have?

"Of course Loyal. Taking a couple of days to think it over is a prudent thing to do. In a couple of days, when you have decided which direction you would like to head in, you can contact me using the same secure method that allowed us to have this conversation. My sincere hope is that you and I can move the Alexander One forward together. Is there anything further you wish to discuss?"

Dean hoped that he had kept Loyal on the phone long enough for the line trace to be completed. Throughout the conversation, he hadn't looked over at Brad to see if the trace was complete. Now that the conversation was ending, there would be nothing Dean could do to extend the call without arousing suspicion. He decided not to look over at Brad so that he could remain focused on the end of the call.

Loyal then spoke. "Again I want to thank you, Mr. B. I'll be in touch."

The line went dead. Dean immediately hung up the phone and asked, "Did we get the trace?"

Brad's look to Dean said all he had to know. He knew the answer to his question before Brad spoke.

"I've never seen anything like it in my life. The trace was bounced over thousands of servers across hundreds of networks. This guy really knew what he was doing. There was no way to trace it back."

Dean wasn't surprised by this realization. He would have been disappointed if his opponent had been easy to identify. If his opponent could create an aircraft that defied gravity, he was probably smart enough to identify a trap. Dean was secretly enjoying this battle of wit. Loyal was going to be the toughest advisory he had ever faced. Dean hoped that his decades of training in the business world prepared him for victory in this contest. He had to change his tactics if he wanted to win. He couldn't let Garrett Michaels go and risk having his identity exposed. Dean knew that he could do one thing that might allow Loyal to be guided to make the right choice. He looked over at Brad. "Your orders have changed. You are no longer to apprehend Ethan Kravis or Risa Castleberry. You are to maintain surveillance only."

Dean knew this was a futile order. He was positive that he would not have another opportunity like he did this morning to capture Kravis or Castleberry. The move to expose Kravis had been calculated. Like a game of chess, Loyal had moved out his queen very early in the game to test Dean's reaction. Once he saw what Dean had done, he withdrew his queen back to her rightful spot next to the king. Dean was very doubtful that he would see Ethan Kravis again until this game was drawing to an end.

"And Garrett Michaels?" Albert asked.

"He will be our guest until this matter is resolved. Make sure that he's comfortable. If his employer calls back, we need a positive endorsement from Micheals."

Dean could taste that victory was near. All he had to do was draw Loyal out of his shell and Dean would take what he most desired. Dean would take his seat among the other super heavyweights of history.

CHAPTER TWENTY

Extreme nervousness set in as I thought about what to say to Risa when she woke up. The whole truth was going to be very difficult for her to believe. I tried to put myself in her situation. If I woke up next to someone I met for less than five minutes and she told me that we had traveled halfway around the world in less than an hour, I would probably jump across the room and strangle the person. At the same time, I really didn't want to start out any chance of a relationship based on a foundation of lies.

The moment of truth was nearing. I had been by Risa's side for more than three hours. Jonah said that the effects of the tranquiller would wear off in a couple of hours. After the second hour of staring at the deep-slumbering brunette, I became nervous when she showed no signs of waking up. I quickly deduced that because she weighted only about 105 pounds, the drugs must have had a more difficult time clearing her system. I became fearful that I would lose her forever once I told her what had happened. No matter what the result of our pending conversation, I was just happy that she wouldn't be harmed.

Risa started to become fully conscious. She tossed and turned in the bed. The thrashing movement caused her sundress to ride up her body, revealing her black lace underwear. I thought about adjusting her dress downward so that there was no appearance of impropriety. I dismissed the thought. It would have been even more awkward for her to wake up with someone fondling her dress than just staring at her. The truth was that the sight of her black lace underwear excited me in the worst possible way. "Stop being a pervert, you idiot," I said to myself as I tried to look away. I got up from the chair that was next to the bed and walked across the massive guest bedroom. I took a seat at the Queen Anne writing desk. I would wait there, facing away from the bed, until she said something. After a couple of minutes of movement on the bed, I heard Risa speak.

"What? Where? Where am I?

The questions Risa had posed where just her audible thoughts and were not directed at me. It didn't appear as though she knew I was in the room. I must have startled her when I began to speak. "Everything is all right. We were attacked outside the convenience store, and I brought you to a safe place to recuperate."

Hearing my voice in the distance, she jerked her head in my direction. She was now propped up in the bed using her arms as leverage. She made the cutest little mouse face as she squinted to see who had spoken. I realized that she was still a little blurry eyed, so I moved a little closer so that she wouldn't have to strain so much to see me. I slowly walked until I was halfway between the writing desk and the bed. I didn't speak. I wanted her to take control of any conversation we might have. The situation might be less strange if she were free to ask any questions she might have.

Risa then said, "Who–?" She stopped herself and squinted to try to bring the person she was looking at into focus. It took a couple of seconds, but then she recognized who I was. "Steve? Where am I? What happened?"

I could hear the fright starting to set in. Risa's eyes darted when she looked around the room in panic. She then looked down and pulled her dress down to a more modest level. I could only imagine what she felt. It was every woman's worst nightmare. I could feel her thoughts, and I felt like I might throw up. The situation looked incredibly bad. I put my hands up as if to indicate, "Hold on a second." I tried to offer any words of reassurance I could think of. "Nothing like that happened. I promise. Please just try to relax. I know how this must look, but I can explain everything."

Risa started to cry. Her tears shook the very core of my soul. I was heartbroken to have caused the panic that she must have felt.

"Please, please don't cry. Everything will be fine. Please."

I felt as if I was going to start crying. I put my emotions in check. One of us needed to remain strong through this difficult situation. Just as I was about to speak again, Risa jumped up off the bed and with amazing speed ran out the door. She couldn't go very far, so I didn't bother to try to stop her.

What have I done? This woman I had fallen head over heels with, who I would protect with every fiber of my being, now thought the very worst any woman could think of a man. She probably thought I was some kind of sicko rapist who had drugged her and taken her to my lair so I could have my way with her. Oh, my God. I felt like going into the bathroom and slitting my wrists. The situation was making me physically ill. I would have given anything to have the ability to go back and convince myself not to take that walk this morning. I wouldn't have met Risa, but I wouldn't have caused her the traumatic experience she was going through.

For both her sake and mine, I had to at least try to right this wrong. I walked toward the door, left the room, and looked in both directions to determine which way she could have gone. Down the hallway I saw David, the head butler. He, no doubt, was sent to keep a watchful eye on the situation. David simply raised his finger and pointed in the direction of the main entrance. I walked past him toward the front door and exited the residence.

Risa was kneeling on the slate path, her head down, with her hands covering her face. I could hear the faint moaning sound of her crying. She didn't look up, but I sensed that she knew that I was approaching.

"Please, Risa." I said in a begging voice. "Nothing bad has happened. Well, actually something bad has happened, but nothing sexual. It's not what you think."

I couldn't find the right words. My thoughts were jumbled, and it caused me to speak in a confused voice. I had to press on. "I'm going to explain everything. I know that you don't know me from a hole in the wall, but please believe me when I say that I will not harm you in any way."

I winced at the ridiculous statement that had just come out of my mouth. It made me sound like a complete psycho. I knew now that anything that I said would do more harm than good. I decided to just shut my mouth and let her speak. I sat down on the slate path about ten feet away from where she had crumpled up in a ball. I took a deep breath of the tropical air and waited.

Risa finally spoke after a couple of moments. "I should've known," she said in a weeping voice. She shook her head and repeated, "I should've known."

"Are you talking to me, or are you just thinking out loud?"

Risa ignored my question and said, "I should've known that for me to have an instant attraction to a man for the first time in years, he would turn out to be some kind of demented rapist or something."

This comment hurt me very deeply. It was one thing for a relationship to fail because of incompatibility; it was entirely different to have a woman think you were the very thing she despised more than anything else in the world. I had to try to set the record straight, even if it meant that Risa would hate me forever. I couldn't let her continue to think that of me. "I'm not what you think I am. I would never disrespect a woman in the way you are thinking. You just happened to be in the wrong place at the wrong time. The people who shot you with a tranquilizer dart wanted me, not you."

Perhaps it was the thought of being labeled a rapist that caused me to speak in a commanding voice. I continued speak in hopes that she would listen to what I was saying. "What I'm going to tell you is going to be very hard to understand. You are just going to have to allow yourself to open up and hear my words. You have gotten caught up in a situation that has put your life in danger. I brought you here to protect you, not violate you. Nothing I say is going to make this situation any easier for you to cope with. I would give anything to go back in time and prevent myself from ever having met you in that store. I only wish we could have met under different circumstances so that you could see that I'm just a normal guy. However, the world isn't perfect. Sometimes you just have to accept a situation for what it is and make the best of it."

I started to stray off topic. My words were getting more and more forceful. I shouldn't be lecturing this frightened woman in a scolding tone. The words were coming from a place of anger deep within me, and I needed to slam on the brakes. I wasn't angry with Risa, I was angry with myself for allowing this to happen. I shouldn't be taking my anger out on her for not better understanding the situation. I made a conscious effort to relax my voice when I continued to speak. In as gentle a voice as I could muster at that moment, I went on to say, "Risa, please look at me."

At first she didn't move. I could hear that her crying had ratcheted down to a slight whimper. It took a couple of seconds, but she started to remove her hands from her face and look up. Her cheeks were moist from the tears that had streamed down her face. Her hair was disheveled and her thin, black-rimmed glasses were crooked. I didn't care. She looked as breathtaking as the moment I first laid my gaze upon her in the store. She lifted her head out of her hands and our eyes locked just as they had in the store. I sat there for a moment transfixed on her big blue eyes. Her eyes were as blue as the thousands of miles of ocean that surrounded the island. What would I give for the privilege to swim in those magnificent eyes for the rest of my life?

"There she is," I said as I smiled in her direction. "I know that this is going to be nearly impossible for you to accept, but you are going to be just fine. I promise."

I was finally getting through to Risa. She was no longer crying. She just sat there looking into my eyes. God, she was gorgeous. She continued to look into my eyes without turning away or blinking. She didn't appear to be angry or sad. She looked like she was in a trance. Her beautiful facial features were relaxed and showed no sign of panic.

When she began to speak, she did so in a soft and barely discernable voice, like she was under a hypnotic spell. "What happened, Steve?"

I realized then that I had started the relationship off with a big fat lie. I figured that she was part of the situation now, so I could tell her my real name.

"Well, for starters, Steve isn't my real name. Steve Hamilton is my cover identity. My real name is Ethan Kravis."

This realization didn't cause the type of shock I thought it would. Risa continued to bore into my soul with those big blue eyes of hers.

"Are you saying that you are some kind of spy or something?" she said with a completely straight face.

I chuckled at the question. It sounded very odd to me to be asked that question in such a serious tone. I broke off eye contact and looked down to the slate path while I played with a pebble. I responded to her question, "Nope, not a spy. I'm a scientist."

Without hesitation, Risa continued. "Why does a scientist need a secret identity?"

"The cover identity was for my protection. I've been working on something that could be extremely damaging to some powerful men's business interests. These are the same men who tried to kidnap me outside the convenience store."

"I guess the fake identity didn't work too well."

I let out a gasping laugh as I took my attention off the pebble I was playing with and looked back up at Risa. "No, I suppose it didn't."

Risa didn't react. She continued to pierce me with her heart-stopping stare. "And these men, who tried to kidnap you, shot me with a tranquilizer dart?"

I didn't detect any sarcasm in her voice. She was simply asking a question without judgment. I didn't know if she believed anything she was hearing. She was like wallpaper, hard to read. "I know it sounds crazy, but it is the God's-honest truth. Do you believe me?"

She paused before responding. It looked like she was processing all that had been said and was trying to come to some conclusions about the bizarre conversation. She did this without averting her eyes from mine. "If I'd heard this story from anyone else, I would've laughed at the thought of it. But–"

Risa paused and slightly squinted her eyes at me.

"But what?" I asked in a curious tone.

"But there is something about your eyes. I can't exactly describe it. It's a feeling I get when I look into your eyes. For some strange reason when I look into your eyes, I can tell that you are speaking the truth.

You have very kind eyes. I know that sounds lame, but it's the truth."

I wasn't sure how to interpret what Risa had said. I just knew that she somehow felt the way I did. Even through this insane ordeal, during the faintest of moments back at the store we had formed an instantaneous bond. The bond was so strong that it was allowing her to look past all the craziness that had transpired after our chance meeting and accept what I had said as the truth.

"It doesn't sound lame at all. I get that same feeling when I look at you as well. I can't describe it, but it feels like I have known you my whole life."

There was no filter between my mind and my mouth at that moment. The words were involuntarily coming out in a wave of uncontrollable emotion. What I had said was incredibly cliché, but I didn't care how it sounded. It was the truth. For the first time since she had reached the island, Risa let out an incredible glowing white smile. I knew in that instant that things were going to be all right between us. We both knew it. We both knew that we had met someone very special. I was so incredibly turned on by this I almost lost hold on our conversation.

"Where are we, Stev–I mean Ethan?"

The question was going to be hard to answer. I decided that if she truly believed what I had already told her, that I should go all the way and tell her the truth about where she now was. I decided that it would probably be a good idea to show her instead of trying to explain. I extended my hand out to her and said, "Let me show you."

She didn't hesitate at all before taking my hand. I helped her off the ground. She used her free hand to adjust her dress and fix her glasses. As I pulled her up off the ground, our bodies touched for the briefest of moments. I could feel her breasts barely graze my chest. The contact lasted only a millisecond, but it sent my mind into a direction it should not have been going. Risa was still in a very fragile state. I didn't want to do anything to break the calm that I had worked so hard to create. Once she was on her feet, I let go of her hand. It was best if I refrained from any additional physical contact until she initiated it.

I started walking down the slate path in the opposite direction of the main house. Risa walked by my side. Once the ocean came into view, Risa let out a gasp and said, "Jesus! Where are we?"

We both stopped and took in the foreboding sight of the vastness of the ocean. I decided to say it like I were ripping off a Band-Aid. "We are on a private island in the middle of the South Pacific Ocean."

"South Pacific? Island?" Risa asked in a confused state. She did a graceful pirouette as she surveyed her surroundings. I glanced over to her, and she had a look of bewilderment.

"Yes. It was the only place I could have brought you, to ensure that you would completely safe from the men we talked about earlier."

"How long was I unconscious for?

"About three hours."

I let that fact sink in and waited for the question that I knew was coming.

"Are you telling me that we somehow made it from Philadelphia to a private island in the South Pacific in three hours?" Risa turned and faced me, clearly skeptical about traveling halfway around the world in such a short amount of time.

"Actually, we got here in a little less then forty minutes. You spent most of the last three hours in bed unconscious from the tranquilizer dart."

Risa looked at me like I had just set her favorite pair of shoes on fire. She began to shake her head and said, "No! No! That isn't possible! I must have been knocked out for at least a day to have gotten here."

I could sense that I was in danger of losing her again. I quickly replied, "It's why those people tried to kidnap us. It's because of the invention. I'm involved with the invention of a new type of aircraft, one that is capable of traveling halfway around the world in a matter of minutes, not days. It's how we got to this island."

Risa stopped shaking her head and looked at me. "I'm trying very hard to believe what you are telling me. I really am. But that–that is just not possible. I'm a teacher and know the laws of physics." Risa started to walk away.

I stood there. I then yelled out, "The Wright brothers!"

Risa stopped, but didn't look back in my direction. She only listened.

I continued, "The Wright brothers were laughed at when they said that they could fly like a bird using only paper and wood. Howard Hughes was thought insane when he proposed the idea of flying coast to coast in a couple of hours. People didn't believe that the SR-71 Blackbird could fly at more than eighty thousand feet at a speed that was never thought possible. Throughout all time people dismissed some of the world's greatest inventions because they just couldn't believe that they were possible. A couple of days ago if you had asked me if I thought that flying to the other end of the earth in less than forty minutes was possible, I too would have dismissed the notion. But as sure as I'm standing here, the invention is very real. Please let me prove it to you."

"How could you possibly prove something like that to me?"

"Just give me a chance."

I slipped my hand into my pocket and took out the key chain Jonah had given me. I pressed the button, hoping that Jonah would make good on his promise to contact me when I used the device.

It wasn't until five excruciatingly long minutes before Jonah came strolling down the slate path. He approached with some caution and said, "Everything all right, Ethan?"

I looked at Jonah and gave him a "what do you think?" type of stare. I was hoping that Jonah would be able to help me out in my desperate situation. I would have never imposed on him, but I had very few choices in the matter.

"Hi, Jonah."

Risa turned to look at Jonah as I spoke to him.

"I was wondering if it would be possible to give Risa a quick ride in the Alexander One. It might allow her to better understand the situation."

Jonah could see the pleading look in my eyes. He looked over at Risa for the first time and said, "Hello, Ms. Castleberry. I'm sorry you got caught up in this mess we find ourselves in currently."

Risa just stood there with her arms folded against her chest. Jonah continued. "I feel that is the very least we could do if it will help ease the tension this situation has caused."

At that moment, I could have run over and kissed Jonah. Thank god for small favors.

"Right this way, Ms. Castleberry," said Jonah as he motioned Risa toward the landing pad area.

Risa hesitated at first, but then started to walk past Jonah and me. Jonah followed behind Risa on the way to the landing pad area. I noticed that it wasn't the same vehicle as the first Alexander One I had been in. It was about twice as long as the first Alexander One that I'd seen. I decided not to make this comment to Jonah as we got closer. This moment was all about Risa. I didn't want to sidetrack the conversation.

As we walked up to the Alexander One, Risa looked surprised.

Clearly she thought that it must be some kind of joke. Jonah opened the passenger door and said, "After you, my dear." Jonah motioned for Risa to take a seat.

Risa looked over at me before she walked over to the open door.

"It's all right. You'll be fine."

I didn't know if my words of encouragement had made the slightest bit of difference, but Risa walked toward the open door.

"Jonah, Risa has been through quite a bit today. Take it easy on her, OK?"

Jonah shot me back a look as if to say, "Yeah, no kidding idiot. I'm not the one who got her into this mess, so stand there and shut up."

Jonah closed the door after Risa had gotten in. He asked me, "Are you coming?"

I thought about it for a second and said, "No. I'll let her experience this alone. I'll be here when you get back."

Jonah nodded and climbed into the driver's seat. A couple of seconds later, the Alexander One vanished from sight. It was amazing to see it disappear right in front of me. So far, I had been inside of it every time it had turned on its electro-chromatic skin feature. A sharp gust of wind gently blew my hair back. Jonah and Risa had just taken off on what I was sure was going to be an unforgettable ride for Risa. My only hope was that the ride would allow Risa to understand the full weight of my words.

CHAPTER TWENTY-ONE

"Your strategy seemed to have worked well, Mr. Schmick."

Hans Schmick sat intently waiting for his trusted friend and closest colleague to continue his briefing. It had been a couple of days since the council meeting, and he was glad to see that his calculated gamble was starting to yield some results.

Hans Schmick was known by the council as Member Number One. He was charged with overseeing the European arm of the council. Born and raised on a rural farm in Germany, Hans never took for granted the way in which he rose to power. Unlike many of the men on the council, Hans prided himself on the fact that he had made his fortune the old fashioned way. He often marveled at the fact that he had accumulated such wealth and power over one lifetime. He knew all too well that the other men on the council had inherited great sums of money from many past generations. The world had been handed to the other men of the council on a silver platter.

When he formed the council thirty-two years before, he found it difficult to choose men he could respect enough to allow them to take a seat beside him. The privileges inherited by many of the candidates made them seem weak in the eyes of Hans. These men had never seen difficult times as he had. As a young boy on the farm, Hans had endured backbreaking labor. After fourteen-hour days tending to the needs of the farm, he would go into the tiny two-room farmhouse and read all night by candlelight. The reading helped him better understand that there was a world that extended far beyond the farm. Hans excelled in his studies as a boy. When the opportunity presented itself, Hans left the farm to study at Oxford in England. It was at Oxford where Hans had developed an extreme hatred for the socially elite. Hans had to work two jobs just to survive. He saw the other students at the school as they walked around without a worry in the world. They always knew where their next meal was coming from.

A year after graduating from Oxford at the top of his class, World War II had broken out and he was summoned back to Germany by the Furor himself. Having been highly educated in an English school, the Nazi party quickly moved Hans up to a high-raking position within the party. His time spent in England cultivated a hatred for the English and their pomp and circumstance. He was more than eager to join the opposition. His position within the Nazi party provided an easy way to accumulate massive amounts of wealth. Over the next several years of the war, Hans stole, looted, and plundered millions from the people the Nazis had enslaved or killed. His advanced education had allowed Hans to hide the money with relative ease.

After the war was over, Hans took the money he had amassed and started a construction company. His company was awarded several large reconstruction contracts. The contracts were to help repair the massive damage that had been caused by the war. His construction company quickly grew into one of the largest in the world. In the mid 1960s, Hans shifted his focus to the oil industry. He took his vast wealth from the construction company and invested money in oil operations. His decision to shift his business interests had been an easy one to make. It was simple for Hans to see that the entire world ran on oil. As nations grew larger, the demand would only increase. He used his investments to consolidate drilling rights in the Caspian Sea. This gave him control over most of the oil within Europe. It was then that he devised a plan to set up similar franchises across the world. This led to the foundation of the council. To date, his decision to form the council had worked to perfection. The council he created controlled virtually all the oil in the world. This made Hans wealthier than he had ever thought possible.

Hans knew now, just as he had known in the mid 1960s, that another massive shift in his business interests was coming. Once he identified the existence of the geomagnetic vehicle, it was only a matter of time before the world knew of its impact. He tried many times over the past several years to find out who had developed the groundbreaking technology. He indirectly contacted every known source he could think of to determine which country had developed the technology. He was shocked to find out that there wasn't even a blip on the radar when it came to such an important discovery. None of his high-placed sources in the world governments knew anything about the anti-gravity aircraft.

It wasn't until a couple of years ago that one of his communication analysts picked up some chatter on the mysterious vehicle. His men had intercepted a secure message that provided a shocking revelation to Hans. The message described that the signature of the aircraft had been detected in California on the West Coast of the United States. It wasn't the message that had shocked Hans. It was to who the message had been sent to that amazed him.

The message had been sent from an advanced research facility to a shell company Hans knew all too well. The shell company was indirectly tied to Dean Bouchard. Member Number Seven on the council had been tracking the mysterious aircraft nearly as long as Hans had been.

Based on the message, Hans had deduced that Dean knew as little as he had about the aircraft. He decided over the next couple of years to continue to monitor his fellow council member in hopes that it would lead him closer to finding the aircraft.

Hans knew that his time on earth was coming to an end. He was growing old and he needed to speed up his search effort. He took the knowledge he had about Dean Bouchard and called an emergency meeting of the council. He decided to inform the council of his discovery to force the council to act. Hans knew that as soon as Dean Bouchard had seen that the council had initiated Plan Alpha, he would be forced to speed up his search efforts as well. Hans could say with relative certainty that both he and Dean shared the same desire. They both wanted to capture this new technology so that they could be the ones to give it to the world. Hans would continue to monitor Dean's communications in hopes of discovering a new clue in the mystery.

Hans shifted his attention back to his second in command while he provided his briefing. Simon had been with Hans through the war. Simon was very aware of Hans's history with the Nazi party. He was one of Hans's closest friends and trusted Simon with his life.

Simon was very thorough when he continued with his briefing. "We have intercepted several interesting communications since the conclusion of the council meeting, sir."

Hans signaled for Simon to continue.

"It seems as though Dean Bouchard has been a busy man since he left the meeting. First he ordered his special operations team to extract a man named Garrett Michaels from a golf club in the suburbs of Philadelphia. Then he tried, but failed, to capture the man that Michaels had played golf with. Lastly, we intercepted a very interesting call between Dean Bouchard and the man responsible for creating the

Alexander One-ah, that is the name of the aircraft we have been tracking, sir."

Hans nearly dropped his cup of tea when he heard what Simon had said. "Excuse me?"

Simon smiled and said, "We have heard the voice of the man responsible for the unexplained aircraft."

Hans couldn't control his excitement. He said excitedly, "Was the conversation recorded?"

Simon withdrew a micro digital recorder and dangled it between two fingers.

Hans eyes widened and he commanded, "Play it."

Hans knew that Dean Bouchard was a very private man. He had spent millions on the most advanced communications systems in the world. As Hans had done with all the council members, he made sure that his companies were used in the construction of their state-of-the-art communication infrastructures unbeknown to them. He ordered his communications company to create a back door in each of the devices that were installed. That would allow Hans unfettered access to any communication the council members had. This was all done without the council member's knowledge and had allowed Hans to keep close tabs on his colleagues. At that moment, he would kiss the geniuses that created the mind-numbingly complicated listening devices if they were in the room.

Hans listened carefully to the message. He ordered Simon to rewind the recording and play it again. Simon did as ordered and played the recording over. Once he was sure that one of the voices on the call was Dean Bouchard, he said, "Who else knows about this recording?"

"Only the analyst who recorded it and us. I made sure that the analyst's supervisor wasn't informed."

Hans shook his head. He had tried very hard to dissuade the other council members against approaching Dean Bouchard at the time of forming the council. The man was unscrupulous in the worst kind of way. Hans had observed Dean's true self on many occasions. Dean was nothing but a rich kid who did anything for power and money.

He had many dealings with Dean when he was first starting out in his construction business. On more than one occasion, Dean had done things that even Hans would have problems doing. Behind Dean's cool façade lurked a violent man. He often chose violence over democracy. Outside of the things Hans had done in the war, he prided himself as being a tough but fair businessman. Dean was much different in this regard. He would stop at nothing to make more money even if it meant strong arming his opponents. Hans had also observed that Dean would go out of his way to disregard the traditions and processes that the council had put in place. This disregard for the rules caused several heated arguments during the annual council meetings. Dean was always the last to arrive for the meetings. Hans always interpreted this as a sign of disrespect. After all, Dean was the last to join the council. They should not have to constantly wait for Dean to start their secretive meetings.

Hans was now in a position to punish Dean for his arrogance. Simon held the evidence in his hand. If this evidence were made public to the council, it would mean certain death for Dean Bouchard.

Hans began to give Simon his orders. "Simon, put that recording in a safe place. If our plans go astray, we may need to use it as means of deflection."

Simon responded, "Of course, sir."

"Were we able to trace the call back to this man who calls himself Loyal?"

"Unfortunately not, sir. He was very good at covering his tracks. The analyst said he has never seen anything like it. Because of this reason, it only furthers my suspicion that this man Loyal is the genuine article."

Hans agreed with Simon. He was disappointed that they could not get the trace but knew that Loyal must have been extremely smart to create such a technological wonder. Hans contemplated his next steps. There wasn't much actionable information from the call. He started by providing Simon with some follow-up items.

"Simon, start traces on Ethan Kravis, Garrett Michaels, and Risa Castleberry. Dig deep into their lives. I want to know everything about them."

Hans paused to wait for Simon's acknowledgment of the order.

"Yes, sir."

"Next, have the analyst who uncovered the message reassigned. I don't want to take any chances that he talks about the work that he has been doing. Relocate him somewhere where we can keep an eye on him."

"Yes, sir."

"Lastly, once you do relocate the analyst, make sure you inform someone else to continue to monitor Dean Bouchard's communications. I want to make sure we intercept the call if Loyal should call back."

"Yes, sir."

"Thank you, Simon. That will be all."

Simon exited Hans's office. Hans sat there and thought through what other actions he could take to obtain his objective of capturing the Alexander One. Hans thought about asking Dean to travel to Germany for a face-to-face discussion. He dismissed this idea because he didn't want to detract from Dean's hunt for the Alexander One or make him suspicious. Then it came to him in a moment of pure genius. Hans would send out a broadcast message to the council members giving them an update on Plan Alpha. He would use the communication to provide some misinformation to Dean Bouchard. Hans was positive that this was the way to go; however, he didn't know what the message should say. Should the message simply say that there were no new leads in the identification of the unknown aircraft? This was sure to make Dean Bouchard feel safe, even though he wasn't. Hans dismissed this idea because it might allow Dean to feel too comfortable with the situation and cause him to slow down his pursuits. Perhaps Hans should provide a few vague details in hopes of keeping Dean motivated to find the aircraft. That sounded like a much better idea to Hans.

Hans took his council-issued black laptop out of his desk drawer. He opened the cover and went through the needed security checks. Once the security checks had been completed, he opened the council inbox and composed a message.

To All,

Re: Plan Alpha

The operation has commenced. Special operations teams have been dispatched and are strategically placed around the globe. All black ops teams are awaiting fresh intelligence. All specialized communication analysts have been briefed. Four persons of interest have been identified and the search for their whereabouts has begun. More details to follow as they become available.

Truly,

Number One

Short, concise, and open for interpretation. Hans was happy with the contents of the note and clicked the Scramble button. Once the message had been fully encoded with a specialized encryption, he pushed the Send button. The little envelope in the middle of his computer flew off the screen as his message traveled on its way around the world.

Hans's big gamble had paid off. He would continue to allow Dean to do his legwork and then swoop in to collect the prize when the right time presented itself.

CHAPTER TWENTY-TWO

As I sat next to the landing pad waiting for Jonah and Risa to return, I had time to reflect on the new information that had developed. It was the first time I took my mind off of Risa and thought about the attempted kidnapping. What did I know about the men who tried to kidnap me?

For one thing, these men were very resourceful. They had the means to blanket the City of Philadelphia with surveillance. The man who tried to capture Risa and me clearly had some type of military training. The man waited outside the store and took a cover position that allowed him to attempt a very effective ambush. He used a tranquilizer dart that wasn't sold in your average gun or hunting store. The events happened so fast that I was having trouble remembering all the details. The only question I knew to ask was, "How?" How had these men tracked me down so fast? How did he even know I was involved with the Alexander One? In addition, even if they knew I was involved, how did they locate me and act so quickly?

These questions swirled around my brain like a tornado. I had always thought that the abrupt change in plans not to return to the golf course would raise some suspicion. Was it possible that these men somehow figured this out and flagged me as someone who knew something about the Alexander One? "Impossible." How would they know that I had any knowledge of the unique aircraft? It was then that I started to see the picture unfold.

These men must have had some way of tracking the Alexander One. It was the only explanation for all that had occurred. It explained how they were able to piece together what had happened in the golf club. It explained how they knew that I had returned to Philadelphia. However, it didn't explain why they hadn't just tried to kidnap me at the house in Society Hill. If they had a means of tracking the Alexander One, surely they would have kicked down the door of the house and taken me away. That revelation was a massive flaw in my theory. Why had these men been able to track the use of the Alexander One at the golf course, but not in Philadelphia or at this island? Surely if they had a way to identify its use, this island would have been raided long ago. I thought I may know the answer, but I would have to ask Jonah when he returned.

As I thought deeply about these questions, I didn't even realize that Jonah and Risa had landed. The Alexander One made absolutely no noise as it touched down on the landing pad. I was startled when I saw the electro-chromatic skin dissolve back to its original visible form. I was standing on the passenger's side of the car. I saw Risa through the window. The door to the Alexander One opened, but Risa just sat there staring straight ahead. Jonah got out of the driver's side door. He looked over to me. I asked, "How did it go?"

Jonah shrugged his shoulders and said, "She didn't say anything, so I'm not sure what she thought."

I walked over and crouched down next to the open door. I could clearly see that Risa was in a state of shock. Knowing exactly how she felt having experienced it only two days prior, there was nothing I could say to make the shock go away. I simply said, "How was it?"

Without turning to me, Risa replied, "I need a couple of minutes."

I knew that Risa would just have to work out what she had just seen. It would take a couple of minutes for the shock to wear off. This provided a perfect time to approach Jonah about my theory of how the kidnappers had tracked me down so fast. I motioned Jonah to come over to my direction. Jonah walked around the back of the Alexander One and headed in my direction. As he got closer, I started walking away from the open car door, and Jonah followed. When we were about twenty feet away from the Alexander One, I began to speak. "I've been giving some thought to the attempted kidnapping."

This seemed to surprise Jonah. He probably thought that I was pulling him aside to talk about the ride he had just provided Risa. I saw that he was listening intently, so I went on.

"At first, I couldn't imagine how these men knew who I was or how they had found me so quickly. I have worked up a theory and was wondering if perhaps you can ask Loyal about it the next time you see him."

Jonah didn't respond with a yes or no. He just continued to listen.

I decided to now expel my theory in hopes of proving or disproving it. "I think that these men who are after me definitely have a way to track Alexander One. It's the only explanation I could come up with that explains how they knew that I was missing from the golf course and that I was back in Philadelphia."

I waited to see if my words had any effect on Jonah.

He thought about this and responded. "The old man has known these men had the capability of tracking the Alexander One's movements for some time."

This was a shocking revelation to me. It sparked several new questions the EyeWonder couldn't answer. I became frantic. I think Jonah could see this in my eyes, so he went on to elaborate on what he had just told me.

"We think that these men are able to track the Alexander One in areas that have a flat topographical terrain. We are pretty sure that identifying the use of the Alexander One in an urban setting is made much more difficult by the buildings. Likewise, we are sure that water muffles the detection completely."

Of course! That makes perfect sense. Jonah's explanation filled in the gaps to my theory perfectly. It was all starting to come into focus.

Jonah went on to explain further. "When the Alexander One operates over flat land, it causes a ripple in the magnetic field of the earth. These ripples spread out uninterrupted if the land is flat enough. This makes it easy for someone to identify where the Alexander One operates if they have the right equipment. The old man thinks, however, that these ripples are obstructed greatly when the terrain is not flat. Therefore, the tall buildings in Philadelphia caused confusion in the signal. Think of it like throwing a rock into a stream. If the stream is flat, the rock will cause an easily identifiable ripple. However, if you were to take that same rock and throw it into a stream that is flowing over other large rocks, the ripples would be very difficult to identify. The ripple in the stream flowing over other rocks would be obstructed from moving outward. With the right equipment, one could probably identify that there was a ripple in this second stream, but would have a very difficult time tracking down its origin. The old man is certain that instead of reflecting the signal that the Alexander One produces, water absorbs these signals."

The explanation was dead on. It explained everything except for one nagging question. If Loyal and Jonah knew all this, why would they have risked using the Alexander One at the golf course? This was question that I had to ask. Just as I was about to ask Jonah, Risa exited the Alexander One. Jonah saw Risa start to approach and said, "Ethan, take care of your guest, and we can talk about this again a little later."

Before I could protest, Jonah turned and started to walk away. As he passed Risa he said, "Hope you enjoyed the ride, Ms. Castleberry."

Risa didn't say a word to Jonah and walked straight toward me. Before I could say anything, Risa extended her arms and took a firm hold of my body. She buried her head in my chest and began to cry. I sensed a subtle difference in the way that she was weeping. These were tears of happiness instead of the fear I had seen earlier. I wrapped my arms around her tight. The warmth of her body pressed up against mine sent my mind into a whirlwind of exotic thoughts. I felt as though our two bodies were one. I could feel her heart beating against my chest. I lowered my head and buried it in her curly locks of hair. I took a deep breath and could smell the sweet citrus shampoo that she used to wash her hair. I lowered one of my arms from her shoulder to the small of her back. The feel of the silky fabric of her sundress excited me. I pulled her closer. The warmth of her body pressed up against mine relaxed every muscle in my body except one. I wanted this feeling to never end. I was so incredibly turned on that I barely heard Risa when she spoke. Her head was still buried in my chest and it was causing her words to sound muffled.

"That was the most incredible thing I have ever seen," said Risa as she hugged me tighter.

I then started to feel her loosen her hug. She withdrew her head from my chest. I could feel one of her hands on the back of my head. She gently pushed the back of my head down. Our lips barely touched at first. The slight contact sent an erogenous shockwave through my entire body. I could feel her nipples growing against my chest. My breathing became more erratic. Our lips met again, this time with a little more purpose. The tips of our tongues touched ever so softly. The feeling was too perfect. My mind was lost in this flawless kiss. I had to use what little self-control I had to resist the urge of moving faster. The urge was getting harder and harder to resist. The delicate caress of her tongue was driving me crazy with excitement. I was completely lost in my thoughts when she moved her head back. I was in a barely conscious state when she spoke.

"Wow," Risa said as she rubbed her hand up and down my chest.

The way she was rubbing my chest only furthered my desires. At first she used her palm. Then she lightly used the tips of her fingernails to gently scratch my chest.

"Ummm. That was amazing," said Risa.

I looked down into Risa's eyes. She had a sinister little grin on her face. I could tell by this look that she too was turned on by what had just transpired. She then spoke in a sexy playful voice. "Ummm. If that is how you kiss, I can't wait to see what else you can do."

Before I could respond, Risa grabbed my arm and was leading me toward the main dwelling. There were no words being spoken. We both knew what was about to happen. These thoughts must have been overpowering, because we started walking faster and faster. The flurry of emotion I was now experiencing made the walk seem incredibly fast. Before I could realize it, we were both standing face to face next to the bed in the master guest room. It seemed that we both knew instinctively what to do at that moment.

Risa pried the button of my blue jeans open. She slowly unzipped the fly and could feel that I was ready for what was ahead. She wrapped her hands around the sides of my jeans and boxers. With one forceful tug she pushed them to the floor. This action caused her to bend down and become eye level with my midsection. She was clearly pleased with what she had seen because she let out a girlish giggle and said, "Ummm."

Risa stood up, and I pulled her close. We kissed softly just as we had on the landing pad. I could sense that Risa was now the one who could not control her desires. She quickly raised my T-shirt over my head and flung it to the floor. I was now standing fully naked in front of her. It was now my turn to undress her.

I slowly ran my hands down the small of her back. My hands passed over her perfectly shaped butt. I could feel the finely toned muscles as I continued to explore this wondrous landscape. My hands had reached her thighs just below her dress line. I started to reverse course and slowly lifted her sundress off her body. I threw the sundress on the floor.

I began to kiss her as I expertly negotiated the clasp of her black lace bra. After a couple of seconds of fumbling, the bra was lying next to the sundress on the floor. I moved back slightly so that I could take in all of Risa's beauty. She didn't shy away when I looked down. It was abundantly clear that she knew what a fantastic body she had. Her body was indescribably beautiful. No tan lines were visible as I glanced at her firm breasts. She used this brief pause to check me out as well. She must have made her determination quickly. She hooked her thumbs around the thin straps of her black lace underwear. She effortlessly pushed the lace panties and they glided down her smooth legs and came to rest around her ankles.

Risa looked at me with her big pale blue eyes. She shot me a sexy smile and without warning pushed me forcefully onto the bed. She quickly jumped on top of me and straddled my midsection. She used one of her hands to guide me into her. I felt like I was back in high school. It was like I was just starting to explore the wonders of sex secretly within my parents' house. Risa started gyrating her hips slowly at first. With every deep breath, she moved faster and faster. She began to moan. I lost what little control I had. I wrapped my hands around her hips and pushed down with growing force. This caused Risa to reach down and grab the muscles of my chest. We quickly found a perfect rhythm in which we moved as one. I could feel myself slipping, but I focused deeply so that this moment would last. Risa was getting close. She dug her fingernails deep into my chest. My hands gripped her hips tighter as I drove her down on me. I felt something inside of me break. All of the fears and emotions that had been building inside of me over the past days were released from my body at that moment.

Risa collapsed on top of me. I could feel the heaving of her chest as she gasped for air. For the briefest of moments, all was well in the world. Risa started gently scratching my chest like she had done prior to the animalistic act that we had just completed. We both sat there trying to catch our breath.

Risa let out a snicker when she began to speak. "Well. That was–umm. That was–"

Risa seemed speechless.

I too didn't have any words to describe what had just happened. All I could utter was, "Yeah. That was–That was."

We both laughed as we lay there completely content with what had just occurred.

Risa then went on to say, "I'm sorry."

Sorry? What did she have to be sorry about? That was the most amazing thing I had ever felt in my life. It was more amazing then going into space. What could she possibly be sorry about? I had to ask. "Sorry? Sorry about what?"

"I'm sorry for jumping you like that. I'm sorry if I hurt you while we–you know. I can't explain what happened. I'm usually very reserved. Maybe it was just a way to cope with the situation. Maybe it was what I saw when Jonah took me up in the Alexander One. Maybe it was my desire to make love to you from the first moment we met. Something in me triggered an uncontrollable desire to act on my emotions. I lost all control, and for that I'm sorry."

I understood what Risa was saying. She was trying to find a way to justify what had just happened. There was a slight panic to what I said next. "Does that mean that you regret what we just did?"

Risa lifted her head from my chest and continued to playfully scratch. She looked at me and said, "I will never regret what just happened for as long as I live. I wouldn't trade that earth-shattering experience for anything."

I was relieved to hear that. She had said all that I needed to hear at that moment. I pulled her close and we began to kiss. Her naked body covered me like a warm comforter. No matter what happened in the days to come, I knew that the brief time we had spent together was worth any danger we might be in.

CHAPTER TWENTY-THREE

Dean Bouchard sat in his large home office and read the message over and over again. He was hoping that rereading it would provide him more insight into how much Hans Schmick knew about the situation. Dean knew that most of the message was fluff. It was the second to last sentence of the message that caused Dean to become nervous.

"Four persons of interest have been identified, and the search for their whereabouts has begun."

What did Hans know about the situation? Who were the four persons of interest? Could Hans have possibly been referring to Garrett Michaels, Ethan Kravis, Risa Castleberry, and Loyal? The questions ate away at Dean. Not knowing the answers to these questions was driving Dean insane. Each time he thought he knew the answers to these questions, he would reread the message again in an effort to validate his suspicions. Dean sat at his desk and agonized over how he should respond to the message. Dean's intuition had always served him well in the past. After reading the message for what seemed like the thousandth time, he cemented one thought in his mind. He could say with certainty that Hans Schmick knew more than he had led the council to believe.

Dean despised the man known as Member Number One from

the moment they first met. Dean always thought that Hans Schmick was part of a lower class of people. His newfound fortunes couldn't hide the fact that he had grown up as a poor farm boy in rural Germany. Dean had descended from royalty. This type of prestige was handed down from generation to generation. Dean was a gentleman through and through. He detested the very thought that someone like Hans could pretend to have this type of nobility and heritage.

Hans's upbringing was not the only quality Dean looked down upon. When Dean was approached by Hans thirty-two years before, he had a full background check done on the man. The type of background check done was not the simple running of a credit report. Dean hired a team to fully investigate every aspect of Hans's life. It was after this that Dean realized how Hans had built his fortune. The reason was physically repulsive to Dean. Hans's entire empire was built on the backs of the millions of people the Germans had killed during World War II. Hans was a high-ranking member of the Nazi party. He used his position to steal from the dead. Instead of using his ingenuity or hard work as Dean's family had, Hans had killed and maimed for his riches. Dean knew that he was no saint. He knew that some situations had called for violence if all other avenues had been exhausted. Dean had ordered the murder of several key people throughout his vast business dealings; however, Dean drew the line far before genocide. Hans had been directly responsible for tens if not hundreds of thousands of murders. This complete disregard for human life proved that Hans was a lower class of human being. He was a thug who had enough smarts to parlay his barbarism into great wealth.

As much as Dean hated the very idea of Hans Schmick, he knew the man was very smart and very unpredictable. There was always a motive to the actions the man took. Dean could not underestimate this man or it would mean certain death. All these thoughts brought

Dean back to the question at hand. How should he respond to this latest communication sent to the council?

Dean was sure Hans had more information about the Alexander One. Instead of focusing on what Hans might have known, Dean decided to figure out how Hans had received his information. If Hans's message was referring to the four people Dean had in his crosshairs, how did Hans find out about them? There were only a couple of possibilities. The most obvious way for Hans to know about the suspects was if he somehow had been monitoring Dean.

Dean thought about this notion but quickly dismissed it. Dean had been far too paranoid when setting up his communications network to allow this to happen. He spread the contracts out among many companies when developing the Lockbox facility. Many contractors only had small portions of the overall project. Dean decided to do it this way so that no one contractor knew the entire scope of the project. The company that had built and installed all the equipment in the Lockbox was as clean as they come. Dean ordered extensive background checks on all of the employees involved with the construction project. He ruled this out as the source of Hans's intelligence.

There was only one other logical explanation Dean could come up with. Someone in Dean's organization may be a mole. Dean became ill at the very notion of this being a possible explanation for how Hans could have known about these four suspects. Dean shook his head trying to dispel this thought from his mind. The paranoia grew within Dean. Could it have been possible that he had a traitor in his organization?

Dean had participated in corporate espionage tactics many times. He often recruited high-powered people within other organizations. He would use these people to obtain inside information about deals that he was involved with. These moles often turned out to be a very wise investment. More often than not these moles would provide critical information that could swing the balance of power to Dean's favor. Again, Dean shook his head to release this thought from his mind. Who could have been in a position to provide this information?

Dean could identify only a small handful of people who knew of the events that had transpired over the last two days. He thought about Albert being the mole. Dean laughed to himself and said, "No way!" He had known Albert almost his entire life. He had treated Albert like a son. He knew Albert far too well. If Albert was the mole, Dean would have picked up on this long ago. Albert was involved in every facet of Dean's business and nothing like this had ever happened before. Albert would have made the perfect mole for Hans. He knew almost everything that happened in the organization. Dean dismissed Albert as a possibility.

There was the six-member special operations team that carried out both missions of the last two days. Dean didn't know much about the men on the team. He knew that Brad had handpicked them and that was enough background Dean needed. Although the team had carried out the missions, Dean knew that they were not privy to the big picture. These men were task oriented. They were given a task to complete, and they completed it. They were never told why they carried out the missions. Dean ruled out all the men on the six-member team.

Dean's thoughts then shifted to Brad Resniki. Dean had known Brad for more than twenty years. He had always thought of Brad as an honorable man. Brad was loyal to a fault. On more than one occasion, Dean had treated Brad with disrespect when he lost his temper. Worse yet, he had done so in the company of Brad's team. Could Brad be the mole? If Dean hadn't received such a cryptic message from Hans, his answer would have been absolutely not. Doubt was starting to fill

Dean's head as he thought about all that had transpired. Brad was knowledgeable of all aspects about what had happened over the past two days. He was visibly upset that he had not been contacted first when the extraction plans were developed. Dean had publicly berated him in front of Albert and Garrett Michaels. Could this public embarrassment have been the final straw?

Dean didn't want to accept this, but his paranoia was taking hold. If Brad was a mole, there was very little chance that Dean would be able to succeed in his overall objective in capturing the Alexander One. Brad was in charge of all of Dean's covert operations. Without Brad, Dean's mission would be severely crippled. Dean had to find out if Brad was a mole.

Dean put away the council provided laptop and locked it in his desk drawer. He then summoned Albert to his office.

A few minutes later, Albert entered the office. Dean motioned for Albert to take a seat. Once Dean was sure that the door to his office was locked, he began to speak. "Albert. I'm afraid that I have some very disturbing news."

This piqued Albert's interest, so he straightened up in his chair.

"It appears as though we may have a leak in our organization."

Albert showed a look of skepticism and replied, "What makes you think that, sir?"

"I received some information that suggests that the council has found out about our activities over the past several days. The only way for them to have this information is for someone to have told them."

Albert took a moment to ponder what Dean had just said. He raised his head and said, "What information did you receive?"

Dean knew that he needed to provide more details if Albert was to be able to help in this situation. He recited the short message that he had received from Hans Schmick verbatim. Once he had completed his recitation, he looked to Albert for some feedback. Dean could tell that Albert was thinking hard about what had just been said to him.

A few moments later, Albert responded. "The message is very vague. Hans Schmick isn't a person you should take lightly. His actions are very calculated. If he divulged this information, there must be a purpose to it. In previous communications he has sent out, does he always speak in such vague terms or is he more specific with his details?"

Dean thought back to all the messages he could remember. Hans typically provided more detail to his messages. Albert had raised a very interesting point. If Hans really knew of four persons of interest, why wouldn't he name them in his message? Given how important this matter was to the council, surely he would try to elicit the council's help in locating these people. But the number four continued to ring in Dean's ears. He had to trust his gut. His gut was telling him that Hans Schmick knew more about the situation then he had been saying.

"He typically provides more detail in his messages. If he knew the four names of the people of interest, based on his past level of detail, he would have provided the names."

Albert went on to say, "So you think by not providing the names, he is making you some type of offer? It would seem to me that if he was willing to keep any information he had about your actions to himself, that he was indirectly trying to strike a deal with you without approaching you directly."

Dean was proud of Albert. He was thinking outside the box. He didn't agree with what Albert was thinking. He quickly dismissed Albert's inference.

"No. I don't think this was his intention. I think that he wanted to convey that he was aware of what we have been doing. He's trying to plant the seed of paranoia in our minds. I have to tell you, Albert, if that was his motive, it has been very effective. I have thought long and hard about who this traitor could be. The only person that I could arrive at was Brad."

Albert's jaw almost hit the floor. He quickly rushed to the side of his longtime friend. Albert started to shake his head while he spoke. "No way! Nope. I would never believe that Brad would knowingly betray you like that, sir. No way."

Dean was surprised at Albert's reaction. This outward display of emotion was very unlike his protégé. Dean was wondering if calling Albert in on this matter was the right thing to do. Dean spoke quickly to bring calm to the situation. "Listen to me. I've known Brad just as long as you have. I have grown to care for and respect him as well. We would be fools if we didn't act on the information we have been provided. There is a way to test Brad's loyalty without his getting hurt. I need you to manage this situation. Can I count on you?"

"Of course, sir" Albert said without a moment of hesitation.

Dean continued. "Good. Now here's what I want you to do. I want you to set up a meeting with Brad. In that meeting I want you to explain that you have received proof that one of the men on his special operations team has been providing information to our enemies. You pick one of the men; it doesn't really matter who. Then you give the order for Brad to execute this man. Brad will strongly protest at first. You must convince him that this is the truth. Manufacture evidence if need be. If Brad kills his man, then we know that he is our mole. If he disobeys, knowing that his life would be in danger, then we know he is not our mole. Understand?"

Albert looked a little confused. He asked, "Shouldn't it be the other way around?"

Dean smiled and knew that Albert still had a lot to learn.

"If Brad kills the man that he has handpicked without protest, it's a way to deflect his actions on someone else. If, on the other hand, he defends his man to the very end, then we can be sure that he would show this type of loyalty to us as well."

Albert looked depressed when he said, "It will be done, sir. You have my word."

Dean smiled at Albert and said, "Thank you, Albert. Please keep me informed about any outcome. You may go now."

"Yes, sir." Albert said as he rose to his feet and left the office.

Dean leaned back in his chair. He understood that this situation was becoming more and more complicated. He was now playing a high-stakes no-limit game against two very formidable opponents. He made the determination that he shouldn't respond to Hans Schmick's message. He didn't want to overplay his hand. Dean knew that his whole plan rested in the hands of one man. Dean hated to have to rely on factors that were completely outside his control. He saw no other way to move his plan along without putting himself and Albert in danger. He just hoped to God that Loyal would make good on his promise and call back.

CHAPTER TWENTY-FOUR

Risa and I made love a couple more times throughout the course of the night. Each time was much different than the first. We took our time and gave ourselves the opportunity to explore each other's bodies. After making love all night, there was no question in my mind. I was deeply in love with Risa.

The phone rang and woke me from a very content slumber. Risa had used my chest as a pillow and was lying very still on top of me. I gently placed her head on the pillow as I reached for the phone.

"Hello?" I said in a sleepy voice.

"Good Morning, Ethan." I recognized Jonah's voice immediately.

"I felt that it would be better if I didn't knock this morning. I'm calling to tell you that it's time for me to brief you on this afternoon's events."

I had completely forgotten. Today was Tuesday, and Jonah had said that he had planned something for us to do. I would have given anything at that moment to have the courage to back out of the commitment I had made to Loyal; however, I was too far involved at this point to do so. I responded to Jonah. "All right. How much time do I have to get ready?"

"I'll meet you in the dining room for breakfast in one hour. Don't be late."

Jonah hung up the phone, and I looked at the receiver. That was kind of rude. Because of the abrupt ending of the phone call, I thought Jonah may have been upset at what he knew had happened between Risa and me. "Oh well, tough shit," I said to myself as I hung up the receiver. Now comes the difficult part. I had to tell Risa that I was going to be leaving the island later that day and that she would be staying. I decided to wake her up in the best way I knew how.

I started lightly kissing her neck. She let out a cute little laugh and said, "Ummm, again? You really must be in good shape."

I stopped kissing and responded in a soft voice, "Good morning, sexy."

"Is it morning already?" Risa said without opening her eyes to look at me.

"Your body probably hasn't had time to adjust yet to the time difference. Your body probably still thinks that it's Monday night, Philadelphia time."

"All my body knows that it just got a wonderfully pleasant workout over the last several hours and is ready for more."

I laughed at her little innuendo. I couldn't remember the last time I had sex three times in one night. What could I say? This unbelievable woman just did it for me. She made my body respond in a way that was involuntary. I thought about using the hour Jonah had given me to continue last night's epic adventure, but it was time to get ready for what I knew was going to be a long day.

"I would give anything to stay with you here all day and night until we were forced to leave the room because of starvation, but I just got a call from Jonah. He and I have to take care of some business. I'll most likely have to leave the island for a little while."

This caused Risa to wake up a bit and look at me. Her curly hair was disheveled, and it made her head look like a dry mop. Normally someone might think she looked kind of funny with her hair the way it was at that moment. I thought she looked like the cutest thing I had ever laid my eyes on. She was clearly concerned when she began to speak. "You're leaving the island? Am I coming with you?"

"I think you would be safer if you stayed here."

I could see a slight panic in her beautiful pale blue eyes. She continued. "How long will you be gone for?"

I really didn't know the answer, but I needed to play it cool. I decided that for Risa's best interest, I would tell a little white lie. "I should be gone only for a couple of hours. I'll be back in time for dinner tonight. You'll have a great time here. You can sleep as long as you want. If you feel like it, you can go out to the beach and lie out. I'll be back before you know it."

Risa seemed to consider this for a moment before she replied. "Are you going anywhere that might put you in danger?"

I leaned in and kissed her on the forehead. I was so happy at that moment. Risa seemed to have ignored her well being and had focused on my safety. That one comment said a lot about where our relationship was headed. "I'll be fine. I'll be back before you know it. You have to make me a promise though."

Risa lay there in silence waiting for my request. I continued, "You have to enjoy yourself here at the island. Think of it as an all-expense-paid dream vacation. Anything you want, you can just ask David the butler for, and he'll ensure that you have it."

She smiled and said, "Anything?"

"Yes, anything."

"So if I ask him for you, he will provide it?"

I knew she was just joking, but it was nice, just the same. I then said something I knew was incredibly cheesy. "He won't be able to give you me, because you already have me. You had me the second I saw you at that store."

Risa buried her head in the pillow and began to scream. She knew just as I did that we were deeply in love. The feeling was indescribable. It makes you do crazy things like bury your head in a pillow and scream at the top of your lungs. I saw the mop top of her head retract from the pillow. She had a sinister little grin on her face. Before I knew it, we were once again engaged in the comfortable rhythm of lovemaking that came so naturally to us the night before.

The next time I looked at my watch, I realized that I had only fifteen minutes left before I had to meet Jonah. I turned to Risa and said, "I have to get ready. I told Jonah I would meet him soon."

As I started to rise off the bed, I felt Risa tugging playfully on my arm. In a whining voice she said, "Just a little longer. Just stay with me for a little longer."

I could tell that she knew I had to go and was just saying this for my benefit. She probably meant it, but the request was made in a half-hearted fashion. She released me from her loose grip, and I walked to the bathroom. I showered and put on a fresh change of clothes. Before I left the bedroom, I bent over the bed and kissed Risa one last time.

"Sleep as long as you like. If you need anything, just pick up the phone, and someone will answer. If you would like to go to the beach, pick up the phone and ask for David. He will be able to escort you down there."

She looked in my direction and said only two words, "Be safe."

I exited the master guest room and headed toward the dining room. As much as I didn't want to leave the comfortable embrace of Risa's loving arms, I was very curious to hear what Jonah had planned.

I entered the dining room, scanned the room, and saw Jonah sitting at the head of the massive table. He was eating some eggs and fresh fruit. He looked up and said, "Everything work out last night?"

I could sense a little sarcasm in his voice when he asked the question. It was well warranted, so I decided to ignore it. "Everything is just fine. What is the plan for today?"

Jonah seemed to appreciate my focus. What little angst he had for the situation seemed to disappear when he spoke. "Have some breakfast before we talk."

I sat down and ate some breakfast. After burning so many calories during the night before, the food did wonders to restore my energy. I signaled to Jonah that I had completed my breakfast. He said, "Ready to find out what we have planned for you today?"

"Ready as I'll ever be."

Jonah stood up and led me into the study next to the dining room. He motioned for me to take a seat. Once I sat, Jonah began to speak.

"Today is the day that you take the first step in introducing the Alexander One to the world. An appointment has been scheduled for you to present a scaled-down version of the Alexander One to an advanced research firm in Atlanta, Georgia."

Jonah paused probably to gauge my reaction. I sat there quietly and waited for him to continue.

Jonah continued his briefing. "The name of the research company is called Transtronics. Transtronics is a research company that has strong ties to almost all technology-related industries. However, Transtronics has a heavy focus on transportation-related advances. They are the tip of the sword when it comes to the automobile industry. They have been responsible for some of the most important improvements the automobile industry has ever seen, from the invention of the taillight to cars that park themselves. They are into everything, when it comes to cars. They are the ideal audience for what you are going to show them."

Jonah once again paused to see if I had any questions. When I had none, he continued. "An appointment has been made for you under your assumed identity. Steve Hamilton will provide them a live demonstration of this device."

Jonah put his hand on a medium-sized plastic case. He opened the case and took out a twelve-inch replica of the Alexander One and a tablet PC. Jonah looked and me and smiled. "This is an exact replica of the Alexander One. It is fully functional in every way. The purpose of the meeting is to show the researchers at Transtronics the Alexander One's capability of geomagnetic flight."

I was shocked that things could be moving so fast. Jonah seemed confident that I would be capable of demonstrating this device seeing it only hours before the meeting. I said without hesitation, "Are you sure you want me to give the presentation? I don't really know how to use it or what to say."

Jonah smiled and responded. "That's what your EyeWonder is for. All you have to do is read the script displayed by the EyeWonder and everything will be fine."

The EyeWonder. "Of course," I said to myself. Loyal would probably create a scripted speech and feed it to my EyeWonder as I provided the demonstration. It was genius. Even if I knew what to say, I still needed to know how to operate the device. I said as much to Jonah. "That sounds like a great plan, but I still need to know how to use it."

Jonah spent the next couple of hours showing me how to operate the mini Alexander One. It was very simple and worked off an electronic joystick display on the tablet PC. Seeing that I had grown comfortable with how to operate it, Jonah asked, "All right, ready to go to the meeting?"

I was so enthralled with the ingenious little device that I hadn't realized what time it was. The question caught me off guard, and I became nervous. Jonah saw this as soon as he asked the question. He looked to me and said, "There's nothing to it, Ethan. We are going to fly over to Atlanta, go to the meeting, and be back in time for dinner."

"Won't whoever is looking for me see the signature of the Alexander One in Atlanta?"

"We have taken the necessary precautions so that our trip will not be discovered by anyone. We'll fly to Lake Lanier just outside Atlanta. We'll rendezvous with a boat in the middle of the lake that will then bring us ashore. Once ashore, a car will be waiting for us. We'll drive to the Buckhead section of Atlanta where the meeting is being held. We will be perfectly safe; I promise."

I had heard that promise before, and it hadn't worked out too well. Thankfully, this time Jonah had seemed to take some extra precautions.

"OK. It seems that you and Loyal have it all figured out. When do we leave?"

Jonah packed up the case with the mini Alexander One and said, "No time like the present."

I wanted to check in on Risa one last time before we left. I said, "I should probably go back to the guest room and change. I don't think it's very appropriate to show up to the meeting in a T-shirt and shorts."

Jonah knew what I was trying to do. He quickly responded. "There will be a nicely pressed suit waiting for you in Atlanta. We wouldn't want it to get wrinkled on the way over, now, would we?" Jonah let out a grin.

I was sure he knew what I was thinking at that moment, because he said, "Risa will be just fine. We have planned a very special day for her that she will no doubt enjoy."

I wasn't sure what Jonah had meant by this, but for some reason I trusted him. Jonah lifted the case by its handle and started walking toward the door.

A couple of minutes later we were at the landing pad. Jonah opened the door to the Alexander One. It was the bigger version of the Alexander One that had brought us to the island the day before. Jonah placed the plastic case containing the mini Alexander One in the back seat. He then opened the front seat passenger's side door and got in. Seeing that he had gotten into the passenger's seat, I asked, "Who's going to be piloting us today?"

Jonah looked at me and said, "You are, Captain."

I was very surprised. I couldn't believe that he could place such trust in my abilities. I got nervous for both of us, so I asked, "Me? You want me to pilot the Alexander One?"

"Nope. I want you to pilot the Alexander Two. The Alexander One is still on your rooftop in Philadelphia. Loyal is going to fly over and pick it up a little later. For now, we are stuck in this bucket known as the Alexander Two."

Wow. Me piloting an aircraft halfway around the world? The thought of it was daunting and scary. I figured that Jonah would be there if I did anything wrong, so I said "What the heck."

Jonah shouted a couple more words of encouragement. "It's easy. You need to learn to fly it if you are going to sell it to the world. I will be here in the event anything goes wrong. Once you see how easy it is to fly, you won't be nearly as nervous."

I walked to the driver's side of the Alexander Two. I got in and looked over at Jonah for some instruction. He pointed and said, "Flip that switch."

As I flipped the switch, the Alexander Two came to life. I heard and felt the familiar low humming vibration below my feet. I was excited and nervous at the same time. Jonah began to explain the instrumentation panel in front of me. I tried hard to listen to his words, but the anticipation of the flight caused me to lose focus. Jonah spent five minutes explaining what each of the buttons on the console did. He then turned to me and said, "All that's left is to plug in the coordinates of our destination on this keypad. Once you do that, you move the joystick in between your legs forward to take off. Once you break through the atmosphere, the Alexander Two will take over and be on auto-pilot until it's time for reentry."

Jonah pointed to the keypad in the center of the console. It sounded simple enough. I leaned toward the keypad, then paused. I turned to Jonah and asked, "What are the coordinates of our destination?"

Jonah smiled and said, "That's a question that your EyeWonder can answer."

I activated my EyeWonder and found the latitude and longitude for Lake Lanier in Georgia. I plugged in the coordinates and nothing happened.

Jonah leaned forward and double-checked the coordinates I had used. Once he confirmed that they were correct, he said, "Looks like we're good to go. Press the Enter button on the bottom left corner of the keypad."

I did as Jonah had instructed and felt the Alexander Two hover slightly above the ground. I felt my stomach tighten.

An electronic voice in the cockpit rang out through the speakers. "Coordinates accepted. Pressurizing cockpit. Pressurization of cockpit complete. You may start primary ascent."

Jonah said, "Push the joystick forward slowly."

I barely moved the joystick, when I felt the Alexander Two start to climb. At first we were moving at only a couple of feet per minute. Jonah said, "You'll need to go a little faster, or we will never make it to

Atlanta. Move the joystick a little farther forward."

I pushed the joystick forward with more force. The Alexander Two climbed at an incredible rate. The feeling caused a massive rush of adrenaline to course through my veins. I was about to pilot an aircraft into outer space.

Jonah chimed in, "You doing OK?"

Without looking at him, I said, "This baby handles like it's on rails."

CHAPTER TWENTY-FIVE

Dean Bouchard was talking on the telephone when Albert burst through the door to his office. Dean was appalled that his protégé had entered his office in such a cavalier manner. He took one look at Albert and said, "Jean-Phillip, I will have to call you back."

Dean hung up the phone without listening to the man on the other end. He quickly asked, "What is it, Albert?"

Albert tried to catch his breath. He had run to Dean's office as soon as he had heard. In a winded voice, Albert said, "The call, sir. The caller you have been waiting for is on the phone in the Lockbox."

Dean catapulted himself to his feet. He had to get down to the Lockbox before Loyal grew impatient and hung up. He came out from the other side of the desk and headed toward the door. Dean and Albert walked at a brisk pace, almost a slow jog. They navigated the maze of hallways and started their descent to the secretive communications room. As they walked down the steps Dean asked, "How long ago did the call come in?"

Still not able to catch his breath, Albert replied, "I was there when the call was answered. I ran up to get you as soon as I realized it. Less than a minute."

Dean's fear grew. He was praying that he wouldn't miss his opportunity to talk with Loyal. He broke into a full jog as they got closer to the door of the Lockbox. Dean and Albert finally reached the door. It took Dean an additional minute to pass the necessary security checks at the entrance. Once the door opened, Dean ran to the command center room. He dove for the SAMSAC terminal and picked up the receiver.

He tried to collect himself before he began to speak. In a winded voice, he said, "Hello?"

There was a pause on the line for a second or two. Dean's heart felt like it was going to explode. He then heard the voice of the man he had come to know as Loyal.

"I'm sorry, Mr. B. Did I catch you at a bad time?"

"No, no. Not at all, Loyal. I wasn't near the phone when you called. I'm truly sorry about the delay."

There was a slight delay, then Loyal finally replied. "I know your house is very large, Mr. Bouchard. I understand the reason for the delay."

Dean was floored. How did Loyal know who he was? Dean felt something he had not felt in a very long time. Dean felt speechless. A feeling of dread came over him. He didn't know what to say, so he said nothing.

Loyal broke the silence. "I can assure you, Mr. Bouchard, you are not the only one with a tremendous amount of resources. I take it from your silence that you didn't expect me to find out who you were."

Dean felt ill. His mind was spinning with questions. If Loyal knew who he was, what else did he know? How did Loyal find out who he was? Did Loyal know anything about the council? Was Loyal in some way connected to the council? Was Loyal Hans Schmick's source of information?

All these questions caused Dean to become dizzy. He took a seat at the console and tried to collect his thoughts before he spoke. "Very good Loyal. I'm very impressed you have been able to identify me. Now that you know who I am, will you return the favor and tell me who you are?"

There was no humor in how Loyal replied when he spoke. "You know who I am, Mr. Bouchard. I'm the man who created the Alexander One. That's all you need to know about me for now."

Dean had no leverage in the situation. Loyal was in charge. All Dean could do was sit back and listen to what Loyal had to say.

Loyal began to speak. "I was calling to tell you that I have strongly considered your offer, Mr. Bouchard."

Every time Loyal spoke his name, Dean winced in pain.

Loyal continued. "I have compiled some background information on you, and I made some very surprising discoveries. I was very surprised to find out that the early part of your career is very well documented indeed, but the last thirty years or so is a complete vacuum. There is very little known about what you have been doing for the past thirty years. Like any good businessman, I like to know with whom I'm doing business. I'm sure a man like you understands this precaution."

Dean couldn't remember the last time the tables had been turned like this. It was usually Dean who taunted his opponents like Loyal was doing. Dean didn't like the feeling of being treated this way. Even in that moment of defeat, he rose to the challenge. Dean responded. "Of course I understand your precautions, Loyal. It's a very natural thing to do."

"Good, then you won't mind filling in some of the gaps for me, would you? Please explain what has been keeping you busy the last thirty years, and it will help me to make a decision."

Dean was slightly encouraged by this last statement. Although

Dean highly doubted that his offer was still under consideration, he knew that he had very little to lose at this point. Dean would provide a vague explanation that didn't mention the council in any way.

"For the last thirty years, I have been involved in business interests that have forced me to withdraw completely from the public eye. My primary interests have been in commodities. The commodities market is extremely competitive, as you know. When one grows a business to the size my family has, you often attract many enemies. For my family's safety, I decided long ago to fly under the radar. I'm sure you must understand my concerns."

Loyal dug deeper into the vague response. "Of course I understand this, Mr. Bouchard. If you don't mind my asking, what type of commodities does your family business deal in?"

Dean recognized the trap immediately. If Dean said that he was in the oil business, it would undoubtedly scare off Loyal. If Loyal knew that Dean controlled one seventh of the world's oil supply, Loyal would know that he would stop at nothing to prevent the introduction of a vehicle that didn't use oil to propel the engine. Dean had to lie.

"My family members have a long history in the commodities business. In the early years, they focused on coal and cotton. Over the years, I have shifted my family's interest to precious metals. The primary focus of my business is now gold and platinum." Dean held his breath. He knew that this lie could end the conversation right then and there. He was relieved to hear Loyal respond.

"Precious metals is a very competitive business indeed. I imagine you must control quite a bit of the world's gold and platinum supply to have amassed such a tremendous fortune. I'm looking at some photographs of your family's Pennsylvania estate, and it looks very impressive."

Dean couldn't tell if Loyal was being condescending or truthful in his praise. He decided not to respond and let Loyal continue.

"The truth is, Mr. Bouchard, that if we were to have somehow connected earlier in our lives, I'm sure we could have made very good partners to one another; however, the kidnapping of my very good friend Garrett Michaels has led me to conclude that you are not the type of man I would like to be in business with."

Dean nearly vomited on the floor. He knew he was about to lose Loyal. He quickly responded. "I'm not the one who killed someone. Your men were the ones who killed one of my employees. I explained to you in our previous conversation my reasons for the distasteful way in which Garrett was brought to me. I admit that this was a dishonest way of handling the situation, but it didn't involve murder."

Dean prayed that this was enough to bring Loyal back into the fold. He patiently waited for Loyal's response.

"You make a very compelling argument. Perhaps I have acted to hastily. The truth is that I could use the influence of a man such as you to provide safe passage through the dangers that exist in the world."

Dean felt a rush of excitement. For a fleeting moment he sensed that Loyal might change his mind. Loyal continued to speak.

"I have no doubt that the men you warned me about are very dangerous. Instead of being their enemy, I would like to invite them into our circle of friendship. I would like them to share in the massive windfall of money that will be created based on the introduction of the Alexander One. Do you think that you could use your enormous influence to convince these men to join us?"

Dean almost laughed out loud. If Loyal only knew what Dean did about these men, he wouldn't have bothered to ask the question. Dean was absolutely certain that if he flatly rejected Loyal's request, he would lose what little opportunity he did have to gain control of the Alexander One. His response to Loyal needed to be somewhere between "Yes" and "No" for it to be believable. He composed his thoughts and began to respond to Loyal. "It's very difficult to say whether these men would be willing to join our effort. I'm afraid that many of their business interests may be threatened if the Alexander One were introduced to the world. Perhaps I could try to convince them that a serious shift in strategy might be within their best interests. If we could somehow solidify our relationship, I would feel more comfortable approaching these men."

Dean was not sure what the next step could be in this situation. He would rely on Loyal to guide his actions. This was uncharted territory for Dean. He had always exerted total control in every situation. Dean hoped that the direction Loyal moved in was possible for him to accept.

"Here's my counteroffer. You make contact with the men you feel would give us the most opposition. Start to plant the idea that now would be a good time to realign their business interests. Explain to them the enormity of wealth that the Alexander One would be capable of generating. If they seem open to exploring this new opportunity, have them clear their schedule so that we can all meet and discuss it in more detail. I will call you back in two days and we will reassess our situation to see if this course of action is feasible. Does that sound like a good takeaway from our discussion?"

Dean had no option in his reply to Loyal. "It sounds like a doable task, Loyal. I'm confident that any setbacks our relationship started with will be quickly dismissed when you see what type of man I really am. Thank you for this opportunity to right any wrongs that I have caused."

"My sincerest hope is that this can be the start of a truly wonderful business relationship. I look forward to our next conversation," said Loyal.

"As do I," replied Dean.

The line went dead. Dean slammed down the receiver to the SAMSAC terminal causing it to shatter in his hand. "God dammit!" Dean yelled as he reflected on his conversation with Loyal. Dean sat in the chair for a moment as he tried to put his emotions in check. He asked Albert to leave him. He needed to be alone while mapping out his next move. He couldn't remember the last time he had been this angry. Dean saw clearly that his once-simple plan was turning into a big-time mess. Nothing was going according to plan. He was losing all control of the situation. Dean sat there in the command center for hours. He thought about everything that had been said by Loyal.

Loyal wanted to bring his potential enemies in on this deal. Why? Did he figure that by doing so, he would eliminate all danger from the equation? Doing so would be a very logical way of ensuring one's safety. If Loyal were as smart as Dean thought he was, why wouldn't he suspect a double cross? Dean knew that the council members were not the type of men to take on new partners. They decimated the competition if given the opportunity. It was very possible that Loyal had underestimated the greed of these men. After all, Loyal did not know who comprised the other six seats of the council. Dean was absolutely sure that no matter how smart Loyal was, there was no way that he knew the council even existed. There was no trace, electronic or otherwise, that would allow them to be identified.

Perhaps Loyal felt like the potential of the Alexander One was so great that any man would be a fool not to jump at the opportunity to share in the vast riches that it guaranteed.

Dean started to develop a new plan. He would do as Loyal had asked. He would organize an emergency council meeting and invite Loyal as a guest speaker. Dean knew that the council would never allow it but it was a necessary part of his new plan. He had to create the illusion of safety for Loyal. If he could just lure Loyal out into the open, he could literally kill two birds with one stone.

Dean's new plan was quite simple. He would call a council meeting and inform Loyal of the date, time, and location. Naturally, Loyal would be suspicions of the meeting. Dean couldn't afford to take any chances. It would have to be the real deal. He needed to assemble the council so that from all outward appearances it would seem legitimate for Loyal's benefit. Once Loyal realized that the meeting was real, he would come out of his shell. This is when Dean would take action. He would simultaneously take control of the Alexander One while he permanently dissolved the council.

The plan solved all his problems in one fell swoop. Dean knew that the most difficult part of the plan was to come up with a way to get the council members to agree to meet. The reason for the meeting must be so overwhelming that it would give them no alternative but to accept the invitation.

Dean was playing a super high-stakes game. It was an all or nothing proposition. He had developed so much wealth that he again questioned his motives. Clearly, one wrong step in his plan could end his life. He reassured himself. If he could pull this magnanimous feat off, he and his family name would be known for the rest of time. It was his legacy to the world. He would not fail.

CHAPTER TWENTY-SIX

Jonah and I had arrived safely in Atlanta and were now on our way to the meeting. The flight over was phenomenal and I was still high on adrenaline. The Alexander Two was easier to operate then a car. All I had to do was plug in the destination and the Alexander Two did almost everything else. The only other process that the pilot had to complete was to tell the computer when to reengage the geomagnetic drive upon reentering the atmosphere. This value corresponded to an altitude. The value varied based on the location of the destination, but was typically around 200,000 feet. Jonah spent most of the flight talking me through the various features of the ingenious aircraft. He showed me how to use the onboard communications system that allowed for in-flight video conferencing. He also showed me some of the built-in safety features. The one feature that really impressed me was the abort feature. If the abort feature was activated, the Alexander Two would travel on autopilot back to the island. This feature was used only in case of emergency and could not be turned off once the abort sequence was started.

The traffic we were stuck in was some of the worst I had ever seen. As we drew closer to the Atlanta city limits, the traffic only got worse. I had never seen so many cars in all my life. The roadway we were on was five lanes in each direction. It was bumper-to-bumper traffic both ways. The long, flat roadway allowed me to see the traffic build-up for at least ten miles ahead of us. We were still about twenty-five miles away from where the meeting was to take place. If this traffic persisted, I knew that we would have a difficult time making the meeting.

Seeing all of the cars on the roadway renewed my sense of purpose. All I could see when I looked out among the thousands and thousands of cars was barrels of oil. It was sights like this that led me to lend more credence to Loyal's ten-year timeline. I looked at the neighboring cars and realized that I didn't see a single car with more than one passenger. I suppose it had been this way for a while, but I just never fully thought it through until Loyal opened my eyes to the epidemic.

The traffic-riddled drive allowed me to gently come down off of my adrenaline high from the flight. I noticed that Jonah hadn't said anything since we started our drive into Atlanta. With my highs from the flight subsiding, it was making room for anxiety to set in. I asked Jonah. "Do you think this traffic will cause us to be late for the meeting?"

Jonah looked at me. I could see a look of anger in his eyes when he spoke. "Do you see now? Look at this craziness."

Jonah extended his arms as he spoke. He was clearly speaking about the traffic. I had never seen Jonah get angry before. Clearly something was upsetting him.

"This madness is a perfect confirmation for what we are doing. The world is committing suicide at an increasing rate."

Jonah was visibly enraged. He was typically very calm, but his true emotions were shown at that moment. That small outburst proved to me that Jonah was committed to our mission. He wasn't just a security guard hired to look after me. He truly bought into what Loyal had sent us to Atlanta to do. Jonah had supported me through difficult times since we had met. The least I could do was try to reciprocate some of that support. I tried to find the appropriate words before I spoke. "It's up to us to try to correct this mess. We will succeed."

Jonah took a deep breath and responded, "We have to, Ethan. This is just ridiculous."

Jonah pointed out at the traffic once again. The anger he was now displaying grew exponentially because he probably had not spent much time in traffic since the Alexander One was invented. I tried to bring Jonah back to the situation at hand.

"This traffic is awful, but we can't start to fix the problem if we miss this meeting. Do you think we will make it?"

This question seemed to snap Jonah back to the here and now. He took another deep breath and responded. "Sorry I lost it for a bit. The sight of this traffic was just so overwhelming that it caused my emotions to get away from me. We have about an hour and twenty minutes until the meeting starts. We should be able to make it."

"OK. That's good." I decided that I should just sit there and let Jonah cool down a bit.

After a couple of minutes, he began to speak. "Let me brief you on what to do after the meeting ends. Once you complete the meeting, exit the building and walk across the street to the parking garage. Take the elevator to the top floor, and I'll be waiting there for you with the Alexander Two. I'm not expecting any trouble, but don't take your time getting to the roof. I want to leave there without any complications."

The plan sounded simple enough, so I said, "The top floor of the parking garage across the street. Got it."

Jonah and I sat quiet for the rest of the ride. We pulled up to the Buckhead Technology complex with only a couple of minutes to spare. Jonah stopped in front of the building and said, "Just go to the main reception and tell them that you are there for a meeting with Transtronics. The reception will make the call, and someone will come down to the lobby to escort you up to the meeting room. Good luck. Loyal is counting on you, Ethan."

I could feel the nervousness starting to build. I really didn't want to let Loyal down. I got out of the car and headed toward the main entrance of the building. I heard the window of the car rolling down and Jonah yelled out. "Hey, Ethan! Are you forgetting something?"

I looked back and said, "Crap!" I had left the mini Alexander One in the back seat of the car. I turned around and collected it from the back seat.

As I reached into the car, Jonah gave me some final words of encouragement. "Don't worry. You'll be great. Have some fun in there. Really sell it."

I gave Jonah a half-hearted smile and again started walking to the main entrance, this time with my precious cargo in hand. I walked through the revolving glass door and up to the large white marble reception desk. Behind the desk was a large woman who was on her cell phone. When she saw me approach, she quickly ended her call and asked me, "Can I help you, sir?"

I told her that I was there to meet with Transtronics. She made a quick call and asked me to take a seat in the seating area off to the side. A couple of minutes had passed when a white-haired gentleman exited the elevator and headed in my direction. He was dressed in a nicely tailored black pinstriped suit. For some reason, I thought that this man would fit in better with a Wall Street investment firm, rather than a group of scientists. He walked up to me, extended his hand, and said, "Mr. Hamilton?"

I almost told him that he must have been there to meet someone else. I then remembered that the meeting had been arranged under my assumed name. My pause caused a look of confusion on the man's face.

"Are you Steve Hamilton?" he asked as he started to withdraw his handshake.

"I am indeed," I said as I extended my hand.

A smile appeared on the man's face when he said, "It's good to meet you. My name is Peter Goldman. I'm the president of Transtronics."

"Wow." I wondered at that moment what Loyal told this company when setting up the meeting. I had never been greeted in the lobby by the president of a company when I was trying to sell the S.T.A.R.E system. We shook hands and I said, "The president of the company; I'm honored. Please call me Steve."

"It's great to meet you, Steve. I typically don't sit in on these types of introductory meetings, but I have been assured that what you will be presenting will change the world. I heard this from a man I know to speak the truth. He wouldn't tell me what you are going to be presenting. I must say that this mystery has caused a lot of excitement. I have assembled all of our department heads, and they are eager to see what you have in store for us. They are awaiting your arrival upstairs. Shall we?"

Through the countless sales calls that I had done for the S.T.A.R.E system, I had become accustomed to walking into a room with a tough audience. Because I knew every aspect of the system that I had built, I knew with absolute certainty that I could address any questions that might have been asked. I didn't have that type of comfort when it came to the mini Alexander One. I had no option but to wing it as best I could. I was confident that every person in that room would be so overwhelmed with what I was about to show them, that the demonstration would speak for itself. With a smile, I said, "Lead the way, Mr.

Goldman."

Peter Goldman nodded at the security guard as we walked toward the elevator. Once we stepped on the elevator, Peter extended his face against an optical reader mounted on the side of the elevator.

"Given the type of work we do, we have oppressively tight security measures, which is why I chose to greet you in the lobby. I thought I would expedite you through all the security checks so we can get right down to business."

I could tell that Peter was excited about the meeting. I knew that it would live up to all the hype that had surrounded it. We arrived at the top floor of the building. We exited the elevator and Peter ushered me to the meeting room. It was a full house. The room had stadium style seating. The fifty or so seats were completely full. There was a table and a podium at the front of the room. I placed the plastic case on the table as Peter addressed the crowd.

"Well, I see that more than just the department heads decided to come to this presentation. I didn't remember extending the invitation to all of you."

The crowd chuckled a little bit. It seemed as though Peter Goldman was a genuinely good guy who cared and respected his employees. Instead of getting angry at the uninvited guests, he seemed to embrace them. I made the determination that Peter Goldman wasn't just a suit. He truly wanted to make a difference in the world and cultivated his people instead of playing the typical role of corporate president. I looked out at the faces in the crowd. There were people of all ages, races, and colors. The audience's nerdy appearance gave me the impression that they were comprised mainly from the research and development staff of Transtronics.

Peter began, "I want to thank you all for coming. As I am sure you are aware, a bit of a mystery has developed over our guest today. Even I do not even know what he is about to present. I've been assured by a very close friend that what we are about to see will change the transportation industry forever. I wouldn't believe this type of bold statement from very many people in the world; however, my friend, who will remain nameless, is one person I tend to believe. Without further delay, I present Mr. Steve Hamilton."

I felt like I was back at MIT listening to a lecture. The crowd gave me a round of applause. I decided to play to the excitement of the crowd before I broke into the presentation. Once the applause had died down, I began to speak.

"Wow! This is defiantly not what I had expected. I was expecting a couple of suits in a stuffy boardroom. I'm happy to see that so many people have taken an interest in what I have been working on. I have no doubt that you will enjoy what you are about to see."

The room was deadly silent. I could see that I was doing a good job at building up the suspense. I decided to give them a little more before I began.

"Imagine if I told you that what I have in this case could save the planet. I know what you are thinking. You would probably think that I was some type of lunatic. I can assure you that once you see what I have brought here today, you will never be the same again. In this case, I have the answer to one of the world's greatest problems. I have the solution that will eliminate the world's dependence on oil. The solution that I have developed is the only real solution that exists to this problem. The use of ethanol, solar, wind, electric, and other alternative fuel sources would only compound the current problems facing the world."

I paused to see if I was building up too much suspense. Some of the faces in the crowd looked a little skeptical. I decided now would be a good time to start reading the script in the EyeWonder. I walked over to the plastic case and opened it. The top of the case was facing the audience, so they couldn't view what was in it. I took the tablet PC out of the case and walked about ten feet away from the table. I pushed the power button on the tablet PC. The display turned on, and I entered in the number ten and pushed the Enter key.

The mini Alexander One shot up into the air and hovered perfectly silently ten feet above the table. The entire room let out a gasp in unison. I looked across the faces in the room. Not a single person who was in the room could seem to register what he or she were looking at. As I glanced at their faces, I eventually made my way to Peter Goldman. He sat there transfixed on the mini Alexander One. He took his eyes off of it just long enough to look over at me. I shot him a broad smile. His look said it all. He had a blank expression on his face. His mouth was wide open in awe. Knowing that I had everyone in that room in the palm of my hand, I continued to read from the script.

"Ladies and gentlemen, please say hello to the Alexander One. The Alexander One is the first geomagnetic vehicle on the planet. Within its architecture lies the answer to the world's problems."

No one said a word. I walked over to Peter and held the PC tablet six inches in front of his face. I pressed a button on the PC tablet and said, "Don't move, Mr. Goldman, OK?"

Peter Goldman didn't respond. I was confident that it would have taken a bulldozer to move him at that moment. I walked back a couple of feet and pressed the key on the PC tablet labeled Call. The mini Alexander One shot like a bullet across the room and stopped six inches from Peter's face. The crowd in the upper rows rose to their feet to follow the action. Peter almost went cross-eyed when the Alexander One stopped in front of him. As he looked in amazement, I continued to read from the script.

"As you can see, the Alexander One has been fully developed and works pretty well."

This comment caused a slight laugh out of the crowd. I pushed a button on the PC tablet labeled Return. The Alexander One hurtled back across the room and came to rest at its original position ten feet above the table. There was the sound of grumbling as the crowd discussed what they had just seen. I let this continue for a couple of minutes. Once I had given the crowd a little time to digest what they had just seen, I decided to bring order back to the meeting.

"Ladies and gentlemen! Ladies and gentlemen, please!"

My yell had caused the room to go silent. All eyes were on me as I began to speak. "I know that everyone must have some questions about what they have just seen."

A young kid toward the back of the room yelled out, "You bet your ass we have some questions, Mr. Hamilton."

The people in the room let out a laugh. This kid had just said what everyone must have been thinking. Peter then chimed in and addressed the outburst. "Please, people. Try to control yourselves until Mr. Hamilton has finished his presentation."

I nodded at Peter to show him my appreciation. With a wide smile, he nodded back as if to say, "Please continue." The attendees took Peter's command to heart and quieted down. I proceeded, "I would like to spend a couple of minutes to explain the fundamental principles of how the Alexander One works. As I said earlier, the Alexander One is a geomagnetic vehicle. It works using the earth as a magnet. The science behind it is fairly simple. The Alexander One is basically a counter-magnet to the earth. Although the concept is pretty easy to understand, the difficult part to solve was its positioning relative to the earth's magnetic field. This is where the bulk of my focus was spent during development."

I could see that the explanation that had been scripted for me was confusing to some of the people in the room. I decided to go off script and explain it in terms that they would better understand.

We spent the next hour discussing the Alexander One. I really enjoyed myself and felt completely comfortable with the audience. They appeared to be very bright and showed obvious excitement at the prospects of the Alexander One.

As we wrapped up the meeting, I decided that it was probably best not to linger in discussion as the crowd disbursed. I motioned to Peter to walk me out before the crowd had a chance to block my escape. He picked up on my sign immediately.

Peter escorted me to the elevator. He couldn't stop raving about what he had just seen. "I've never seen anything like that in my life. There is absolutely no doubt in my mind that what you showed us today will change the world for the better. I would do anything if you allowed me the opportunity to help you bring the Alexander One to market. Anything!"

Peter was a good guy. I'm sure what I said next saddened him greatly. I took out the business card that Jonah had given me and said, "I have several more meetings scheduled to present the Alexander One. I'm sure others will be interested as well. Here's my business card. Develop a plan for how you would intend to bring the Alexander One to market and I will consider it carefully."

Peter took the card and had a look of disappointment on his face. We reached the lobby of the office building and he followed closely behind me as I walked toward the front entrance. I turned to him before he could speak.

"Peter, I can see that you have a close bond with your employees. There's no question in my mind that this is one of the main factors that will go into my decision making process. I have to know that I can trust the company I choose to partner with. From what I observed in the meeting, you seem like a very trustworthy individual. This will be weighed heavily when I make my decision, I promise. I'm sure you must realize that Transtronics is not the only company out there that would jump at this opportunity. Think about how you would approach the rollout and give me a call."

I felt bad about saying this to Peter. The truth was that I really hoped that whatever Loyal's plan was for the Alexander One, it involved Peter.

Peter said, "I'm very confident that the plan I come up with will knock the cover off the ball, Steve."

Peter extended his hand and said, "Thank you so much for taking the time to speak with us today. I'm positive that my team will jump at any opportunity you extended to us."

"I really enjoyed it," I said as I shook his hand. I turned and started walking toward the parking garage across the street.

As I walked away, I heard Peter yelling in my direction. "You won't be sorry if you choose us Steve, I promise."

I smiled at the unabashed display of public begging as I crossed the street. I made my way to the top floor of the parking garage. Things had gone very well in the meeting and my spirits were high.

Jonah must have sensed that I was pleased, because he said, "You look happy."

I got in the Alexander Two. As soon as I was situated, Jonah started up the Alexander Two and quickly left Atlanta. Once we were out of any possible danger, Jonah began to talk in a very excited voice. "You did very, very well."

"How do you know the meeting went well?"

"There's a camera and microphone embedded in the mini Alexander One. I watched the whole thing. You were terrific!"

I wasn't completely surprised by this revelation. "I think it went really well. Everyone was obviously very impressed."

"Of course they would be, but you sold it so well. You are a natural."

I took what Jonah had just said as a compliment. I was happy that he had cheered up when compared with his mood this morning. We spent the rest of the flight discussing the particulars of the meeting. Jonah was nearly in tears when he described the look on Peter's face as the Alexander One stopped six inches from his nose. The pleasant conversation made the flight back to the island go by very fast. I was relieved that things had gone so well and that I would soon be seeing Risa again.

We touched down on the island at a little before midnight local time. Jonah said that everyone had held off eating dinner until we arrived. We went inside the main dwelling and headed toward the dining room. The anticipation of seeing Risa was rising. Jonah and I entered the dining room. Risa was standing in the corner talking to Loyal. My jaw almost dropped to the floor when I saw her.

She looked unbelievably sexy. Her curly brown hair was expertly done up in a bun. Long strands of hair draped down the side of her face. She had on bright red lipstick that accentuated her perfect white smile. She must have lain out in the sun all day, because her skin possessed an even darker tan than it did that morning. She was wearing a long, black evening dress that hugged her body in all the right places. Her beauty overwhelmed both Jonah and me as we entered the room. We both stood at the door staring at her. She turned and looked in our direction. Our eyes connected from across the room. I saw the sparkle of a diamond necklace that was positioned perfectly around her neck. She was so beautiful I almost fell over. Before I could make my way over to her, Loyal raised a flute of champagne in the air and said, "To our heroes who have returned so gallantly from the field of battle."

Risa gave me a devious little smile as she lifted her glass of champagne and took a sip. Jonah handed me a glass. Loyal walked over as I continued to look at Risa. He stopped in front of Jonah and me and said, "I'm very pleased with your performance today, Ethan. You did a perfect job."

I looked to Loyal and said, "Thank you, Loyal. Your approval means everything to me. I really didn't want to let you down."

"I noticed that you strayed quite a bit from the script."

I suddenly had a feeling of concern, but it quickly passed when I heard what Loyal said next.

"It was brilliant. You assessed the situation and you took the absolutely correct steps to address it. I doubt very highly that anyone could have done better then you in that meeting."

Risa must have felt a little left out of the conversation. She came toward our little huddle and stood behind Loyal.

Loyal said, "Jonah, I need to discuss a couple of things with you. Do you have a moment?"

Loyal led Jonah to the other side of the dining room in an obvious attempt to give Risa and me some time to catch up.

She glided closer and said, "Well, Mr. Hero, I'm glad to see that your meeting went well." Risa leaned over and gave me a slight peck on the cheek.

A waft of her perfume pleasantly tickled my nostrils. I had to concentrate to maintain control of my bodily urges. As she withdrew from this innocent kiss, I looked at her and said, "There are no words that I can use to describe how unbelievably beautiful you look tonight."

Risa blushed. She used her pale blue eyes to scan me from head to toe before she responded. "You don't look that bad yourself, sexy."

"God, grant me the strength to make it through this dinner quickly," I thought. Her words, the way in which she said them, could mean only one thing. I needed to change the subject before I lost all control. "It looks like you had a good time today."

Her response was excited and unrehearsed. "Today was incredible. It started with a full body massage and only got better from there. After the message, I tanned on the beach for a while. When I came back to the house, there were closets full of beautiful clothes to try on. I then was treated to a personal spa. I had my hair, nails, and makeup done. Then I picked out this dress for you. Do you like it?"

Risa batted her eyes at me and struck a sexy model-like pose.

I almost stuttered when I responded. "Do I like the dress? Are you kidding me? If you only knew what I was thinking right now. For lack of better words, you are simply the most beautiful woman I have ever seen."

I put my hand on her hip. The satiny fabric of the dress drove me wild. I leaned in and gave her a small kiss. I was completely caught up in the moment when Loyal interrupted.

"Who here is hungry–for food?"

The pause in Loyal's comment caused Risa and me to laugh. I felt like a teenager who had just been caught by my parents. We shifted our focus off each other and onto Loyal.

Loyal motioned to the table and said, "Come, let us dine upon today's small victory."

Risa and I sat across from each other, which afforded us the opportunity to shoot each other dirty looks throughout the course of dinner. The food was good and the company was great. I was relieved see that Risa was enjoying the company of her newfound friends. The conversation at dinner covered many wide-ranging topics. We seamlessly made the transition into new areas of conversation. The conversation was never forced and it flowed very naturally. I had experienced this only with people I had known for a long time. It wasn't until the dinner was coming to a close that Loyal said something that surprised me.

"It's very easy for me to see that you two have formed a very strong relationship over the past couple of days."

The blunt comment took both Risa and me by surprise. We both looked in Loyal's direction as he elaborated on his thoughts.

"There's nothing more important in this world then true love. If one has love–"

Loyal was cut off in mid-sentence. He started to cough violently.

Jonah rose from his chair with a look of concern. He walked behind Loyal and put his hand on Loyal's shoulder. Jonah leaned over Loyal and said, "Are you all right?"

Loyal waved his hand in the air. He got the coughing fit under control and took a drink of water. In a hoarse voice, Loyal said, "Yes, yes. I'm fine, Jonah. Please sit back down. I'm not going anywhere."

Jonah did as instructed.

Loyal took a couple of seconds to clear his throat. Once he looked a little better, he said, "I just got a tickle in my throat. I'm fine."

The rough nature in which Loyal had been coughing had given everyone at the table a scare. We all relaxed as he continued what he was saying before the fit started.

"As I was saying, I can see very clearly that you two are in love. Hold on to that feeling and make it last."

Risa and I looked at each other. What Loyal had just said was the obvious truth. It was a little embarrassing to hear out loud, but it was undeniable.

Within a couple of minutes after Loyal's statement, the dinner party that I had so enjoyed broke up. Risa and I retreated to our rooms for what promised to be another night of incredible passion.

CHAPTER TWENTY-SEVEN

Hans Schmick was in his office meeting with two Saudi Arabian royals when Simon entered. Hans had a look of incredulity when he saw the interruption. He took one look at Simon and cut his meeting short. Simon would have never interrupted such an important meeting if the reason wasn't earth-shattering. Hans apologized profusely to the two Saudi royals. "I'm afraid something extremely pressing has come up that I must address right away. Would you consider postponing the rest of our discussion until later today gentlemen? I have something upstairs that will keep you occupied until then."

The two Saudis looked at each other and smiled. Hans's extra-circular activities were the main reason the men traveled to Germany instead of forcing Hans to come to Saudi Arabia. Hans had always gone above and beyond with the women he chose for his guests. They were often young models in desperate need of money. Blond and blue-eyed girls were very hard to come by in the Middle East. In Germany, they were in abundance. Hans would pay upwards of one hundred thousand dollars a day for the girls who were not typically prostitutes. For that amount of money, very few of the models could resist.

The two men couldn't get out of the room fast enough.

Hans pressed a button to call his secretary on the intercom. "Hello,

Lee. Could you escort our guests upstairs and ensure they have everything they need?"

"Right away, Mr. Schmick"

The two gentlemen fled the room with growing anticipation on their faces. They couldn't wait to see whom Hans had chosen for today's entertainment.

Now that the two guests were pleasantly distracted, Simon closed the door to Hans's office and said, "Sir, I know you hate to be bothered during such important meetings, but there is something you really need to see. I didn't think it could wait."

This piqued Hans's interest. He motioned Simon to come and sit down in a chair across from his desk. Simon walked over and chose to stand to deliver the update.

"We have a very significant development pertaining to Plan Alpha."

Before Simon could continue, Hans cut him off and said, "Did this Loyal person call Dean Bouchard back?"

Simon could barely contain his excitement when he continued. "Even better, sir."

What could be better then hearing directly from the creator of the Alexander One again? Hans decided to let Simon continue uninterrupted.

"We received this a little over an hour ago." Simon held up a USB memory stick.

"What's that?"

"This is a USB memory stick. It is like a floppy disk you put in a computer."

Hans was not the most technical person. He only learned just enough about computers to survive. He had no idea what a USB memory stick was, so he said, "Get on with it Simon. Save me the explanation and tell me what caused you to interrupt my meeting."

Simon walked over to the flat panel TV. It was sitting on top of a credenza in the corner of the office. He plugged the pen drive into the USB port on the side of the TV and said, "The USB device isn't what I wanted to show you. The video footage on it is what is going to make you very happy, sir."

Hans walked over to the TV as the video started. He saw a man in a meeting room talking to an audience of fifty or so people. He listened intently as the meeting progressed. As soon as the camera caught a glimpse of the curious object floating in the middle of the room, Hans nearly fell to the floor. Hans asked his trusted colleague, "Is that what I think it is?"

Simon couldn't contain his excitement any longer. He nearly yelled when he spoke. "Without a doubt, you are looking at a miniaturized version of the Alexander One."

Hans was dumbfounded as he continued to watch the video. The small aircraft zipped across the room as if it were a controlled bullet. The tiny aircraft stopped right next to an audience member's face, and then shot right back to its place over the table. Hans then asked, "Where did you get this video?"

"You'll never believe it if I told you, sir."

Hans momentarily took his eyes off the video to shoot Simon a cold stare. The games Simon was playing were starting to irritate Hans.

Simon must have seen the look and continued the update. "About six hours ago, a man named Steve Hamilton waltzed into one of our advanced research firms and made this presentation."

Hans was in shock over what he just heard. Impossible, he thought. Simon continued his briefing. "This footage was taken at Transtronics. It's one of our research think tanks located in Atlanta, Georgia. The presentation is spectacular, but that isn't the most interesting thing on the video."

Hans looked at Simon with growing anticipation. Hans greeted Simon's pause with another impatient look.

Simon continued. "The most interesting thing on the video is the true identity of Steve Hamilton. Facial recognition proves with ninety-nine point nine percent accuracy that Steve Hamilton is actually Ethan Kravis."

Hans's knees buckled as he looked for a chair. Simon rushed to get a chair and bring it to Hans. Simon slid the chair under Hans as he sat. Hans was deep in thought when he spoke next.

"Are you saying that the man we have been conducting a world-wide hunt for strolled into one of my companies and gave a presentation on the very invention seven of the world's most powerful men are spending millions to destroy?"

"That's what I'm saying, sir."

Hans's mind was bombarded with millions of questions. There were so many questions this turn of events had caused that he was nearly paralyzed by information overflow. Before his mind had a chance to completely shut down from the overload, he started to ask Simon some of the questions that were forming. "Why now?"

Simon looked perplexed with the question. He asked, "What do you mean 'Why now'?"

"Why did Steve Hamilton decide to present the Alexander One now?"

"Perhaps he could sense that Dean Bouchard was closing in on him and he had to take action."

Hans thought that Simon had provided a logical explanation. Hans decided to challenge Simon with another question.

"Do you think that Ethan Kravis is actually the Loyal character that Dean Bouchard has been speaking with?"

"I can tell you with certainty that they are not the same people. I had our communication techs run the video against the voiceprint from the intercepted call. The voice of Ethan Kravis on the video does not match the voice from the intercepted call."

Hans was impressed with Simon's thoroughness. He continued his line of questioning. "Were we able to locate Ethan Kravis after the meeting?"

"No, sir. We received the video too late after the meeting had concluded."

"Who sent us the video?"

"No one at the company sent us the video. It was discovered during the nightly backup process. All of the company's data is stored on remote servers for disaster recovery purposes. This is how we keep tabs on our shell companies without directly interfering in the business. Transtronics, along with our other companies, back up their data to our data centers in Germany. We have specialized programs that run through all the data and flag anything that may be of interest."

Hans had invented the process long ago, so he knew it all too well. This was how the council could control so much of the world's oil. The council controlled the flow of information and information was power. Hans skipped forward to his next question. "Do we have any additional leads?"

Simon smiled. He turned off the video and advanced to the next piece of data stored on the USB drive. "We're lucky that Transtronics uses CRM software, or we probably wouldn't have gotten our hands on this piece of information."

The TV screen displayed an imprint of a business card. Hans looked at it like it was a brick of gold he had found in a pile of horse manure.

Simon continued. "Transtronics uses an electronic CRM system.

CRM stands for Customer Relationship Management. This software is basically a huge contact database used to store all the contact details Transtronics does business with. We found this business card in the president's private contact list."

Hans stared at it for a moment. It was the business card of Steve Hamilton. The business card was very plain. It said only his name and a phone number. Hans asked, "Did you try to find out anything about the phone number?"

"Yes, sir. We didn't attempt to call it yet. We contacted the local phone company and tried to find out who owns the number. They said the number doesn't exist."

"What do you mean?"

"Phone numbers in the United States have eleven digits if you include a one at the beginning of the number. The number on the business card has twelve digits. It's not an international number, either. Our techs think that it's an IP address."

Hans looked confused and asked, "A what?"

"IP address stands for Internet protocol address. IP addresses are used for many things, including secure satellite phone transmissions. When you enter the address into the right equipment, it can open a secure line of communication with another party."

Hans pondered this revelation. He really didn't know much about computers, but he trusted his loyal confidant. "Do we have the needed equipment to make the call here at the house?"

Without hesitation, Simon responded. "We can make the call anytime, sir. Just tell me when and where, and I'll set it up."

Hans decided that there was no time like the present. He turned to Simon and said, "I'm going to watch the video of the presentation a couple of times. When I am finished, I would like to make that phone call from the communications room. That should give you a couple of hours to prepare for the call. I want the call recorded, and I want a trace done."

Simon nodded. "Everything will be ready to go by the time you have completed your analysis of the video."

As Simon was leaving the office to go make the necessary preparations, Hans stopped him and said, "How do you get the video back on the screen?"

Simon glanced over to the TV screen. The image of the business card was still displayed. He walked over to the TV remote and turned on the video. He explained to Hans how to operate the controls to fast forward, rewind, pause, and restart the video.

Once Hans got the hang of using the remote control, he said, "Be prepared to make the call in two hours."

Simon nodded and left the office.

Hans watched the video twice. He was amazed at what he saw and heard. Ethan Kravis was a natural salesman. He was charismatic and full of energy when he spoke. He built an immediate relationship with the audience. Most of all, he truly believed in his product. "Why shouldn't he?" Hans thought. It's only one of the greatest inventions mankind has ever seen. Hans was excited at the prospect of talking to its creator. He had no doubt that the IP address Simon had described led to the man known as Loyal.

After Hans had viewed the entire video three times, he had seen enough. He turned off the TV and withdrew the USB drive from its side. Hans didn't want anyone to accidentally see the valuable video on the device. He walked to his desk and called down to the communications room. Simon answered the phone on the first ring.

Hans asked, "Are we set up down there?"

Simon replied, "Ready any time you are, sir."

Within a couple of minutes, Hans was in the communications

room. He sat down in front of the phone receiver and waited for Simon to provide his direction.

Simon began to speak. "I thought it best that we have no one else in the room. The communications analyst explained to me what I needed to do to place the call. I'm ready anytime you are, sir."

Hans spent the last two hours thinking about what he would say if someone answered the phone. He couldn't remember the last time he felt this nervous. He collected his thoughts one last time and said, "Place the call."

Simon hit a couple of buttons and said, "Pick up the phone receiver, and you should hear the call being placed."

Hans picked up the receiver and held it to his ear. He heard the phone ringing. It rang about seven times before it was finally answered. The man's voice on the other end sounded like the man Dean Bouchard had talked with. Hans knew that he couldn't mention the call that he had intercepted between Dean Bouchard and this man named Loyal. He decided to play it dumb. When the call was answered, he began to speak. "Hello, is this Steve Hamilton?"

There was a pause on the line that caused Hans's heart to skip a beat. The man on the other end finally spoke. "No, this isn't Steve Hamilton."

Hans took a calculated risk and said, "Oh. I'm terribly sorry. I must have dialed the wrong number."

Hans knew that one didn't accidentally dial the wrong satellite phone number. The equipment needed and the process taken was too complicated to make such an error. By saying this, he was hoping to elicit a specific response. If the person on the other end hung up, it would mean that he was waiting for a specific caller. If he responded, then Hans would know that he wanted to speak. Hans held his breath for a response.

"Satellite phones are rarely dialed incorrectly. To whom am I speaking?"

Hans knew that this man would find out his real name just as he had found out Dean's. He hoped that by being truthful at the outset of their relationship, it would build trust between them. Hans responded, "My name is Hans Schmick. Now that you know who I am, please tell me who you are."

"My name is Loyal, Mr. Schmick. How did you obtain this number?"

Hans thought of giving some convoluted answer, but again decided to tell the truth. "I own Transtronics. I just reviewed some video that was taken today in one of our meeting rooms. Needless to say, the presentation provided by Steve Hamilton has caused quite a commotion. It is you that I have to thank for this, isn't it, Loyal?"

Instead of answering Hans's question, Loyal replied with an unexpected question of his own. "I was led to believe that Transtronics was owned by the Macktel Corporation. Are you sure you want to start this conversation off with a lie, Mr. Schmick?"

Hans thought about his answer carefully before responding. He knew that if he told Loyal about how his shell companies operated, it might jeopardize the anonymity that the council had carefully crafted over the last thirty-two years. However, he couldn't lead Loyal to believe that he was a liar. Hans responded in a simple, yet vague manner. "I have many business interests that span many different companies. Transtronics happens to be one of those companies in which I have a vested interest."

"I see. Why are you calling?"

Hans was confused by the question when he responded. "I thought the reason would be clear. I'm very interested in the Alexander One. If you were in a position to discuss a possible partnership, then I would love to have that conversation. Are you in that position, Loyal?"

"I am indeed in a position to determine the fate of the Alexander One, Mr. Schmick. What is it that you propose?"

Hans was surprised when Loyal asked the question so bluntly. Hans knew that the conversation may eventually come to this, but he was caught off-guard when it had happened so quickly. He scrambled for the reply that he had worked up earlier. "I'm prepared to offer you everything that you need to bring the Alexander One safely to market. With my resources, we could have the Alexander One mass produced within a matter of months. You will not have to spend one cent in this effort. If you sign an exclusivity deal with me, I'm prepared to give you seventy-five percent of the profit that the Alexander One generates. With no out of pocket expenses and seventy-five percent of the profit, I know for a fact that no one will be able to match my offer."

There was a pause while the offer floated out in the air for a bit. Hans knew that his offer was too good to pass up. There was no way that Loyal could turn him down.

Loyal began to speak after thirty seconds of consideration. "That's a very impressive offer. I'm almost inclined to accept the offer right now. However, it's recently come to my attention that there are some very dangerous men who are after my invention. This has caused me to become a little paranoid, I'm afraid. I don't think that I can proceed with any deal until I'm certain that these men no longer wish to bring me harm. Do you understand my concerns?"

Hans knew perfectly what Loyal had just said. He quickly responded so that he could keep the conversation moving in a positive direction. "I can truly sympathize with your reluctance to proceed. What if I were to tell you that I know those men personally, and I could guarantee that your concerns would be addressed permanently?"

"I would say that if you could provide proof that this concern was addressed permanently, I would have no other choice but to accept the generous offer that you have made."

Hans felt a wave of joy flow over him. He could almost taste the victory. He responded in an almost hysterical voice. "Loyal, I have a feeling that we will make a wonderful team. I will need a couple of days to obtain it, but you will soon receive proof that these men will no longer be of any concern to you. Once I address this issue, should I contact you using the same method as this call?"

"I will be eagerly awaiting your call, Mr. Schmick. Until then."

"I look forward to it. Please call me Hans. Partners address each other as equals. I cannot wait to change the world with you, Loyal."

"And I you, Hans."

The line went dead. Hans looked over a Simon and said, "We got him. This deal is as good as done, Simon!"

The joy that Hans was exhibiting was contagious. Simon started clapping at the performance Hans had just given. Simon said, "Bravo, sir. You really closed that deal. Excellent, sir."

It was a little too soon to celebrate. Hans thought about his next move. How was he going to prove to Loyal that he was no longer in danger? He knew that merely killing the rest of the council members wouldn't provide proof. After all, the world didn't know who the men truly were. What would it matter if the world knew who these men were after they were dead? The council would be permanently disbanded at that point. Hans had all the records needed to prove who these men really were. The plan was simple. He would call an emergency meeting of the council and have them killed. He would put together some documentation for Loyal that explained who these men really were. Once Loyal was comfortable that his life was no longer in danger, Hans would work with Loyal until the first production version of the Alexander One was ready. Once that happened, Hans could easily have a terrible accident befall his new partner. Hans would then control the greatest invention ever witnessed by man.

The plan was perfect. It was very doable for Hans to execute. The only difficulty would be to secretly strike a deal with the security firm that was put in charge of the council meetings. This was one aspect of the plan Hans would not have full control over. He needed to somehow coerce the security firm to allow the assassinations to occur. Hans would give this some thought over the next day and arrive at an answer. For now, he would celebrate his minor victory.

CHAPTER TWENTY-EIGHT

I stared at Risa as she lay next to me quietly sleeping. She was everything I was looking for in a woman. She was drop dead gorgeous for starters, but her looks only triggered my lust. I realized that I loved her for reasons that extended far beyond her looks. There was just a feeling that I got when I was around her. I can't really explain what this feeling was because I had never experienced it before. The only thing I knew for certain was that I wanted to spend every minute of every day with this woman for the rest of my life.

Risa opened her eyes. I felt a little weird at first. I could only imagine how uncomfortable I would be if our roles would have been reversed. Risa covered her face as she smiled and said, "What are you doing?"

I was caught. I decided to go with it.

"I was just staring at you to assure myself that I wasn't dreaming."

Risa came out from behind her self-made disguise and said, "Well I thought that you were supposed to wake up from a dream if someone pinched you. I know I did more than pinch you last night."

I let out a laugh and said, "You sure did, Ms. Castleberry."

Risa laughed.

"I'm sure you hear this from lots of guys, but you are the most beautiful thing I have ever had the privilege of laying my eyes upon."

I was a little embarrassed at my cheesy line, but it was the absolute truth. She was simply the most amazingly sexy and beautiful woman I had ever seen. Risa didn't seem embarrassed by the comment.

"I hear that at least twice a day. You are going to have to come up with a better line than that to get in my pants, mister." She let out a playful giggle. She looked under the covers of the bed and said, "Oh. You must be very smooth. It looks like I don't have any pants on to get into."

Her flirting was driving me crazy with excitement. I really wanted to focus on learning more about this mysterious woman I had fallen head over heels with. As much as I wanted to spend every second of every day making love to her, I needed to build up the non-physical side of our relationship. To date, our relationship was almost all physical mixed in with some moments of sheer terror. This type of relationship doesn't last forever. I needed to get to know Risa, or this whirlwind lust-driven relationship might start to lose steam. I continued along the lines the conversation was headed.

"I know that it sounds cheesy, but I'm serious. Last night when I saw you in that dress, I really was thinking that I had never seen anything so beautiful."

I decided to cool it. I had no doubt she knew how beautiful she looked. I couldn't run the risk of overstating the obvious.

"I know that you probably say that to every girl you bring to a private island in a top secret flying magnet."

I was glad to see that she responded in a joking way. She said something that surprised me.

"You know that you are pretty damn sexy yourself, Mr. Kravis. I know without a shadow of a doubt that you definitely don't have any problems with the ladies. You looked like a male model in that suit last night."

I was taken aback by her comments. I really didn't know how to respond. I was happy when Risa continued to speak.

"How did a man of science get such a nice body? I thought all of you guys were little nerds who walked around with pocket protectors. I've never met a six-foot-four-inch nerd with a body like yours."

I was embarrassed at this excessively nice observation. Girlfriends of my past had made similar comments, but I never took them too seriously. I thought that they were just being nice. I decided to respond with a sense of modesty. "The truth is that my lab provides all the workout I need during the day. Whether it is moving equipment around or running around collecting results, I seem to always go home exhausted."

"You are solid muscle and have quite a lot of stamina. Whatever you have been doing, you should keep it up."

"How about you? I know that you must work very hard to maintain that amazing body of yours. What do you do to keep such an amazing figure?"

I saw that Risa was flattered by my observation. "During the school year, it is pretty easy. I get a crazy workout trying to keep up with my students. I'm typically exhausted by the end of the day. During summer break, I try to go to the gym at least three times a week."

I decided to give her a taste of her own medicine when I spoke next. "Well, whatever you have been doing, you should keep it up."

She gave me a love tap in the chest and said, "Don't make fun of me. The truth is that I haven't had a solid relationship for a long time. I'm a little rusty, not a smooth operator like you. Nobody has a pickup line that good. Hey, baby, want to take a ride in my spaceship?"

I laughed at her little joke. "Ha! Did you like that one?"

She followed up her first joke with another joke. In a deep voice she said, "Hey, baby, stick with me, and I'll show you the world."

I was in a full out laughing fit that I couldn't contain. My laugh must have been contagious, because she starting laughing as well. As I gasped for air, I said, "Stop! Stop! You are going to make me pee."

We settled down after a minute of intense laughter, and she became serious and said, "You really didn't need any of those smooth lines. I fell pretty hard for you as soon as I saw you in that store. I could have sworn you said the word 'laughter' out loud. This is what really caught my attention. After I took one look into your beautiful blue eyes, I was hooked. I knew it as soon as I looked at you."

I knew she meant what she had said. I felt the same way. I looked into her eyes and said, "I felt the same thing. I couldn't explain the feeling I had if you asked me now. Something just clicked. Does that sound weird?"

She held my stare when she spoke. "It's the sanest thing I have heard over the past couple of days. I felt it too. It was like I was drawn to you. Like all the planets had aligned and we were destined to meet. It was like fate, if you believe in that sort of thing."

"I never believed in fate before. But with all that has happened, I'm not so sure anymore."

Risa and I continued to look at each other without saying anything. It was like a magnet was drawing us together and wouldn't allow us to separate. I lost track of time, but it must have been a full minute or two since last we spoke. Risa leaned into me and gave me a simple kiss. She then popped out of bed and said, "Let's go for a walk on the beach."

Risa stood there egging me on. All I could do was look at her perfectly tanned body. She leaned over and grabbed my arm.

"C'mon, lazy bones. There will be plenty of time for that later. Let's enjoy the amazing tropical weather."

Risa literally dragged me out of bed. Her petite one-hundred-and-five-pound frame was a lot stronger then it appeared. Once she dragged me out of bed, she led me to the shower. We took a long, hot shower while we took turns washing each other's bodies. Every swipe of the soapy washcloth was a new adventure. I could have stood in that shower all day, but she finally turned off the water. She exited the shower and threw a towel in my face.

"Dry off, hot stuff," she said as she used a towel to start drying off her legs.

I really liked her take-charge attitude. If it were up to me, I would have lain in bed until we both had no option but to leave the room. As I dried myself off, Risa walked over to the armoire. She picked out a solid blue swimsuit and a Hawaiian floral shirt. She threw the items on the bed and said, "Put those on."

I looked over at the items she had chosen and said, "Do I look like Magnum P.I. to you?

She smiled and said, "Oh, who cares what you are wearing? This island is about as private as you are ever going to get. No one will see. Besides, I think you will look cute in them. The shirt will accentuate your eyes."

As long as she thought I looked good, I didn't really care what I was wearing. I walked over to the bed and put the swim trunks and shirt on. When I looked over at Risa, she was just finishing adjusting her tiny black bikini. The sight of her in that tiny bikini made my heart beat faster. I said, "Yikes! Did you ever think of becoming a swimsuit model instead of a schoolteacher? You must drive your students crazy with a body like yours."

She smiled and struck a pose as if she were modeling it for me. When she was finished, she walked over and kissed me on the top of my head. I was sitting on the end of the bed, and she stood in front of me. I couldn't help myself. I pulled her toward me and started to kiss her perfectly flat stomach. Risa grabbed my head with both of her hands and said, "The beach. If you keep doing that, we'll never make it to the beach."

I was happy with her apparent self-control. That fact was that it would be good to get out of the room and enjoy a relaxing day on the beach. Risa walked over to the closet and put on a black tie-wrap skirt over her bikini bottom. She then put on a halter top to cover up the top of her bikini. She turned to me and said, "All set?"

I motioned to the door and said, "After you, gorgeous."

Risa meandered toward the door. I followed behind her. She was about to open the door when she suddenly spun around and grabbed me. She used the lapels of my ridiculous shirt to pull me close. We kissed. Without warning, she pushed me back and said, "Sorry about that. We're going to the beach."

Risa adjusted her skirt and turned around. She opened the door and I stood there for a second. That blatant sexual outburst left me yearning for her again. What she had just done wasn't fair to me. I figured that maybe she was conflicted about whether she really wanted to leave the room. Well, it was too late now. I exited the room and caught up to her. As we approached the front door, David the butler intercepted our escape. He positioned himself in front of the massive wooden doors that led to the outside. I thought that maybe he would interrupt Risa's and my plans to go out to the beach. I was relieved when he spoke.

"Good morning, Mr. Kravis. Would you or Ms. Castleberry care for some breakfast?"

Risa and I stopped. She looked at me. I decided to respond.

"Risa and I thought that we would do some exploring on the beach. Would it be possible to have some food sent out there? If it will be a problem, please don't go to any trouble."

"No trouble at all. What type of food would you like me to send out?

"I'd like some fresh fruit, if you have some. If not, I'm sure anything will do. Risa, do you want anything in particular?"

Risa looked at David and smiled. For the first time since I met David, he smiled back. Risa was truly astonishing. She had that affect on people. People instantly took a liking to her. Last night when Jonah and I arrived at dinner, I could see that Loyal had really been enjoying her company as well. Perhaps in Loyal's case, it was a little easier to understand. After all, he didn't seem to leave the island that much. The company of a young, exceedingly beautiful woman would make it an easy sell. But I could tell that Loyal was truly happy to talk to Risa.

Risa began, "Good morning, David. If it wouldn't be too much trouble, maybe I could have one of those delicious fruit smoothies that you made for me yesterday."

"It would be my pleasure, Ms. Castleberry."

"I told you yesterday to call me Risa. There's no need to be so formal with me, David." Risa gently patted David on his arm.

David let out a beaming smile and said, "As you wish, Risa." David nodded. He seemed as smitten with Risa as I was. As David looked over to me, I saw his smile disappear and his normal stoic face appear in its place. He said, "If that will be all, I will go make arrangements to have your breakfast brought out to the seating area on the beach."

David did a sharp about-face and walked away. I looked over to Risa, and we both giggled. We exited the front door and were immediately met with a blast of tropical humid air. It was only ten o'clock local time, but already it must have been pushing one hundred degrees.

"Holy Christ, it is like Dante's inferno out here," I said as I started to waft my shirt.

"Oh, don't be such a baby. You'll get used to it. If you are good, I'll let you apply some baby oil when we start to sun ourselves."

Risa looked back at me and gave me one of her devious smiles. The looks she gave me made my heart flutter. It usually took me at least two or three months in a relationship to get those kinds of looks. Our bond had grown so close in such a short amount of time, that I was sure that she was the one. It was so natural that it felt almost too right. I felt like I had known Risa for years, even though I had known her only for a couple of days. I responded to her frolicsome little taunt. "You have to stop putting those images in my head. I won't be able to control my actions."

"If you lost control, it would make us even, based on what I did to you that first night."

Again she was taunting me with sexually charged images. That first night was the most incredible night of my life. A piece of me left my body and would never return for as long as I lived.

Risa seemed to know where she was going. She led me right down to the beach and over to a small dining table that had been set up. I commented, "You seem to have mapped out this place pretty well."

"I had some time to explore yesterday while you were off saving the world." Risa smiled as we took a seat at the table. "This Island is so beautiful. It's almost a shame that others will most likely never get to experience it. I feel really fortunate to have been invited to stay here."

I could tell that Risa meant what she said.

She scanned the area. "Sights like this that makes it easy to fight for the survival of the world. Back in Philadelphia, you kind of lose perspective. You turn on the news, and all you hear is that so and so was murdered last night or such and such exploded. If what you say is the truth about the Alexander One, you really could do a lot to save all of this." Risa raised her arms and motioned to the ocean.

I wasn't sure where this all was coming from, but she seemed a little emotional about what she had said.

She then said, "Don't laugh at me. I know that I'm not making sense, but don't laugh."

I think Risa had interpreted my smile as a laugh. I quickly said, "I'm not laughing at you by any means. I was simply thinking that everything I will be doing, I will be doing for us. So that we can have kids and not have to worry if the world might end before they grow old and die."

I couldn't believe what had come out of my mouth. I had known Risa only for two days, and I had already mentioned kids. What is wrong with me? What was I thinking?

Risa responded in a reassuring tone. "Wow. Kids? Really? After two days?"

I quickly tried to backpedal. "Yeah, I don't know why I said that. I'm sorry. I was just trying to–I don't know. I was trying to–" I couldn't find the words. I was embarrassed.

She looked into my eyes and said, "I feel it too, you know."

"What?" I said.

"I feel it too. I don't know why, it's only been two days since we met. However, I feel like we were made for each other. I feel like it's a very real possibility that I would want to have your children."

It was my turn to be in shock. I couldn't believe what I had just heard. She said it so bluntly that it caused me to lose my concentration. Just as we shared that intensely adult moment, a servant came over and placed a ton of food on the table. I looked at the platters of food and I said, "My gosh, I hope others will be joining us."

Risa and I both laughed as the server kept putting down platters of food. There were bagels, eggs, sausage, biscuits, lox, cream cheese, and on and on. The food just kept on coming. It reminded me of a hotel buffet. The situation was so comical that it went a long way to break the tension of the serious discussion that Risa and I had been having.

When the servant was done, there was practically no room left on the table for our plates. I said to the young woman, "Most of this food will go to waste. Please take some of it back to the kitchen before it goes bad."

Risa and I chose a couple of items, and the rest was taken away. Once we were alone again, I decided not to bring up the subject of kids again unless she did. She sat staring at me as she drank her fruit smoothie. I decided to break the tension by saying, "Is that any good?"

Without a word, Risa got up and walked over to me with her fruit smoothie in hand. She jumped in my lap and took a sip. She then lowered her head and started to kiss me. I could taste the icy fruit drink from her mouth. When the fruity taste subsided after a moment, she leaned back and looked into my eyes. She said with a completely serious face, "I would really like to be the mother of your children."

This comment, if said by any other woman that I had ever known, would have made me throw the woman to the sandy beach and I would have run for the ocean. Instead, a warm feeling of calm passed over my body. I knew that she was the one. I knew that I wanted to spend the rest of my life with this woman. I was so sure of this, I said, "I love you."

The words felt so natural, that I wasn't scared at all when I said them. I saw a small tear in her eye and she said, "I love you too."

"This situation is crazy, isn't it?"

"What do you mean by that?" said Risa.

"I feel like I have been looking for someone like you my whole life. Now, we are caught up in this crazy situation, and you happen to come along. The timing is really bad."

Risa's body got tense. "Timing," she said with a hint of panic.

"What's wrong?"

"With all that has happened over the last couple of days, I forgot about my summer preparatory meeting. I need to be at my school tomorrow."

"What would happen if you miss the meeting?"

Risa shook her head and said, "I can't. It's too important. My students are counting on me. If I miss the meeting, I won't have enough material when they arrive back at school."

"C'mon. Do you think it would really hurt if the students didn't learn how to finger-paint for a couple of weeks?"

This comment was not sitting well with Risa. She pinched my arm and said, "Don't dismiss how important a schoolteacher's job can be. Who do you think will be running this world in thirty years? My third-graders do more than learn to finger-paint. They are at a precarious age. They are starting to learn how to interact peacefully with others. If they miss out on this lesson, you get things like, well, every war that has ever commenced throughout time. I have a duty to my students and I won't disappoint them."

Risa's conviction excited me. Her forceful statement only cemented my opinion that she was a fundamentally good human-being. She truly cared about her students. This made what I was about to say even more difficult. "I'm not sure if you will be able to attend your meeting. It will be too dangerous."

"I didn't ask for any of this to happen. I've really enjoyed my time with you. As much as I would like to stay here at the island with you, I can't. If you truly love me, you will help me convince Loyal that I need to go to Philadelphia tomorrow."

"How long will the meeting take?"

"Two-to-three hours max."

"Can you attend the meeting by phone?"

"No. It's a collaborative meeting. We construct the school's curriculum on a white board in the teacher's lounge. If I'm not there, I won't be able to see what is going up on the white board. I have to be there in person."

I took a deep breath. This situation just got much more complicated. It was clear that Risa's life would be in danger if she went back to Philadelphia, but who was I to stop her? She clearly had a strong opinion about what needed to be done. I kissed her on the cheek and said, "I'll talk to Loyal about it. We'll figure something out."

Risa hugged me and said, "If every argument we have can be settled so easily, you and I will have a great future together."

CHAPTER TWENTY-NINE

Dean Bouchard couldn't take his mind off of how close he was to achieving his goals. All that was left for him to do was to set up a meeting with the council and plan their executions. Dean had figured it all out. He would send out a meeting request to the council for a completely unrelated matter.

Over the past couple of years there had been several unexplained attacks on oil production facilities controlled by the council. These attacks occurred all over the world. The media had always blamed the attacks on disgruntled locals in the area of the facilities. However, the council knew that the attacks were planned and executed by someone or some organization far more intelligent than the below-average citizens of the area. The attacks required a highly coordinated break-ins and military-grade explosives, which ruled out the impoverished people who typically lived in the area of the production facilities.

Even with the near limitless resources, the council was still unable to identify the perpetrators. These attacks had always been counter to the council's goals. The council had always tried to keep the price of oil low. These attacks caused unwanted stress in the oil markets, which in turn raised the price of oil. Although it provided a higher profit margin for the council in the short term, members feared that the higher price of oil would expedite the rate at which the world looked for a fuel alternative.

Dean knew that finding the perpetrators of these attacks was paramount to the council. The council couldn't allow the attacks to continue, for fear of losing its grip on the world's primary energy supply. If Dean could convince the council that he had new information about the attackers, it would surely warrant an emergency meeting.

Dean walked into his office and locked the door. He withdrew his council-issued laptop and turned it on. He opened the Email inbox. Dean's eyes widened when he saw that he had an unread message. He became very confused by what he saw.

To All Council Members,

Re: Plan Alpha

In just a few short days, the special operation teams have preformed wonderfully in the tasks in which they have been assigned. I am happy to report that the subject of Plan Alpha has been fully addressed. I request an emergency meeting to fully brief the council on all the events that have transpired. Please make every effort to attend the meeting in person. The normal RSVP process is to be followed. As the process states, if everyone responds to this meeting request in the affirmative, no further communications will be sent. If someone is unable to attend the meeting or doesn't RSVP, the meeting will be rescheduled and a follow-up communication will be sent. The details of the meeting location are as follows:

When: Friday 12:00 P.M. MST

Where: Facility 61: Scottsdale, Arizona, USA

I know that this is only two days from now. Given the impact that this issue could have on the council's interests, I am confident that everyone will find the time to attend.

Truly,

Member Number One

Dean read the Email again. What had Hans meant when he said, "I am happy to report that the subject of Plan Alpha has been fully addressed?"

This latest turn of events was not sitting well with Dean. He couldn't figure out why Hans had sent out the invitation. Dean sat at his desk motionless, pondering what could have precipitated the communication.

Dean nearly knocked over his cup of tea when he heard his office phone ring. The loud ring jarred Dean, as he was deep in thought. Dean picked up the phone. "Yes?"

Albert's frantic voice shot through the phone receiver like a sonic boom. "Sir, we're getting another call down here in the Lockbox. It's coming in on the same IP address as the previous call."

Dean scrambled to shut down and lock up the council laptop. As Dean departed his office and made his way to the Lockbox, he couldn't help thinking that the message he had received and the timing of this call from Loyal was very curious. Had Hans somehow destroyed the Alexander One? Was Loyal calling him to tell Dean the bad news?

Dean's anxiety over the situation was growing exponentially. He needed some information, and he needed it now. He broke into a full jog as he made his way to the Lockbox. He desperately needed to talk with Loyal and didn't want to spoil his opportunity.

Dean made it from his office and into the command center of the Lockbox in record time. Brad was sitting at the console and Albert was standing beside him. Albert said, "He's still on the line."

Dean grabbed the receiver and in a winded and frantic voice said, "Hello? Hello? Are you there, Loyal?"

Neither Albert nor Brad had ever seen Dean act from a position of weakness before. The way in which Dean answered the phone shocked both of them.

A couple of seconds passed before Loyal began to speak. "Hello, Mr. Bouchard."

"Hello, Loyal. Everything all right?"

Dean winced. He had just given Loyal two indications that he knew something might have been wrong. The way in which Dean answered the phone and the question he asked would clearly indicate that he knew something about the situation was amiss.

"I'm afraid I have some bad news, Mr. Bouchard. I have decided to reconsider your proposal. New information has come to light, and I no longer feel that you can provide the type of protection that I require. I felt that I should make you aware of this decision as soon as possible. My decision is final. This will be the last time we talk."

Before Dean could say a word, the line went dead. Dean was furious. He threw the phone receiver in the direction of the closest wall. Instead of hitting the wall, the coiled phone cord caused the receiver to spring back toward the direction from which it had been thrown. The receiver hit a monitor on the console, cracking the glass screen. The phone receiver shattered in several large pieces. Albert and Brad stared at Dean with wide eyes.

Dean clinched both of his fists and screamed, "God damn it!"

Dean walked over to a small table off to the side of the command center. He wrapped both of his hands around the edge of the table and hoisted one side in the air. The papers on the table flew up in the air as the table crashed into the wall.

"Sir! Sir! Please calm down," pleaded Albert from across the room.

Dean looked over to Albert. There was fire in his eyes. Dean could feel himself slipping into a psychotic rage. His chest started heaving. He kicked some of the papers on the ground and nearly put his foot through the wall. He walked over to the pieces of shattered phone and stomped on them. A primitive battle cry filled the air of the Lockbox.

Dean focused his attention on Brad. Brad rolled his eyes at the outburst. Brad was a trained killer. He could easily handle Dean if it ever came to that. He was speechless when he heard what Dean said next.

"You! You did this to me!"

Dean pointed at Brad from across the room.

Brad quickly protested this accusation. "What? You think that I had something to do with this?"

Albert chimed in before the situation did irreparable damage to Dean and Brad's relationship.

"Sir, Brad and I had that discussion we talked about. I'm one hundred percent sure that Brad has not betrayed our confidence. He said that not only would he give his own life to save any one of his men, but also he would take his own life if you asked him to. I've known Brad for too long not to believe him. He's a man of his word. There's no way this situation was caused by him. I'd bet my life on it."

Dean took his focus off Brad and looked back at Albert. Albert's hands were raised in front of him. He was gesturing Dean to calm down. The look on Albert's face seemed to dissipate some of Dean's craziness. Dean understood that Albert would never lie to him. He loved Albert as a son. He was his most trusted confidant. Albert's assurances were all that were needed to restore some order in the room. Still breathing heavily from his outburst, Dean sat down. He focused on getting his breathing under control before he spoke.

"If it's not Brad, then how did Hans get so much information?"

Before Albert could answer, Brad said, "This is bullshit. Is that all you can say?"

An employee had never addressed Dean this way. He knew that the very thought of Brad being a traitor went against everything that

Brad had ever stood for and this had upset him greatly. Dean looked at Brad and apologized.

"I'm sorry, Brad. You were the only logical answer I could come up with. The other alternatives are too far outside the realm of possibility."

"That apology isn't good enough this time. I have known you for twenty years. I have done everything you have ever asked, no matter how distasteful it was. I have carried out hundreds of operations for you and never failed. I've killed at your command. To think now that I would betray the trust that we have built is unforgivable."

Dean looked at Brad. He could tell that their relationship would never been the same again. Dean had caused Brad to lose his trust. Brad had a look of incredulity in his eyes. Dean had to work fast to try to repair this trust. He decided to do something that he had never done in the thirty-two years since the council was created. He decided to tell Brad about the council's business without receiving permission first. Dean didn't agree with some of the processes that the council had put in place over the years, but this was a rule that even Dean strongly believed in. He addressed Brad when he spoke.

"Brad, you may not believe me when I say this, but I am truly sorry that I suspected you as a mole. What we have been working on is so important that it started to change the way I think. It has me questioning everything and everyone. The only person I trust without any hesitation is Albert. If Albert tells me that I can fully trust you, I have no choice but to believe him.

In an effort to win back your trust, I'm going to tell you some things that very few people in this world know. It's perhaps one of the most closely guarded secrets ever held by man. I hope that once I tell you about these secrets, it can somehow restore our confidences in one another. Do you think that by my telling you these closely guarded secrets, this will allow us to rebuild the trust that has been broken over the past couple of days?"

Dean watched as Brad considered his offer. Brad had been with Dean for a long time. On many occasions, Dean was sure that Brad had overheard council-related conversations. Brad was already privy to a lot of information he shouldn't know. It was a desperate time. Dean needed to bring Brad back to his side if he was to be successful in his mission.

Dean used this offer to extract additional information from Brad. If Brad was too eager to learn about the council, this would indicate to Dean that Brad truly wasn't the mole. If Brad showed no interest in learning more about the council, this could mean that he had more information then he originally disclosed.

Brad said, "Anything that you have said or do say to me is always held in the strictest of confidence. If you would like to tell me more about the council, I'd be happy to listen."

Without hesitation Dean responded. "Yes, but would telling you more about the council's business help to repair our relationship?"

"The mere fact that you have offered to share your deepest and darkest secrets shows a true sign of trust. If you choose to tell me more about the council, it would be abundantly clear to me that you have full trust in our relationship."

Dean thought about Brad's response for a moment. The many years that they had spent together shaped this man of combat into a very good politician as well. The council's days were numbered no matter what happened, so it would not be too harmful to divulge some of the details to Brad.

Dean spent the next two hours explaining to Brad the council's true purpose. He detailed the true impact the council had on the world. Dean described how extensive the council's tentacles had grown to be. Dean validated what conspiracy theorists had suspected for years. Out of the seven billion people on the planet, Dean and six other men controlled much of the known world. He freely admitted to Brad that he controlled one seventh of the world's oil. With the profits from its oil enterprise, the council subsequently reinvested its massive amounts of money in hundreds of other businesses. These investments made it easy for the council to work its way into every other aspect of human existence. This strategy only tightened the council's grip on the world.

When Dean was finished explaining all of this to Brad, he asked, "Do you have any questions?"

Brad responded, "If you have all of this wealth, why do you need more? Why do you need to capture the Alexander One?"

Dean smiled and said, "Because I want to matter."

CHAPTER THIRTY

I was pretty nervous as Risa and I sat at the dining room table eating dinner with Jonah and Loyal. Risa had convinced me that stealing the Alexander Two and taking a joy ride to Philadelphia was not feasible. She was the voice of reason. The logic she used made all the sense in the world. There was no doubt that if we had taken the Alexander Two without Loyal's permission, we could be jeopardizing one of the most important inventions ever known to man. Clearly there were evil men who would love to get their hands on the technology. Risa convinced me that there was no other alternative but to broach the subject at dinner. I needed to ask Loyal if he could arrange a flight to Philadelphia that evening. I was still drunk with love. I knew exactly what his answer would be and it made me angry.

We were about an hour into dinner, and I hadn't been nearly as jovial as the night before. I think Loyal realized this, because he stopped the conversation and asked, "There seems to be something on your mind tonight, Ethan. Would you like to share it with the rest of us?"

All eyes at the table were on me. I knew that it was now or never, so I responded. "A rather important matter has come up, and I'm not sure how to handle it."

Loyal looked at me, then to Jonah. He replied, "As you could have probably gathered, I'm good at solving puzzles. Perhaps I can help solve your problem."

This was my opening. Loyal was correct. He was the only one with the power to solve this particular issue. I threw caution to the wind and pressed on. "When I accepted your offer to join you, I did so knowing the risks involved. I was, and still am, willing to accept those risks. I'm still fully on board to help bring the Alexander One to market. The problem is that Risa didn't have any choice in her involvement. She was whisked away into our world and her old world wants her back."

"What do you mean by that?" asked Loyal.

"Risa is a school teacher. Tomorrow, there's a mandatory meeting for the teachers. Risa has vigorously stressed to me the importance of the meeting. She has made it clear that missing the meeting is not an option. She must be back in Philadelphia by tomorrow morning."

I shied away from Loyal in anticipation of his rejection. I glanced over to Risa. Her expression told me all I needed to know. My attempt to convince Loyal to allow Risa to leave the island was pathetic. Risa's cold stare reinforced this fact.

Loyal didn't dismiss the request right away. I didn't know if that was a good or bad sign. Trying to avoid eye contact with Risa, I focused my attention back on Loyal.

Loyal cast his eyes upon Risa and said, "It's a very difficult position we find ourselves in, my dear. The truth is you didn't know what you were getting into when you entered that convenience store. I feel terrible for what has happened. However, now that you are involved, it's far too dangerous for you to return to Philadelphia. I trust that if your students or fellow teachers knew the full circumstances, they would forgive your absence. I cannot allow you to go to Philadelphia tomorrow. I'm sorry."

I was relieved. I respected Risa's allegiance to her students, but my selfishness overrode this feeling and wanted her to stay within the safe confines of the island. I shifted my eyes from Loyal over to Risa. I took one look at her and I knew she was not going down without a fight.

Risa said, "So, I'm going to be held here against my will?"

Jonah chimed in, "It's for your own good. For better or for worse, you are involved now. There's too much at stake to risk you or Ethan being captured. If this were to happen, it would end badly for everyone."

Risa took a deep breath and calmly said, "You might not believe me when I say this, but what I do is just as important as the Alexander One. By introducing the Alexander One, you are trying to solve a huge problem in one fell swoop. The impact I have as a teacher may not be as significant in the short term, but in the long run it's everything. My students are the future. Without a good teacher, they'll perpetuate the social discontent. This malfeasance can be directly attributed to poor education. These children are the building blocks of our society. If you construct a foundation with faulty material, it will eventually collapse. I need to be at my school tomorrow to ensure that doesn't happen."

The forcefulness of Risa's words caused everyone at the table to look at her. I was witnessing a new side of Risa. Beneath her attractive exterior was a lioness. She was passionate about what she believed in and was willing to fight for it. This new dimension of her personality only fueled my desire for her. She was going toe-to-toe with Loyal and holding her own.

Loyal cleared his throat. "Your argument is very strong. Your position is clear. It doesn't change my decision, but I applaud your fervor. I cannot permit you to go back to Philadelphia, my dear."

Risa pouted and threw her napkin on her plate. She rose up off her chair and said, "It looks like I have a long swim back to Philadelphia. Please excuse me."

"Wait," commanded Loyal.

Risa stopped.

Loyal looked at Jonah, and then at me. Loyal's eyes asked for my opinion without speaking. I shrugged my shoulders.

"Please sit back down," said Loyal in a soft-spoken voice. "If you insist on going back to Philadelphia, I will not stop you. This isn't a prison. If you do decide to leave the island, I want you to be fully aware of the possible consequences. Your life will be in danger. We can offer you some protection, but it will be nothing compared to what we can offer you here. Do you understand the ramifications of your decision?"

Risa sat back down and replied, "I understand. If I didn't think that the meeting was so important, I'd skip it. My students are that important to me. Personally, I think you are overstating the danger I would be in if I returned to Philly."

"Jonah, what are your thoughts on this matter?" Loyal asked. "Do you think we can provide Risa sufficient protection during the meeting tomorrow?"

Jonah chuckled and said, "I think it's ludicrous to allow Risa to attend this meeting. Only bad things can come from it. If she decides to go forward with leaving the island, I cannot be party to it. It's way too dangerous."

Risa interrupted, "Life is dangerous. Walking across the street can get you killed. Cancer, guns, violence, car accidents–these cause thousands of deaths a year. If everyone were worried about death, nothing would ever get done. What is important is that you have to live life as if every moment is your last."

"Those words have more truth then you realize, my dear," said Loyal. He looked at Jonah with an expression I didn't understand. I could tell that Risa's words were getting through to him. Loyal and Jonah locked eyes. It was clear to me who was in charge.

Jonah made one last ditch effort to make his position clear. "I agree that life is dangerous. All people can do is try and limit their exposure to something that may harm them. Allowing Risa to leave the island for something as insignificant as a teacher's meeting is asking for something bad to happen. I'm truly sorry. I have been tasked with everyone's safety and I cannot condone this type of behavior. It causes far too much risk."

Jonah stood up and placed his napkin on his plate in a casual manner. When he spoke, his tone was one of caution, not anger. "I think that I've made my position clear. I'm against this, and I know with relative certainty that something bad might happen as a result. If you decide to move forward, I cannot be a part of it. One of the other men will need to provide security."

Jonah walked out of the room without another word. His warning had been duly noted, but I knew this wouldn't dissuade Risa.

Loyal considered Jonah's reaction. He looked at Risa and said, "I have to tell you that on matters of security, I listen to Jonah above all else. He seems pretty sure that something will happen if you decide to move forward. Is this a risk you really want to take? Before you answer, let me say that I support you regardless of what you decide."

Risa had a look of calm on her face. I raised my eyebrow in an effort to subtlety ask her what she thought.

She answered Loyal. "My students need me. I'm going to that meeting."

"I'm going with you then," I exclaimed.

My statement was met with a chorus of pleads from Risa and Loyal. I held up my hand and said, "I need to go back and check on my house and business. I also want to be there to make sure nothing happens to Risa. This matter is not open for discussion."

Within an hour, Risa and I were on our way to Philadelphia with our new security guard. The guard's name was Leon, and he barely spoke. We reached Philadelphia at a little after eight o'clock in the morning local time.

Leon followed the Delaware River until we reached the Ben Franklin Bridge. A couple of minutes later, we were touching down on the roof of the Society Hill townhouse. I prayed to God that our approach into Philadelphia over the river dissipated enough of the Alexander Two's signal. The last kidnapping attempt took fifteen hours to coordinate. If Risa could get through her meeting within four hours, I was confident we would be fine.

"Your meeting starts in two hours. We can relax here until you need to leave."

Risa and Leon followed me through the rooftop door. Once we arrived at the third floor mezzanine, Risa said, "Holy crap. You live here?"

Risa leaned over the banister and scanned the atrium. I placed my hand on her shoulder and said, "I wish I could take credit for picking this place out. This is my safe house. Jonah and Loyal set me up here while this whole situation works itself out."

I moved to Risa's side. She was in a trancelike state. Her eyes were transfixed on the stain-glass skylight. I leaned over the railing and said, "Not bad, huh?"

"Not bad at all, Mr. Kravis. I could certainly get used to living in a place like this. It's magnificent."

Leon interrupted and said, "I'm going to do a quick sweep of the premises. You two wait here. I'll be back in a couple of minutes."

Leon walked off. Once he was out of earshot, I cupped Risa's butt and said, "You know, I haven't christened the bedroom yet. Is that something you may be able to help me out with?"

Risa turned to me. She rubbed her body up against mine. I placed my hand against the small of her back and pulled her closer toward me.

Our sexual momentum was arrested when Leon interrupted. "This floor is all clear. I'm going to check out the other floors."

Risa and I chuckled like adolescent school children. Risa backed up and said, "It wouldn't be fair to Leon if we excused ourselves for the next two hours. I think it would be best if we stayed close to him. It was one thing for me to come back to Philly. It is entirely different now that you are here. We need to remain vigilant."

I wanted Risa in the worst type of way, but knew she was right. We needed to remain alert. I took Risa by the hand and said, "Would you like a tour?"

"Leon told us to stay here."

"He checked out this floor already. We can start the tour up here."

Risa gave me a coy look. I raised my hands and said, "I'm just going to show you around. I wouldn't even dream about jumping you with our first guest in the house."

Risa slapped my chest and said, "I better be the only one you are dreaming of, buddy."

I put my arm around Risa and guided her around the top level of the townhouse. She seemed very impressed with the beautiful home. We reached the threshold of the master bedroom. Before I opened the door, I said, "Don't laugh."

"What do you mean by that?" Risa opened the door and gasped. "Oh my, God. This bedroom is an exact replica of the one at the island. Wow, do you think Loyal uses the same decorator for each of his homes?"

Leon startled me when he quietly came up behind Risa and me

and said, "The other floors are clear."

"Thanks Leon. I'm going to give Risa a quick tour of this place. If you are thirsty, please don't be shy about helping yourself to a drink from the refrigerator."

"Thank you, Mr. Kravis, but I'm not to leave your side."

"C'mon, Leon. Please call me Ethan. Mr. Kravis is my dad's name."

"The same goes for me. Please call me Risa."

Leon stood there. After an uncomfortable silence, Risa and I continued our expedition. We descended upon the second floor. I don't know why, but I felt like I was evaluating a new home with my wife. I'd known Risa for only two days, but it felt incredibly natural. My spirits rose every time Risa uncovered a new treasure in the house. I pictured what it would be like in fifteen years when our kids slammed their doors shut after losing an argument. I imagined myself coming home from a hard day's work, putting down my briefcase, and being greeted by Risa with a simple kiss.

I snapped back from this pleasant daydream when Risa said, "This place is extraordinary. When can I move in?"

It was obvious by her tone that Risa said this in jest. I replied, "How about we swing by your place after your meeting and gather up some of your stuff?"

Risa laughed, but I was deadly serious.

She looked at me and stopped laughing. "You are joking, right?"

"I don't think I am."

"We've only known each other for forty-eight hours. In a week or so, you may come back to earth and decide that we moved a little too fast."

I shrugged my shoulders. "The only way that would happen is if you decide it. From my perspective, I'm sure I want to live with you. I have never been so sure of anything in my life."

"That's a big step, buddy. I think you better take some more time to consider it. I'm not saying no to the idea, but you need to be sure. Plus which, you don't even own this place. When whatever you are doing ends, do you think Loyal is going to give you this place?"

"Oh, I get it. You'll only move in with me if I lived in a place like this. Do I have that right?"

Risa pinched my arm. "That's not what I'm saying and you know it. I don't enjoy moving. If we do decide to do this crazy thing, I want to make sure I don't have to go through it again. Ask me again when you are absolutely sure. Once I move, I don't plan on leaving for a long time. Got it, mister?"

"So, does that mean we are going to swing by your place this afternoon?" Before Risa could respond, I leaned over and gave her a kiss.

Leon cleared his throat. Poor Leon. I felt bad for subjecting him to the conversation Risa and I were having.

Risa giggled. "Sorry about that Leon. Totally not cool. Let's continue the tour."

We spent the next half hour exploring every nook and cranny of the townhouse. The expressions on Risa's face were priceless as she moved from room to room. It was nearing the time of Risa's meeting. We stopped in the kitchen and helped ourselves to a cold soda before we embarked on the mile-long walk to the school.

We congregated at the kitchen table. Everyone, including Leon, seemed to be in a good mood.

I brought the cheerful discussion to an end when I said, "Let's review our plan of action one more time."

Risa rolled her eyes. "Again? We've been over this a million times. We are going to walk to the school. If anything happens, we should meet back here. After twenty minutes, if someone doesn't show up, we get in the Alexander Two and fly back to the island."

"I mean it, Risa. If I'm captured, I want you to leave me and get somewhere safe."

"Whatever. Nothing is going to happen. Just relax, though guy."

The shrill of a beeper sounded. Leon shot to his feet and said, "There has been a perimeter breech. You two get up stairs to the third floor, now! I'm going to check it out."

I grabbed Risa by the hand and yanked her off the chair. We sprinted toward the staircase and bound up the stairs, two at a time. We reached the second floor. A huge crash came from the front door. I glanced back and saw the door splinter into several pieces. It told me all I needed to know. The alarm was the real deal.

"C'mon. Move faster," I yelled. I tripped on a step, causing me to fall face-first on the staircase. Risa helped me up. I used this split second to peek back at the first floor. Three men dressed in all black stormed through the front door. Leon charged them and leveled the first intruder with a bone-crunching right hook. As soon as Leon connected with his punch, one of the other men raised a gun in Leon's direction. I heard several pops in short succession. I looked over at Leon and he was falling to the ground.

Risa and I arrived at the third floor. We turned the corner and ran towards the stairwell leading to the roof. We were making good time. The men in black were on the first floor and we had a huge head-start on them. If we could make it to the Alexander Two, we would be all right.

I rammed the door to the rooftop will all my weight. The door flew open. "Get in! Get in!" I yelled as we approached the Alexander Two. The passenger side of the car was facing the rooftop door. I released Risa's arm from my death grip and ran around to the driver's side. Both doors opened, and I threw myself into the driver seat. As Risa was climbing in, I slammed the abort button on the dash. Risa had fallen backwards out the door, a tranquilizer dart lodged in her back. I reached out for her as she slumped to the ground. Two men ran full speed toward us. I tried to jump out of the Alexander Two before it took off and headed back to the island. I would have rather died right then and there than to have left Risa. The driver's side door was closed and wouldn't open. I frantically tried to open it, but it was no use. The passenger's side door closed and the Alexander Two was taking off. What had I done?

As I left the rooftop, I saw the two men carrying Risa away. I was inconsolable at that moment. I tried to stop the Alexander Two from flying back to the island. I had to get her. Nothing would matter if I couldn't live with Risa. The world could shrivel up and die for all I cared. I felt a flood of emotion wash over me. I began to weep. I had to do something to stop this madness. There was only one thing that I could think of at that moment.

I turned the dial on my watch to nine o'clock and pressed the winding mechanism. I had no idea what effect it would have on the events that had just transpired, but I had to do something. Within ten seconds of my activating the distress signal, the onboard communications panel of the Alexander Two came on. I could see Loyal's face looking at me.

"What happened, Ethan?" Loyal asked.

"They took her! They took Risa!" I yelled so loud that I scared myself.

"Who took her?"

"Three men came to the townhouse. We ran, but they shot her with a tranquilizer dart."

I could barely speak the words. I was grasping for air between sobs.

Loyal then said in a calm voice. "All right, Ethan. It will be OK. We will get her back. I promise. Where's Leon?"

"OK? OK? Does it really look OK to you? I wish I had never met you. If we don't get her back, I won't be able to live. I know this is all my fault, but you have to help me. We have to get her back!"

"We will, Ethan. Where is Leon?"

"They took him too."

"OK. We will get her back. How long until you get back to the isl-and?"

"I just took off. A little less than an hour. Is there any way to stop this thing and go back to Philadelphia?"

"Not if you used the abort function. It overrides everything else onboard. Come back to the island, and we'll get this figured out."

"I'm sorry Loyal. This is all my fault. I should have never agreed to let Risa return to Philadelphia."

"Look at me."

I wiped my eyes and looked into the small video monitor.

Loyal continued, "I won't let anything happen to Risa. Try to relax and I will see you when you get back to the island."

I tried to control myself, but it was useless. I couldn't think straight. The flight back to the island was going to be sheer hell. The screen in the cockpit went black. I would have forty plus minutes to think about Risa's kidnapping. I never in my life felt as vulnerable as I did at that moment.

CHAPTER THIRTY-ONE

Dean was sitting in the Lockbox in anticipation of the call he knew would be coming. Brad and his men had redeemed themselves after their first attempt at kidnapping Ethan Kravis failed. Although this time they didn't capture Ethan Kravis, they did manage to get Risa Castleberry. Dean was thankful that Brad had connections to military men for hire around the world. The contracted team was out of Philadelphia. The three-man team was composed of active and retired Special Operation Forces out of Willow Grove Air Force Base. The men were contacted and deployed within fifteen minutes and worth every penny. The reports that Dean had received said that Kravis and Castleberry were at a townhouse in Society Hill. The technical analysts were becoming more accustomed to deciphering the Alexander One signal. Decoding the jumbled signal took only a couple of minutes. Kravis made a huge mistake when he guided the craft over the Ben Franklin Bridge. This error allowed the technical team to pinpoint Kravis's location.

Dean knew that Risa was an important piece of the puzzle. He finally had the leverage that he had been searching for with Loyal.

The SAMSAC terminal rang. Dean looked over at Brad before answering. On the second ring, Brad said, "You can pick up the receiver anytime you are ready."

Dean cherished the position of power in which he found himself. When he answered the phone, he did so with a boisterous voice. "Hello, Loyal. I'm so glad you decided to call me back."

"That wasn't a very nice thing you did, Mr. Bouchard. Risa has nothing to do with the Alexander One."

"On the contrary. She now has everything to do with the Alexander One. You see, she is my insurance policy. She ensures that you proceed with our previous arrangement. I truly wish that the circumstances had not come to this, Loyal."

"How do I know that Risa will not be harmed?"

"Please, Loyal. The girl means nothing to me. However, I know she is important to you and she must be very important to Mr. Kravis."

"Life is important to me. All forms of life. I want you to return Risa to me unharmed."

Dean reflected on the tone of Loyal's voice. Although Dean didn't know how close Risa and Loyal were, he suspected from the tone of his voice that he cared what happened to her. This was a positive sign for Dean.

"Fine. That is a reasonable request. Now I have a request of my own. I think you are smart enough to figure out what I want. I want you to make good on our original deal and let me help you usher the world into a new age. I want to be the one to introduce Alexander One to the world. I'm a reasonable man. My original offer still stands on the same terms. I'll protect you from the evil men I know to exist in the world. In addition, I will fully finance the production of the Alexander One. As an added bonus, I will release both Risa Castleberry and Garrett Michaels."

"As a show of good faith, release Risa and Garrett now, and I will reconsider my intentions."

Dean thought about Loyal's counteroffer. He knew that he couldn't release his only real bargaining chips before the Alexander One was in his hands. He decided that Garrett Michaels was not nearly as important as Risa Castleberry. As long as he still had Risa Castleberry, he still had his leverage.

"Loyal, let's be reasonable. I'll tell you what. I'll release Garrett Michaels as a sign of good faith. When you deliver the Alexander One to me in person, I'll release Risa Castleberry. Does that sound like a deal?"

"How do I know that you will protect me from these evil men you speak of?"

"That's simple. You will come to a meeting where the men will be gathered. We will do the swap there, and you'll witness that they will no longer be a threat with your own eyes."

"Are you saying that you will kill these men at this meeting?"

"Me? Kill? I don't kill people Loyal. That's why I pay extraordinary sums of money to some of the most elite soldiers money can buy. There're very talented and enjoy their craft. They'll be the ones to remove our roadblock."

"When and where is this meeting?"

"I think it best if I wait until a couple of hours prior to the meeting to give you that information. I wouldn't want you to get any delusions of grandeur and try to take out the men who attend this meeting yourself. All you have to know for now is that the meeting will be held in the United States. I'm confident that with a couple of hour's notice, you will be able to get just about anywhere in that wonderful machine you built. Is this a fair assumption?"

"Yes."

"Good, then. Do we have a deal?"

"Prior to my coming to the meeting, I want proof that Risa has not been harmed. When you call me with the details of the meeting, I would like to speak with her."

Dean thought about Loyal's request for a moment. Did providing contact with Risa have any impact on his overall plan? Dean concluded that as long as Risa was safely in his possession, there would be no harm in allowing them to speak.

"That would be fine, Loyal. When I contact you with the details of the meeting, I will let you speak with Risa. You will see that I'm a man of my word and that she has not been harmed."

"All right. Now talk to me about Garrett Michaels. When and where will he be released?

"He's being transported to the same place where I found him as we speak. He should be there waiting for you by the time we finish our discussion."

"That's good. If you try to pull anything when we pick him up, our deal is off. The most important thing is that the Alexander One be made available to the world. It's more important than Garrett Michaels and Risa Castleberry. Do you believe me when I say this?"

"I understand. You'll see in due time that this will all work out if you follow my plan. You will be rich beyond your wildest dreams. You'll have saved the ones who matter most to you, and the Alexander One will change the world forever. I'm a businessman despite what you may think. I'll live up to my end of the arrangement. Will you do the same?"

"As long as you keep good on your promises, I will keep mine."

"Splendid, then. How can I contact you to provide the details of the meeting?"

"You can call me on a new IP address." Loyal relayed the new IP address to Dean.

Dean motioned to Brad to ensure that he had taken down the information. Brad nodded his head and gave Dean a thumbs up.

"That will work, Loyal. The meeting will be held tomorrow, so please be on standby."

"The sooner the better, Mr. Bouchard. I want Risa back as soon as possible."

"Yes, yes. Not to worry. You will get Ms. Castleberry back tomorrow. Perhaps then Mr. Kravis and Ms. Castleberry can get back to whatever they were doing."

There was a pause on the line. Dean didn't know why he made that comment. He didn't want to aggravate the situation any more than he already had. He held his breath as he waited for a reply from Loyal.

"Perhaps, Mr. Bouchard. We will speak again tomorrow."

Before Dean could say goodbye, the line went dead. Dean gently placed the receiver back on the SAMSAC terminal. He looked over at Albert and Brad, and with a grin from ear to ear said, "We got it. We got the Alexander One."

Albert clapped at the performance. Brad was a little more reserved. He simply nodded his head and looked at Dean. There was only one more detail of the plan that Dean needed to address. He needed to plan for the assassination of the council members. This was not going to be an easy task. However, if there was one person who could plan such a difficult operation, it was his trusted chief of security. Dean turned to Brad, "I know that this is short notice, but I have a very difficult assignment for you that will require all your ingenuity and training."

This piqued Brad's interest. He sat up in his chair and waited for Dean to continue.

"I need you to plan a mission. The objective is to kill the other six council members."

Dean saw the looks of concern on Brad's and Albert's faces and tried to reassure them. "I know that it sounds like an impossible task, even if you had six months' notice. I can say with certainty that this is a very dangerous operation, and some of your men may die. We are only going to get one chance at this. We have to take the opportunity. Can it be done?"

Brad replied, "Before I can answer that, I need to know as much as you know about the security measures in place for these meetings. What can you tell me?"

"The full details of the security precautions are not fully divulged to the council members for this very reason. I can tell you that there are extraordinary security measures in place. From what I have been told, there's constant satellite surveillance on the meeting area. Teams of men are deployed sporadically in a one-mile radius from the meeting area. Their orders are to shoot to kill if they spot any threats. All the security is handled by Hans Schmick. He's the founder of the council and is known as Member Number One. That's all I really know. "

Brad probed deeper. "How do the men get to the meeting?"

"Well, Albert typically drives me. I'm not sure who drives the other council members, but I did notice that they are typically the same men at each meeting."

"Are these drivers armed?"

"Considering their cargo, I think that they would be. I know that Albert never carries a gun, but I think that he could without being stripped of it. No one frisks the drivers when we arrive at the meeting."

"So if my math is correct, we are talking about twelve targets. The six council members and their drivers."

"That is correct."

"Have you ever been to this meeting facility? What is the terrain like?"

Dean had never been in the meeting facility, but he knew the area quite well. He was an avid golfer and Scottsdale was home to some of the nicest golf courses in the country. Dean made it a point to drive by the facility the last time he was out there playing golf. "I have never been in the facility itself, but I have driven by it. From the outside, it looks like a small one-story office building. It's located on the very northern tip of Scottsdale. The last time I was out there, it was very secluded. There were no other buildings in the area. The building is set back about a half mile from the Carefree Highway. It's a long road that runs perpendicular to Pima Road, the main artery in Scottsdale."

"Is there a parking lot at the facility or is there a parking garage?"

"There's a parking lot in front of the building. No parking structures are attached."

"Talk me through what you do when you arrive at a typical meeting."

"The council has a tradition. All seven members pull up and form a circle with their cars. Each member exits the car and walks to the middle of the circle. Once the area is swept for electronic surveillance devices, we enter the facility together. The drivers wait in the cars until the meeting is over."

"Do the drivers exit their cars at all in this process?"

"Yes, they typically open the doors and stand in front of the car until the electronic sweep is completed. The only one that doesn't leave the car is Hans's driver. He's the one that orders the sweep to be performed."

"Are there any high-rise buildings around the facility? Any buildings that are higher than the meeting facility?"

"No. The facility is located in the middle of the open desert. Unless the rapid development of Scottsdale has moved that far north, it should be relatively flat in the area."

"Crap."

"What's wrong?"

"The only plan I could develop on such short notice requires an elevated platform over the target area. If there is none, we have no plan."

"There are no buildings in the area, but Scottsdale is in a valley. It's surrounded by mountain ranges."

This got Brad's attention. "How far away are the mountains?"

Dean tried to picture the place. He hadn't paid attention to this detail when he drove by.

"Actually, I have a better idea." Brad turned to the console in the Lockbox and pulled up the topographical satellite image of the area. He turned to Dean and asked, "Where's the facility?"

Dean guided Brad through the streets until the satellite image had the facility within view. Brad measured the distance between the facility and the mountain that faced the front of the building.

"A shade under two miles. That will be stretching it," said Brad.

Dean could tell that Brad had a rough idea of what he would do. He let Brad think and study the map for a couple of more minutes before he asked, "What are you thinking Brad?"

Brad took one more look of the satellite image before he responded. "I'm assuming that you will be in the area, correct? Meaning that we can't just unload a couple of bombs on the area and call it a day, right?"

"That is correct. I need to be at the meeting with the girl, so that Loyal doesn't back out of the deal at the last second."

"Well, I see only one option then. It's the safest way to take out a well-protected target. We will need to set up snipers in the mountains and take out the targets with specially designed fifty-caliber supersonic rounds. It'll be a hell of a shot, but I know some of the best snipers in the world can do it."

Dean considered Brad's plan. He knew that a single two-mile shot was next to impossible. Brad was now talking about twelve shots from that range. Dean didn't like the plan. There was too much that could go wrong. "Twelve shots from two miles away? That doesn't sound like a very high success rate."

"Until about two years ago, I would have agreed. However, a new type of high-velocity ammunition was developed. It was designed to travel up to three miles and has proven very accurate. I'm confident that the snipers can hit their targets. All the bullet has to do is make contact, and the impact will be devastating to the target. Even if the sniper were to hit someone in the arm, the bullet will do the rest. Since this is the case, we no longer need the accuracy of a head shot to take out the target. This increased target area increases the chances of success dramatically."

"I don't know. We have only one opportunity to get this right. If we fail and even one council member escapes, we'll all be dead."

Brad protested, "I'm saying that we can do this and succeed. Have I ever failed a mission like this before?"

Dean could sense Brad's irritation. He knew that this was the only plan that could be developed on such short notice. He thought long and hard about the plan and then came to a decision. "All right, Brad. I guess this is our only option. If you tried to raid the area, you would most likely encounter resistance. The mountains are far enough away to fall well outside the one-mile perimeter of the security team. Do you have all the equipment and men you need to pull it off tomorrow?"

"The equipment will be no problem. I think the best option for us will be to have a six-man team. One sniper for each council member and his driver. The question I need to figure out is which snipers I should hire for the job. I'll have to give it some thought and get back to you on that."

Dean knew that Brad was better at deciding the details then he would be. He hoped Brad was correct in his assessment of the situation. Everything was riding on a successful mission. Dean gave the final order. "Please do everything that you can to ensure success. Money is no object. You have an open checkbook. Let me know what I can do to help."

Dean was uncomfortable when he saw the ominous look on Brad's face. He prayed that their rocky relationship could endure this critical task. Once Dean had the Alexander One in his possession, he would send Brad on a permanent retirement.

CHAPTER THIRTY-TWO

Two men in a black Mercedes entered to main gate of Ravens Valley Golf Club. They pulled up to the clubhouse and searched for Garrett Michaels. The valet approached the car and the driver rolled down his window.

"Good morning, gentlemen. Would you like me to park your car?"

The driver replied, "We are here to pick someone up. Would it be all right if we stayed with the car while my friend here goes to look for him?"

"Sure. If you tell me his name, I might be able to find him for you."

The driver looked at his passenger. The passenger gave the driver a nod. The driver said, "That would be great. The member's name is Garrett Michaels. Have you seen him today?"

"I sure have. He was dropped off about an hour ago. He told me to say that he was at the bar if anyone should ask about him."

"Good. Would you mind going into the clubhouse and telling him that his ride has arrived?"

The driver he handed the valet a fifty-dollar bill. The valet's eyes widened. "That is a big tip, sir. I don't think I would feel right taking such a large tip for such a small task." The valet started to hand the money back to the driver.

The driver held up his hand and said, "Don't worry about the money. Please just go and get Mr. Michaels."

The valet ran to the front door of the clubhouse without any additional protest. Within a couple of minutes, the valet returned with Garrett Michaels in tow. The passenger in the black Mercedes exited the car and held open the rear door. Without a word, Garrett Michaels entered the vehicle. The passenger shut the rear door and got into the front seat. The black Mercedes sped off.

Two minutes went by without a word spoken. The passenger in the front seat of the car turned around to face Garrett Michaels. In his hand he had a device that looked like the handheld metal detectors that airport screener's use. He extended the scanner in front of Garrett Michaels' face and scanned his entire body. The scan was thorough and took about a minute. Once the scan was complete, the passenger in the front seat said, "We're clear. There are no signals being transmitted."

Garrett immediately began to ask questions. "Who are you guys?"

It was now the driver's turn to speak. "We were sent by Jonah to pick you up."

"Where are we going?"

The driver looked at the passenger before responding. A moment passed before the driver spoke again. "We are going to drive around while you speak to Jonah."

The passenger in the front seat turned around and handed Garrett something that looked like a PDA cell phone. Once Garrett had the object in his hand, the driver provided additional instruction. "Press the square button."

As soon as Garrett touched the button, a crystal clear image of Jonah appeared. It took a moment for him to realize it, but this was a handheld video-conferencing appliance. Garrett was surprised when

Jonah started to speak to him.

"Hello, Garrett. I'm glad to see that you survived this little ordeal."

Garrett was flustered. He really didn't know how to respond. He was nervous that Jonah would be angered if he found out that he had betrayed his employer's confidence. Garrett thought about how much he should tell Jonah about Dean Bouchard. "Hello, Jonah. I'm also glad that I survived this assignment. I've got to be honest with you, it was touch and go there for a while."

"How did Dean Bouchard treat you while you were held captive?"

"It took a while for the effects of the tranquilizer to wear off, but besides that, I was treated humanely."

Jonah nodded his head in approval before he spoke again.

"So Dean Bouchard didn't harm you in any way, except for the initial abduction?"

Garrett knew that he would have to come clean about the two hundred and fifty million dollars. He was now in Jonah's possession, so he needed to do everything he could not to aggravate the situation further. He took a deep breath and decided to lay it all out on the table for Jonah. "Dean Bouchard not only treated me well, he paid me a tremendous amount of money to tell him everything I knew about the Alexander One. My only options were death or extreme wealth. I had to tell him, Jonah."

Jonah considered this truthful admission. Garrett Michaels was in an untenable situation. He was flip-flopping between allegiances. Jonah continued to ask questions. "How much did he pay you?"

Garrett went into a dream-like state thinking about his newfound pot of gold. When he said the amount, there was wonder in his voice. "Two hundred and fifty million dollars. Half was already paid and the other half will come once he gets the Alexander One."

The driver heard this and let out a whistle. Jonah ignored the interruption and continued his questioning. "Two hundred and fifty million dollars. That's quite a bit of money. What did you tell him?"

"You know what I told him. I told him everything I know, which, as you know, is not very much."

"Start from the beginning and don't leave out any details. I want to know everything you talked about."

Garrett told Jonah everything that he could remember from the first conversation between himself and Dean Bouchard. Jonah listened patiently and didn't interrupt. Garrett went into great detail about the information he provided. He explained that he told Dean about the Alexander One and how he thought it worked. How it had a skin on the exterior that could make it invisible. Garrett concluded his summary of the conversation by saying, "I really didn't tell Dean Bouchard much, because I didn't know much."

Jonah started to ask probing questions. "You said that you were stripped of all personal items when they abducted you. Did they give them back to you when you were released?"

Garrett had almost forgotten about the specially made wristwatch and EyeWonder. He reluctantly provided the answer to Jonah's question. "No. Dean Bouchard still has the watch and the EyeWonder."

Jonah had a look of disappointment on his face. He continued his line of questioning. "Did he ask any questions about the EyeWonder?

"He didn't ask any direct questions about it. He only said that they detected a slight signal emanating from the device and that they had to take it out and place it in a special box that trapped any outgoing signals from escaping. He thought that it was a contact lens. He asked why I had only one, and I made up an excuse. I'm pretty sure he has no idea what The EyeWonder does."

Garrett knew that the little device would destroy itself if anyone tried to reverse engineer it. The question was aimed to illicit a response out of him.

Jonah followed up Garrett's response with another question. "So, you didn't tell him what the EyeWonder does?"

Garrett was offended by the question. He then made sure that his answer left no doubt in Jonah's mind that he was telling the truth. "I didn't tell Dean Bouchard what the EyeWonder is or what it does. He didn't ask, so I didn't tell."

"Fair enough. What can you tell me about the environment in which you were held?"

"The house was one of the most magnificent structures I've ever seen. Although I wasn't allowed free access to most of the rooms, the rooms that I did see reminded me of a European palace. The rooms were furnished with extremely high-end antiques, and everything was in museum-quality shape. Dean Bouchard is clearly a man with tremendous wealth."

"How about other people? Did you speak with anyone else while you were there?"

"Outside of my interaction with Dean Bouchard, there were two other people who seemed to be integral to his operation. There was his chief of security. His name was Brad. He also operated the phone when I made the call to Judge Lawrence. I have no doubt that Brad was the one who led the operation to have me kidnapped. He seemed very capable of planning such a task.

The second man appeared to be Dean's assistant. His name was Albert. Albert didn't say a word during any of the times I saw him. I got the impression that Albert was privy to every detail of Dean's business interests. He was the one who completed the wire transfer of the one hundred and twenty-five million dollars."

"Was there any discussion between Dean and Brad?"

Garrett thought back. He then realized that he left out a major fact when telling his story to Jonah. "When we were making the call to the judge, Brad was there to ensure that the call wasn't traced. He told Dean that the call should not be able to be traced. Dean went crazy and yelled at Brad. He said that he didn't pay for 'should.' He only paid for 'will.' It was a tense moment between the two of them, and I was a little embarrassed for Brad."

"Why were you embarrassed for him?"

"Dean was yelling at him like a child. Brad seemed like a proud warrior. Being talked down to like that didn't seem to sit well with him."

"I have one more question for you. When you were being held captive, did you ever meet a woman named Risa?"

"I only saw two women while I was at the house. They were maids. They were Hispanic, but I didn't hear their names."

"So you didn't see a woman who may have appeared to be a captive like you?"

Garrett immediately answered, "No. No one like that. Only workers in the house."

Jonah spoke in a much more serious tone. "Thank you for providing me all you know about the situation, Garrett. I'm truly sorry you got caught up in all of this. I must tell you that I'm very disappointed with you. As part of your contract with us, you signed a nondisclosure agreement. This agreement clearly states that you will not divulge any information pertaining to your assignment. If you remember correctly, I stressed this fact several times when you first started as a contractor with us."

Garrett didn't like where this conversation was headed and he had to defend himself as best he could. "Wait one second. My life was in danger. If I didn't tell Dean Bouchard all he wanted to know, he would have killed me."

"This is the reason why we paid you so much for your discretion. You were made very aware of the consequences of speaking about the Alexander One to anyone. I'm sorry, old friend, but you will never get to spend your newfound blood money."

The passenger in the front seat turned around and held a twenty-two caliber gun with a silencer at Garrett. Garrett dropped the handheld video-conferencing device and threw his hands up. He yelled out, "Wai–"

The cold thud of the silenced gun rang out. The bullet struck Garrett Michaels in the center of his forehead. Garrett's body slumped over motionless in the back seat of the car. The passenger in the front seat picked up the handheld video-conferencing device from the floor in the back seat. He looked at Jonah and said, "Mission completed, sir."

CHAPTER THIRTY-THREE

The forty minutes it took to get back to the island felt like an eternity. I wasn't sure what to do or say once I landed. As I approached the island, I looked out the windows and saw two figures standing next to the landing pad. Jonah and Loyal were outside waiting to greet me. The Alexander Two gently touched down, and I scrambled to open the door. The cabin hadn't fully depressurized, so the door lock hadn't disengaged. I started to pound on the window and scream. "Let me out of this thing!" I yelled as Loyal and Jonah walked over.

The electronic voice within the vehicle finally announced that the Alexander Two was fully depressurized and that I could exit the vehicle. I opened the door and bounded out. Before Loyal and Jonah could say a word, I frantically yelled the question. "Where is she? Where is Risa?"

I knew I needed to calm down and think rationally. It was the only way that I could help to get her back. Before Jonah or Loyal spoke, I took a deep breath and tried to contain some of the emotion that was oozing out of me so freely.

Loyal was the first one to speak. "We know that this is going to be very difficult for you to handle, but you have to trust us. I personally have grown to like Risa in the short while that I have known her. She's a beautiful example of what humanity should be. She is funny and compassionate, and she puts other people's needs before her own. You may not believe this, but I want to see that she survives this just as much as you do. We will do everything that we can to ensure she is returned safely."

Loyal's practiced speech did little to calm my nerves. All I could think of was her. If anything happened to her, I didn't think that life would be worth living anymore. I suddenly felt the weight of the world crashing down on me. The impact of the situation was so great that it caused my knees to buckle. I stumbled backwards. Before I could fall to the ground, I felt the cool skin of the Alexander Two at my back.

Jonah came to my aid. "Whoa, Ethan. I think we better get you inside." Jonah grabbed me by the shoulders, lifted my arm and put it around his neck. He helped me walk toward the house.

After about ten feet, I lifted my arm off of him and said, "I can walk. I'll be fine."

The three of us quickly made it back into the house. We arrived at the study off the side of the dining room. Jonah motioned for me to take a seat. Dread filled me as I waited for him to tell me how going to Philadelphia was a bad idea. However, instead of saying "I told you so," Jonah had words of comfort. "We will get her back, Ethan. It will require some large sacrifices on our behalf, but we will get her back."

"If by large sacrifices you mean handing the Alexander One over to the men who have Risa, I can't allow that to happen. It is too important to the world." I looked at both Jonah and Loyal directly in the eyes so that they knew I meant every word of what I said. No one spoke for a minute until Loyal broke the silence.

"So you would sacrifice Risa's life to protect the Alexander One?"

Without hesitation, I answered. "It's abundantly clear how much I love Risa. I would gladly give my life in exchange for hers. However, the Alexander One is greater than any one life. Even the possibility that it may save the world from a catastrophic fate is worth protecting with everything, even if includes my life and Risa's."

I couldn't believe what I had just said. It was like the response was hardwired into my brain. However, I knew with absolute certainty that it was the truth. Loyal and Jonah looked at each other, and for the briefest of moments, I thought I saw a hint of a smile between them.

Loyal coughed violently. It was a coughing fit like I had witnessed a few nights ago at dinner. Jonah sprang to his feet and gently placed Loyal into a chair.

I ran over to the wet bar and got a glass of water. I brought it over to Loyal and handed it to him. He took a sip, but it seemed to fuel the coughing spasms. It was a full minute before Loyal could bring the coughing under control. A look of worry was on Jonah's face.

Once the coughing subsided, I had to ask an obvious question. "Are you all right, Loyal? That cough didn't sound too good."

Loyal was still recovering from his episode. Once he had regained control of his body, he answered the question. "I'm fine. The smell of the saltwater outside sometimes tickles my throat. Jonah and I were out there for a while waiting for you, and it must have caught me. I'll be fine in a moment or two. Let's focus on the issue at hand."

I didn't know if I believed Loyal's explanation, but he was right for refocusing our efforts. Seeing that Loyal had seemingly recovered, I started to ask questions. "Do we know who took Risa?"

I looked at Jonah as I asked the question. He appeared to know the answer to this question, but was reluctant to answer. I took this as a sign that he did know, so I rephrased the question. "Who took Risa?"

Jonah looked at Loyal before he spoke. Loyal gave a slight nod, and Jonah began to speak. "A man by the name of Dean Bouchard took Risa."

I was fairly certain that I knew the answer to this next question, but I had to ask anyway. "What does Dean Bouchard want?"

Jonah seemed disappointed at the question, but answered. "He wants us to deliver the Alexander One to him. He has said that if we do this, that he will release Risa unharmed."

I was very surprised at this answer. The answer itself was obvious, but something was amiss. "Are you saying that you have spoken to the kidnappers since they took Risa?"

Jonah looked at Loyal. It looked as though Jonah was uncomfortable answering the question. Loyal recognized this and answered the question. "Yes. We spoke to Dean Bouchard while you were on your way back here."

I realized then that there was a lot more to this story that I was currently not privy to. I needed to know more so that I could help solve the problem at hand. Seeing that Loyal was not going to expand on his answer, I asked the most obvious question I could think of at that moment. "There is clearly a lot going on that you have not told me. I think I have earned the right to know what you know about the kidnapper. What do you know about Dean Bouchard?"

"We only became aware of Dean Bouchard's existence a couple of days ago. He contacted us through a mutual acquaintance. His proposition was simple. He wanted to help bring the Alexander One to market. Truth be told, we were very close to arriving at an arrangement with him until a better offer came our way. Dean Bouchard is not a man who takes failure lightly. This is why he tried to kidnap you at the convenience store. It's why he has taken Risa captive. He needed leverage to negotiate with and thinks that Risa provides him this leverage."

I was starting to get the picture. There were still a lot of missing details, but the explanation given by Loyal seemed to fit. I could have spent hours asking Loyal questions, but I really only cared about one thing. "How do we get Risa back without sacrificing the Alexander One?"

"You have had a very tough day. Why don't you let Jonah and me worry about how to get Risa back? I'm afraid that your emotions will cloud your judgment. I'm very happy to see that you are willing to put the safety of the Alexander One above all else. It only confirms further what I already had known to be true. Your selfless actions show that you know how important the Alexander One could be to the world. This is the exact reason why you were chosen for this opportunity. Because of this reason, I have full trust in you. Do you have the same level of trust in me?"

I thought about this question. A week ago I didn't even know this man. Within the past week, I have seen glimpses of his genius. He has introduced me to things in this world that I never thought possible. It could only stand to reason that if he were willing to share these discoveries with me, I couldn't help but to fully trust him.

"I trust you."

"Good. Then you have to do as I say. Let me and Jonah worry about this problem. I need you to go to your room and get some rest while Jonah and I work this out with Dean Bouchard. Would you do that for me?"

I resisted the temptation of telling Loyal to go to hell. There was no way I could sleep with Risa's life in the balance. I trusted Loyal, but it didn't mean that I could sit idly by and do nothing. "I trust you, but I'm not sure I can do nothing while you and Jonah tend to the issue. I know I will not be able to sleep. Going back to the room and sleeping is an impossibility."

Loyal sat in his chair and looked at me. "I'm sorry, but Jonah and I need to focus on this. There's more than Risa at stake here. I can't have you interrupting us while we move forward. Now, this is going to feel strange to you at first. We are going to help you relax."

I felt a strange sensation in my legs, as if my legs were paralyzed. I tried moving them, but nothing happened. I looked up at Loyal. "What's happening to me?"

Loyal spoke quickly. "We are shutting down your body. The Nanobiotics are putting your body into sleep mode, like a computer. You'll be fine."

A wave of panic grew inside me as the effects of the Nanobiotics slowly crept up my body, like I was slowly being dipped in a hot bathtub of water. It would have felt good if I weren't so terrified. The strange sensation reached my arms, and they went limp. Before the Nanobiotics reached my head, Loyal said one last thing.

"When you wake up, everything will be better. I promise."

I could feel myself slipping into unconsciousness. I tried to fight it as long as possible, but everything became black. The last thing I felt was Jonah's hands catch me as I started to fall forward off the chair.

CHAPTER THIRTY-FOUR

Hans Schmick was aboard his private 747 on his way to Arizona for the council meeting. He was deep in thought about the latest turn of events. The most recent call intercepted between Dean and Loyal had enraged him. Hans knew that not only was he in danger of losing the Alexander One, but Dean was planning to kill the council members at the meeting. The situation was problematic for Hans because the call didn't define how Dean hoped to accomplish his coup.

Hans knew that Dean would never get the chance to kill him now that he had uncovered the plan. He needed to figure out a way to take this important information and use it to his advantage. Hans's many years in the business world dictated that the more you knew about a situation, the greater the chances would be that it could result in your favor.

How was Dean planning to take out the council? It was the question that had been on Hans's mind the entire flight. Would Dean simply send a car with a bomb to the meeting? Would he come to the meeting and let his driver try to kill the council members and their drivers? There was only one real solution Hans could think of. Dean would have to take his targets out from long range. It was the only plan that made sense. Dean wasn't privy to the security measures in place.

Rather than risk being exposed before his plan was set in motion, Dean would opt for a plan that called for a team to sit outside the surveillance area. The kill shots would be extraordinarily hard to make, but it was the safest way to execute the plan. Hans sat there thinking of how he would respond to such a plan.

Simon entered the main cabin. He approached Hans and said, "Sir, we are receiving a call through the secure satellite phone. The man calling claims to be Dean Bouchard's chief of security."

An alarm sounded within Hans. It was very suspicious that he was being contacted by a man claiming to be Dean Bouchard's chief of security, given what he knew was going to happen the next day. It was a long-standing rule that had never been broken since the council was created. There was to be absolutely no direct contact between any of the council members except through the secure laptops they had been issued. Hans immediately felt as though this call might have been a trap. However, with the council seemingly on the verge of unraveling, Hans had no choice but to take the call. He looked at Simon and gave his order. "Simon, I'm going to take the call. Can you bring the satellite terminal in here?"

"Of course, Sir."

Simon left the main cabin. He returned with a black briefcase that contained the secure satellite receiver. Simon placed the briefcase down on the table in front of Hans and opened it. After a minute of punching numbers on the keypad, the call was ready to be taken.

"You may pick up the receiver any time now, sir," Simon said as he slid the briefcase closer to Hans.

Hans picked up the receiver and listened for a voice on the other end. Within seconds, he heard the voice of the unknown caller.

"Hello. Is this Hans Schmick?"

"Speaking. Who is this?"

"Hello, Mr. Schmick. My name is Brad Resniki. I'm the chief of security for a man you know very well."

Hans was growing impatient with the cloak and dagger display of bravado. He wanted the man to say what he had to say and be done with it. "This call is highly unadvisable. Perhaps you can tell me what you want, Mr. Resniki."

There was a pause on the line before Brad began to speak again. "I have some information that would be very valuable to you. I have no doubt that this information would help you in your efforts to secure the Alexander One."

Hans sat up in his chair. This man knew a lot about the situation. Perhaps his information would be helpful after all. Hans decided to hear him out. "All right. You've got my attention. What is this information you speak of?"

"Before I tell you, we need to come to some sort of arrangement. I'm afraid that once I tell you this information, I may become unemployed. I need to secure my future before we continue."

Hans cut in and asked, "Is this what this is about? Would you like a job within my organization?"

Brad laughed. "Mr. Schmick, I'm an old warrior. I'm afraid the time has come for me to think about retirement. I've been working for men like you and Dean Bouchard my entire life, and it's now my turn to leave the business. My deal is simple. The information I have for you is very valuable. In addition to providing you this information, I'm willing to act on it on your behalf. The price for my information and services is five hundred million dollars."

Hans almost choked when he heard the amount. He already knew that there was going to be an attempt on his life the next day. That information would not be worth anything. Hans responded to Brad's offer.

"That's a preposterous amount of money for information. I doubt very highly that anything you could say would warrant such an astronomical sum."

Brad went quiet. He was not skilled in the art of high finance deals. He was a skilled warrior, not a Wall Street banker.

Hans took the silence as a moment of weakness. He didn't want to overplay his hand either. There could be valuable information that Brad had, but he couldn't divulge what he knew about the situation. The conversation was at a standstill. Neither side wanted to relent.

Hans finally broke the silence. "I can tell that you are not accustomed to negotiation tactics. I'm afraid that I must get some sleep now. Tomorrow is going to be a long day for me, and I need my rest. Good night."

Before Hans could hang up, Brad said, "Your day tomorrow may not be as long as you might think, Mr. Schmick."

"Now we are getting somewhere," Hans thought. Brad had just tipped his hand early. Hans would use this to his advantage. "What does that mean? Is that a threat? Did you just threaten me? Are you saying that my life is in danger?"

With a revived sense of purpose, Brad continued. "Not at all. I'm simply saying that the information I have is worth your full attention and five hundred million dollars."

Hans was tired of playing games. He decided to expedite this conversation. "The fact that Dean Bouchard is going to try to kill me at tomorrow's meeting isn't worth anything to me, since I already know this to be true. You'll have to do a lot better than that if you ever hope to get rich off of it."

"You seem to be very observant, Mr. Schmick. Dean Bouchard does want to kill you tomorrow, but that was only half the information I was going to provide. The other half was for the services I can provide given this information. You see, I'm the one who is in charge of killing you. I know when, where, and by whom you will be killed. How valuable would it be if I turned the plan against the man who is trying to kill you?"

Hans had the answer he had been searching for all night. A simple double cross. Dean Bouchard would never see it coming. This would be very valuable indeed. The money it would cost would be a pittance compared to the profits the Alexander One would generate. Hans was eager to make this deal, but couldn't show too much eagerness or the price might go up. He responded to the offer. "I would say that that type of action would be valuable to me. I'm sure we can arrange something if you were to make good on your offer."

Without hesitation, Brad replied. "Yes. That 'something' you speak of is five hundred million dollars. Half now and half upon completion. I will divvy up the money as I see fit among the men who will carry out the mission."

Hans was still skeptical about the timing of the call. He felt that it may have been a trap. Dean Bouchard was cagy. He might have been using Brad as a go-between to get information. He wasn't fully convinced that Brad would deliver even if he transferred the money. He had to have assurances before he committed to the deal. "How do I know that you'll make good on what you have offered? Am I simply to accept your word that you will carry out this operation for me? You have to see that this proposition is sketchy at best. After all, I don' know you. You may not even be who you say you are."

"I see what you are saying, Mr. Schmick. I have nothing I can offer to prove what I'm saying is the truth. Let's just consider this a good faith deal. If you transfer the two hundred and fifty million dollars, I'll live up to my end. If you don't, I'll know that the deal has been rejected. I don't like rejection, Mr. Schmick. Unfortunately I will be taking my anger out on you if you fail to enter this agreement. I'm very good at what I do, and I can guarantee that you will die tomorrow if you don't take this deal."

Hans rolled his eyes at this blatant threat. A fly that landed on his golf ball as he was about to hit it caused him more concern than Brad Resniki. Everything else being equal, it was the best plan he had at the moment. The money was inconsequential to Hans. Two hundred and fifty million dollars was a minuscule percentage of his net worth. It was a rounding error on his books. If Brad were to make good on his end of the bargain, the risk of losing two hundred and fifty million dollars was well worth the reward. Hans decided that he would take the deal and see how it all played out.

"First, let me tell you for future reference that someone like me doesn't respond to threats. I didn't get to where I am by submitting to the will of others. This tactic may work in your line of business, but it rarely works in mine. That being said, I have decided to take you seriously. You will have the first installment in your account within an hour. If you complete your mission as advertised, you will have the rest of your money."

Hans heard a large exhale on the other end of the phone.

Brad responded. "You won't regret your decision, Mr. Schmick. My word is all I have in this world, and I promise you that you are paying for something that is as good as done. Just stay in your car until me and my men take care of business. Before you exit your car, transfer the remaining balance, and you will never hear from me again."

This was not what Hans had in mind. He quickly interrupted Brad's last instruction. "I will only transfer the remainder of the funds after I'm safely away with the Alexander One in hand. This is non-negotiable. I have shown you an extraordinary gesture of good faith on accepting your deal based on your word. You must now reciprocate and accept this new term, or I'm afraid our deal is off."

"Very well. I will accept your last term. I'll be monitoring the account for the first installment. If the money is in the account, I know that we have a deal. Are you ready for the account information?"

"I'll give the phone to my assistant. He will ensure that the wire transfer goes through. I look forward to the conclusion of our business. If you do what you say you can do, you will have your money. Good night."

Before Brad could say another word, Hans gave Simon the phone. Hans saw Simon take down the account information. Once Simon had completed the call, he hung up the phone and looked to Hans for direction.

"Transfer two hundred and fifty million dollars to the account. Be sure to put a tracer on the wire. If this man doesn't make good on his end of the deal, I want to get that money back."

Simon nodded and asked, "Do you think he will do it? Do you think he will turn on Dean Bouchard?"

Hans looked out the window of the plane. It was pitch dark outside. The only thing he could see as he spoke was his reflection in the glass of the window. "I don't know, Simon. I don't know. If Brad Resniki does do what he says he can, it would be a perfect solution to our problems. If not, I fear we may be in trouble."

CHAPTER THIRTY-FIVE

Dean waited patiently in the living room of his Scottsdale ranch. With the council meeting only hours away, his nervous energy was building. There was a lot that could still go wrong with his plan. He needed as much information about the situation as he could get. He decided that it would be a good idea to talk with Risa Castleberry. He called Albert on the intercom. "Albert, would you bring Ms. Castleberry to me?"

Albert responded in the affirmative.

Risa Castleberry was escorted to the living room where Dean sat. Two large bodyguards flanked her as she entered the room. Dean ogled Risa as she entered. He stood up and said, "Good Morning, Ms. Castleberry. Please have a seat."

"I prefer to stand."

"Come now, my dear. Don't make this any more difficult than it has to be. I'm on old man. Can't you pretend that you are enjoying my company?"

Risa didn't appreciate Dean's attempt at humor. She stood there and pierced her pale blue eyes into Dean from across the room.

Dean saw this look from Risa and almost laughed. "You're far too pretty to scare anyone with that look of anger, my dear. Please sit down."

Dean motioned to a couch directly across from where he was sitting. Risa hesitated at first, but then sat as requested.

Dean watched her carefully. She was graceful, even given the difficult circumstances. Once Risa was firmly in her seat, Dean engaged her in conversation. "Well, first let me say that I'm sorry we had to go to such lengths to bring you here. If there was any other way, I would have much preferred that. I trust you know what this is all about, don't you?"

Risa didn't say a word.

Dean thought that this newfound sense of heroics was just plain stupid. She had nothing to gain by not talking. Dean sat quietly waiting for an answer. After a moment had passed in silence, he decided to change his tactics. "You must be hungry. Can I get you something to eat or drink?" Dean looked up at Albert and said, "Albert, would you have the chef prepare Risa some breakfast?"

"Of course, sir," Albert said and left the room.

Risa was going to be a tougher nut to crack than Dean had expected. He just needed to get her talking, and the rest of the conversation would fall into place. "If you aren't going to talk, perhaps you will listen. My name is Dean Bouchard. I have been working with Loyal on the Alexander One. There are some very evil men who would like nothing more than to kill Loyal and destroy the Alexander One. Your kidnapping was for your protection."

Dean observed a slight look of confusion on Risa's face. He had used what he knew about the situation to his advantage. Everything he had said was a lie, but it would provoke a response, even if Risa knew it was not true. Dean didn't know how much Risa knew about the Alexander One or Loyal. This was the most difficult part about constructing his web of lies. Dean continued. "It was my responsibility to look out for you while you were in Philadelphia. These men I told you about were after you and Ethan, and I had to act."

Risa shook her head and finally spoke. "I don't believe you. Loyal said that you were the evil man looking to kidnap us."

With the first thing she said, she gave up a big piece of information. She has been in direct contact with Loyal. Dean needed to know where Loyal operated from. He continued his questioning.

"I don't believe that Loyal would say something like that. He specifically told you my name when he explained this to you?"

"I guess he never said your name specifically. However, I still don't trust you. I will never trust a man who kidnaps me."

This was a fair point, Dean thought. This conversation was going nowhere. Albert returned with a tray of food and placed it in front of Risa. They tray was filled with scrambled eggs, toast, yogurt, fresh fruit and cereal.

Dean saw her reluctance. "Please eat something. Despite what you may think of me, I'm not a barbarian. This isn't a POW camp in Vietnam. There will be no torture or starvation. Please eat; we have a long day ahead of us."

Risa looked at Dean, then back down at the food. She started to pick at the eggs. As she started eating, she asked, "What will be so long about today? Are we going to play some golf or something?"

Dean was encouraged that the food was starting to loosen Risa up. He decided to dangle a carrot in front of her in hopes of continuing a fruitful discussion. "In a couple of hours, we will be going to a meeting. At that meeting, you will be released. You should be home in time for dinner with your boyfriend."

Risa stopped eating.

Dean could read Risa's expression like an open book. He knew that he had her attention now. He would use this temporary chink in her armor to extract as much information as possible. "That is the truth. You should be back with Ethan tonight if all goes well at the meeting. To ensure that things go well, I need you to answer some simple questions for me."

"Do you think I can't tell when someone is playing on my emotions? You aren't as cleaver as you may think."

"I'm sure someone as beautiful as you attracts the attention of many male callers. It's apparent that you are use to men trying to manipulate you. Don't confuse this exchange as your average dalliance. I'm not the type of person who takes rejection lightly. You would be well advised to answer my questions."

"Ask your questions." Risa said as she crossed her arms.

Dean saw this dramatic change in posture. He knew that what he had told her had worked. He didn't waste any time. "How long have you known Loyal?"

"The first time I met both him and Ethan was after you tried to kidnap me the first time. Ethan and I met in the convenience store. When we went outside and you shot me with a dart. Ethan thought it best to take me to a safe place and recover."

Dean sensed she was telling the truth. He said, "Do you make it a habit of picking up strangers in convenience stores?"

"I didn't pick up anyone. We talked for a couple of minutes, and the next thing I knew, I woke up in a strange place."

"Where did Ethan take you after the convenience store incident?"

"I don't know where it was that he took me. I was unconscious when we traveled there, thanks to your tranquilizer dart."

Dean thought that was a fair answer, but was sure that Risa knew more. He decided to press on. "Was this place in a hot or cold climate?"

"All I know is that it was on an island and it was hot as hell."

"How long did it take to get there?"

Risa frowned and said, "I have no idea. I was unconscious remember?"

"How long did it take to get to Philadelphia from the island?"

Risa lied. "I don't know. I was drunk and passed out. Next thing I knew, I was back in Philadelphia."

"You're not helping your cause by lying to me. It can only hurt you. Are you sure you don't want to revise your answer?"

"You're lying to me. I'm just reciprocating. You start telling me the truth and I'll do the same."

Dean had enough. He knew that Risa was not going to be helpful. His attempts at gaining information were futile. He decided that it wouldn't really matter if things went according to plan later. Dean stood up and looked at Risa. "I can tell that you don't want to cooperate with me. I hope that your lies don't come back to haunt you later."

Risa rolled her eyes. "What does it matter anyway? Nothing I say will have the slightest impact on this situation. I've known men like you before. No matter what I say or do, you will do what you want. You might as well kill me now and get it over with."

Dean realized that the conversation was over. He motioned to the two guards to take her away. The two enormous men did as instructed. Without protest, Risa left the room.

"Albert, ask Brad to join us. I want to review the plan one more time. After the review, we will need to call Loyal and provide specifics about the meeting. Please have the SAMSAC prepped for the call."

"Yes, sir."

Albert left the room briefly to retrieve Brad. Dean sat back down in his chair to think about his discussion with Risa. She mentioned that she was taken to an island. This was good information, but not very helpful. The Alexander One could probably reach anywhere on earth within the time she was unconscious. However, if things didn't work out today, he could use his research company to do satellite reconnaissance of every island in the world. The effort would take years, but at least it was a clue to Loyal's whereabouts. Deep in thought, Dean didn't realize when Brad and Albert entered the room.

Albert spoke softly as if not to startle Dean. "Sir, Brad is here as requested." Albert placed his hand on Dean's shoulder.

Dean snapped out of his deep thought and turned his attention to Brad.

"Brad, can you provide an overview of the plan for today again?"

Brad was noticeably jolly as he began to speak. He placed a blown-up satellite image of the area on the coffee table and began to give his briefing. "Here's a satellite photo taken of the target area yesterday. At the center of the photo is the meeting place. The concentric circles radiating out from the meeting place are in one-mile increments. Approximately two miles away, I will place six snipers due east of the target area. This is the only vantage point with a clear shot at the targets."

Dean interrupted. "When will you commence firing?"

"We will open fire only after the exchange for the girl has been completed and the Alexander One is on the ground without a driver. Once you are comfortable that these conditions exist, raise your hand in the air. That will be our signal to engage and take out the targets."

Dean thought that it was a rather simple plan. He would have thought that taking out the council members would have called for a more dramatic plot. The simpler the better. The only part of the plan that Dean was unsure of was how to make the trade for Risa. Loyal would most likely ask that she be released prior to landing. However, if Dean did this, what would prevent Loyal from taking off? Dean also knew that Loyal would probably not land before he was sure that Risa was safely away. He decided to raise this question with Brad. "What is the best way to make the exchange for the girl?"

"The craft has to land prior to your releasing the girl. In addition, you have to draw the driver out of the vehicle before you let her drive off. It's the only way to ensure you can take control of the Alexander One."

Brad was right. It would be a high-stakes game of chicken when it came to the swap. Dean had to be strong and not give in, regardless of what Loyal requested. He had to make this point clear when they called Loyal in a couple of minutes. Realizing that Brad had fully explained the mission, Dean said, "It's time to make the call to our guest of honor. Albert, could you bring in the SAMSAC terminal and Risa?"

Albert left the room. As Brad and Dean sat there, Dean decided to use the free time productively.

"So, Brad. Do you think the mission will be a success?"

Brad didn't look up from the satellite image when he replied. "I have no doubt in my mind that the mission will yield positive results."

Dean was elated to hear Brad's positive response. Albert entered the room with Risa and the SAMSAC terminal. He placed the SAMSAC terminal down on the coffee table and motioned for Risa to take a seat. Risa sat on the couch. She saw the large plastic case that housed the SAMSAC terminal and said, "I thought you said that you wouldn't be torturing me. What's in that case?"

Dean realized how the case must have looked and quickly reassured his guest. "We have your ticket home in this case. We are going to be calling your friend Loyal to arrange for your pickup. If he asks, I hope you will be truthful and tell him that we have treated you well."

Risa put her hand over her mouth to hide her laugh. She responded to Dean's request. "Treated me well? You shot me with a tranquilizer dart, twice!"

Dean looked at Risa with a serious stare. He didn't fault her for being angry, but he needed her to cooperate in order for his plan to succeed. "I trust you know what I mean. You do want to go home tonight, don't you?"

"Of course I do."

"Then if Loyal asks, say you are in good health and have been well fed."

Risa sat there quietly as Albert prepared the SACSAC for the call to Loyal. He completed entering the IP address that Loyal had provided and motioned for Dean to pick up the receiver. The satellite phone rang three times before Loyal answered it.

"Hello, Mr. Bouchard. Have you called to tell me where the meeting is to be held?"

"Good morning, Loyal. That is indeed the purpose of this call. The meeting is being held in Scottsdale, Arizona. The meeting is precisely two hours from now at noon local time. The exact coordinates of the meeting are–"

Albert handed Dean a piece of paper with the latitude and longitude coordinates. Dean put on his reading glasses and recited the information.

"I'll be there at noon. Let me speak with Risa."

Dean handed Risa the phone receiver.

She took the phone receiver and put it to her ear. "Hello?"

"Hello, my dear. This is Loyal."

"Hi, Loyal."

"Are you all right? They didn't harm you, did they?"

Risa looked at Dean and said, "No. I'm fine."

"I'm very glad to hear that. This will all be over soon. I promise. You have to promise me something. You have to promise to take care of Ethan. He will be lost without you."

"Of course I will, Loyal. But you will be there too, right? He needs you too."

Before Loyal could respond, Dean snatched the receiver out of Risa's hand. Dean motioned for Albert to take her away. Without protest, Risa got up and left the room. Once Risa was safely out of the room, Dean said, "Are you satisfied that Risa is unharmed?"

"Yes."

"Good. Then listen to me. We need to discuss how the swap will occur. I will be brief, because the clock is ticking and you need to get going so you won't be late for the meeting. I have given it much thought. The way in which we swap is non-negotiable. You will land and exit the Alexander One before I allow Risa to drive off. That is the only way I can be sure that you will not take off when she is a safe distance away. Is that understood?"

"Very well, Mr. Bouchard. Just know that there is a code that you will need to start the Alexander One. I'll land and exit the Alexander One, but you will not receive the code until Risa is safely away. Without the code, you will never get the Alexander One to work. There are also safeguards against reverse engineering the aircraft."

Dean was impressed that Loyal had thought this through. "Very good, Loyal. We'll just have to trust each other, I suppose. I will hold up my end of our deal."

"If that is all, I must be going. I'll see you at twelve noon in Scottsdale, Arizona."

The line went dead. Dean thought that this was not a very friendly way to end the call. However, if he got the Alexander One, he would disregard the insult. Dean placed the receiver back in its cradle. He looked up at Albert and Brad with a broad smile across his face.

"We're almost at the finish line. Make sure your men are ready for a sprint, Brad."

"Oh, don't you worry, sir. My men will get it done," said Brad with an eerie smile.

CHAPTER THIRTY-SIX

I had trouble focusing when I woke up. I was lying in bed in the master guest room. I didn't feel sore or have a headache. In fact, I felt refreshed from whatever had knocked me out. I could barely remember what had happened. The last thing I remember was Loyal telling me that the Nanobiotics were shutting my body down. I looked down at my watch and realized that it was eleven P.M. local time. I had been unconscious for only about an hour and a half. It took me a couple of minutes to clear my head, but then it all came flooding back to me. Risa had been kidnapped!

The need to find out the latest on Risa propelled me out of bed. It was then that I realized a small blinking red dot on my EyeWonder micro display. This was curious to me, because the EyeWonder was in the off position. The blinking red dot was signaling me to do something. I turned on the EyeWonder to see if it still worked. The display turned on, and the blinking red dot continued. Next to the dot was a message. It simply read, "You have one unseen video message."

After a couple of incorrect commands, the video message finally opened. The message was from Loyal. Loyal was sitting in the study and I could hear Loyal's voice, clearly, like I was listening to him with headphones on.

"Hello, Ethan. I trust you are well when you receive this message. I know that inquisitive mind of yours has already asked how you can hear a message from the EyeWonder. I'm confident you've already figured it out. Am I right?"

I hadn't figured it out, but then it hit me. The Nanobiotics must be working in conjunction with the EyeWonder. Small electrical impulses must be emanating from the EyeWonder and transferring the voice signal to Nanobiotics located near my ear canal. Very impressive. The message from Loyal continued.

"Ah, yes. You must've figured it out. That is why you were chosen for this little adventure, Jonah, and I have invited you on. We recognized your talent as soon as we reviewed your source code for the S.T.A.R.E. system. The code you wrote was nearly perfect. You gave your creation life with your source code. The buildings in which your system is installed now have the ability to see, hear, taste, smell, and touch. This was made possible because you lent a piece of yourself to your code. You are very gifted in this regard."

The heartfelt compliments were great, but I wasn't sure where Loyal was headed. All I wanted was an update on Risa. I sat down on the bed and viewed more of the video.

"I'm afraid that all good things must come to an end. I have recorded this video to you so that I could tell you some very important information. I'm sorry that I will not be able to provide this information in person. If all goes according to plan, Risa will be back in your arms by tonight and I will be dead."

What? It wasn't possible. Loyal was far too important to the world to die. I had to stop whatever he was planning. I attempted to get up off the bed, but his words stopped me from moving.

"I know what you must be thinking. You must think that I'm too important to sacrifice myself for Risa. The truth is that I'm doing this for much greater reasons. One small benefit of my actions will be the safe return of Risa. I must admit that I was very happy when I saw that you two were so deeply in love. It renewed my sense of right and wrong. It validated everything that Jonah and I have been working on for so many years. I am so very glad that you and Risa could aid me in fulfilling my destiny. Do not mourn my loss. Embrace it. Know always that with my death comes life. I fully expect that you and Risa will live a moral life. That you will lead this world away from the path of self-annihilation that it is clearly heading down. That you will not only love each other, but love all forms of life as well. You will devote your entire life to ensure that the human race survives this difficult time in history. I know that this is a lot to ask, but I have all the faith in the world that you will exceed this lofty expectation. I'm willing to bet my life on you, Ethan. I'm that confident that you are the right person to ensure my wishes are carried out properly."

Loyal was marching off to his death, and his final wish was for me to take over where he had left off. I felt extremely honored to aid Loyal with his last request. I was certain that I could never achieve the accomplishments that he had attained. However, I was willing to spend the rest of my life trying.

Loyal continued. "I know that this is a lot to ask of you. You have been exposed to this secretive world for less than a week. You have seen only a glimpse of the constant tug-of-war that exists between the world's power brokers. It's a game that will take you some time to master. I'm not going to leave you empty handed. You may have more of a resource in Jonah than you may have previously thought. Listen to Jonah. He's smarter then you may think."

As Loyal said this, he gave a wry grin. I wasn't sure how to interpret this facial expression. The message appeared to be ending. Loyal had tears in his eyes when he spoke next.

"Well, I'm afraid my time is up. This is the last time we will get to speak. By the time you get this message, I'll be on my way to meet with Risa's kidnappers. At this meeting, I'll be executed and the men will attempt to steal the Alexander One. I can promise you one last thing before that happens. I will not allow them to take my life before Risa goes free. This is my lasting gift to you. Please accept this gift with my greatest love and affection. Goodbye, Ethan."

The video message cut out. I sat for a moment and thought about what Loyal had said. I was overwhelmed by his sacrifice. He was willing to die for Risa's and my well-being. I felt my eyes start to tear. I wasn't sure if they were tears of joy or anger. As much as I loved Risa, I needed Loyal to accompany me on the journey he had planned. I didn't think I could be successful without him. He was clearly the smartest man I had ever met. The Alexander One, Nanobiotics, Eye-Wonder, and the P.A.S.S. technology were so far beyond my realm of understanding that his knowledge would be irreplaceable. I decided that my tears were tears of anger. I couldn't allow Loyal to sacrifice himself, even if it meant that Risa would have to be killed.

I sprang off the bed, left the master guest room, and looked around. David the butler was sitting in a chair at the end of the hallway. He rose to his feet and walked toward me. "Jonah would like to see you. I'm to bring you to him."

David turned and walked toward the back of the house. Not a word was spoken as I followed. David arrived at a door. When David approached that door, the lock automatically disengaged. David entered the doorway. A long concrete-lined hallway extended about one hundred feet. David took long strides down the hallway. As we reached about a fourth of the way down the hallway, I heard the lock behind us reengage. This was a part of the house that I had never been in before. I tried to think what direction we were headed in. I knew that we had to have been walking to the rear of the main house. The length of the hallway suggested that wherever we were going was located underneath the rock face that was visible from the outside.

David and I approached the door at the other end of the hallway. David opened the door and motioned for me to enter. Once inside, David closed the door behind me and didn't enter the room in which I was standing.

I looked around at the massive room. This room was clearly where Loyal conducted most of his business. It was like Loyal's personal bat cave. I looked to my right, then my left. The sides of the room were covered with colossal banks of servers. They were unlike any servers that I'd ever seen before. I could barely feel a slight vibration. Most data centers that I had ever been in were extremely loud. The fans that ran to keep the processors cool were deafening. These servers were virtually silent. Thousands of blinking lights on the servers were visible through the glass walls. I focused my attention to the front of the room. Monstrous movie screens lined the top of the walls. One of the screens displayed a satellite image. The screens were tracking an object as it moved across the earth. I was mesmerized by the scale of the room. I continued to stand at the entrance.

Someone yelled out. "Down here, Ethan."

I couldn't tell where the yell had come from. I started to walk toward the large movie screens. As I moved forward, I could sense that I was on the upper level of the room. I walked to a staircase and looked down. Jonah was sitting in front of an enormous console of computer screens. The console was on the ground floor of this massive command center. I was elevated two stories above him. Jonah looked up and yelled out, "Down here."

As he said this, he waved for me to come down to him. I bound down the steps two at a time. I approached the console from the rear.

Jonah turned around and said, "Take a seat here." Jonah patted the seat next to his.

Before I sat, I asked him an obvious question. "What is this place?"

Jonah continued to look at the monitor in front of him when he answered. "This is my command center. I do a lot of things in here, one of which is to track the Alexander One and Two."

"So you know that Loyal is going to trade the Alexander One for Risa?"

"Yes. That's Loyal and the Alexander One right there." Jonah pointed up to the big screen at a blinking dot on the satellite image.

I ignored where he was pointing and asked, "And you are OK with this? Loyal is going to die, and the Alexander One will be captured by the men we were trying to keep it away from."

Jonah looked at me. I could tell that he felt the same way I did about Loyal.

Jonah began to explain. "You know it's funny. His name isn't Loyal, you know. When he met with you, he took some liberties with the script I had prepared for him."

"What do you mean the script that you prepared for him?"

Jonah ignored my question and continued. "For our conversation now, I will call him Loyal so that it doesn't confuse you further. Loyal has been with me for the last forty-two years. He has been my best friend through some very difficult times. That may be the reason why he decided to tell you his name was Loyal. He has been very loyal to me over the years."

I was confused. Jonah appeared to be in his mid-thirties at most. There was no way that he could have known Loyal for forty-two years. I thought Jonah must have misspoken, so I decided to clarify what he had said. "Did you mean to say that you have known Loyal for the last thirty years? Forty-two years is a little too long. You can't be more then thirty-five years old, Jonah."

Jonah smiled at me. If there was a joke, I didn't get it.

Jonah continued. "No, I didn't misspeak. I have known Loyal for forty-two years. I met him when I was nineteen. Back then, he was just an idealist hell-bent on changing the world."

Jonah seemed to cherish this memory.

I thought that he was delusional. "That's impossible. That would make you sixty-one years old."

"Given all that you have seen this past week, would that be too difficult to believe? I'm sure if you think hard enough, you will come up with an answer."

I couldn't believe what Jonah had just said. Then it hit me. My world came crashing down like a plane with no engine. I replied with a barely audible voice, "The Nanobiotics."

"Very good, Ethan. I knew there was a reason why I picked you for this mission. You have the ability to see beyond what is known to be logically correct and think for yourself."

It couldn't be. Was Jonah really saying what I thought he was? He said that this was his command center. He said that Loyal had joined him. He said that he had picked me for this mission. I felt the room start to spin. All this time, he was the one who planned all of this. He was the one who developed this mind-blowing technology. It wasn't true. It couldn't be. I shook my head and got up off the chair.

"It can't be. You? You planned all of this? You created the Alexander One?"

"Yes, Ethan. I created all of this."

Jonah raised his arms in the air displaying the massive command center.

I backed away from him. It was too difficult for my brain to understand. I couldn't see how he could have created such sophisticated technology in his lifetime. Jonah then said something that almost put me in a state of shock.

"You don't think that I could have created such sophisticated technology in my lifetime?"

Did I just ask that question out loud? How did he know what I was thinking? Without my saying a word, Jonah responded.

"I'm sure if you think really hard, you will know how."

I was dizzy from all the images of the past couple of days. Jonah met me for the initial meeting at the golf course. Jonah was the one who explained how the Alexander One worked. Jonah gave me the EyeWonder. Jonah injected me with the Nanobiotics. Jonah picked Risa and me up at the convenience store. He had been there every step of the way, guiding my actions. Again Jonah spoke without my saying anything.

"Yes, Ethan. Every step of the way."

"Stop doing that! Stop reading my thoughts!"

"Relax, Ethan. Just relax. Everything will be fine."

"Fine? Fine? I don't think Loyal will be fine."

Jonah's tone was passive. He sat back in his chair and looked down at the floor when he spoke. "Loyal has been my best friend for most of my life. Do you think this is easy for me? The truth is that Loyal is sick. He has lung cancer. This will be his last act of heroism. I fought with him about it for a while, but he's a hopeless romantic. He wouldn't be denied this opportunity to save your budding relationship with Risa."

"No. What about the Nanobiotics? Why didn't they work for him? How could he get lung cancer?"

Jonah was visibility upset. He squeezed the bridge of his nose and shut his eyes when responding. "Loyal was the first subject injected with the Nanobiotics. I developed the Nanobiotics when I was thirty-three. Loyal was already in his late sixties. I thought that the design was complete. I found out only a year or so ago that there was a minor flaw in the Nanobiotics that are responsible for cancer cells. The flaw was discovered too late. The revised software couldn't do anything for Loyal. His cancer had progressed too far." Jonah started to tear up.

"The coughing fits at dinner and in the study," I said, as if the pieces of the puzzle were coming together. It was making more sense to me.

Jonah just nodded his head.

"It isn't your fault, Jonah."

Jonah looked up at me for the first time since we started talking about Loyal. "I know it isn't my fault. I'm not upset because I think it's my fault. I'm upset because I know that I'm about to lose my best friend. Loyal was more to me then a friend. In the early years, he was the only one who understood me. When I first realized I had a unique gift for science and mathematics, my brain worked more quickly than my mouth. Almost everyone thought that I was retarded because I couldn't speak down to their level of intellect. This caused me to speak in gibberish. So many ideas and concepts were flowing through me that my brain couldn't filter the thoughts fast enough. I would find myself saying one thing, then the next sentence would be something completely unrelated. Loyal was a professor at MIT at the time. I had written a paper on new concepts of micro-computing and sent it to him based on the work he was doing. This was back in the late nineteen-fifties and no one had ever even heard of microprocessors.

Instead of dismissing me for a nut job as the rest of the world had, he came and found me. He helped me channel my talents while teaching me how to act in social environments. He left MIT and joined me full time. Together we ushered in a new era. Together we developed much of the computing technology in the world today. We picked certain people to be the public faces for our discoveries. Loyal and I have installed many of the world's richest people into power. They helped spread our technology into every crevice of the world. We held back certain technologies so that we could maintain control of the limitless amounts of data that were compiled. We have done this many times over the years, with many different inventions. That is why you are here. You will be our public face for the Alexander One. You, and you alone, will introduce the Alexander One to the world. You will singlehandedly resolve the impending oil crisis."

I was speechless. I really didn't know how to respond to what Jonah had just said. The story seemed so farfetched that it might have actually been true. I needed to make sure I heard correctly. Before I could ask, Jonah answered the question.

"It's all true, Ethan. Very few people in the world know this to be true."

All this time I thought that Jonah had been reading my body language. He had always seemed to know what I was thinking and reacted on it.

"The EyeWonder. If it can read my thoughts to answer a question, you can interpret my thoughts and hear them as I think."

Jonah seemed to take pleasure in this statement. "Like I said, we develop the technology and hold back its full potential for ourselves. That's just one example."

I was starting to see what he was telling me. Jonah was one sick genius. He developed computers and had them distributed all over the world. He then used his P.A.S.S. technology to sneak in and out of networks undetected. Very smart.

"So what will be held back from the Alexander One?"

"Several things. For starters, the scaled-down version will be able to lift only a couple feet off the ground. The world at large isn't ready for orbital flight yet."

That sounded like a logical explanation, but there was one thing that was really bothering me about this whole situation. I decided to ask Jonah. "Why go through all this trouble? Why not just leak the design of the Alexander One over the Internet? Once it is out there, there would be no stopping it."

"There are a couple of reasons why this would not work."

Just as Jonah was about to explain, a voice came over the speakers of the command center.

"Approaching the meeting coordinates."

It was Loyal. He was about to land somewhere in the western United States.

Jonah turned to me and spoke. "I promise that I will answer all your questions later. I need to focus on the last part of the plan. You want to make sure Risa survives this, right?"

"Of course."

"OK. Then sit here and do as I tell you." Jonah patted the seat next to him.

I walked back to him and sat in the chair.

Jonah responded to Loyal. "Roger that. Let's get this done with. Commence landing sequence. Engage geomagnetic drive at one hundred and eighty thousand feet. Good luck, and God speed, old friend."

CHAPTER THIRTY-SEVEN

The rest of council members were already at the meeting facility when Dean pulled up. Hans cursed under his breath when Dean arrived to a council meeting late again. This was the last time he was going to be disrespected by Dean Bouchard. Dean's black Maybach completed the circle of cars. Now that all the participants were there, the drivers exited the cars and opened the rear passenger doors. Each of the council members exited their vehicles and walked to the center of the circle. There were looks of shock when Dean exited the car with Risa in tow.

Hans, who was still in his car, saw Dean with Risa. He remembered what Brad had said about exiting the car, but he had to calm the anger that he was sure was to come from the other council members. In the thirty-two year history of the council, there had never been an unauthorized outsider brought to the meeting. Hans exited his car and joined the circle. Hans knew of Dean's plan to trade Risa for the Alexander One, but had to act his part.

Member Number Three addressed the infraction without hesitation. "Member Number Seven, who is this outsider that you have brought to the meeting? The rules are very clear when it comes to strangers attending the meetings. Guards!"

Several of the drivers pulled guns from their shoulder holsters. They trained the guns on Dean and Risa.

Dean held up his hands and said, "Wait! I can explain. I think once you hear who I have with me and what she can do for the council, you will welcome my infraction."

Hans brought calm to the situation. He knew that if he allowed Dean or Risa to get killed, he would never get his hands on the Alexander One. He came to Dean's defense.

"Stand down, gentlemen. I knew that Member Number Seven was going to bring this outsider to the meeting. Her capture was the result of Plan Alpha. Let him explain, and it will all be clear in a moment."

Dean looked at Hans. Hans must have thought that he still had control over this situation. Dean became nervous when he heard Hans's order. He somehow knew that he was bringing Risa to the meeting. Tension filled the air. Dean decided that he would have to play along with Hans's ruse or both he and Risa would be killed. Dean began to explain. "The council's primary goal over the past week was to hunt down and destroy the threat identified in last week's meeting. Well, this woman is our answer. In a few short moments, the unique aircraft known as the Alexander One will land here. The driver will be the man who invented the aircraft. Once he has landed, this woman will be released, and we will have the Alexander One in our possession."

The council members looked at each other in amazement. They seemed very pleased with what was just announced.

Risa looked at the faces of these old men. She had no idea what was going on, but she didn't like what Dean had just said. She noticed one of the old men ogling her. She looked at him with disgust. Risa then felt a short burst of wind coming from the center of the parked cars. The council members were in discussion about this latest turn of events. The electro-chromatic skin of the Alexander One faded away. All of the jaws on the council members' faces went slack when they saw the Alexander One in front of them. There wasn't a word spoken by anyone. The driver's door of the Alexander One opened, and Loyal got out.

Even Dean Bouchard was in shock with what he saw. He didn't even try to stop Risa as she ran to Loyal and hugged him. She started crying as she squeezed him tighter.

Loyal reassured her. "Now, now, my dear. It will be all right. Everything will be fine. You must get in a car and drive as fast as you can away from here. Keep driving until you run out of gas. You must do this for me. You must return to Ethan and love him unconditionally. He will need you now more than ever. Will you do this for me, Risa?"

Risa was still sobbing. She lifted her head from Loyal's shoulder and replied, "Yes, of course I will, but it doesn't have to end this way. They have what they want. Why can't you just come with me back to the island?"

Loyal smiled, wiped the tears from Risa's cheeks, and said, "I truly wish I had more time to spend with you and Ethan. I knew this was a one-way ticket when I landed. These men will not allow me to leave. Now you must get in that car and drive as fast as possible. Go now, my dear."

Loyal looked at Albert and said, "Give Ms. Castleberry the keys to the car."

Albert looked over at Dean. Dean nodded.

Loyal gave Risa a gentle nudge in the direction of Dean's car. Albert tossed her the keys as Risa ran past Dean who was standing there still clearly in shock with what he had just seen. As Risa passed Dean on the way to the car, Dean raised his hand. A split second later, Dean's head exploded from the impact of the supersonic fifty-caliber round.

The arterial spray hit Risa as she ran to the car. One by one the council members and their drivers were mowed down by sniper shots choreographed so quickly that no one had a chance to take cover.

Risa looked back at the massacre unfolding. She ran to the driver's seat of the black Maybach. It was like everything was happening in slow motion. Albert was standing next to the driver door. As Risa approached, Albert's chest exploded and the window of the car shattered. Risa's mind was racing so quickly that panic had not yet set in. Albert's body flew five feet away from the car with the impact of the round. Risa crouched down as she got into the car. She turned the ignition and the black beast came to life.

She took one last look at Loyal. Loyal looked back at Risa and winked. Loyal and one other man were the only two people left standing. Blood and body parts were everywhere. Risa slammed the car into reverse and jammed her foot on the accelerator. For such a large car, it had a lot of power. The tires screeched as the car started moving backwards. Risa cut the wheel hard, and the car swung in the opposite direction. She threw the car into drive and sped away from the meeting facility.

Hans saw that Risa was safely away, and he raised his hand to signal Brad that his mission was completed. Hans would spare Risa's life and keep Dean's end of the bargain with Loyal. Hans hoped that Loyal would see his show of good faith and that it would encourage him to form a relationship with him. Hans looked back at Simon, who was sitting in the driver seat of Hans's car. He indicated for Simon to roll down the window.

Hans ordered, "Make sure that the security detail doesn't move in on our position. Order them to stand down."

"Yes, sir."

Hans turned his attention back to Loyal. He studied the seemingly fragile man. Loyal didn't look frightened. Hans had seen the effect a fifty-caliber round had on a human body many times during World War II. He could only surmise that Loyal had seen battle as well. The sight of bodies being ripped apart did not shake Loyal as it would an average person. "Hello Loyal. It is very curious that you would not run for cover when the shooting began. Why is that?"

Loyal looked at Hans. He simply replied, "I figured that if you killed me, you wouldn't be able to use the Alexander One. After all, you heard what I told Dean Bouchard this morning. If you don't get the code, the Alexander One won't operate."

Hans was not surprised at this answer. He could sense that Loyal was keenly aware of how Hans had obtained his information. Hans's curiosity was getting the best of him. He was intrigued with this little man that he knew nothing about. He wanted to find out more. "Who are you, Loyal? You are clearly one of the most gifted minds the world has ever seen. How come I have never heard of you?"

Loyal smiled at Hans. Hans seemed to be very calm for someone who had just witnessed the savage murder of his comrades. Loyal indulged Hans with an answer. "I'm a lot like you, Hans. I'm someone who works behind the scenes. My greatest strength is my anonymity. I help point people in the right direction without their knowing it. I believe that this is very similar to what you and these men have been doing with the oil markets over the past several decades. Isn't that correct?"

Hans was impressed. This answer only seemed to fuel Hans's desire to know more about Loyal. He wanted to know how much Loyal understood about the council. Hans walked up to Loyal and stopped ten feet in front of him. He looked Loyal directly in the eyes when he asked his next question. "How did you find out about this council's purpose? We went to enormous lengths to keep our involvement hidden from the world. Not even someone with your level of technical expertise could find any electronic evidence of our involvement with the oil markets."

Loyal shook his head at what Hans had just said. He replied. "You just explained how I was able to figure out what your council has been doing for the last thirty years. You did too good of a job covering your tracks. You and your council created a vacuum. Your group was like a black hole in the universe. Astronomers can't physically see that a black hole exists, but they know they are out there because they can see the effects they have on their surroundings. I must say that I'm very impressed with your ability to conceal your actions. I have been trying to find out who you and your council members were for quite a long time."

Hans considered this explanation. Loyal was a smart individual indeed. This simple explanation made perfect sense to Hans. Hans nodded his head in approval. He started to think out loud in hopes that Loyal would confirm his suspicions. "So you used Garrett Michaels to make contact with us. You knew that we could track the Alexander One. You left Garrett Michaels at the golf course for Dean Bouchard to kidnap. This opened a line of communication with someone on the council."

Hans started peeling back the layers one by one. "With the communication established, why did you allow Ethan Kravis to go back to Philadelphia? Surely you knew that he would be in danger based on what happened with Garrett."

Loyal stood there and smiled. He didn't respond.

Hans continued to follow the path of logic that he was on. "You let Ethan go back to Philadelphia to meet the girl. She was a plant? You wanted Dean to know about Risa?"

Again, Loyal said nothing. He just stood there and let Hans figure out what had happened.

"Ethan and Risa get rescued, and Ethan falls in love with her. You send Ethan to Transtronics, where he provides a presentation on the Alexander One. But why? Why go public with the Alexander One, if you knew it would get back to me?"

Hans thought about this for a moment. When he found the answer he was looking for, he raised his pointer finger in the air. He nodded and furthered his reasoning. "You knew that I was involved with Transtronics. You knew that I would see the presentation and contact you. Up until then, you had been dealing only with Dean Bouchard. You wanted to open an additional line of communication with me. But why?"

"You already know the answer. You asked why I didn't run for cover when the shooting began. Why do you think I didn't run?"

Hans pinched the bridge of his nose. He painfully answered, "You wanted to talk with me because you planted some type of line tap on my satellite phone. You needed an open line to plant the bug. By doing so, you became privy to my conversation with Brad Resniki. You knew that everyone was going to be shot, so you didn't take cover."

Loyal nodded. Hans continued. "But why would you allow Ethan and Risa to go to Philadelphia? You knew that Dean would capture one or both of them. Why would you allow this to happen?"

Loyal knew the end of this conversation was nearing. He used his EyeWonder to track Risa's progress in her escape. She was about three miles away. Loyal focused his attention back on Hans.

Hans continued to peel the layers off of Loyal's plan. "You let Ethan and Risa travel to Philadelphia because you knew that one of them would be captured. You needed to give Dean Bouchard a worthwhile bargaining chip. You planned it so it would not raise suspicion when you agreed to come to this meeting so freely."

Loyal was impressed that Hans was deciphering his puzzle so quickly. It was clear to Loyal that Hans was a master tactician himself. Loyal cut in and confirmed what Hans had said. "All that you have said is correct."

Hans tilted his head to the side. He didn't understand why Loyal had gone to such enormous lengths to get invited to a council meeting. As soon as Hans asked himself this question, a wave of panic hit him. His body froze and his eyes widened. Hans looked at Loyal. Their eyes met.

Loyal could see the fear building in Hans. He let out a beaming smile.

Hans turned back and ran toward his car, but it was too late. A slight hiss came from the Alexander One. Loyal held up his arms. He did not feel anything when the shockwave from the blast vaporized every molecule of his body.

CHAPTER THIRTY-EIGHT

"Oh my god! Oh my God! Oh my god!" I couldn't believe what I had just seen. Jonah and I watched the whole scene unfold on the satellite image. All of the men at the meeting were dead. Loyal had talked with the only other man left standing for a couple of minutes, and then the entire screen filled with white light. A moment passed and there was an unmistakable shape taking form on the satellite image, a shape that the world had seen only a couple of times before in all of history.

The mushroom cloud of a nuclear explosion was growing at a sickening rate. I looked over at Jonah, who was mesmerized by the image. The look on Jonah's face was not one of shock, but one of awe. It was clear to me that Jonah had known that this explosion was going to happen. I rose to my feet, but almost fell back down.

"You sick bastard! You did this! You just detonated a nuclear bomb in Arizona!"

Jonah looked over at me. The look on his face was eerily calm. His reply was soft-spoken and short. "Yes."

I felt like I was on the verge of vomiting. My head started spinning out of control. I grabbed the back of a chair to help steady myself. "All those people! You just killed all of those people! You just killed Risa!"

I had never felt so alone in the world. This event shook my very being. This nuclear detonation could throw the world into a tailspin. The fear and panic caused by the explosion would take decades to repair. I flopped down to the floor of the command center and asked Jonah, "Why?"

Jonah looked down at me. His voice was distant when he responded. "To restore the balance."

This response made absolutely no sense. How would detonating a nuclear bomb on American soil restore any semblance of balance in the world? It would surely do the exact opposite. "You are nuts, Jonah!"

I felt like killing Jonah with my bare hands. Before I could act, Jonah explained his reasoning.

"This was the only way to remove the two obstacles that were preventing us from going public with the Alexander One. Drastic times call for drastic measures."

I had no idea where Jonah was headed. He had just taken everything I had ever loved in the world.

"Loyal and I have tried several ways to push the world in the right direction over the years. We tried to do so without causing any real harm. We've carried out countless missions that would raise the price of oil to such a high level that the world would have no choice but to develop alternatives. Each time we did, there was an unexplained counter force that worked to keep the price of oil low. For the longest time, it didn't make sense to us. We didn't know who was doing it and why. We scoured the earth trying to find out how the unexplained force worked. About five years ago, we narrowed our search down to a group of men who controlled virtually all of the oil on earth. These men kept the price of oil in check so that the world wouldn't have a reason to develop fuel alternatives. If left unchallenged, these men would have bled the earth dry."

All of what Jonah had just said was interesting, but it didn't even come close to explaining why a nuclear bomb needed to be detonated and why Risa had to be killed. Instead of interrupting, I let Jonah continue his explanation.

"When we found out that this group existed, we knew that nothing we did would allow us to guide the world in the right direction. These men had amassed too much wealth and power. Attacks on their oil refineries were like shooting a tank with a BB gun. We needed a way to remove these men from power and raise the price of oil to an exorbitant level. This is the plan we came up with."

Jonah pointed at that screen. The mushroom cloud was still hanging over the city of Scottsdale. Jonah's logic was still not making sense to me.

"How does killing tens of thousands of people accomplish your goal?"

"The men at that meeting were the people who controlled the world's oil. They called themselves the council. There will be absolutely no trace of their existence after the blast. The explosion will cause a worldwide panic."

I was starting to see the logic of Jonah's plan. This one action remedied both the impediments Jonah had explained. I picked up where Jonah had left off.

"So the bomb kills this council and causes a worldwide panic. Whole countries stockpile oil, thus driving the price up. In turn, there is an oil crisis the likes of which the world has never seen. This would create the opportune time to introduce the Alexander One."

I thought about the plan. I decided to challenge Jonah on his logic. "The plan you created is very logical. However, you are not taking one extremely important factor into account."

Jonah raised his eyebrow and motioned me to continue.

"You have discounted the will of the people. Humans adapt and overcome. This trait is encoded in their genes. What makes you think that they will not be able to adapt to an elevated price of oil?"

Jonah smiled. He reached forward and flipped a switch on the console. The large display at the front of the room changed to a financial news network. The reporter was frantic in her reporting of the events that had just happened. Jonah turned to me and continued to explain, "The plan didn't merely address the council and the initial panic of the people. When we contacted the council members to arrange this meeting, we infiltrated their networks. We used the P.A.S.S technology to plant a program that would ensure that the price of oil remains elevated. As soon as the blast occurred, it triggered the program. We took the trillions of dollars that the council had amassed and started buying oil futures."

I looked up at the screen and the ticker on the bottom displayed the current price of oil. I could say only one thing when I saw the amount. "Holy shit!"

The price of oil that had been hovering between one hundred and one hundred and fifty dollars a barrel had skyrocketed to nearly three thousand dollars a barrel. As each second passed, the price continued to rise.

Jonah continued. "I wanted to give the world a taste of what it would be like if oil ran out. At these prices, the world will shut down. No one will be able to afford oil. We will gradually bring the prices back down, but the psychological damage will be done. There will be only one way that the world will be able to adapt to these prices."

"The Alexander One," I said out loud.

Jonah nodded his head.

I was still overwhelmed at the thought of furthering this agenda with the use of a nuclear device. I raised myself up off the floor and sat in one of the chairs at the end of the console. I put my head in my hands and felt as if I were going to cry. "All of those innocent people in Arizona are dead. They are just normal, everyday people going about their lives. They didn't deserve this." I gestured to the screen.

Jonah said something next that shocked me even more than the image on the screen. "Not nearly as many people have died as you may think. Once the situation settles, you will see that less than one hundred people will die as a result of the bomb. The fission core of the Alexander One was relatively low yield, as far as nuclear explosions go. The explosion equates to less than two kilotons, only about fifteen percent of the destructive force of the bombing of Hiroshima in World War II. The blast radius was only a few city blocks. Because it was in a fairly unpopulated area, there was not much collateral damage."

Jonah pressed a button on the console. The news broadcast reverted back to the satellite image. "Do you see those small arrows around the image of the area? Those are the wind speeds and directions. The prevailing wind is blowing south to north at fifteen miles an hour." Jonah panned the satellite image north of the blast area. "The small amount of radioactive material that was released by the blast will dissipate over the barren desert. You will see over time that the damage wasn't nearly as bad as you may think now."

This did a little to settle my feelings. If this truly was the case, then why explode the bomb at all?

Jonah answered the question without my asking it aloud. "When the papers and news programs report on the explosion, people will only be able to see this image. They will not care how many or few people have died. All they will see is the mushroom cloud and the words 'nuclear explosion.' This alone will fuel panic."

"But you said that you did this to bring things back into balance. It will have the exact opposite effect on the world. The panic will cause rioting and mass hysteria. The world will spin out of control if people think that major cities are being bombed with nuclear devices."

Jonah and I looked at each other.

"Do you remember what Loyal said to you when you first arrived at the island?"

"He said quite a bit that I remember."

Jonah ignored my comment and continued. "He said that he was neither good nor evil. He existed to bring balance to the world to help stave off self-annihilation. Do you remember his saying that?"

I nodded.

"Well that is the absolute truth. The world is addicted to oil. The consumption of oil is growing at an unsustainable rate. This growth heavily tipped the scales of balance. The unhindered consumption of this natural resource is causing irreparable damage to the earth. We needed to do something drastic to bring this behavior back into balance. You may not agree that innocent people should have died to accomplish it, but I can assure you that this action will end up saving more lives than you may think.

Think of how many innocent people throughout history have died over oil. You don't have to look back in history very far to understand what I'm talking about. Africa is being ripped apart by Civil War. America has waged war on the Middle East while Russia is invading their neighboring states. The one hundred dead people from this bomb will pale in comparison to the number of people who perish in those conflicts. The potential benefit to the world is far greater than the few people who were just sacrificed. With this little bit of evil, good will prevail, and balance will be restored. "

"It isn't just the one hundred people who died today. What about the people who will die when the food they need can't be transported because of lack of fuel? How about the people who start killing gas station owners to steal their gas? What about the cities that depend on oil to generate electricity? There's much more collateral damage than you may think."

"Every country has a least a six-month supply of oil in reserves. Within minutes, you will see every president, prime minister, king, sultan and sheik holding press conferences assuring their people that life will continue. They will freeze the stock markets and institute martial law. There will be some fallout, but over time you will see the balance return. In fact, you will be on the front lines helping restore this balance."

Jonah reached down below the console. He lifted a box to the console and placed it between us. I didn't move or ask what was in the box. Jonah patted the top. "In this box is the solution to the world's problems. These are the detailed patent applications for the Alexander One. Loyal and I want you to fulfill your promise. We want you to take these patents and introduce the world to the Alexander One. You will guide the world into a new age. You will bring calm to the masses with this invention. You will save the world from itself. Given all that you have seen over this past week, will you still accept this opportunity to make a difference in the world?"

"A week ago I would have been fully behind this plan. But I'm not sure I can do this without Risa. She opened my eyes to life. With her gone, I'm not sure that the world is worth saving."

Jonah smiled for the first time since his good friend Loyal had been killed. I think he understood what I was saying. Jonah reached down to the console and flipped a switch. The main display in the room returned to a satellite image of the earth. The familiar red dot was blinking on the screen. Jonah turned to me and said, "Loyal keeps his promises. The red dot is the Alexander Two and it's carrying some precious cargo back to the island. Does this make your decision any easier?"

I had never felt so relieved in all my life. The blinking red dot moving across the world was Risa coming back to me. I turned my attention to Jonah and said, "I guess you are right. I have no excuses not to accept your offer."

CHAPTER THIRTY-NINE

It had been six months since the shockwave of the explosion rocked the world. Just as Jonah had promised, the world had kept spinning. The first couple of weeks were rife with riots and looting. Within a month, balance came back to the world.

Reflecting back on the past six months, I could say with absolute certainty, that it was the busiest time in my life. All the sacrifices and hard work had led to this very moment. I could hear the seventy-thousand-plus crowd chanting as Peter Goldman started his introduction.

"Thank you all for staying here for the halftime show. I know that this time is usually reserved for getting food and going to the restroom. I'm glad that ya'll have decided to stay here and witness history being made. The past six months have been very difficult for the world. Since the unexplained nuclear attack in Arizona, the world has been brought to its knees with the skyrocketing cost of oil. Well, I'm here to tell you that this will no longer be your concern. Out of this tragic event, a new idea has been born. The unprecedented cooperation of the world's governments has allowed us to speed up the development of the world's very first geomagnetic vehicle. Ladies and gentlemen, I'm honored to present the Loyal Traveler."

The cheers of the crowd swelled. I looked at Risa, who was sitting in the passenger's seat of the newly renamed Alexander One. Risa smiled at me, and I leaned over to her and gave her a kiss.

"Are you ready to do this, sexy?"

Risa looked at me and said, "We mustn't keep the world waiting."

I gently maneuvered the Loyal Traveler down the player's tunnel of the Georgia Dome. Even the two football teams stayed on the field during halftime to witness history being made. As soon as we emerged from the tunnel, all seventy thousand people rose to their feet and let out a deafening cheer. My new partner, Peter Goldman of Transtronics, continued his speech.

"Here it is, folks. Here's the invention that will save the earth and cure our addiction to oil forever. The Loyal Traveler doesn't need gas. It doesn't need oil of any kind. All the parts have been manufactured from recycled products. This vehicle never needs to be refilled or recharged. It's the safest and least expensive form of transportation on the planet. The governments have agreed to heavily subsidize the cost of the vehicle, so it will cost you a fraction of a new, gas-powered car. You can trade in your gas guzzlers, and we will recycle your old car to produce new Loyal Travelers. We're at the dawn of a new age, and I'm ecstatic to be able to unveil this new technological wonder in my hometown of Atlanta. The eyes of the world are on you, my friends."

Peter's sales pitch was a smashing success. The noise generated by the crowd lasted for the next thirty minutes. Risa and I floated around the field so that the crowd could get a better look at the Loyal Traveler. So many emotions were bubbling inside me, that I didn't know what to feel.

My only regret was that Loyal wasn't with us to witness the reception of his and Jonah's invention. After we drove around the field a dozen or so times, I stopped the vehicle in the center of the field.

Risa turned to me and asked a surprising question. “Do you remember what you asked me back in the convenience store when we first met?”

I could barely hear the question over the chanting of the crowd. I looked at her and raised my shoulders.

Risa yelled so that I could hear her over the crowd. “You asked me if this was the start of something special. Well, I can say with certainty that this will be the most special day the world has ever known!”

Risa leaned into me and gave me one last kiss. We exited the Loyal Traveler and joined Peter on stage. Peter’s staff formed a circle around our elevated platform. Peter yelled into the microphone, “Ladies and Gentlemen, no words can describe how happy I am to present the inventors of the Loyal Traveler. Mr. and Mrs. Ethan Kravis!”